"Why did you kiss me?" Rex asked.

Despite getting to bed well past a decent hour, despite the eternities of socializing Rex's evening had demanded, that question had robbed him of sleep.

"You kissed me first, sir," Eleanora replied.

A gratifyingly nonsensical answer. "I kissed you because a gesture of affection under the circumstances seemed appropriate. I hope I did not offend."

The ever articulate, always competent, not-to-be-daunted Mrs. Hatfield looked away. "You did not, and I hope I did not presume."

"You rather did," he said, tossing his scarf around his neck. "I adore you for it. Feel free to presume again whenever the mood strikes you."

He left her by the window, looking once again quite self-possessed. She was doubtless deciding how to explain to him that yet another trusted hireling was plundering the ducal coffers. So why was Rex's imagination fixed instead on images of Eleanora Hatfield plundering the ducal person?

D0032204

PRAISE FOR GRACE BURROWES AND THE ROGUES TO RICHES SERIES

"Grace Burrowes is terrific!"
—**Julia Quinn, #1 *New York Times* bestselling author**

"Sexy heroes, strong heroines, intelligent plots, enchanting love stories…Grace Burrowes's romances have them all."
—**Mary Balogh, *New York Times* bestselling author**

"Grace Burrowes writes from the heart—with warmth, humor, and a generous dash of sensuality, her stories are unputdownable! If you're not reading Grace Burrowes you're missing the very best in today's Regency Romance!"
—**Elizabeth Hoyt, *New York Times* bestselling author**

WHEN A DUCHESS SAYS I DO

"An unusual pair of smart and worldly but reticent lovers; a modern sensibility about themes of consent, class, and disability; and a surprising and adventurous plot make Burrowes's latest Rogues to Riches Regency satisfyingly relatable nerdy escapism…will warm readers' hearts to the core."
—***Publishers Weekly,* starred review**

"A romance of gentle yearning and fulfillment balanced out by a suspense plot and a fast-paced third act."
—***Kirkus Reviews***

"Readers will root for these two wary people as they learn to trust each other with their foibles and their truths. With revealing dialogue, games of chess and subtle sensuality, this romance sings."
—***BookPage***

MY ONE AND ONLY DUKE

"Skillfully crafted and exquisitely written, Burrowes' latest is pure gold; a brilliant launch to a promising series."
—*Library Journal,* **starred review**

"Burrowes is a writer of towering talent."
—*USA Today* **Happy Ever After**

"A delicious read. Best of the Month pick."
—**Apple Books**

ALSO BY GRACE BURROWES

FOREVER
AND A DUKE

A Rogues to Riches Novel

GRACE BURROWES

FOREVER

New York   Boston

This book is a work of fiction. Names, characters, places, and incidents are the product of the author's imagination or are used fictitiously. Any resemblance to actual events, locales, or persons, living or dead, is coincidental.

Copyright © 2019 by Grace Burrowes

The Lady in Red copyright © 2017 by Kelly Bowen

Cover illustration and design by Elizabeth Turner Stokes. Cover copyright © 2019 by Hachette Book Group, Inc.

Hachette Book Group supports the right to free expression and the value of copyright. The purpose of copyright is to encourage writers and artists to produce the creative works that enrich our culture.

The scanning, uploading, and distribution of this book without permission is a theft of the author's intellectual property. If you would like permission to use material from the book (other than for review purposes), please contact permissions@hbgusa.com. Thank you for your support of the author's rights.

Forever

Hachette Book Group

1290 Avenue of the Americas, New York, NY 10104

read-forever.com

twitter.com/readforeverpub

First Edition: November 2019

Forever is an imprint of Grand Central Publishing. The Forever name and logo are trademarks of Hachette Book Group, Inc.

The publisher is not responsible for websites (or their content) that are not owned by the publisher.

The Hachette Speakers Bureau provides a wide range of authors for speaking events. To find out more, go to www.hachettespeakersbureau.com or call (866) 376-6591.

ISBNs: 978-1-5387-0027-3 (mass market), 978-1-5387-0028-0 (ebook)

Printed in the United States of America

OPM

10 9 8 7 6 5 4 3 2 1

ATTENTION CORPORATIONS AND ORGANIZATIONS:
Most Hachette Book Group books are available at quantity discounts with bulk purchase for educational, business, or sales promotional use. For information, please call or write:

Special Markets Department, Hachette Book Group
1290 Avenue of the Americas, New York, NY 10104
Telephone: 1-800-222-6747 Fax: 1-800-477-5925

*To those for whom math is not a
strength*

Acknowledgments

For this book to reach my readers, I rely on the good offices of many publishing professionals. My editor, Leah Hultenschmidt, continues to be a joy to work with (even when I'm doing my temperamental artist impersonation), and the whole crew at Grand Central Publishing keeps coming through for me, book after book. I am enjoying the living peedywaddles out of the Rogues to Riches series, in part because I have such a wonderful team to work with. That said, the real foundation upon which my joy rests is you, the reader. You allow me to turn storytelling into a calling, and to claim as a profession work that I absolutely love. Thanks for that. Endless, heartfelt thanks, and happy reading!

FOREVER
AND A DUKE

Chapter One

"Eleanora Hatfield is like the fellow who extracts a bad tooth," Joshua Penrose said as he set a brisk pace down the walkway. "Your very survival means you allow him to inflict his special brand of agony, though you dread each encounter."

"Not a flattering analogy to apply to any female, Penrose." Wrexham, Duke of Elsmore, paused to examine a flower girl's offerings at the corner. He and Penrose weren't due at the bank for nearly a quarter of an hour, after all.

"How are you today, Miss Marybeth?"

She had the usual offerings—carnations for the lapel, tussy-mussies to take on a courting call, nose-gays of sweet pea and lavender, small sprays of muguet-des-bois.

"I'm in good health, Your Grace. And you?"

He chose a little arrangement of violets and mouget-de-bois. "I'm preparing to prostrate myself before that great institution known as Wentworth and Penrose. Very imposing financial organization. I must look my best. What shall we choose for Mr. Penrose?"

Penrose bore Marybeth's inspection with an impatient twirl of his gold-handled walking stick. Marybeth considered him with an odd gravity for a mere girl, then passed over a bright red carnation arranged as a boutonniere.

"The gentleman would disdain to wear more than one simple flower. He hasn't your ability to wear posies, Your Grace."

"What a wise young lady you are."

She smiled, which also made her a pretty young lady. Rex would ask his cook how soon they could hire a new scullery maid, for a London street corner wasn't safe for the poor and lovely.

"Go on with ye, Your Grace. I've other custom to see to."

That was the point. Rex enjoyed cutting a dash, but a duke's choice of flower stall could mean the difference between the flower seller's family eating meat that week or going without.

"And well you should have other custom, when your inventory is so impressive." He paid a little generously, and would have sauntered on down the street, except that Penrose was trying ineffectually to affix his carnation to his lapel.

"Let me," Rex said, taking the flower in one hand and the pin in the other. This necessitated holding his own boutonniere with his teeth.

Penrose's expression had *For God's sake, Elsmore* written all over it, poor fellow.

"You've been working with Walden for too long," Rex said, stepping back. "A little color in a gentleman's daytime attire preserves him from utter forgettable-ness. I notice your partner always has flowers on his desk when I call upon him at the bank."

A detail, but telling. Quinn Wentworth, Duke of Walden, had been raised in the slums and was known to pinch a penny until it took a solemn oath never to be spent again. And yet, the man paid good coin for the lilies of the field.

"Walden wants the bank's customers to feel comfortable," Penrose said. "About Mrs. Hatfield."

"The bringer of agony." Rex tipped his hat to a pair of dowagers, and because they smiled at him, he also tipped his hat to the pug one of the ladies held. This occasioned giggling from two beldames who probably hadn't giggled in public for decades.

"As long as Mrs. Hatfield is competent to find the errors in my books," Rex went on, "and she can do so without alerting the London *Gazette*, I will consider myself eternally in her debt."

Perhaps he could make the fearsome Mrs. Hatfield giggle or at least smile. The day—and the night—went ever so much more smoothly when the ladies were smiling.

Penrose tried to walk more quickly; Rex refused to oblige him. They were early, the autumn weather was gloriously temperate for the time of year—a false summer that could not last—and what awaited Rex at the bank was hardly cause for eagerness.

"Mrs. Hatfield," Penrose said, "is one of those annoying people who can glance at an entire page of figures and spot where somebody read a three as a five. Her acumen is unnerving, and she doesn't understand how unusual she is."

Penrose was a lean, tall blond who did justice to exquisitely tailored morning attire, especially now that he'd deigned to adorn himself with a lowly carnation. His origins were vague, but he looked every inch the London nabob. Rex knew Penrose's partner better than he knew Penrose, but he trusted both men.

Under the circumstances, Rex had no choice but to trust them.

"Isn't it in the nature of an eccentric," he said, "to believe themselves the pattern card of normality? One of my aunts collects shoes. She goes on and on about them, and no matter how often the subject is changed, she brings the conversation back to shoes as if no other topic merits discussion."

"You dare not refer to our Mrs. Hatfield as eccentric," Penrose said, looking about as if checking for eavesdroppers. "She will reciprocate with her own opinion regarding you, the king, the Corn Laws, and half the bills pending in Parliament."

"You are protective of your auditor," Rex said. "You needn't be. I respect ability wherever I find it." Then too, beggars could not be choosers, especially not ducal beggars.

They came to another intersection and Rex flipped the crossing sweeper a coin. "How's business, Leonidas?"

The boy caught the vale in a grimy paw. "Right stinky, Your Grace, thank you very much."

"Glad to hear it. Try calling your enterprise odoriferous instead. You'll sound like a duke."

"Odor-ripper-us," Leonidas replied, grinning.

"Almost. Odor-if-or-us."

"Odoriferous. My enterprise is odoriferous and that means my job stinks. Thankee, Your Grace."

Penrose made a sound that might have been distress and cut across the street the instant a coach and four had rattled past.

"Enterprise and enterprising were last week's words,"

Rex said. "He likes big words, and I like to cross the street without stepping in horse droppings. A fair exchange."

That observation spiked Penrose's guns for about six paces, then, like the stalwart financier he was, he regained his verbal footing, more's the pity.

"Regarding Mrs. Hatfield," he said. "What she has, Your Grace, goes beyond ability. She was one of our first customers, because she had known His Grace of Walden previously. His reputation for fair dealing preceded him, which is why, when her statement arrived with a mistake amounting to tuppence, she demanded to see the bank partners. She looked about at the clerks, pointed a finger at one of our most promising lads, and accused him of failing to focus on his duties."

"Imagine that, a bank ledger failing to hold a fellow's attention." Rex knew of no stronger soporific than column after column of figures. He'd inherited the Dorset and Becker Savings and Trust at the age of twenty-one, a singular irony when a man had little aptitude for bookkeeping and inadequate time to tend to his own finances.

"Mrs. Hatfield looked at a dozen young fellows," Penrose went on, "all dressed about the same, and picked out the one who'd made a minor error. When we went back through his work—at her insistence—he'd made two other mistakes, one for eight pounds. His calculations were usually so accurate that the man assigned to verify them hadn't paid adequate attention either."

Penrose had clearly been fascinated with this two-penny drama, while Rex simply wanted to be done with the day's business. No previous Duke of Elsmore had ever had to bother his handsome head about two pounds, much less tuppence.

Hence, Rex's present difficulty. "How did Mrs. Hatfield identify the culprit?"

Penrose paused at the foot of the steps that led to his bank's impressive double doors. "The young man had taken on a second job copying a silk merchant's daily receipts each evening. His clothing was rumpled from having been slept in. He was pale, his eyes were slightly bloodshot, and he had a wax stain on the cuff of his shirt though the bank uses lamps rather than candles in the counting room. She not only spotted those details immediately, she also connected them to her missing tuppence. The boy was tired and his work grew sloppy as a result."

"Mrs. Hatfield sounds impressive." Also like she'd get on well with the aunties. Rex could picture them, a quartet of unrepentant old besoms, cackling like the Fates over tattle and tea.

"Impressive is the right word. I feel it fair to warn you she does not generally hold aristocrats in high regards, sir."

"Neither do I, Mr. Penrose. Always a pleasure to make the acquaintance of a woman of sound sensibilities. I'm sure we'll get on famously."

* * *

"My grandmother, whose good opinion of me ranks among my greatest treasures, pounded a few simple rules into her progeny." Eleanora Hatfield spoke calmly, as one must when addressing one's misguided employer. "Foremost among her rules is to never involve myself in the affairs of the peerage. Peers are trouble, and dukes the worst of the lot."

Quinn Wentworth, who had the great misfortune to be the Duke of Walden, drummed his fingers on the blotter of his massive desk. His nails were clean now, but Ellie had known him when he would have literally dirtied his hands doing any honest work.

"You don't mind involving yourself weekly with the bank's wage book, Eleanora Hatfield, and I number among the realm's peers."

Ellie wanted to pace and wave her hands, but had learned long ago that women were denied the luxury of speaking emphatically, if they wanted to be taken seriously. Of course, when she spoke moderately, she was also brushed off at least half the time, particularly by her own family.

She remained seated across from the desk, hands folded in her lap. "Correct you are, Your Grace, and look how you thank me for making a single exception to Grandmama's cardinal rule. You shove me out the door to chase down a missing penny for some fop who cannot be bothered to tally his own estate books."

"Madam, we are not shoving you out the door." His Grace adopted the wheedling, now-be-reasonable tone that made Ellie want to shut herself in the bank's vault. When Walden spoke to her like that, his blue eyes all earnest innocence, her grandmother's sage advice might as well have been instructions for the care and feeding of spotted unicorns.

"A few weeks," the duke continued, "a month at most, and you'll have His Grace of Elsmore's situation put to rights. You glance at a set of books and see what's amiss with them. Your powers of divination are legendary. For you to ferret out the problem with Elsmore's family accounts—"

"Need I remind you, sir, that I am a *bank* auditor. I will have no truck with a ducal family's ledgers."

Walden sat back, a financial king comfortable in his padded leather throne. "You inspect my household books. You do the monthly reconciliations for Lord Stephen and other members of the Wentworth family."

"You cannot help that you've become a duke," Ellie shot back. "I've overlooked that sad development for the past six years, and I'm willing to continue to extend you my tolerance because you are a decent man, you pay honest wages, and your title was none of your doing."

Her profession of loyalty had apparently sent her into some sort of verbal trap. A slight shift in His Grace's expression, a hint of a smile in his eyes, foretold her doom.

"Elsmore cannot help his birthright either. Is our own Mrs. Hatfield, defender of balanced ledgers and retriever of lost pennies, really such a snob?"

Not a snob. Sensible. "When did we lose you?" Ellie retorted. "You were one of us, born to scrape out a living as best you could, fated to dread cold and consumption along with most of the rest of England. Now you ask a favor from me on behalf of one of *them*."

The duke's smile died aborning, replaced by the signature Quinn Wentworth glacial dignity.

"You lost me," he said, "the moment I held my oldest child in my arms. Elizabeth will make her come-out someday, God willing, as will her sisters. Elsmore was the first peer to acknowledge my title, the first to leave his card. His mother and sisters call on my duchess. When my Bitty makes her bow, she'll have her pick of the bachelors, in part because several years ago, Elsmore opened doors for the Wentworth family."

That recitation sealed Ellie's fate.

If His Grace considered himself indebted to the Duke of Elsmore, then Ellie's job was forfeit should she refuse this assignment. Quinn Wentworth was loyal to his employees, but he was fanatically devoted to family.

A quality to be respected, most of the time. "I love working for Wentworth and Penrose," Ellie said. "I love the smell of the beeswax polish on the wainscoting, love how sunlight comes through the windows because you insist they always be clean. I love…"

She loved the sense of safety here, of having a worthwhile place and knowing it well. Her family could cheerfully racket from one misadventure to another. Ellie had to have peace, order, and respectability.

"You love how the clerks live in dread of your raised eyebrow," His Grace said. "Love knowing which messengers favor licorice candy and which prefer peppermint. We're your family, so on behalf of that family, I ask you to extend a courtesy to another institution. If one bank fails, all banks suffer, and rumors about His Grace's personal finances would send Dorset and Becker straight into the cesspit."

He had her there. A bank might start the week solvent and, on the strength of nothing more than club gossip about a single bank director, end the week floundering.

"I don't want to do this. Why can't Elsmore's solicitors manage this task?"

"I didn't want to be a duke, Eleanora. Elsmore's solicitors should already have seen any irregularities in the estate books. That they either failed to notice them or declined to mention them means the lawyers can't be relied on. This project should be your idea of a holiday. Say you'll do it, and I'll introduce you to Elsmore."

Wentworth and Penrose had given Ellie a job when most banks considered women fit only to scrub the floors after hours. There were exceptions of course. Lady Jersey ran Child's Bank. Her Grace of St. Alban's managed Coutts, but Ellie was neither a countess nor a duchess. Quinn Wentworth and Joshua Penrose had opened the door to respectability for her, and thus, Ellie would always be in their debt.

"I'll have a look at Elsmore's estate books," she said,

"and maintain my duties here. In the evenings, His Grace must make available to me any document I request."

"Elsmore's holdings are more complicated than my own, and a few hours of an evening won't allow you to do justice to the task. I'll inform Milton that you've taken a month's leave to deal with a family matter."

That Walden was willing to part with Ellie's services for a month told her volumes about his sense of indebtedness to Elsmore. All that remained was to be introduced to the mincing fop who'd mucked up simple math relating to bales of wool and boxes of candles.

"Wentworth and Penrose cannot audit itself over the next month," Ellie said. "Who will mind the books here while I'm gone?"

"You'll be gone for only a month."

"Two weeks, during which the tellers will notice that I'm away from my post. They won't mean to make errors, but every one of them occasionally does. You do too." About twice a year, which was amazing, considering the sheer volume of calculations His Grace performed. He not only kept his hand in as a bank director, he owned half a dozen properties, and oversaw a few charities as well.

The duke paused halfway to the door. "What do you suggest?"

Ellie got to her feet, because putting off the inevitable was not in her nature. "Did you honestly think to let the books go for even *two weeks* without a reconciliation? Did you expect me to merely skim a few pages when I returned from this frolic for Elsmore? Haven't I taught you any better than that?"

"Two weeks isn't so long," the duke said. "I'll keep a close eye on the bank in your absence."

Ellie marched up to him. "Not good enough. You are

the managing director for the institution and you still post entries from the head teller's ledger to the bible if Mr. Penrose is otherwise occupied. You will have Lord Stephen review the books in my absence. If there's an error, he'll find it."

Lord Stephen was the duke's younger brother, a genius of protean interests, and a right pain in His Grace's arse. Ellie rented rooms in one of his lordship's properties, and while his lordship had a genius's share of impatience with lesser mortals, Ellie trusted him to review the books.

"By choosing Lord Stephen to hold the reins, you are punishing me for asking a favor of you," His Grace said, "and yet the work—finding inconsistencies in the books— is your greatest delight in life."

He always smelled good, of flowers and spices. Ellie hadn't realized that until Jane, Her Grace of Walden, had listed a pleasant scent among her husband's many adorable qualities. The notion of anybody adoring a duke...

"My greatest delight in life is looking after the books at *my* bank, Your Grace. Tidying up after some prancing buffoon with too much money and not enough meaningful work is my idea of a penance."

His Grace opened the door and gestured for Ellie to precede him. "Come along, then. Elsmore is kicking his heels with Penrose in the conference room. I'll introduce you to your penance."

Just like that, the battle was over and lost, and Ellie's next two weeks taken hostage. "I will start Elsmore's audit on Monday."

"Elsmore will be overjoyed to hear it."

"And well he should be."

His Grace allowed Ellie to have the last word, which was prudent of him.

Joshua Penrose stood when Ellie entered the conference room, as did another man. Ellie took one look at the stranger and cursed herself for a fool, though Elsmore bowed politely and thanked her for being willing to "lend her assistance."

She'd been wrong, and she *hated* being wrong. Elsmore was neither a fop, nor prancing, nor a buffoon, and two weeks in his employ would be the longest fortnight of her life.

* * *

Rex had waited in the Wentworth and Penrose conference room like a brawling schoolboy awaited a headmaster's judgment, though no schoolyard pugilist had ever enjoyed such luxurious surroundings. The walls were wainscoted in oak and covered with green silk. The floors sported first-quality cream, gold, and green Axminster from wall to wall. The furniture was heavy, well padded, and polished to a gleaming shine.

This might have been any conference room in any bank, except—Rex hadn't noticed this until he'd been in the room many times—the windows were clean, inside and out, despite being one floor above a busy street. London coal smoke dirtied everything it touched, from laundry to ladies' gloves to Mayfair mansions.

The result of clean windows, though, was a rare sense of light and freshness within Wentworth and Penrose's walls. Unlike most commercial establishments—including Dorset and Becker, come to think of it—this bank was maintained to the standards of a wealthy domicile rather than a busy shop. The difference was both subtle and profound.

Cathedrals, unheated and often set apart from major cities, had the same clean, benevolent light.

The Duke of Walden himself held the door for a small-ish female who preceded him into the room as if he were her footman rather than a wealthy peer.

Rex liked women—almost all women, which was handy when a fellow was knee-deep in sisters, aunties, and cousins of the feminine persuasion. He would have stood had any female joined the meeting, because manners were the least courtesy the ladies were due.

With this woman, a man would sit about on his lazy backside at his peril. She did not walk, she marched, plain gray skirts swishing like finest silk. Her posture would have done credit to Wellington reviewing the troops before a battle. She wore her dark hair in a ruthlessly tidy bun; a pair of spotless spectacles perched halfway down a slightly aquiline nose.

She had the figure of an opera dancer and the bearing of a thoroughly vexed mother superior.

Rex took in these details—and interesting details they were—as the lady crossed the room and snapped off a shallow curtsey. She declined to offer her hand, as was a woman's prerogative.

He bowed, and for once refrained from smiling at a female. He had an arsenal of smiles. Friendly, flirtatious, bored, condescending, menacing—that one was not for use with the ladies—but this woman would likely slap him silly for such posturing.

The Duke of Walden dealt with the introductions, and all the while, Mrs. Hatfield studied Rex as if deciding where to take the first bite of him.

"Elsmore at your service, madam. A pleasure to meet you."

She aimed a glower down that not-exactly-dainty nose. "Likewise, Your Grace."

"We'll leave you two some privacy," Penrose said. "Would not do for Wentworth and Penrose to be privy to the concerns of a rival institution's director. Your Grace, madam, good day."

He trundled off to the door, a tutor much relieved to turn his charge back over to the nursery maids. Walden followed him but paused before leaving.

"I'm down the corridor if I'm needed." He sent Rex an unreadable look, then left, closing the door.

"Which of us do you suppose would be calling upon Walden for aid?" Rex asked. "I don't quite count His Grace a friend, but I have asked this favor of him, haven't I?" Rex wasn't sure anybody considered Walden a friend, and Walden appeared to prefer it that way.

Mrs. Hatfield opened a drawer at the head of the table and withdrew several sheets of paper and a pencil.

"The favor you seek is from me, Your Grace. Applying to my employers was mere courtesy. Shall we begin? I need to know exactly what evidence you have of errors in your bookkeeping, and the sooner we embark on that discussion the sooner you can get back to"—her gaze flicked over him—"whatever it is you do."

"I'm sure your time is valuable," Rex said, pulling out a chair for her. "I appreciate that you're willing to take on this project."

He more than appreciated it. If his personal books were problematic, whether due to errors, bad accounting procedures, or something else, his own solicitors hadn't noticed. Rex would explain the situation to them only after he grasped how the inaccuracies had arisen and what to do about them.

Mrs. Hatfield looked at the chair, then at him, her air of annoyance fading into puzzlement. "You need not act the dandy with me, sir. I am entirely capable of managing both my skirts and a chair. One can, if one dresses sensibly."

Eleanora Hatfield did everything sensibly. Rex knew this from the tiny dash of lace at her collar, from the small, plain watch pinned to her left sleeve—an odd but practical location—and from the ink stain on her right thumb.

She was painfully sensible, while he was...painfully worried about his wretched, blasted, bedamned family finances.

"Holding a chair for a lady is not acting the dandy, madam, but rather, being a gentleman. If the fellows at this institution have inured you to discourtesy, shame upon them, for I am unwilling to commit the same transgression." This skirmish over a chair mattered. Rex needed her help, but he would not be treated like a pestilence when he'd committed no wrong.

Her brows drew down, and fine dark brows they were too. Nicely arched, a little heavier than was fashionable. As she rustled closer, he considered that she wasn't so much annoyed with him as she was flustered.

"Does nobody hold your chair, Mrs. Hatfield? Mr. Hatfield has much to answer for."

She sat as regally as a cat settling onto a velvet cushion, tidied the blank paper into a stack, and took up the pencil. "Mr. Hatfield is none of your concern, Your Grace. Tell me about your situation and spare no details. My discretion is absolute, and I gather the situation is becoming urgent."

The situation, in Rex's opinion, had passed urgent some time ago. If his instincts were to be trusted, and they generally were, the situation now qualified as dire.

Chapter Two

Rex began a recitation of the family's history, which as far as titleholders were concerned, went back for three dreary centuries. The previous Elsmore peers had had a knack for coming down on the right side of political dramas, which had started them off with an earldom, and then seen them elevated to ducal honors. By then, the family had founded the Dorset and Becker Savings and Trust, though the Dukes of Elsmore had known better than to keep exclusive control of the institution in their own hands.

Other venerable families had shares in the bank, allowing Rex's ancestors to retreat to the gentility of directorships and quarterly meetings. Younger sons and cousins involved themselves in the business as employees. Thus the institution remained a family venture, and solved the conundrum of what to do with spares and relations unsuited for the church or the military.

"This arrangement has served us well," Rex said, "and also served the bank well."

Mrs. Hatfield scratched away with her pencil for a moment. "If your books aren't balancing, then some aspect of the dukedom is not in good repair. Somewhere in your ledgers, a cross-tally isn't done, a series of entries is not verified. Bookkeeping is both an art and a science, and yours has fallen into disrepair."

She spoke gently, as if diagnosing him with a serious illness.

"The problem is doubtless minor," Rex replied, "but over time, small amounts can add up. The Dukes of Elsmore have always had a sterling reputation, as has any financial institution we take an interest in. I am determined to uphold that tradition."

An auditor ought not to have such pretty eyes. Mrs. Hatfield peered over her spectacles, looking like a solemn little owl, except that an owl's eyes didn't slant like a cat's, or shade toward a velvety chocolate. Nor did an owl have a capacity to appear concerned over a few missing quid.

"How did you first notice something amiss, Your Grace?"

"A few details that literally didn't add up." And a persistent suspicion that a prudent peer would spend less time waltzing and more time with an abacus. "A tally here, a shortfall there. Must we trouble ourselves over those specifics now?"

Mrs. Hatfield put down her pencil. She checked her watch and compared the time with that told by a great monstrosity ticking away on the mantel. Rex had the sense she was choosing her words, or perhaps counting to ten.

"The word auditor comes from the Latin *audire*," she said, "meaning to hear. An auditor *listens*, Your Grace. In former times, we listened to the accounts read out while we kept tallies in our heads. Now we not only pay attention to the books, we also attend to what happens around those books. Anybody can make a mistake in calculations or transcription. You can see a seven where I see a one. But if what's occurring is something other than random errors, then I must discern the pattern, and that means I need all the information you have."

She spoke so earnestly, as if instructing a slow scholar who very, very much needed passing marks.

Rex rose, having tolerated as much inactivity as he could. "You want to know how much I lost at the club last night? What I spent at the haberdasher's? What baubles I purchased for my current *chère amie*?"

"Yes, though I doubt you have a mistress in keeping at present."

A frisson of unease had Rex pretending to examine a sketch of a small girl with a large dog. In a few strokes, the artist had caught the dog's protectiveness and the child's trust, also her resemblance to the current Duchess of Walden.

"Mrs. Hatfield, you cannot possibly divine that I'm without a current attachment merely by looking at me."

"Of course not," she said, using a penknife to sharpen her pencil point. "I merely read the newspaper. You are escorting only the most eligible of the blue-blooded young ladies these days, but not singling any woman out for special attention. Your set considers it good form to approach marriage without other entanglements, and you are of an age to take a wife. You have no direct heir, no younger brother even. Hence, my conclusion. Now, might we resume our discussion of your books?"

Rex's social life apparently did not interest her beyond

what was reported in the tattlers, but then, the vast, cease-
less whirl of his entertainments seldom interested him. He
wandered back to the table and sent the lady a questioning
glance.

"Mind if I sit?"

"Your Grace, if you insist on silly rituals we will
accomplish little. You must treat me as if I were a
chambermaid or a footman, an employee, though one who
labors with her mind rather than her hands. No more of
your chair-holding, bobbing about, or pretending you need
my permission to sit."

Her handwriting was painfully neat, her attire painfully
plain, and yet simple manners flustered her.

Rex remained by the chair to her left. "As a boy, I
slurped up proper deportment with my morning porridge,
and as a peer, I hold myself out as an example of British
manhood at its most refined, at least when a lady is present.
With you, I must tend to the silly rituals or I will lose my
good standing in the Decorous Dukes club."

That salvo earned him not even a hint of a smile. "You
may sit." She set her knife aside. "Sir."

"Don't pout," he said, patting her wrist. "A man who
insists on showing you common courtesies is not the worst
fate that could befall you. Once you've concluded your
little inquisition, our paths will hardly cross." A pity, that.
Eleanora Hatfield did not want to dance with him or learn
his opinion regarding the weather. That alone made her a
rarity among his female acquaintances.

She held the pencil, now dagger-sharp, poised over the
paper. "I am loath to contradict my betters, but your path
and mine will cross frequently," she said. "Until I have
solved the problems besetting your accounts, our paths will
be one and the same."

* * *

Ellie liked sitting at the head of the conference table. In the usual course, this allowed her to have a partner on either side of her, so they could all three peruse the same ledgers or documents.

With Elsmore, she wished he'd taken the head—most men would have—so she could sit at the foot.

He smelled not merely clean, but expensively clean and masculine. His shaving soap bore the scents of sandalwood and God knew what. Some exotic orchid that doubtless only bloomed under a blue moon in the deepest jungles of darkest South America. On a woman, the scent would be too heavy. On a man it faded to a reminder of morning ablutions and a promise of evening waltzes.

"Then there's my little Ambledown," Elsmore said. "I love that place. Anybody would."

He'd been listing properties for the past thirty minutes, and the odd thing was, he knew them all as if he'd spent most of his life at each one. The sheep farms in Cumbria, the castle in Peebleshire, the hunting box on the edge of the New Forest, the modest estates he managed for his aunts and cousins.

"Who does the accounting for Ambledown?" Ellie asked.

"The housekeeper, and she sends me monthly reports. You'd get on well with her."

Elsmore did this, tossed out casual lures that sparkled before Ellie like golden apples: *Why would I get on well with her?* He seemed to admire this housekeeper—he certainly trusted her—and he smiled when he spoke of her.

"If I could show you one property," he said, "it would be Ambledown. My grandmother used it as a dower house, and my sisters and I ran wild there with the neighbor children. My parents liked for us to be near them in London—Ambledown lies in Surrey—but not underfoot at the town house."

His smile had grown so wistful, Ellie paused in her note-taking and indulged in a single personal question. "How did your grandmother feel about having young children underfoot?"

"We were the curse of her old age, the tribulation she had to endure for sins committed in past lives. She told us that regularly, while making certain we had good tutors, sound ponies, and other children to run amok with."

Oh, to have had a grandmother able to tease her grandchildren like that. "When did you last look over the books from Ambledown, Your Grace?"

He propped his chin in his hand. "Who ran amok with you, Mrs. Hatfield? When you were a little girl in pigtails, much smarter than your brothers but not yet confined by the strictures of decorum, who tempted you to climb trees, roll down hillsides, and play pirates in a punt tied to a stump?"

The first part of the question—Who ran amok with you, Mrs. Hatfield?—might have been flirtation or worse, an announcement of male interest. Except that the rest of the duke's question, about a little girl in pigtails, was genuine. He regarded Ellie in some puzzlement, his blue-eyed gaze roving over her as if trying to discern who she reminded him of.

"I had not the luxury of running amok, Your Grace." Her family had done more than their share of that. "My upbringing was most humble. Tell me more about Ambledown. Any tenancies?"

Ellie pretended to study the notes on the page while she reminded herself why her upbringing had been so humble. Humble and perilous.

"Six farms," he said. "Possibly five. I've asked the land steward to look for a buyer for one of the farms. The tenants decamped for America and failed to apprise the steward of their plans. Neglect resulted."

Ellie set down her pencil. "No, neglect did not *result*. You employ a steward, and his job is to ensure your resources are well cared for. An entire family leaving a district for foreign shores doesn't happen in the dead of night. Livestock must be fed and watered. A milch cow cannot go for more than a day without attention. Chickens must be let out of the henhouse to forage for daily sustenance or they soon die. No farmer worthy of a ducal tenancy would simply walk away from his animals unannounced."

Elsmore studied her from the place at her left hand. No smile lightened his expression, and though he wore a small bouquet of violets and lilies of the valley on his lapel, Ellie had the sense that even without his rank, he'd be a formidable man.

"You were raised in the country," he said.

"Yorkshire." She regretted that admission as soon as she'd made it. "How many other properties do you have, Your Grace?"

"In England? That's the lot of them, as far as I know."

In the name of fractions, decimals, and ratios... He'd listed a dozen pieces of real estate, all of them income-producing, all of them staffed year-round except a fishing cottage with twelve bedrooms near Sunderland that had only a couple as caretaker.

"You have foreign properties as well, Your Grace?"

He waved a languid hand. "Vineyards in France and Portugal, a villa in Italy I've never laid eyes on, a forest in Bavaria. My progenitors believed that if the family had need of something—wool, lumber, brandy—we had best have the means to secure it. Hence, the dukedom developed a tendency to sprawl."

Sprawl. He referred to a small kingdom as *a tendency to sprawl* and did so in a tone between apologetic and disgruntled.

"Various cousins help oversee the foreign bits," Elsmore went on. "Cousin James occasionally jaunts up to Scotland for me—he's the nominal heir, hence my willingness to impose upon him—and he stops in at the fishing cottage en route."

"And across all of the properties, investments, businesses, and what not, how much money would you say has gone missing?"

Elsmore looked around the room, as if he'd misplaced his hat. "Not much, a few thousand pounds? All I know is, this year's harvests were good, my tenants pay their rents on time, seed and feed prices have dropped since Waterloo, and yet my expenses grew while my income declined, even after I account for fluctuations in corn prices. The discrepancy is five thousand pounds at most, but I cannot justify it."

Long practice allowed Ellie to jot that figure down as if all those zeros were commonplace. "That's in total, or this year?"

"In the past twelve months. I was hoping you might be able to take a peek at what happened prior to that." He sounded so hopeful, so...charming.

I will kill Quinn Wentworth. Ellie put down her pencil, tidied her notes into a stack, and chose her words carefully.

"Your Grace, while I understand the delicacy of your position, and I wish I could help you, this task exceeds my abilities. I'm sorry to disappoint you, but I really must decline the assignment."

He rose, braced his hands on the table, and leaned close. "No, Mrs. Hatfield, you really must not."

She got to her feet and went nose-to-nose with him. "Yes, I must. I absolutely must decline this assignment."

* * *

Joshua Penrose ambled into Quinn's office. If the door was open, anybody was welcome to intrude on Quinn, provided they came on bank business. If the door was closed, the angel Gabriel would have been taken severely to task for interrupting.

"No shouting from the conference room," Joshua said. "What do you suppose they're up to?"

Quinn had left his door open precisely to monitor developments down the corridor. The conference room sat between his office and Joshua's, but by design, the walls allowed little sound to carry.

"I expect Mrs. Hatfield is interrogating Elsmore more thoroughly than he was ever quizzed at Eton."

"Harrow. The Dorsets are a Harrow family, and they've been known to send the occasional younger son to Cambridge."

"How broad-minded of them."

Quinn's younger brother Stephen occasionally lectured at Cambridge, also at Oxford and various Continental institutions. He was in London at present, though he no longer stayed at the ducal town house when in the capital.

Joshua took a love seat situated beneath a window and helped himself to a biscuit from the tray on the low table.

"Eleanora is doubtless interrogating, but what is Elsmore doing?"

"Reciting," Quinn said, giving up on the lease agreement he'd been reading. "Or confessing."

"Why did he come to us?" Joshua said. "Why not have a

word with the army of solicitors he employs, why not set a
cousin or uncle to the task? A thorough examination of the
books could be a simple exercise in prudence, a modern
measure for modern times. We have an auditor on staff
and have nearly since we opened our London doors."

They didn't have merely an auditor, they had Eleanora
Hatfield, the most observant, logical, financially astute
person Quinn had the pleasure to know.

"Family money is delicate," he said. "Discretion must
be assured, and solicitors can be put in situations where
loyalties are divided."

"When did you start speaking duke-ish?"

"In plain banker-ish, the source of Elsmore's problems
might lie quite close to home. He describes the situation
as trivial—one tally a little short, another even less than
that—but the problem is significant enough that he's handling it both quietly and with the most competent resource
he could bring to bear. Don't mistake Elsmore's charm for
a lack of shrewdness."

Joshua munched another biscuit into oblivion. He
favored raspberry glazes and had been known to add butter
even to those.

"How does Elsmore know of our Mrs. Hatfield? Eleanora fancies herself something of a secret weapon."

"I might have mentioned her over steak and port." To
Elsmore, in whom Quinn placed as much confidence as he
did in any peer.

A muted exchange of words sounded through the wall
behind Quinn's desk.

Joshua was on his feet in the next instant. "I'll not have
him intimidating her. If Elsmore thinks his rank entitles
him to rude behavior with an employee of Wentworth and
Penrose, he is sorely mistaken."

Quinn remained seated. He was married, he had three daughters and two sisters. "Wait. Elsmore will not get the better of this exchange."

Joshua paused, hand on the door latch. "How can you tell?"

"Firstly, he is in no position to bargain. Eleanora has no use for peers of any stripe, while Elsmore would not have asked for our help unless he had no alternatives. Secondly, they must sort themselves out without an audience lest somebody be needlessly humiliated."

"If Elsmore belittles Mrs. Hatfield, even implies a casual slight…"

"Joshua, it isn't Mrs. Hatfield's dignity that's imperiled. Have another biscuit and tell me what you think of this lease."

The exchange from the conference room continued in muted, emphatic tones. Joshua brought the tray of biscuits to the desk, picked up the lease, and took a seat.

* * *

The common view of dukes was likely that they were refused little and indulged much.

Ha.

Mrs. Hatfield glowered up at Rex as if he'd threatened to burn the Union Jack, curse out loud in the nave of St. Paul's, and—high crime, indeed—announce that two plus two equaled five.

"I am not up to the challenge you put before me." She hurled that thunderbolt with such absolute certainty that Moses would have scampered down Mount Sinai intent on scribbling her words at the bottom of his stone tablets.

Or possibly across the top.

"You audit this entire bank," Rex said. "I'm told you not only audit the ducal estate books, but you also supervise the ledgers for every member of the Wentworth family. His Grace of Walden—not noted for praising anybody or anything except that family—has sung rhapsodies to your acumen."

Great brown eyes framed in long lashes and swooping brows showed momentary confusion.

"You exaggerate, sir."

Most women adored honest compliments and didn't get enough of them. "Walden himself claims you have saved Wentworth and Penrose much embarrassment and even more liability. You are the conscience of this whole institution and the confidante of a fabulously solvent dukedom. You *can* help me. You simply choose not to. Why?"

She clearly had her reasons. Mrs. Eleanora Hatfield likely did nothing without at least three sound reasons rounded to the nearest unassailable conclusion.

She subsided into her chair. Rex stayed on his feet.

"I know the Walden dukedom," she said. "I've had years to learn its patterns and peculiarities. I know the people who populate it. His Grace has taken me with him back to Yorkshire, so I can make the acquaintance of the staff at the ducal seat and instruct them on proper accounting. His sisters, Lady Althea and Lady Constance, have established their accounts in keeping with my guidance. Your situation, however…"

Her gaze fell to a dozen pages of meticulously penciled notes.

"That you don't know my situation is an advantage," Rex said. "I am familiar with the patterns and personalities. You will bring the fresh eye."

"I would help you if I could, but your financial picture is very different from the Walden holdings."

"Certainly it is. Walden's duchess could buy and sell me with her pin money."

Mrs. Hatfield stole a glance at him, then checked her watch. That glance told him she was re-arranging her artillery, choosing the words best suited to conveying a difficult message to a difficult duke.

"The two dukedoms differ, sir, in that the Walden money hasn't had three hundred years to develop bad habits and poor deportment. People deride new money as if it doesn't spend as well as the other kind, but give me new money over old any day. New money has no dark past, no airs and graces, no social bonds that transcend law and custom to afford it powers money ought not to have."

What an extraordinary perspective, and how passionately she adhered to it. "You disdain to help me because my lineage dates back centuries? Walden outranks me. His title is thirty-seven years older than mine, and yet you work for him. What is it that truly troubles you? You must know I will pay handsomely for your services."

She rubbed her fingers across her forehead, the first sign of human frailty he'd seen from her.

"Listen to me, Your Grace. The Walden dukedom had but five properties when I undertook its rehabilitation, none managed by family. His Grace and I, or Lord Stephen and I, went property by property examining revenue and expenses. We sacked the stewards whose books were suspicious—which was all of them—and hired people whom I could train to keep proper books."

She switched to using her thumb to make slow circles on her temple. "Bringing that situation to rights was relatively simple. The Wentworth family books have always been spotless, and the bank has always been well run. By comparison..."

She sent him a look of sheer pity, which was both novel and unsettling. Nobody pitied a duke. "By comparison?"

"The situation with the Walden dukedom was like a seventy-four gunner that needed some caulking below the water line. We looked in the usual places, sealed up the boards, and made a basically sound vessel seaworthy again."

"And my dukedom?"

"A splendidly appointed seagoing yacht to appearances, full of your family and employees on holiday. The vessel hasn't had any maintenance since the day it was launched, is not scheduled for dry dock anytime soon, and has headed for the open ocean while taking on water in three dozen places, with a storm bearing down fast."

Rex liked that she was honest. He did not like that her opinion confirmed his own suspicions. "I still seem to have pots of money."

"If you can gradually diversify your holdings beyond crops and livestock, you will likely always have pots of money, but you do not have control of that money to the extent that you should. I would have to undertake extensive study to ascertain how much of the problem is due to plain error and how much comes from other sources."

That much honesty was a bit daunting.

Rex resumed his seat. His solicitors muttered about cits in trade, standards being abandoned, and England always needing her farmers, and yet, land rents had been dropping since the war had ended. Mrs. Hatfield advised diversification, while she refused to render aid.

"Other sources of the bookkeeping problem," he said slowly. "Sources such as theft?"

"Embezzlement, theft, graft, schemes...yes. When a sum such as you have mentioned is leaking from your books, you are very likely being fleeced."

That conclusion had hovered at the edge of Rex's mind like a persistent housefly, an explanation that fit the facts but not the logic or the intuition.

"Then that's all the more reason why you must help me. If somebody familiar to me is stealing from the family coffers, I cannot be expected to see the patterns you allude to."

She closed her eyes and she might have murmured something in French. "To untangle your situation could take months, and I do not have months to lend you."

"I do not have months to borrow from you either. Repairing my yacht, as you term it, has become urgent. We'll resolve it before the Season has ended." His mother, sisters, aunties, and cousins sailed with him on that yacht. Taking on more water was unacceptable.

Mrs. Hatfield's glower was back. "*We* shall do no such thing. I have a job, and my first loyalty is to Wentworth and Penrose. I have no desire to become your financial bullyboy, restoring order to your books by main force."

No bullyboy had ever approached his duties with such an air of feminine exasperation. No bullyboy had such fine brown eyes or had the power to distract Rex with an ink-stained thumb.

Mr. Hatfield was a lucky fellow, and not simply because his household books were in order.

"May I trust your discretion, madam?"

She tested the point of her pencil against her fingertip. "A bit late for that, Your Grace."

She was trying not to smile. The battle was waged mostly in her eyes, though a certain quirk of her lips betrayed the conflict as well. Rex batted aside a desire to *make* her smile, not only because that pursuit was irrelevant to the present discussion, but also because he'd likely fail.

"I am of an age to marry," he said.

She waved a hand in a do-go-on motion.

"I have no younger brothers, and thus must take a wife. My sisters in all likelihood will take husbands before I myself am married."

"The aristocracy marries. This is hardly a confidence, Your Grace. You've mentioned any number of cousins employed on your various properties, several at your bank. I'm sure one of them is eager to oblige if you fail to produce a legitimate son. Fortunately, you have aunties to ensure your choice of duchess is sound, and I wish you the joy of your courtship."

Perhaps Mr. Hatfield was not such a lucky man after all. His wife clearly held the institution of marriage in no affection whatsoever, though the fault for that might lie at the feet of the husband.

None of your business, old man.

"I will take a wife and at least make a good faith effort to see to the succession."

She stuck the pencil behind her ear. "Such a sacrifice on your part, *seeing to the succession*. Never did mortal man engage in comparable heroics for such a noble cause at such great risk to his own well-being. I commend you for it."

Not even Rex's male cousins would have fired that salvo, though the lady had a point.

"Forget about me, then," Rex went on, "but recall my three sisters. Any one of them could bring a fellow up to scratch at tonight's soiree, and I could be in settlement negotiations next week. What do you suppose a detailed examination of my books would reveal?"

Mrs. Hatfield gazed into the middle distance, as if counting butterflies dancing on imaginary sunbeams. "Looming chaos, thinly veiled graft, perhaps even somebody hoping to make you look like the thief."

Ye thundering heavenly choruses, Rex had not thought of that. "You have a pessimistic view of life."

She went to tidy a lock of hair by sweeping it over her ear and had apparently forgotten about the pencil, which sailed onto the table and clattered past her reach.

"An auditor's lot results in an unflattering view of human nature, sir."

Rex took a moment to assess strategy. An assertion of rank would likely provoke not simply a smile but gales of laughter. Nobody told this woman what to do, not even the Duke of Walden. She apparently prowled the bank at liberty, poking her nose wherever she deigned to poke it.

She was a stranger to flattery or perhaps its sworn foe.

Attempted bribery would earn him summary eviction from the premises.

What did he have that Mrs. Eleanora Hatfield—and Mr. Hatfield, if any such fellow existed—wanted badly enough to take on the challenge of untangling his books?

"If you will aid me, madam, and put my books to rights, I will deed to you or to the party of your choice ownership of Ambledown in fee simple absolute. The property carries no mortgages, and I assure you it is profitable. Being so close to London, I've bided there frequently and can vouch for the integrity of my retainers and tenants."

He'd surprised her. Those swooping brows rose, then knit. The brown eyes stared at the errant pencil in the middle of the table. She straightened in her chair, pursed her lips, and shook her head.

"I cannot leave my post at Wentworth and Penrose, sir, not for the length of time required to investigate your situation. My employers expect loyalty from me, and—"

"Let's ask them, shall we? Ask them if you can take a leave of absence. I will double your salary." If she put the dukedom on sound footing, he could afford to give her three of the smaller estates and be ahead for having done so.

She rose and snatched up the pencil. "Stop that. Stop trying to bribe me."

"Offering the very compensation you've longed to earn isn't bribery. Do you know what rumors of my personal insolvency would do to my bank?"

"Yes."

She likely did not know what rumors of insolvency would do to his mother, aunts, and sisters. Rachel had been out for "several" years, and she'd had no offers for the past two. Mama was worried, Rachel was quietly despairing, and Rex was supposed to bring all to rights with a smile and a nod.

Mrs. Hatfield paced, the pencil once again behind her ear, and Rex held his peace. He'd told himself that tending to the books was so much financial housekeeping, but then he'd taken a closer look at the figures and admitted he had a problem. Watching Walden's auditor wrestle with the decision to aid him confirmed that the problem was significant.

Significant to the point of social disaster.

The family could remain handsomely solvent and still be ruined, which meant a dozen cousins, three blameless old women, and several uncles would suffer from the taint of scandal. The cousins would likely have to leave the bank's employ, the aunties would withdraw from society. Rex's sisters would be doomed to rural spinster-dom.

And then the bank would fail.

Unless Eleanora Hatfield took his situation in hand, and even then, scandal might still be unavoidable.

"I'll help you," Mrs. Hatfield said, coming to a halt before the unlit hearth. "I will give you two weeks. You will pay twice my salary for those two weeks because I will very likely work twice as many hours as I ought. I will devote myself entirely to a review of your domestic books."

That was an ideal compromise. The banking community was small and gossipy, though Mrs. Hatfield taking a short leave of absence was of no moment, and Rex was confident that she'd not abandon a project halfway through.

"You are turning up your nose at Ambledown?" Was that arrogance on her part, foolishness, or something else?

"I am not a country squire, Your Grace."

Neither am I, more's the pity. "What if two weeks isn't enough?"

"Don't be greedy," she said, gathering up her papers from the table. "I will give you two weeks and report my findings. You will give me complete access to your personal finances and to your time."

The analogy of the tooth-drawer came to mind. "Of course. When do we begin?"

"Immediately."

Chapter Three

Contrary to the myth at Wentworth and Penrose, Ellie could not ingest facts and figures without limit. She was sharpest and most efficient when she alternated careful work with periods of quiet reflection. If the weather was pleasant, she left the bank for a time at midday.

The excuse of record was to tend to errands, but her real agenda was to clear her head. She would sit watching pigeons in a public square or wander market stalls at the nearest fashionable arcade. Polite society provided an endless, fascinating pageant to a woman who'd come of age intimately acquainted with life in the slums.

An entire afternoon spent with His Grace of Elsmore had exceeded Ellie's tolerance for new information, and thus she was pre-occupied on her way home.

His Grace wore the fiction of a heedless aristocrat well. The elegantly whimsical nosegay on his lapel, the gold pin in his lacy cravat—not a rearing stallion, but a rearing unicorn. The small talk strewn about during what should have been a purely business meeting.

He was not an idle, stupid bore, more's the pity.

"Have you missed me, long lost dearest Eleanora?"

Ellie marched on without stumbling, barely, despite the tall young man who'd appropriated the place at her elbow. Jack was a clerk today, blending seamlessly with all the other clerks and shopgirls hurrying home to their suppers. He wore a lanky, slightly rumpled mien, his signature good nature beaming from his blue eyes. His dark hair was longish, but clean and recently combed.

"Throughout all of creation," Ellie replied, "down through the mists of antiquity and forward into the dimly perceivable future of the race, I have not nor will I ever miss you."

"What a gift you have for the understated endearment." Jack tipped his hat to a lady in a fancy bonnet, and of course, she smiled back at him.

"What a gift you have for showing up where you're not welcome."

He kept up with her easily. Ellie could not outrun him, could not scold him into slinking off to the back alleys and stews where he belonged. Jack knew well how to appear respectable, usually the better to behave with complete disregard for the law.

"Some thanks I get for my tender concern, Eleanora. One would think we were strangers."

"One wishes we were strangers. What do you want, Jack?" Other than to remind Ellie that she would never be free of the past. Jack and Mick left her in peace just long enough that she began to hope, and then they pounced.

"I seek only to brighten my day with the merest glimpse of your countenance, dear cousin. To reassure myself that the object of my concern yet thrives, despite the distance between us."

"You're not rolled up," Ellie said, as Jack charmed another passing lady into a smile. "When you lack funds, your cuffs aren't clean, your boots aren't polished, and you pawn your watch." She'd taken in those details at a glance.

"Do you know how I treasure you, dearest Eleanora? Do you know how I wish right now you would take my arm in the fashion of two people companionably disposed toward each other?"

"If I gave you my arm, you'd return it missing a hand."

He laughed, and Jack had such a charming laugh, damn him. "I had occasion to chat up one of the lads at your bank over a steak and kidney pie. He said our Mrs. Hatfield was in the conference room all afternoon with some nabob, which got the clerks to speculating. Wasn't just any nabob either, though the boy of course hasn't memorized Debrett's."

Jack nearly had.

"You will leave Peterfield alone, Jack, lest you cost him his position." Peterfield was the newest messenger, and therefore the hungriest. Not ten years old, still finding his feet among the other lads. Still hanging on every word of gossip that dropped from the indiscreet lips of the clerks when they thought they were private over their nooning.

Ellie would have a stern word with Peterfield. Jack, like most career criminals, eschewed certain behavior as beneath his dignity. Fortunately for Peterfield, abducting pretty little boys to sell them to the brothels fell into that category. Peterfield had been lucky—this time.

"I undertook a good deed," Jack said, "bought a poor lad a meal, and you castigate me for it. Where is your Christian charity? You were brought up better than this."

No, she hadn't been, not after the age of eleven.

Ellie turned the corner onto her own street, and Jack stayed right by her side. He was apparently feeling bold—or desperate.

"Lord Stephen is in town," Ellie said. "I gather he'll be staying for some time." She gathered no such thing. His lordship—her landlord—came and went as he pleased, where he pleased. Eleanora balanced his books. She did not pretend to know his plans, nor did she want to.

Jack came to a halt though Ellie's rooms were two streets on. "You do know how to spoil a man's day."

Jack and his associates would never set foot in the bank, and he'd give Lord Stephen's property a wide berth. Between those two islands of safety, Eleanora made a quiet, useful life.

"I need a favor, Ellie."

"You need a sentence of transportation."

He patted her shoulder. She barely refrained from drawing his cork. She could do it too, and had on more than one occasion.

"Nothing bad. I simply need you to point out a certain lady to me."

As Jack's favors went, that sounded innocuous enough, but then, they all did at first. "I am a clerk at a bank," Ellie said. "I do not mingle with ladies."

Jack smiled at her, which was utterly wasted effort. She'd fallen for his charm once, half a lifetime ago. Even then, she'd seen the determination in his eyes despite his smiles.

"You mingle with a duchess," he said, "and she mingles with ladies. Go for a walk in the park with Walton's duchess and express idle curiosity. Her Grace will babble as all the fine women do, and you can tell me which pretty face I need to watch for on some dreary Wednesday night."

Ellie resumed walking, a shipwrecked sailor swimming doggedly for shore. "Whether you are planning to steal the lady's jewels, forge her portrait, or sell her secrets, I want no part of it."

He could do all three. He *had* done all three, at various times, and he was by no means the worst of the lot. Almack's held their assemblies on Wednesday evenings, suggesting Jack was looking for a plump pigeon to fleece, one way or another.

"I kept a roof over your head, Eleanora. A pretty little thing new to London would have been ill-used and you know it."

Whatever his scheme, it was apparently borne of desperation. Jack reverted to his Great Protector speech when he was pockets to let.

"We squatted," Ellie retorted. "We bided illegally in condemned buildings. We scavenged the middens of the hotels, clubs, and great houses." Because Ellie had had the sense to know where the best scraps would be and the boldness to root for them.

The smell of kitchen waste still had the power to make her ill.

"She needn't attend Almack's then," Jack said. "But nobody gets into that place without having substantial blunt. Makes choosing a mark much simpler."

The artist in Jack loved the spectacle of society balls. He stood outside the great houses of Mayfair gawking along with the rest of London's idlers, and polite society— the hostesses were too ignorant to realize they invited a wolf to their windows—preened for his amusement.

"Whatever scheme you're hatching this time, I want no part of it." One street to go, then Jack would tip his hat and bid her farewell, pray God.

"Stubborn. How I adore a stubborn woman." He patted Ellie's arm as her doorstep came into view. "You can take the woman out of the stews, but she'll never be a lady. Waltz around at your bank all you please, little Ellie, and that won't change who your people are. Walden ignores what he knows of your past, but should our history become public, you'd find yourself without a post and you know it."

The pity in Jack's voice nearly undid her. He wasn't sneering, wasn't even threatening. In his way, Jack was reminding Ellie that when all of society turned their backs, family was still family.

"I'm careful, Jack. You be careful too." She opened her reticule, intent on passing him a few coins, because Jack would never admit if he was down on his luck. He had much more of a conscience than Mick did, though that wasn't saying a great deal.

He stayed her with a hand on her wrist. "I am always careful, dearest Ellie." He touched his hat brim and sauntered off, taking a portion of Ellie's hard-won peace with him. When they'd courted—such as the destitute courted—he'd had the same ability, like a soldier marching to war. His partings were a little wistful, a little brave, and entirely for show.

Ellie could never hate him—she had tried to—but she could resent him, and be terrified of his endless capacity for illegal schemes. Mick was a thoroughly charming bounder, while Jack was shrewd, occasionally ruthless, and oddly principled. Mick would leave Jack to deal with consequences, and Jack, being Jack and the oldest of the cousins, in-laws, and step-relations, would take those consequences on the chin without complaint.

Ellie's father had had the same stoic quality, and just look how that had turned out.

* * *

"I do fancy a proper dinner," Cousin Howell said, grabbing for a strap as Rex's coach swayed around a corner. "Excellent wine, everything served hot, pretty ladies to keep the mood cheerful."

"You fancy Lady Joanna Peabody," Eddie replied.

Howell and Eddie were brothers, and Rex had long ago concluded that it was the sworn duty of siblings to provide truth at the most inconvenient public moments.

Rex's oldest sister, Rachel, leapt into the affray. "Lady Joanna is lovely," she said. "Quite accomplished on the violin, an excellent watercolorist, and more witty than the two of you combined. Of course Cousin Howie fancies her."

Howell and Eddie were not twins, but they might as well have been, so closely did they resemble each other. They were blond, a touch over medium height, and blue-eyed, a matched set sharing the backward-facing seat with Rex.

Their wardrobes told a different tale. Howell was sober to a fault, his linen tied in a simple knot, his walking stick a plain oak article with a dull pewter handle. He'd been dubbed Howell the Hopeless in the schoolyard. Eddie, by contrast, cut a dash and had styled himself Edward the Elegant. His cravat pin, sleeve buttons, watch chain, and walking stick all sported ornate gold fittings. Howell wore no boutonniere. Eddie's lapel was adorned by a bouquet of tiny purple orchids with gold foil wrapped about the stems.

Howell looked like a footman in his Sunday finest, unaccustomed to riding inside so fine a coach. Eddie looked like he owned the coach or aspired to.

Lately, half of Rex's waking hours had been spent

rolling around London in wheeled conveyances crammed with his cousins, aunts, and uncles. He also escorted his sisters at least once a week, more if Mama was insistent.

And that didn't count her goddaughters, who were legion, and not a one of them married yet.

"Howie fancies who and what he cannot have," Edward said, elbowing his brother as if they were eight years old. "That's his specialty, pining from afar. Next he'll be penning sonnets and wandering beneath the full moon."

Howell refrained from retaliation, proving that even Dorsets eventually matured.

"Howell appreciates good company," Rex said. "A fine quality in any gentleman." Though too much fine company left Rex longing for the peace and quiet of Ambledown.

"And whose fine company are you appreciating these days, Elsmore?" Cousin Eddie had the most annoying smirk. "The fellows at the club were talking about starting a pool, and your name figured prominently in the discussion."

"How gratifying to know that my marital prospects or lack thereof provide amusement to my peers." Rex had spoken more sharply than the moment called for, but ye gods...A Gloucestershire cheese-rolling was more decorous than polite society on the topic of an unmarried duke.

Rachel sent him a look, one she'd been sending him frequently in recent weeks. Part warning, part commiseration.

"Elsmore will take a bride when he's good and ready," she said. "A man with eleven male first cousins needn't be overly worried about his title's succession."

"Ah," said Eddie, "but not a one of us eligible male cousins is married yet. Perhaps I should drop James's name into the betting pool."

James, the cousin who at present had the honor to be the Elsmore heir, showed no signs of succumbing to Cupid's arrow. When Rex escorted his party to the ducal theater box, he did spot James across the theater and one tier down. At James's side sat one of London's most exclusive courtesans, the rest of her court crowded around her. The ducal contingent ignored James's coterie, though James himself would be cordially acknowledged should he appear alone in the passage.

Rex generally avoided the corridor, but at the interval, Mama of course had plans for him.

"We must greet dear Lady Wollmerton. Come along, Elsmore. If you want the latest *on dit*, you could ask for no finer source."

Rex did not want the latest *on dit*, or even last week's *on dit*. He rose and edged around a pair of lady cousins arguing about hats.

"Of course, Mama. Rachel, are you joining us?" *Please, grant me at least one ally.*

"Don't be daft." Rachel waggled gloved fingers at him and blew him a kiss.

After Mama had stopped to admire the coiffure or whitework or necklace of five successive—unmarried—goddaughters, Rex turned her back toward the box.

"Have we really nothing better to do than parade about a chilly passage pretending to be thrilled to see people we saw twice last week?" he murmured.

"Nonsense, darling." Mama smacked his arm with her fan. "What is a ducal son for, if not parading about at the theater? I do think Rachel will soon bring that nice Lord Jeremy up to scratch."

Mama had thought Rachel would bring Nice Lord Somebody or Other up to scratch for the past five years. Rex had a firm understanding with his sisters, however. They married whomever and whenever they pleased, not before. If his ducal authority meant anything—and he wasn't sure it did—it meant that he could preserve his sisters from the dreaded advantageous match.

"Lady Guilfoyle." Rex bowed and endured a re-recitation of the same gossip he'd already heard several times in the past half hour. Lord Pritchard's heir had stumbled into the Serpentine on Sunday trying to rescue a lady's glove from peril. As a result—how unfortunate!—passersby had been treated to the sight of a soaking wet male form, and the glove—even more tragic!—had been ruined.

"But you know," Mama said, "if one must be subjected to the particulars of the male physique, at least the specimen on display was a credit to his gender."

Titters, faux kisses, bow-and-curtsey, smile, repeat.

Rex returned his mother to the box, the play resumed, and all the while, he had the oddest urge to make his excuses, walk back to the ducal residence, and closet himself with the ledgers he was collecting for Mrs. Hatfield. Those ledgers held truths about him and about his dukedom, while increasingly, the theater box held only a vast, inane boredom.

As did the ballrooms, the musicales, the carriage parade, the gentlemen's clubs, the soirees, the card parties, Almack's—God spare a hapless duke from Almack's—the Venetian breakfasts, and churchyard socializing. Perhaps titled men took up parliamentary responsibilities in defense of their sanity.

The lady cousins continued to feud, Eddie teased his brother while Howell pretended to watch the play, and Rachel and Mama pretended to ignore James and his paramour, who politely ignored them in return.

On stage, Tony Lumpkin made up boisterous songs about the joys of life after inheriting a title, while the boring, dutiful character Hardcastle lamented the status of an observer, doomed to watch others laugh and joke away their days.

* * *

Elsmore set three thick ledgers bound in green leather on the bank's conference table. "We have a problem."

"You have a problem." Ellie had tossed away half her night considering the dimensions of his problem. "I am generously attempting to solve it for you."

He unbuttoned his greatcoat, a many-caped sartorial wonder that would have fetched significant coin in the re-sale shops.

"And I am endlessly grateful for your efforts," he said, draping a scarf over a peg beside the door. His hat went on another peg, his coat on the third. Thus did he gradually assert dominion over a space Ellie would have said he could never claim. "I have every confidence you will succeed, but I cannot continue to deliver my personal accounts to this institution, day after day."

He wore morning attire, and he wore it very well. Whereas Quinn Wentworth dressed with the sobriety of a wealthy undertaker, Elsmore knew how to achieve style without appearing foppish. His boutonniere today was a pink rosebud and a few sprigs of lavender. His two watch fobs were anchored in their buttonholes with tiny sapphires mounted in gold. Jewels for daytime were an unusual choice, but on him, the effect was fashionable. The silk ribbon banding his top hat was dark blue, and his morning coat indigo.

He had an innate sense of style that other men likely envied, and women would notice without putting a name to.

"How am I to conduct an audit without seeing your books, Your Grace?"

Ellie's notes were spread across the table, but she'd taken the desk this morning, the better to have an abacus, spare paper, and blotter between her and the duke.

"You will see my books, of course, but you cannot see them here." He studied himself in the pier glass and ran his hand through his hair to eliminate the creases caused by his hat. The result was slightly tousled and—drat the man—dashing.

"Do you impugn the security of Wentworth and Penrose, Your Grace? Nobody on these premises will so much as peek at your blessed books. They are safer here than in your own estate office." Ellie was safe here too, and that was not a detail.

He poured a cup of tea from the service on the sideboard. "Do you take milk or sugar in your tea?"

What had that—? "I've had my tea for the morning, thank you." One cup from the bakeshop. Plain.

He added sugar and milk. "Join me in having a second. The morning will be long."

Based on his expression, his evening had been long. His eyes were tired, his mouth bracketed in grooves. He'd not smiled since coming through the door. He set the cup and saucer by Ellie's elbow, along with a table napkin and the plate of shortbread.

"Do you customarily wait on others, sir?"

"Would you believe I am the realm's best-dressed lackey? I have three younger sisters. They took my education seriously." He held his own cup of tea beneath his nose and inhaled. The bank stocked a good black tea, and the baked goods were delivered fresh from the shop across the street. Ellie typically did not indulge, which left more for the tellers and clerks.

"Please have a seat," she said, lest he resurrect that battle when they had work to do.

He took a chair from the conference table and set it before the desk. "About our problem."

"Send the books with a footman," Ellie said. "I will keep a list of questions, and you can either send me written answers or drop by when your schedule allows. Daily would be best, or even twice a day."

The tea was piping hot and strong without being bitter. Elsmore had added the perfect portion of sugar and milk, too, or perhaps the novelty of being served by a duke made the brew especially satisfying.

"You take yours plain?" Ellie asked.

"Sometimes plain is best. I cannot entrust my books to a footman."

"Why not?"

He crossed his legs, making the chair creak. "Because I never have. If I'm to conduct this audit discreetly, then the last thing I should do is draw notice by violating my personal routines. I bring a wage book with me to my club on occasion, or a quarter's worth of the housekeeper's accounts out to Ambledown if I'm biding there for a few days. You have asked for every single household ledger I possess, going back at least a year."

He closed his eyes and took a sip of tea. This morning, he was without flirtation, charm, or humor, and that should have been a relief. Auditing ducal books was not a lark. And yet that other version of Elsmore, full of small talk and smiles, had been easier to spend time with.

Ellie could be annoyed with a charming duke. A weary, beleaguered duke was an unsettling companion.

"You'd rather not deliver your account books to this location?" Ellie asked.

"The largest problem is the location. Wentworth and Penrose is a rival institution, and if I'm seen bringing my books to a lengthy appointment here day after day, talk will ensue. Neither your bank nor mine wants talk, and gossip would be a fine recompense to your employers for their generous assistance."

My generous assistance. Ellie pushed the plate of shortbread toward his side of the desk. "And the rest of the problem?" Something bothered him, possibly something beyond his havey-cavey, harum-scarum account books.

"My complete, utter, and unrelenting lack of privacy."

"I don't understand. You are a duke. You wave a manicured, be-ringed hand and the realm orders itself accordingly. Everything from the King's spending money to the poor laws to the courts organizes itself at your whim and pleasure."

He pushed the shortbread back to her side of the desk, using a hand that bore not a single ring. "Is that what Walden would have you believe?"

Ellie took a piece. Breakfast had been bread and butter several hours ago. "His Grace is not a typical exponent of his rank."

"Your view of a duke's life is understandable, but not applicable in the present case. My comings and goings are noted by my three siblings, by any of the several cousins who work at my bank, by my mother— whose acumen outstrips human explanation—my valet, my butler, my house steward, my footmen, my coachmen, and any number of gossips among whom my personal secretaries prominently number. I meet you here again at my peril."

Ellie broke the shortbread in half and got crumbs on the page she'd been tallying. "What do you propose?"

He pinched the bridge of his nose, then pushed his thumb and forefinger up to stroke out over his brow. "I keep a house off of—"

"No."

A frigid pair of blue eyes regarded her from down the length of a ducal nose. "I beg your pardon?"

"You cannot be seen to frequent this bank, and I will not be seen to frequent your...your love nest." Ellie was blushing, surely for the first time in fifteen years. "My reputation means much to me, Your Grace, and unlike you, I cannot expect polite society to turn a blind eye to bad behavior or even the appearance of bad behavior."

Then too, Mick and Jack would notice, and they would never believe Ellie's explanation.

Elsmore pinched the bridge of his nose again. "For God's sake, the property has been empty for months. The housekeeper alone bides there and she knows better than to gossip."

"What has that to do with anything? If I meet you during daylight hours, the worst assumptions will be made about me precisely because the property has been unused in some time. Talk can ruin a woman as surely as it can ruin a bank."

He stared at her as if she had two heads, one adorned with snakes, the other with horns. "What do you propose?"

Normally, Ellie liked puzzles, but not when they were presented by an unhappy duke. "Does the audit itself bother you, or is something else amiss?" Was he pale? Ellie well knew the scent of a man who'd overindulged the previous evening. All she detected on Elsmore's person was his shaving soap and a hint of lavender.

He finished his tea, doubtless stalling while he framed half truths. "I spent last evening with family and friends and the company was not at all restful. A slight megrim—"

"No megrim was ever slight, Your Grace. Give me your hands." Ellie held her hands out across the desk and waggled her fingers.

He *regarded* her. "You interrupt me more than all three of my sisters put together."

"Your hands, sir."

He held out his hands. "You give me more orders than they do, you contradict me, you scold me... What are you doing?"

Ellie took his hands in hers and found the muscle between the thumb and palm on each one, then pressed hard.

"I'm using my granny's trick for easing a megrim. It doesn't always work immediately or entirely, but it can't hurt and it's much safer than a patent remedy." And it cost nothing, always a consideration.

Though Ellie should have realized that Granny's trick meant more or less gazing into the duke's eyes while holding hands with him across the desk.

The odd familiarity seemed to bother him not at all. "Your grip is strong, Mrs. Hatfield, and your husband is a lucky man. Would he mind if I brought my books to your home?"

"What? You cannot bring the books to my home."

"You never receive callers? Your husband never receives callers?"

As firmly as Ellie pressed her thumb and forefinger into Elsmore's hands, even more assuredly did she feel his curiosity intruding into her privacy. She let go of him and sat back.

"I have no husband."

The duke clenched and unclenched his hands, big masculine paws that closed into capable-looking fists for all the lace at his wrists.

"No Mr. Hatfield. I see."

No, he did not. He did not see that even the tiny scrap of respectability that went with appropriating a married woman's form of address was precious. Housekeepers were invariably addressed as Missus. Women who ran their own shops were frequently Missus, and a husband need not come into it in either case.

"I have rooms in proper lodgings in a proper neighborhood. You should not call upon me..." Though in truth, Lord Stephen's establishment boasted certain amenities. "I hcsitate to tell you this."

"We either solve the immediate dilemma or I might as well run an ad in the *Gazette* that I'm so distrustful of my own employees I've asked a competitor to look into my personal books. Dorset and Becker won't last a fortnight thereafter, but I'll have my audit."

Still, Ellie dreaded the thought of Elsmore in her parlor, even for the time it took him to deliver a few ledgers or answer the odd question. Jack would watch and wait, and sooner or later, he'd draw the wrong conclusions.

"You were right to arrange an audit," Ellie said. "Your books are askew. I already know that much. A system that allots to each factor a limited area of responsibility has ended up limiting accountability as well."

"Somebody is stealing from me. You have barely scratched the surface of my ledgers and you know that already." His attitude was philosophical acceptance of another problem to be solved rather than anger or even annoyance.

Ellie was annoyed enough on his behalf that she'd decided to make an attempt to straighten out his books as a matter of professional pride. Two weeks was insufficient for a thorough audit, though she could get a sense of where the problems might be buried.

"I strongly suspect irregularities, but an auditor does not leap to conclusions. My lodging house is in an old neighborhood and has its own coach house and stable. Lord Stephen purchased the building in part because it affords him at least one private entrance that I know of. If you were seen on the premises, the assumption would be that you were calling on him."

Elsmore considered his empty teacup, then rose to set it on the sideboard. "That will serve. Thank you. More tea?"

"Please."

Nobody called on Ellie at her private lodgings. She was not friendly with the other tenants beyond a polite nod at the front door, and she barely used the kitchen facilities on the lowest level. Lord Stephen had the whole top floor of the house, and the attics were available to house domestics, but Ellie almost never crossed paths with his lordship.

She would have to explain Elsmore's calls to him though.

The duke set a fresh cup of tea by Ellie's elbow and took away the one she'd finished. "Shall we to the books, Mrs. Hatfield?"

"I have a few questions first."

He settled into his chair. "Do your worst. I'm to meet two uncles at the club for luncheon, and I'm yours until then."

He would never be hers, nor could Ellie imagine wanting him to be—even if he did fix her tea exactly how she liked it, dress with exquisite good taste, and have warm hands.

Chapter Four

Rex could not imagine that a bank would stock a better class of tea than a ducal household did, and yet, Wentworth and Penrose served a lovely blend. He had eschewed breakfast rather than escalate the megrim that had plagued him throughout the night.

As Mrs. Hatfield launched into the first volley of questions, he allowed himself a small piece of shortbread.

"We will make a map of any employees who handle your money," she said. "Like this." She sketched a series of boxes connected with arrows, the boxes labeled by person—butler, housekeeper, porter, and so forth. "The greater risk is in the areas where you pass money downstream rather than as money flows upstream to you."

"Why?" The concept of a money map made intuitive sense, for all its novelty. Did other large households use this approach, and if so, why had Rex—a bank director and a duke—remained ignorant of it?

"Downstream money is more vulnerable," Mrs. Hatfield said, "because you will likely know how much rent is due from a tenant. Stealing a bit on the path between the tenant and your pocket would thus be difficult. You are less likely to know what coal and candles cost, and will probably never have a conversation with the suppliers of those commodities regarding their prices."

Many, many arrows led from the ducal coffers into other hands, even for the London household. The housekeeper, house steward, valet, ladies' maids, butler, under-butler, first footman, and head porter all had accounts, some mere pocket change, some enormous. Rex's sisters and his mother had pin money, and so did the aunties and three lady cousins. The family accounts originated at the bank, but required management at various points along the way.

Four male cousins at university had allowances, and Eddie, Howell, and James, in addition to duties at the bank, also each managed a rural property.

And at every distant holding, another flight of arrows sprang from another pot of ducal gold.

"I can eliminate some of the potential areas of concern," Rex said, pulling the chart of London boxes to his side of the desk. He took another bite of shortbread and washed it down with sweet, milky tea. "My butler, for example, has never put a foot wrong in forty years of service. I inherited him from my father, and he served as first footman to my grandfather."

Mrs. Hatfield took the chart back. "We eliminate no one. In fact, you should have somebody check my work when we've concluded this exercise."

The shortbread seemed to help with Rex's upset stomach, or perhaps actually doing something about his books was helping.

The patient compassion in Mrs. Hatfield's gaze helped not at all. "I know my staff, madam."

She took off her glasses and produced a plain handkerchief to polish them. "Your Grace, we have a problem."

"Please do elucidate." Without her glasses, her features took on different proportions. Her nose called less attention to itself, her eyes looked larger. Even the contour of her lips softened.

"You know the particulars of being a duke. You've spent your whole life learning that role, and it comes to you now as naturally as a hound chases a hare. I can claim the same expertise when it comes to accounting, particularly crooked or inept accounting. You are no more qualified to tell me how to do my job than I am qualified to be a duchess."

"And yet"—he waved his hand, which nobody save himself bothered to manicure—"you presumed to tell me of the many privileges associated with my office."

"And you corrected me, because my perspective is limited to that of somebody who is employed by a duke, who has tea with a duchess every Friday, who has observed ducal holdings for years at very close range, and yet, I was in error."

She stated her error baldly, no mincing about or draping euphemisms all over it. The honesty was refreshing, though, like a tonic, not exactly palatable.

Rex took up one of the pencils from the silver tray and drew a sheet of blank paper near. He crossed an ankle over a knee, used a ledger book for his easel, and began sketching the woman who boldly lectured him.

Corrected him, rather.

"Do you know the insult my butler will suffer if I impugn his integrity?" Rex paused to take another sip of tea rather than launch into a lecture of his own. Mrs. Hatfield could not possibly grasp the delicate workings of a large, wealthy domicile. "An affronted butler can set off a cascade of burned toast, sour wine, feuding housemaids, and warring footmen. The upheaval would rival the English civil wars."

Mrs. Hatfield's eyebrows were her most interesting feature. Most people's eyebrows were not perfectly symmetric. Hers were two exactly matched swoops that added elegance to the intelligence in her gaze.

Why had such a woman—competent, well mannered, even pretty—no husband? She hadn't said she was widowed, simply that she had no husband.

"Your Grace, please attend me."

He glanced up to find her gaze had grown quite severe. "You have my undivided attention." *And you have eyes that should not be hidden behind a pair of spinsterish spectacles.*

"You observe that you have no privacy, and yet, if I asked you which clubs your cousins belong to, could you tell me? If I asked you which tailors, modistes, or bootmakers they use, would you know?"

"Not in the usual course." Howell and James favored Hoby boots, but then, most of fashionable London did. Rex had sponsored James for membership at some club or other—the Explorers, or was it the Charitable Knights?

"Nonetheless," Mrs. Hatfield said, "those cousins all know your movements, your preferred merchants, your schedule, your clubs. Your servants know details far more personal than those. People who have less, who *are* less, keep a close eye on people who have more. Children are more observant about adults than conversely. Women are vigilant regarding the actions of men because we have to be. The same is not true in the opposite direction, not in any flattering sense."

Her words resonated with Rex's experience and, more than that, organized a vague sense of frustration into cause and effect. He had responsibility—he had *power*—but not privacy. When had he chosen to strike that bargain with life? Had he even had a choice?

"You are saying whoever is fleecing me has had long acquaintance to learn my habits. That describes most of my staff."

She folded her arms. "And all of your family."

Rex sketched the curve of her jaw, which angled cleanly, then flowed into a firm chin. "There, I must protest, madam. You will not impugn the honor of my family again, lest you inspire me to a display of temper." Not that he'd had any such displays since the age of about, oh, six?

"I would *at least* raise my voice if a family member betrayed my trust," she retorted. "I'd not be sitting on my elegant backside, swilling tea, and doodling. I'd throw fragile objects, provided they weren't worth much. I'd kick the wall and curse. To entrust another with money is an intimate act of faith. One's security, one's future, one's … I needn't tell you."

She thought his backside elegant. He could venture a similar opinion about hers, except that he sought to live to a vigorous old age.

"Don't forget that my dignity will also suffer when I find out which employee has been dipping a hand into my coffers. Dukes are supposed to have endless reserves of dignity."

"Dukes are people," she said, taking up her pencil of doom. "I thought that condition applied only to His Grace of Walden, a rarity among his peers. My theory no longer fits the available facts, for you are nearly as stubborn as he is."

Rex took a moment with her nose. Noses were easy to get wrong, easy to relegate to an afterthought, but a whole countenance could be rendered either noble or ridiculous by an artist's handling of the nose.

"Did you just pay me a compliment, Mrs. Hatfield? I daresay you did. You admitted me into membership in the human species, a very exclusive club indeed. I cannot recall when last I was so cleverly flattered."

He finished the tea and realized he'd finished the short-bread as well. Mrs. Hatfield put her glasses back on, but Rex decided not to draw her wearing them. The lady on the page was intriguing, even beautiful, but she was not smiling. Glasses would make her look too severe, too unhappy.

"We must consider your family members among those responsible for mishandling your funds, sir."

"Who is stubborn now, Mrs. Hatfield? Do you think I wouldn't notice if my sisters were padding accounts? Am I so oblivious to my own cousins that they could steal from me, abuse my generosity, and have me none the wiser?"

Rex might resent his family, find their company tiresome, and even nip out to Ambledown occasionally to escape them, but he knew them well enough to trust them.

"You need not feel ashamed, Your Grace. Your holdings are vast, your family large. We'll find the source or sources of the irregularities and then you can decide what to do about them."

Sources, *plural*? "My family is above suspicion, Mrs. Hatfield. I'll grant you that errors occur, miscalculations can be carried forward, but I pay sufficient attention to my loved ones that the misbehavior you suspect them of could not happen. Give me that much credit, at least. We limit our investigations to retainers, employees, and factors."

She drew another arrow that ended in a question mark and then two more. One for each sister? *Preposterous.*

"We can start with your staff, Your Grace."

A prudent cease-fire on her part, and doubtless not the last time Rex would have to limit her zeal with an application of common sense.

"I applaud your thoroughness, Mrs. Hatfield, and your diplomacy. More tea?" The brew, the shortbread, and the passage of time had apparently routed his megrim.

She drew another outward arrow on his money chart and labeled it with yet another question mark. "Will you purloin my next cup too?"

What in creation was she—? Rex looked at the cup in his hand. *Hers*, the one he'd fixed with milk and sugar. Empty. He'd drunk from her cup and finished her tea without even noticing his error.

* * *

"What do you suppose Elsmore's real problem is?" Lord Stephen Wentworth asked. "The situation must be serious, if he's come to us for aid."

Quinn passed his younger brother a glass of lemonade, an unusual choice for a day when autumn had turned up chilly, but then, for Stephen to navigate across Quinn's family parlor with a cane in one hand and a hot drink in the other was perilous to himself and the carpets.

"His Grace did not come to us," Quinn replied, pouring himself a glass. "I've sung Mrs. Hatfield's praises from time to time, and Elsmore asked to hire her temporarily. I merely brokered the arrangement as a courtesy."

Stephen hooked his cane on the arm of his chair. "Does Elsmore think she'll share particulars about how you and Penrose run the bank?"

Stephen's intellectual appetites were prodigious, a polite way of saying that he was curious about everybody and everything, sometimes obnoxiously so. That lively curiosity had saved his life, in Quinn's opinion, and resulted in any number of mechanical inventions.

"Elsmore will soon learn better if he thinks to compromise Mrs. Hatfield's loyalty, though I don't take him for the underhanded kind. How was Paris?"

"Paris is redolent of cat piss, as usual. The French can create marvelous roads, exquisite art, and incomparable ladies' fashions, but they cannot eradicate the stink of the alley from their fair city. What did darling Eleanora make of this temporary assignment?"

Only Stephen would dare refer to the lady so familiarly. "She was reluctant at first, but she cannot turn her back on sloppy account books. Enforcing order and accuracy are her passions."

Stephen drew his finger around the rim of his glass. "A bloody boring ambition, if you ask me. Have you never wondered how she came by it?"

Quinn took the opposite armchair and weighed his obligation to a loyal employee against his obligation to an equally loyal—if inquisitive—brother. Stephen on the scent of a conundrum was a force of nature.

"I knew Eleanora Hatfield in York," Quinn said. "She was Ellie Naylor then."

Stephen had been eight when John James Wentworth had finally perished from too much gin and not enough decency. Quinn hoped that his brother's childhood memories were dim and few, though nobody could forget what having a monster for a father had been like.

"Naylor rings a bell," Stephen said, sipping his drink. "I recall an old chap with a white beard, ink-stained hands. Not a bad sort. Mrs. Naylor once gave me a slice of bread with jam. I knew from that moment on that should I survive to adulthood, I would enjoy bread and jam three times a day if I had to commit hanging felonies to have it."

So much for dim memories. "The Naylors were no more respectable than we were, but Mr. Naylor certainly lacked our father's violent nature."

"Hard to be *less* respectable than we were, Quinn."

What to say? "We were destitute, Stephen, but we weren't criminals. Papa was a lazy, mean drunk. I never regarded that as an excuse for his children to break the law."

Stephen shot Quinn a wry glance. "Just the opposite. You once spanked my lame little backside for stealing a currant bun."

He would recall that. "The only time I raised a hand to you. You could have been transported for stealing that bun, Stephen. At least give me credit for waiting until you'd finished eating the damned thing."

No matter how wealthy Quinn became—he was scandalously wealthy—the sheer terror of being a poor lad in the back alleys of York would never entirely leave him. For a younger brother with a bad leg, transportation would have been a death sentence, and at the time, Quinn would have been powerless to intervene.

"You *watched* me eat that whole bun before you dressed me down, Quinn?"

"The treat would be just as stolen if you ate it or not, and you were starving." Too proud to beg, too infirm to work, Stephen's lot as a child had been heartbreaking.

How hungry had he been, to risk thieving when he could never have outrun pursuit?

Stephen shifted in his chair, pulled a pillow out from behind him and laid it on a hassock, then propped his foot on the pillow.

"I wish to hell it would just damned snow," he said. "This rain is a misery."

"You'll stay in London for the winter?" Quinn put the question casually, but Jane fretted over Stephen, and preferred to have him near when winter set in.

Stephen traveled for months at a time, then circled back through London for long, unannounced visits. He no longer bided in the Wentworth town house when he was in Town, which was a blessing—mostly.

"I have to remain long enough to look over the bank books, don't I?" Stephen replied. "Mrs. Hatfield has spoken, and I reject the great honor of being her understudy at peril to my well-being."

"Jane likes her." Quinn's duchess was friendly to nearly everybody, but her genuine liking was a precious rarity.

"I like Eleanora Hatfield, when I'm not terrified of her, and I have raised misanthropy to a mythical quest. Why were Naylor's fingers ink-stained, Quinn? I know that's a significant detail, but I can't recall the particulars. Was he a printer?"

Damn Stephen's voracious curiosity. "He was a talented artist fallen on hard times after some sort of scandal. More than that, it has not been necessary for me to recollect. Eleanora never judged me for being the offspring of a foul-mouthed, gin-drunk fiend. I do not judge her for her antecedents, and we've both benefited from that arrangement."

A footman came in to light the lamps and build up

the fire. Soon, the children would be turned loose from the nursery, and Quinn's favorite hour of the day would arrive. He suspected Stephen called later in the afternoon because that meant a chance to visit with his nieces, upon whom he doted.

"Naylor was an artist fallen on hard times after a scandal," Stephen murmured. "His hands were *always* ink-stained, and even living in the most rotten neighborhood of devil-begotten York, his missus could afford to share bread and jam with my thieving little self."

Like tumblers in a lock clicking into place, Quinn could feel Stephen's prodigious intellect closing in on a deduction.

"We are a long way from York, Stephen, and it was a long time ago."

"Naylor was a forger," Stephen said, saluting that conclusion with his drink. "Apparently, a successful one. Eleanora the Incorruptible has rogues and scalawags for family. I'll bet that makes for a very interesting Christmas dinner."

Quinn brought the pitcher of lemonade over from the sideboard. "Conjectures like that can get a man called out and leave a bank without the finest auditor in the realm."

Stephen used his walking stick to snag the afghan draped over the back of the chair Quinn had vacated.

"Give it up, Your Perishing Grace. Word of a gentleman, honor of a Wentworth, solemn promise of a reformed stealer of currant buns, I'll never mention this to anybody outside the family. If anything, my regard for Mrs. Hatfield swells to even more impressive proportions when I think of how far she's come. A man might shed a dubious past with hard work and good luck, but a woman's reputation can never be rehabilitated."

"And yet," Quinn said, as the soft thunder of small feet reverberated from the corridor, "Mrs. Hatfield is formidably respectable. Prepare for an invasion."

Stephen set his drink aside just as the door burst open, and three small female whirlwinds all attempted to climb into his lap at once.

* * *

Ellie's life was a constant balance between appreciating the comforts of her station and warning herself not to grow attached to them.

The Duke of Walden, for example, had sent his town coach back for her at the end of the day, a courtesy he observed in nasty weather often but not always. Instead of spending her evening with chilly feet, her boots stuffed with old newspapers, her cloak steaming before the fire, she could curl up with a book and a bowl of good, hot soup from the chop shop.

Those luxuries were not yet to be hers, for His Most Inconvenient Grace of Elsmore had handed her into the Walden carriage and climbed in after her. She automatically took the backward-facing seat, which resulted in being seated beside him.

"A gentleman yields the forward-facing seat to a lady," he said, rapping on the roof.

"An employee yields the higher station to nearly everybody." Ellie reached past him to pull down the shades. Darkness had fallen and the interior lamps were lit. Anybody peering through the windows would see her seated inside with a gentleman other than her employer.

She should be in high dudgeon about that, but in her present mood, she was mostly hungry and tired.

"Do you suppose we can argue over seating for the entire journey?" Elsmore mused. "I think we could. We've taken each other's measure, thrown out a few exploratory punches, and can have a proper set-to now that we've warmed to the challenge."

That analogy flattered nobody. "I do battle with dirty books, Your Grace, not with peers." Grandpapa had attempted that folly and come off much the worse for it.

"We could wager the choice of seat on a coin toss."

"I never wager." Ellie's entire life was a risky bet, and she'd lately wondered if that would ever change.

"We could both take the forward-facing seat."

"Regardless of which bench you occupy," Ellie said, "you will be at my figurative elbow until this auditing exercise is completed." He'd intruded into her dreams and accompanied her on her noon ramble, too, more cause for a sour mood. "Where you choose to seat yourself is of little moment, but you will not tell me where I—"

He switched seats. "I can compromise, Mrs. Hatfield. I can refrain from arguing with a lady. Your devious turn of mind will conclude that I yield this point for the sake of conserving my shot and powder. Notwithstanding your suspicions, my objective is to lighten our discourse with occasional frivolity rather than to vex you."

The coach pulled away from the curb, the horses at a walk.

"You seek to be silly?" Ellie did have a devious turn of mind, no need to take offense at that truth when the same quality kept a roof over her head.

His Grace's expression remained utterly serious. "Dukes are never silly."

This duke was. "Good to know. Auditors are never frivolous."

Ellie shared a smile with Elsmore, which felt both silly and frivolous, also slightly dangerous. She smiled at the bank's messenger boys, but never at the clerks, tellers, managers, partners, or directors. For Jack, she mostly attempted expressions of indifference, though they often eluded her.

Traffic in the early evening was horrendous, and thus the coach moved at the barest crawl. The rain drummed on the roof while Ellie explained what her first review of the Ambledown books had revealed.

"You make many of the entries yourself," she said. "You are on the premises frequently enough to note whether what you see in the books matches what you experience when you dwell there."

"I'm in London more often," Elsmore countered, his smile nowhere in evidence.

"The London household is much larger, and I daresay you are distracted from its functioning most of the time. At Ambledown, how do you spend your days?"

He took off his top hat and set it atop the pile of ledgers on the seat beside him. "I ride out in the mornings and visit with tenants if the weather's fine. I call on my neighbors, I work in the library or the conservatory—the conservatory is warm and has excellent light. I frequently walk the home farm and the home wood. I attend services with the neighbors. At Ambledown, I sleep well, probably a result of greater physical activity and cleaner air."

"You see? You ride your acres personally, you occupy the public rooms, you don't reserve them for company. You take all of your meals at the manor rather than breakfast, lunch, and dinner at your clubs or among your social acquaintants. You *live* at Ambledown while you're there, you don't squat."

Elsmore lowered the lamps on either side of the coach. "I *come to life* at Ambledown. I can think there, I can go for three consecutive days without dressing for damned dinner. I know the domestics by name, and the menus are the plain fare I prefer, not six removes of French ridiculousness drowning in overly rich sauces."

And yet, he'd offered to transfer the estate to her? "We all need a safe place, a place where we can be ourselves. I'm glad you have Ambledown." She was even gladder that of the entire tangle of ledgers, wage books, and tallies, Ambledown's accounts had been honestly kept.

"How long have you lived in London?" Elsmore asked.

Well, yes. Small talk was safer than unintended confidences, and Ellie had long since settled on an answer to this question. A quarter hour of chit-chat and she'd be in her slippers before the fire, no dukes in sight.

"I came down from York when Wentworth and Penrose moved its headquarters south. I was with the bank in York, and had seen enough northern winters." She *wished* she'd come to London when the bank had moved to the capital. That had not been the case. She'd been sent south with Pammie, Jack, and Mick when one of Grandfather's chancier schemes had collapsed, and thank heavens she'd found employment clerking for a mercer soon after.

"Why is there no Mr. Hatfield?" Elsmore asked.

"Because I prefer it that way." Mostly. How could she explain Jack, Mick, and Pammie to a Mr. Hatfield? How could she keep a husband safe from her family's relentless mischief?

And yet, Ellie considered herself in the confidence of the Duchess of Walden, and that good lady became positively luminous on the topic of domesticating with her duke. In the presence of the Wentworth offspring, the duke himself was shockingly affectionate, and had been known to laugh out loud.

Elsmore shifted his legs, which even in this behemoth conveyance, brushed Ellie's skirts. "I might prefer not to have a wife, at least for the present. The Duke of Devonshire appears determined to maintain his bachelorhood and he's a notably sanguine soul."

The coach rounded a corner and picked up speed, which caused the stack of ledgers to slide. Ellie reached for them at the same time Elsmore did, so her hand was trapped beneath his. She couldn't pull back until the coach was again traveling straight.

Ellie's inherent curiosity absorbed Elsmore's personal details rather than the awkwardness of the moment. According to his account books, the black glove covering her much-darned brown mitten had been made for the duke at Halverston's. His top hat was a Dunsmore creation, and he'd recently ordered three more just like it.

His soap came from Belleville's Emporium, a custom blend for which he paid dearly. Note to the margin: Did he pay *too* dearly?

She catalogued those facts as his words wedged past her perceptions to bump up against her weariness: *I might prefer not to have a wife, at least for the present.*

She took two of the ledgers onto her lap and passed him the other two. "I thought this whole endeavor of sorting out your books was so you could take a wife without fear of scandal."

"It is, and your initial findings tell me the exercise was long overdue. I am obligated by my station to marry, and my dear mother would gladly see me wed to any suitable *parti*."

Ellie acknowledged a pang of envy toward the suitable

parti, a woman who'd doubtless share many smiles with Elsmore and care not one whit that he had no privacy whatsoever.

Time to return to the topic of business. "I'll show you Lord Stephen's private entrance and how to use his lift. How shall I summon you if I have questions?"

"You don't summon me."

The rain intensified, from a persistent drenching into one of London's signature downpours.

"Fine then," Ellie said. "I'll conjure answers from my imagination when I don't know what a pair of initials means. I'll make a jolly guess at any questionable entries, and two weeks from now, you can assure yourself your estate has been thoroughly audited, when in fact, I've simply joined the endless procession of retainers—but not relations, for they would never pilfer from an itinerant family head with acumen as astute as yours—who take your money and provide less than you deserve for it."

He had driven her to forgetting herself. Again. "Forgive me," Ellie added. "I am weary and famished."

Was he also hungry and tired?

"What I meant, madam, is that you cannot summon me and maintain the privacy necessary to your task. All of my correspondence is handled by the butler, who collects it at the door from whoever retrieved it from the posting inn. From the butler's keeping, a footman takes it to my office, where either my personal secretary, my real estate secretary, or my commercial secretary will open it. If one secretary is out on an errand, the other two will open anything that seems urgent or worth gossiping about."

Three secretaries handled his correspondence? That was not good at all.

"I can see you drawing more arrows, Mrs. Hatfield. Entire flights going skyward from my pockets."

She wanted Elsmore out of the coach, but the horses had apparently forgotten how to trot. She wanted her bowl of soup—even plain porridge would do—and she wanted for Elsmore's money to remain in his pockets until he chose to send it elsewhere.

"Do you have any idea where the practice of mapping money began?" she asked, even knowing her mouth was about to outstrip her better judgment.

"In your fertile imagination?"

"In the larcenous imaginations of successful embezzlers, Your Grace. The smart ones won't begin the complicated, dangerous, and time-consuming crime of stealing from an enterprise until the entire financial vista is sketched in, complete with rivers of coin, mountains of cash, fields of neglect, and clouds of inattention. They start with the simple map, and they embellish with relevant details over time. They ease their scheme across the landscape like a changing season, subtle at first, but destructive of the previous order. Your canvas is an embezzler's delight."

Ellie was clutching at the ledgers in her lap too tightly, the better to deal with fatigue and exasperation. Her head had begun to ache, and finding something to eat had become imperative.

Now the horses lifted into a trot, which added jouncing and swaying to her discomfort.

"I will pay a call on you each afternoon," Elsmore said, after a beat of rainy quiet, "or morning if you prefer. You set the time, and I will abide by it as best I can. If you must contact me otherwise, send me a brief, general note from a Mr. Patrick Entwhistle. Avoid using a Wentworth and Penrose messenger to deliver it and keep the content vague."

"I can do that."

They traveled the rest of the distance without conversation, the rhythm of the rain nearly putting Ellie to sleep. Before that mercy could befall her, Elsmore was handing her down from the coach. The cobbles in the porte cochere were slick, and she accepted his assistance without a fuss—for now.

"This way," she said, leading him into the carriage house. "The whole edifice was one grand house until about thirty years ago. Renovations were undertaken piecemeal, until his lordship bought the building."

The porte cochere attached the carriage house to the back of the main building. Those coming and going thus had privacy, which Ellie valued as much as the relative luxury of her apartment.

She showed Elsmore where the spare key was and explained how to work Lord Stephen's lift. Moments later, His Grace stood with her in her modest parlor, holding the ledgers while Ellie lit candles and hoped the cat hadn't left any feline calling cards of an inappropriate nature.

The duke set the ledgers on her desk. "This is where you'll work?"

"For the next two weeks." The premises were chilly, but not frigid. Lord Stephen's rooms on the next floor up were always kept roaringly warm, as were the rooms of the writer living on the floor below. Ellie benefited by proximity, though she also lit the parlor stove on truly cold days.

"I have a question for you, Mrs. Hatfield." Elsmore lounged back against her desk, a battered old article rescued from some alley.

The cat emerged from under the sofa and sniffed at Elsmore's boots. The beast was all black with green eyes, an aloof creature by nature, but drawn to novelty.

"That is Voltaire," Ellie said. "She's quite the mouser."

Elsmore picked up the cat, who nuzzled the wool of his lapel as if he were her long lost kitten. "A worthy companion. I'm curious about something."

The cat commenced purring and rubbing her head against His Grace's chin.

"I've asked you many questions," Ellie said. "I suppose you are permitted to ask me a few in return." The chop shop across the street would be open for another hour, but they sometimes ran out of soup at the end of the day. Ellie did not fancy a dinner of stale bread any more than she fancied watching the cat flirt with the duke.

"This is a very friendly feline, but then, animals usually like me."

Ellie liked him. Liked that he was slow to anger, liked that he had a sense of humor. She liked that Elsmore was trying to manage his situation responsibly, and liked—grudgingly—that he insisted on courtesies. This liking was yet another problem, because an auditor must remain disinterested if she was to be effective.

Not, of course, that she'd *do* anything about liking him.

"How is it that a woman so closely associated with one of the wealthiest bankers in London, a woman entrusted with more responsibility than many titled men will bear in a lifetime, has intimate knowledge of an embezzler's trade? I find that very curious."

The only sounds when Elsmore fell silent were the cat, purring contentedly in his arms, and the rain beating against the windows.

Chapter Five

Mrs. Hatfield took an inordinate amount of time unpinning her bonnet, fussing at her hair, and removing mittens and gloves. Rex ought to leave her to her privacy, but seeing her in her own surroundings outshone the tired charm of rare steak and stale gossip at his club.

"The essence of effective auditing is simply paying attention," she said, hanging her bonnet on a hook beside the door. "Paying attention to patterns, and to details that contradict those patterns. Clerks, for example, are humble fellows by trade. They thrive on being told exactly which work to do, in what order, with what specific goal. They accept modest wages, but should be paid enough that they need not compromise their honor for their next meal. Any clerk whose behavior does not fit that pattern bears closer scrutiny."

Why did no one explain this to a peer's heir, for he would employ many clerks? "So the sullen, tired, restless clerk bears watching?" Fortunately, Rex could think of no one in his employ who fit that description.

The humid weather had dealt Mrs. Hatfield's severe bun a few blows, turning ruthless order into tendrils, waves, and an errant curl or two. She smoothed her hair over her ears, which did nothing to tame the chaos.

"One watches the surly ones, but the better thief will be too cheerful, too punctual. He will announce to his fellows that he loves his position—which he does—and hopes to spend his entire career seeing the employer's enterprise thrive—which he also does."

Well, damn. That described nearly every retainer on every property Rex owned. "How do you tell the difference between the happily loyal and the cheerfully untrustworthy?"

"Careful observation, luck, and determination, Your Grace."

She unbuttoned her cloak next, and without thinking, Rex drew it from her shoulders, gave it a shake, and hung it on the drying pegs beneath the mantel. A small silver teapot sat in the middle of the mantel, a sketch on either side in plain wooden frames. He wanted to study those drawings, but not when Eleanora could see him doing it.

He braced himself for a scold as he passed her a shawl that had been draped over the back of a reading chair. "Shall I light the fire?" he asked, for want of anything else to say.

By the limited illumination of a few candles, she looked weary. "I'll be going out again, just across the street, and I don't light the hearth until I'm in for the night."

Eleanora Hatfield, like much of London, had no cooking facilities in her domicile. Of course, she'd go out to fetch a hot meal.

"I'm still dressed for the weather," Rex said. "I'll get us some food, while you consider a strategy for organizing our efforts over the next two weeks."

He bowed and left before she could argue. By the time he returned, she'd curled up in a chair, her shawl about her shoulders, her hearth crackling. She'd also fallen asleep.

He dealt with the cat first, unwrapping a morsel of fish and leaving it on its paper in a corner. For himself and his hostess, salty fried potatoes came next and slices of hot roasted beef followed. The scents were humble and tantalizing, and apparently enough to tempt Mrs. Hatfield from her slumbers.

"You bought beef and potatoes."

She looked at him as if he'd served her one of those fancy dinners Mama made such a fuss over. Four removes, three feuding chefs, footmen run ragged, the sommelier pinching the maids, and all the guests more interested in flirtation than food.

"Voltaire has started on the fish course," Rex said. The cat was, in fact, growling as she ate, and sounding quite serious about her meal.

"Her manners were formed in a hard school," Mrs. Hatfield said, sitting up. "Where are my—?"

Rex passed her the spectacles, though he preferred her without them.

"Have you cutlery," he asked, "or do we shun etiquette for the sake of survival?"

"In the sideboard." She took a plate from him. "I can put the kettle on if—you brought wine."

"A humble claret, but humility is a virtue, I'm told."

The shared meal reminded Rex of something that ought to also be part of a peer's curriculum: Some people had the luxury of chatting and laughing as abundant food was put before them. Other people had such infrequent acquaintance with adequate nutrition that the notion of focusing on anything other than appreciation for food was a sort of blasphemy.

Eleanora Hatfield ate with that degree of concentration. She did not hurry, she did not compromise her manners, but she focused on her meal with the same single-mindedness she turned on her ledgers.

"You have known poverty," Rex said, buttering the last slice of bread and passing it to her. "Not merely hard times or lean years. You have known the bleakest of realities."

She took the bread, tore it in two, and passed half back to him. "There's no shame in poverty."

"I doubt there's much joy in it, either."

"We managed, and I am impoverished no longer." She launched into a lecture about concentric rings of responsibility, redundant documentation, and heaven knew what else. Rex poured her more wine, put an attentive expression on his face—he excelled at appearing attentive—and let his curiosity roam over the mystery of Eleanora Hatfield.

She'd known hardship, and she'd probably known embezzlers. She'd decided to wrap herself in the fiction of widowhood or wifehood, but not the reality, and she was truly passionate about setting Rex's books to rights.

The longer she talked about the many ways his estates could have been pillaged—while he'd waltzed, played piquet, and debated the Corn Laws—the more he appreciated her fierceness and the more he wondered how she'd come by it.

"When should I call upon you tomorrow?" he asked, rising and gathering up the orts and leavings of their meal.

"At the end of the day," she said, standing to take the greasy paper from him. "I'll use this for kindling, and I leave any empty bottles in the alley for the street children to sell. In cold weather, their lives grow more perilous than usual."

She drew her shawl up and looked away, as if those last words should have been kept behind her teeth.

Rex shrugged into his greatcoat, wrapped a cashmere scarf about his neck, and pulled on gloves lined with rabbit fur. Autumn had not only turned up nasty, winter was in the offing.

"I want you to consider something," he said. "Something in addition to the many ways my trusty staff is bilking me of a fortune."

"Not all of them, we haven't established that."

Not yet. Anybody seeking to steal from the Elsmore fortune was doomed to eventual discovery, now that Eleanora Hatfield was on the scent.

"Please consider a theoretical question: If instead of allowing my coffers to be pillaged by the enterprising thieves in my employ, I had donated that money to charity, where would you have me put those funds?"

He had her attention now, and having Eleanora Hatfield's attention was not a casual state of affairs.

"You are asking about thousands of pounds, Your Grace."

"No, actually, I am asking for your trust. You will soon know all of my secrets, Eleanora. You will know where I have been lax, where I have been less than conscientious about my duties. You will know who has betrayed me. Not even my priest knows me that well, not even my siblings. I am asking much of you, and in return, all I can offer is an assurance that your secrets would be safe with me."

Her gaze was momentarily dumbstruck, then puzzled, then troubled. "Thank you, Your Grace, but in my line of work, I can afford to trust no one."

Interesting choice of verb—*afford*. "You like it that way."

"I need it that way."

How honest, and how lonely. Elsmore brushed her hair back over her ear, and when she did not protest that presumption he bent nearer. She stood still, eyes downcast, though he well knew she was capable of pinning back his ears.

"Eleanora?"

She closed her eyes, and he realized that was as much permission as he would get from her. He kissed her cheek and let himself out into the chilly corridor, pausing only long enough to make sure she locked the door after him.

As if her mind had imparted its restlessness to his own, he walked the distance to his home, turning over questions and ignoring the persistent freezing drizzle. Two streets from his own doorway, he took off his gloves and scarf and left them in an alley.

Why had he kissed Eleanora Hatfield? Even a chaste gesture such as he'd bestowed on the lady was an intimacy, and with the least intimacy-prone female he knew. Why cross that line? Why blur those boundaries? His musings yielded no satisfactory answers, but then, a man who failed to notice his trusted staff dipping into his coffers, a man who overlooked drinking from the wrong teacup, was probably overdue for an audit of his own sentiments and motivations.

*   *   *

Friday arrived on schedule, though Ellie awoke slightly groggy for having had two glasses of wine the night before.

"And good claret it was," she muttered to the cat. "I saved you some scraps of beef too."

Voltaire had liked the duke. She watched Lord Stephen from the safety of her windowsill on the rare occasions when he happened by, and most other visitors sent her scurrying under the sofa.

"Don't get attached to Elsmore," Ellie said, putting the scraps on a piece of paper for the cat. "We will determine where the ducal vessel is leaking, and he'll be on his way, married to a suitable *parti*."

She allowed herself a pot of tea to go with her jam and buttered bread, and settled in for a morning of absolute bliss among the ledgers. Drawing conclusions from too little information was a good way to miss important patterns, and Elsmore's books were a puzzle in any case.

A messy puzzle. After pleasant hours with the ledgers, Ellie pondered that conundrum as she walked to the Wentworth town house. She was still pre-occupied when Jane, Duchess of Walden, swept into the room, a big, black hound at her side.

"Your Grace." Ellie curtseyed, stifling the impulse to curtsey to the dog as well. Big dogs with big teeth should make anybody respectful, though the duchess's pet was always beautifully behaved.

"Eleanora." The duchess wrapped her in a hug. Her Grace was taller than Ellie, and quite self-possessed, but she also had a bewilderingly maternal quality. "I so look forward to your weekly calls. Starting next Friday, I will send my coach for you. The weather grows too chilly, and you have better things to do with your time than hike across London."

"I like hiking across London." When Jack kept his distance. "I spend too much time hunched over figures and account books. Fresh air keeps me sane."

"Many a mother has said the same thing. I am convinced

that Mayfair's proximity to Hyde Park is more than half its attraction for those who can afford the surrounds. Are we having tea or chocolate today?"

Ellie had never had chocolate until the duchess had served it one frigid afternoon nearly a year ago. "Chocolate would be lovely, Your Grace."

When the tray arrived, and they were assured of privacy, Her Grace switched to French. Simple phrases that were easily mimed: Would you like more chocolate? Please and thank you. Today is cold, don't you agree? Wodin is a fine dog. Yes, he is very fine. In return, Ellie explained the financial instruments and transactions that Quinn Wentworth gloried in with the natural affinity of a lamb at spring grass.

When the small talk had been thoroughly reviewed, Ellie tried a question she could not ask anybody else.

"Pourquoi les ducs sont-ils si compliqués?" Her syntax was questionable—Ellie still wasn't quite sure what syntax was—but the duchess smiled.

"Why are dukes so complicated? Is it the duke who's complicated, Eleanora, or the dukedom—*le duché*? My Quinn is not complicated at all. He thrives on hard work, expects honesty and fair dealing from all who do business with him, and he'd die to protect those he loves."

"Did His Grace of Walden tell you...?"

"That your services are on temporary loan to a peer with a delicate problem. Yes, he's told me, and believe me, Walden does not like having the bank's arbiter of accuracy off the premises. Tell me about your complicated duke."

British dukes numbered less than three dozen, and Her Grace doubtless had a good idea who among them had claimed Ellie's time.

And her interest. He'd also claimed a brief, maddeningly chaste kiss.

"His Grace's holdings are spread out all over Britain," Ellie said, "and even on the Continent. He has more than twice the properties His Grace of Walden owns, and his family sprawls like topsy over the lot of it. He has aunts in dower cottages, widowed cousins living on quiet lanes in Chelsea, other cousins among the employees of the various enterprises he owns or oversees...I knew there were people with such wealth, but I'd never met one."

Had carefully avoided making their acquaintance, in fact.

"How is your duke's wealth different from what you see every day at the bank?" The duchess poured another cup of chocolate, and as good as the first cup was, Ellie always preferred the second. The chocolate was so rich as to approach bitterness, and nothing complemented that richness as well as warm, buttery shortbread.

"He's not my duke."

The duchess made an elegant picture with her delicate china, engraved silver, and expensive attire, but the look she gave Ellie over the tray was plain enough to decipher.

"You have speculated, Eleanora. We all start off by speculating. It's harmless, though I don't advise anything more than speculation where handsome, hot-headed, half-pay officers are concerned."

Her Grace's first husband had fit that description.

"The duke in question is simply a variety of ledger book I haven't come across before. He's more complicated, more complex. His Grace of Walden belongs with you. If he sold off his shares in the bank, donated all of his properties to charity, and set up shop as a blacksmith, he would still be every bit as much yours as he is now. With this other duke..."

The duchess sat back, stroking a hand over the head of the dog sitting by her chair. "A duke is not a favorite reticule, Eleanora, or a new bonnet. He's a flesh and blood man with hopes and fears and needs the same as any cobbler or yeoman."

Eleanora could speak the language of numbers at a great rate, but expressing unfamiliar sentiments took significant thought.

"I meant he belonged *with* you, like the rich chocolate goes with the marvelous shortbread. Like a good claret and perfectly cooked beef. Why are my analogies all about food? I meant that you and Walden belong *with* each other—forever, not simply for as long as he's the duke of this or that. I did not mean that you own each other."

The duchess studied Ellie over the rim of a fine porcelain teacup, looking at her the same way Ellie regarded a ledger kept in a crabbed hand. The numbers might be accurate, or they might be all widdershins. Only careful study and determination would reveal which.

Ellie tried again. "I cannot see this other, complicated duke ever belonging *with* anybody the way he belongs with all those estates, accounts, ventures, and cousins. He is titled, but it feels to me as if his estates and relatives and siblings have title to him, not the other way 'round. You and Walden belong *with* each other, come what may, forever and ever, amen. The rest is mere trappings to you both."

"What a burden it must be," the duchess said, "to have such an observant mind. You cannot help yourself, you take note of everything and everybody around you. You describe my relationship with His Grace better than I could myself."

When Elsmore had stood so close to Ellie, the scent of

his shaving soap still detectable late in the day, she had noticed little, save utter amazement that he was about to kiss her. She could admit to finding him attractive, but hadn't entertained the possibility that the attraction might be reciprocated. She'd braced herself for disappointment, for a brief pawing that would reveal Elsmore to be as heedless and self-absorbed as the rest of his gender, and then...

Soft warmth against her cheek, a moment of closeness, and a quiet click of the door latch as he'd left her in solitude.

His kiss had been perfect. Respectful, sweet, surprising...

"You pose an interesting topic," Her Grace said, sipping her chocolate. "I could never have envisioned myself married to Quinn Wentworth, much less becoming anybody's duchess, but you are exactly correct: Were he a blacksmith, a pawnbroker, a candlestick maker, I would choose to be his wife, and choose only him to be my husband. Who or what, I wonder, belongs with you, Eleanora?"

"Ledgers are my lot," Ellie replied. "We get on well, and I am never bored in the presence of sums and tallies. The benefit of our association is that my expenses are paid and my cat and I eat well and regularly. That is as much perpetual bliss and forever after as one lady needs."

"Have some more shortbread," the duchess said, holding out the plate. "I suspect you are in need of the fortification."

"Thank you." Ellie took two more pieces, because she was, indeed, in need of fortification. Elsmore might kiss her again or he might not. Either way, she'd need to be strong and sensible, and never lose sight of the fact that she could not have forever after.

She of all women knew better than to pine for a duke, much less both forever *and* a duke.

The duchess, as was her habit, walked Ellie to the door, and insisted on sending her home in the ducal coach. The weather was threatening more rain or possibly even sleet, so Ellie accepted.

"And Eleanora, promise me something," Her Grace said, re-arranging the drape of Ellie's plain wool scarf.

"I will be back next week, you may depend upon it." Ellie treasured this odd, comfortable association, and suspected Her Grace did too.

"Of course you will, but beyond that. *Soit prudent. Les ducs peuvent être dangereux.*"

The reminder was timely, also wise. "Yes, Your Grace. I know." Better than most, Ellie well knew that titled men could be dangerous. "I will be very careful. You needn't worry about me, or about the duke."

* * *

"Your Grace, I feel it only fair to warn you that continued intransigence on your part will serve no purpose other than to aggravate me past all bearing. You will not care for the consequences."

Rex leaned over Mrs. Hatfield's desk, his hands braced on the blotter. "Madam, do you know what the consequences are for aggravating a duke?"

She tidied a stack of foolscap. "Indeed, I do. An annoyed duke will fume and splutter like a rejected flirt. He assays brooding silences and gimlet-eyed glowers, while all the mice cower and attempt to placate him. That drama goes dull after the third performance."

Rex straightened. "Do you mean to tell me that His

Grace of Walden carries on like that before bank employees?"

Next, she took up a penknife and pared a fresh point on her pencils, one by one. "Of course not, but the bank has among its patrons a sprinkling of titled ninnyhammers. Their tantrums exhibit a lamentable sameness."

Rex resumed his seat, half amused by her self-possession, half awed by it. "I am not having a tantrum. You postulate that my own sisters are stealing from me. Allow me to be affronted on behalf of all concerned."

The quill pens were her next project, each one sharpened with a few deft strokes of the knife. "Not stealing. I did not say stealing. Your sisters look to be engaged in one of the oldest ploys known to womanhood for amassing private funds."

Her fingers weren't ink-stained today, but she had turned back the cuff of her right sleeve, revealing a slender wrist. A tiny smear of ink graced the soft, pale underside of that wrist.

"And you posit that my siblings learned this scheme from my own mother." A simple enough plan, as Mrs. Hatfield had explained it: Mark down in the books that pin money was spent on dresses and, indeed, order and have delivered a garment or three from some fashionable establishment, complete with a detailed invoice marked paid in full.

Return the garment for coin rather than credit. Pocket the coin.

"I suggested you investigate the possibility," Mrs. Hatfield said, folding her hands like a dame school headmistress. "Have a look at the invoices and consult your memory to see if any of the dresses described ever graced the persons for whom they were sewn. The modiste your sisters favor is renowned for being *very understanding* about returned merchandise, and even the Duchess of Walden doesn't go through dresses at the rate your sisters do."

Rex's head had begun to pound before he'd left the hallowed corridors of Dorset and Becker that afternoon. An argument with his valet over the choice of cravat pin hadn't helped—Rex did not favor gaudy displays— and now this: allegations of pilfering aimed at the present Duchess of Elsmore and her daughters.

"I cannot recall what my sisters wore at breakfast much less to the last ball. They have an endless progression of pretty frocks, and it is my pleasure to pay for the lot."

Mrs. Hatfield's gaze bore into him with the thou-art-doomed implacability of a cat beholding a caged canary. "Then have a look at their wardrobes, Your Grace. Trouble yourself to wander into their dressing closets at the odd hour, and seek out the last three dresses for which you have paid. If that is beneath your consequence, have a word with the lady's maids. They are typically given cast-off clothing to sell, and they know their mistress's wardrobes quite well."

He pinched the bridge of his nose. "The notion that I'm to skulk about, spying on my sisters, attributing nefarious schemes to them and to my dear mother is insupportable."

Mrs. Hatfield folded her arms. "The notion that you'd rather be stolen from than attempt a discreet inventory of a single wardrobe suggests the problem is your pride rather than family honor."

The throbbing at Rex's temples became an anvil chorus, some of which involved self-recrimination for that pride. "Do you never give quarter? Never show mercy?"

She smiled. Not a grudging quirk of her lips that masked impatience, but an impish, self-satisfied smirk that lit her eyes with mischief.

"I *am* showing mercy, you daft man. I'm starting with

the harmless, predictable adjustments women make to maintain some control over their funds. When you can take that medicine without complaint, we'll move on to more troubling symptoms."

Clearly, *she* wasn't troubled by sororal pilfering. "This is harmless and predictable? Misrepresenting what funds are used for? Pocketing coin in secret?"

"The only person from whom the scheme has been kept secret is likely yourself. The modiste can resell the dresses, and the clients returning the merchandise give the same shop their considerable legitimate custom. Think of this as a banking system for the ladies, and nothing you fellows need concern yourselves about."

"What use have my sisters for ready coin?"

The humor faded from her gaze. "The coin is only part of it, for most women. The possession of independent funds, the exercise of ingenuity necessary to amass those funds, the use of relative invisibility not as an insult but as an asset, that's the heart of the transaction."

I cannot recall what my sisters wore to breakfast...

"Let's assume the scheme is ongoing," Rex said. "The sums involved must be modest, and if I arrive to a family meal blind to my own siblings, then they deserve to dip an occasional hand into my pocket in compensation."

Mrs. Hatfield rose and went to the sideboard, rummaging in its cupboards. "What or who has given you yet another headache?"

My family. "How can you tell?"

"Your eyes. They aren't... Usually, you look out on the world with a benevolent tolerance. You are annoyed today." She set out a mug and crushed some dried herb or other into a strainer, then swung the kettle from the fireplace and poured steaming water into the mug.

She passed him the brew.

"What is this?"

"Peppermint with a dash of feverfew. You have to hold the cup in your hands while it steeps if the remedy is to be most effective."

Rex complied rather than earn yet another scold. The warmth comforted, the scent soothed. "I had a meeting at the bank today."

Mrs. Hatfield closed the account book on the blotter. "Banks and meetings, meetings and banks. I loathe meetings. While everybody is gathered around listening to their superiors bleat about some procedure they've concocted without consulting the underlings, nobody is doing the work that keeps the bank in business. Better to send around a decree—the managers and partners do as they jolly well please most of the time anyway—and leave the clerks to their labors."

Well, yes. Rex had made the same point more than once. "An account was closed last week amid some irregularity."

She took the seat beside him rather than resume her place at the helm of the HMS *Accurate Ledgers*. "I was afraid of that."

Not good, when Mrs. Eleanora Hatfield predicted trouble. "Tell me the rest of it, madam."

"If your personal books are vulnerable, then it stands to reason that your commercial establishments will also be victimized. In all likelihood, schemes set up several dukes ago are still bearing fruit, and as each generation of factors and stewards sees what the one before got away with, they add a new layer of inventiveness to the means by which your dukedom is robbed."

She emptied the pen tray of its contents and used it as a saucer for the strainer. "Have a taste."

"It's too hot."

"It's meant to be hot."

Rex liked arguing with her. That realization dropped into his mind amid the miseries of the day with the unexpected beauty of a late-blooming rose dusted with the first snow of the season. He tried a sip of the drink, which was both calming and refreshing.

"Dorset and Becker does business with many old and respected families," he said. "That's another way of admitting that some of our customers are a bit eccentric."

"Go on."

"Mr. Purcell Butterfield is elderly, reclusive, and very particular about his accounts. His transactions are usually handled by mail. He used to send us banknotes torn in half. One half delivered one week, the other the following week, the better to reduce the chances of a mishap with the mails."

"Many a poor family does likewise when resorting to the post. Drink your tisane."

Rex also liked when Mrs. Hatfield fussed at him in the usual female manner. "Mr. Butterfield came into the bank last week and closed one of his accounts in person." Rex would have set the mug on the desk, but Mrs. Hatfield passed it back to him.

"You have to hold the mug. My grandmother claims something about the heat in your hands helps with the headache. The person who closed the account wasn't Mr. Butterfield. You learned that when the real Mr. Butterfield came into the bank today intent on closing the same account."

"Well...yes."

"The Butterfield who closed the account *seemed* elderly," she went on. "The weather having turned, he arrived swathed in scarves and a hat, wearing a nondescript greatcoat with the collar turned up. If he's a careful sort of swindler, he wore finger gloves beneath his mittens. He might also be bearded, stooped, and wear tinted spectacles, so your teller can barely describe the man who first came in to close the account."

She'd even got the tinted spectacles right. "Has the same scheme been attempted at Wentworth and Penrose? Perhaps Mr. Butterfield's impostor is working a city-wide swindle." A marginally cheering thought.

"Stealing a wealthy old man's identity is not complicated when that old man has removed himself from society. His son, secretary, or favorite nephew could pull it off. When the schemer disappears into the night, the old fellow realizes that his funds are at risk. By that time, it's too late."

Rex finished the last of his tisane and saluted Mrs. Hatfield with the empty cup. "I am apparently the only bank director in all of London unaware of even the simplest frauds. How in the hell is every teller to know every customer at sight?"

"They can't," she said, taking the empty mug from him and setting it on the sideboard. "But there is good news. The bounder who duped you will not run the same rig on you again. He doesn't dare."

"He'll move on to another bank?"

"Very likely to another city, even another country. How much did he get?"

"A couple hundred pounds and half of my self-respect."

"It could have been thousands, but a smart crook doesn't want to carry that much ready cash. Because the bank will cover the loss rather than publicize its error, the injured party is the bank, not the old man. Criminals prefer to steal from institutions rather than people, the honorable ones, anyway."

She knelt to poke up the fire, and the cat leaped down from the reading chair to strop itself against her skirts.

"On that disheartening note," Rex said, "I should be going. I'm expected at the theater later this evening." Where the hum of gossip all but obscured the dialogue from the stage half the time—not that Rex was interested in the dialogue. "How does a thief decide which old man to impersonate?"

"Cautiously. Impersonation is a long game, involving employment in the household of the dupe, or a careful observation of him. Will I see you tomorrow?"

"Yes, though I hope you rest from your labors on the Sabbath."

She brought him his greatcoat and held it up for him. "I do. Even I know that the mind needs periods of repose. Enjoy the theater."

She passed him his scarf, then his gloves.

"Do you ever go—to the theater?"

"I do not," she replied, picking up the cat. "I sometimes think about attending an opera, but the seats are dear, and it's not a venue a woman can frequent on her own."

"The *opera*, Mrs. Hatfield?" Rex took satisfaction from knowing this about her, from knowing that even she had an unfulfilled wish or two.

"Don't take a two-hundred-pound rig too much to heart, Your Grace. If that's the worst setback the bank experiences, your institution will thrive for generations. The tellers should be instructed to chat up every customer and get to know their situations. Keep the fires going in the public areas so nobody has an excuse to remain swaddled in a disguise."

She carried all of this wisdom around in her head, as easily as Rex carried the ducal succession in his. Her knowledge was useful while his...

"This whole business will get worse, won't it?" he asked, hand on the door latch. "You will soon make me face far more than a few returned dresses and some loose pin money."

Mrs. Hatfield cradled the cat against her middle. "Your entire problem might be a matter of loose pin money going awry in three dozen directions, or it might involve that plus more sophisticated schemes. We'll have a better sense of that by this time next week."

So yes, the reality of his books would soon grow considerably worse. "Do you know how much I value your honesty?"

"As much as I value your coin?"

More. Far more. He didn't dare say that to her when the admission was something of a shock even to him. "Until tomorrow afternoon, Mrs. Hatfield."

She touched his sleeve. "An audit is a difficult tonic, Your Grace, but the sooner you take it, the greater the likelihood your sons and grandsons will be spared the same problems. We'll get your dukedom sorted out."

She went up on her toes and kissed his cheek, then held the door for him, and waved him on his way.

Chapter Six

"Pamela, tell me the truth," Ellie said in her sternest Your-Sister-Knows-All tones. "Did Jack play the Old Man on a fellow named Purcell Butterfield?"

"Now, Eleanora, you mustn't be wroth." Pamela plucked the infant from Ellie's arms, and Ellie let the child go. "The baby will be upset by your harsh words, and then I'll get no peace."

"My words are not harsh. I'm merely asking a question."

Pamela took the only other seat in the sitting room, and one-handed began to unbutton her bodice. The child waved tiny fists, while two older siblings played some game involving pebbles on the threadbare hearthrug. The only spot of grace about the place was a pair of sketches hanging beside the door, one of Pamela, one of the two older children.

Jack had done both and had likely completed each one in less than five minutes.

"Who knows what Jack and them get up to?" Pamela asked, putting the child to her breast. "They have the sense not to gabble about it. Jack has been looking like a clerk lately, a proper secretary. He takes honest work sometimes, but then his reputation catches up with him."

"Or his criminal tendencies do."

Pamela stroked the baby's downy crown. Another redhead, from the looks of him. "Easy for you to judge, Ellie. You were lucky. Jack works hard, and he'd work honest all the time if he could. You're not to tell him I said that."

The little apartment smelled of boiled cabbage and bacon, the signature scents of Ellie's later childhood.

"Do you hear anything from York?" Ellie asked.

"Had a note last week. It's on the mantel."

"You had a note and you didn't tell me?"

Pamela wrapped the infant more closely in his blanket, which had been a gift from Ellie to Pamela's firstborn.

"Slipped what's left of my mind. You try having three babies in six years. Makes ya fair daft, it does."

Pamela could affect the speech of a Mayfair debutante when she chose to, but here at home, the broad vowels of Yorkshire shone through.

"I wish they'd write to me," Ellie said, taking down a single folded sheet of foolscap. Grandmama crossed her letters to save on postage, but she still had the handwriting of a lady. Ellie carried the note to the window, where grimy glass let in weak sunshine.

"The usual," Ellie murmured. "Grandpapa dislikes the cold, Grandmama's knees bother her. She hopes the winter won't be as snowy as last." No hidden messages, no encoded directions for Jack or Pamela or Mick, no word that any of the cousins had been arrested. *No bad news*, thank the celestial powers. "I wish they'd move south."

"You wish Jack would move north, and probably me and Clyde as well. Mick has nipped off to Bristol or Antwerp, I forget where."

Meaning Mick was safely away, if he'd impersonated Mr. Butterfield.

Clyde was a charming Scotsman, which in Ellie's experience was a redundant term. Charming and unscrupulous were, alas, also often found in close proximity.

"What is Clyde up to these days?"

"Odd jobbing, man of all work," Pamela said, switching the baby to the second breast. "He drives a cab for any fellow who's down with an ague, he shovels coal, sweeps crossings...this and that."

Clyde Andrews was also a cheerful and affectionate father, a faithful spouse from what Pamela said, and he only got drunk on the Sabbath, when no work was to be done for hire.

Ellie did not trust him, though she distrusted him less than she distrusted her cousins. "Keep Clyde away from Jack, Pamela. Jack is not a good influence." Though to Ellie's knowledge, Jack had never involved Clyde in an illegal scheme. Clyde was the sole support of three children and thus, according to Jack's reckoning, not a man to be taking on risky ventures.

"Our cousins are enterprising lads, Ellie. We don't all have your good fortune. Ouch." Pamela gently batted the child on the nose—very gently.

"I am lucky," Ellie said. "I am also careful, and I work hard."

"You wouldn't have to work so hard, but you alone of all the Naylors insist on ignoring opportunity when it all but falls into your lap."

"I ignore the opportunity to end my days with a rope around my neck."

The oldest child glanced up from the pebble game, then looked to her mother.

"Aunt Ellie is cross this morning," Pamela said. "She works too hard."

The middle child scrambled to his feet. "Aunt El rides in fancy coaches with fancy gentlemen!" This occasioned dancing about and general shrieking on the parts of the older two. "Cousin Jackie says Aunt El rides in a fancy coach with fancy coves!"

"Both of you go play on the landing," Pamela said. "Go now, before you upset the baby."

"They upset me," Ellie said, when the door had been stoutly slammed by the departing children. "Has Jack been spying on me?"

Fancy gentlemen, the children had said, *plural*. Not the occasional coach ride shared with His Grace of Walden, but gentle*men*.

"Jack keeps an eye on us all. Grandpapa told him to."

"That was more than ten years ago, and Grandpapa told me the same thing. I don't lurk in alleys watching what you get up to."

"Take the baby," Pamela said, passing the infant over. "I can't say Jack has been lurking in any alleys, but you do ride about in fancy coaches. I saw you myself just yesterday. The Walden crest is well known, and there you were, pretty as a princess in the middle of the afternoon."

Ellie put the baby to her shoulder and softly patted his little back. "Her Grace lends me the carriage on occasion when the weather is inclement."

"In-clem-ent," Pamela drawled. "You really have left Yorkshire behind, haven't you?"

The baby was precious and sweet, and to have this

argument when the little fellow was due to drift off for a nap struck Ellie as wrong.

"If Jack is spying on me, then I have dragged Yorkshire and all its miseries right to my own doorstep, haven't I? Tell him to leave me alone, Pamela, or he could ruin everything I've worked years to build."

A bank auditor with criminal connections would not be a bank auditor for long. The Wentworth and Penrose owners would give Ellie generous severance, and they'd regret cutting her loose, but they would think first, last, and always of their bank's reputation.

"You want the grandparents to move down to London, but you want Jack to pretend he's a stranger. Fine way to treat a man you were once engaged to."

Not this. Not now, when the baby was sighing so sweetly near Ellie's ear. "He left me for one of his schemes, Pamela. You know that. Left me without a word in parting, and came jaunting back three months later with no explanation and little apology."

A bullet dodged, though Ellie would never say that to Jack. She kept her peace on the matter not to spare Jack the guilt and shame of having abandoned her, but because it flattered him to think she'd pined for him.

"Men do what they must," Pamela said, buttoning and tucking in her bodice. "How are matters at the bank?"

"The same. Wentworth and Penrose thrives, and I pride myself on contributing to its good standing. One word from Jack, and I have no livelihood and no reputation."

The baby gave a tiny burp, then a sigh.

"They are always so good for you," Pamela said. "The babies, that is. Jack simply looks after you for old times' sake."

No, he did not. Ellie wasn't sure what exactly Jack was about. She refused to have anything to do with his schemes, and he refused disappear from her life. He was like a half-tame dog. She worried when he dropped out of sight for too long, but she wasn't comfortable when he was underfoot either.

"Our family was respectable once, Pammie. We can be respectable again, but not if Jack and his cohorts keep running their rigs."

Pamela stared at the door. "The little heathens have gone upstairs to bother Mrs. Hilton. Where that woman gets her patience, I do not know. I think I might be expecting again. Mrs. H says I have the look."

"Mrs. H is on the nest," Ellie said. "She sees babies everywhere. For your sake, I hope you haven't conceived again so soon."

Pamela tied her bodice ribbon in a bow. "Clyde can be persuasive."

But could he provide adequately for the fruits of his persuasion? "Take this," Ellie said, passing over a gold sovereign. "For the children."

The coin disappeared into one of Pamela's pockets. "You needn't, you know. Mick left us a bit of a windfall before he went traveling. We'll be in clover through the New Year."

An eternity of good fortune by the standards of a Naylor. "Keep the coin. Winter is long and coal is expensive." Ellie passed the now-sleeping child to his mother. "Don't you ever want better for your children, Pamela? Want them to grow up without the fear that their uncle might end up transported or worse?"

Ellie wanted better for her nieces and nephews, and for her sister and cousins.

"No, Ellie, I don't. We were respectable a lifetime ago, and then, because the nobs can literally get away with any-thing, we weren't respectable any more. We could all toil away, minding the rules, working ourselves to death, and maybe our grandchildren would someday be halfway acceptable. Then another earl or duke or even a bloody shop owner could start making accusations, and we'd be ruined again. That's how it works. Enjoy your fancy coaches while they last."

Ellie had no argument to that reasoning because it was based on experience and fact. "They aren't my coaches."

"They aren't your fancy gents either," Pamela said, passing Ellie her coat, "but not a one of us would begrudge you a little time spent lightening their pockets. We'd cheer you on, in fact."

"It's not like that."

"Maybe it should be like that, Ellie. You ever think of that? If you're not inclined to marry, you should at least enjoy the occasional frolic and be paid for your troubles. Nothing illegal in that, and the fancy gents have more coin than they know what to do with."

"Frolics have consequences. I'll keep my job at the bank, thank you very much." Until some cousin or in-law ended up drenching the whole family in scandal once more.

"Come see us again soon," Pamela said, offering Ellie a brief, one-armed squeeze. "Come around on a Sunday, and we'll set a place for you."

Ellie left without committing to that plan, because another mouth to feed was another mouth to feed. She'd made it two streets past the corner before Jack fell in step beside her, looking every inch the modest clerk.

"So who's the new fancy gent, Eleanora? Have you taken to collecting dukes now?"

"None of your business, and I'll thank you not to spy on me. Don't bother begging me to hand an innocent young woman into your keeping either, Jack Naylor."

"I didn't want to trouble the woman, only borrow her purse for a bit. Though as to that, an older lady might have more jewels and coin. I'm not particular about the lady as long as the purse is worth my while."

The game Jack contemplated was uncomplicated: Have some urchin steal a lady's purse when she was in a public location. Give dramatic chase, then return the purloined item on a cloud of selfless gallantry. Because returning stolen items was to be encouraged, a reward usually followed. What the scheme lacked in certainty it made up for in simplicity and immediacy of the benefit, if any benefit was to be had.

Best of all, the urchin took all the risk, and a very significant risk it was. Too often as children, the cousins had done the snatching, and Ellie had done the worrying.

"So Mick has departed this sceptered isle for the nonce?" she asked.

"He took a notion to travel, as restless young men sometimes do."

"After he took a notion to work a rig on a Mr. Purcell Butterfield?"

The name had Jack stopping in the middle of the walkway. "How do you know about that?"

In the name of fractions, decimals, and irrational numbers. "Shall I share my suspicions with the magistrate?"

"Nora Naylor, for shame." Genuine dismay colored Jack's features, or as close to genuine dismay as he ever came. "A bank can stand to lose a few bob to an enterprising fellow with family to look after. Not like the old cove was out a single farthing."

Despair and exasperation stole the last of Ellie's self-restraint. "Some teller is likely *without a job* because of Mick's scheme, and that man has family to feed too—

family he worked hard to feed. If the bank doesn't fire the teller for being too honest to sniff out your crooked scheme, then his pay will be docked until the day he dies, and all of his peers will hold him in contempt. He might well have been let go without a character, and then Mick with his little scheme is no better than the Earl of Winston, is he? Victimizing the blameless for his own gain, going merrily on his way and leaving other lives in ruins."

In this neighborhood, nobody would pay attention to family members having a public spat, but Jack looked up and down the street anyway.

"Watch your mouth, Ellie. Mick works hard, but unless you're respectable and you have all the pretty letters in your pocket, you cannot find decent work, not decent work that pays."

"You're saying you'd take honest work if it was offered? You, Jack?" Ellie resumed walking though she wanted to take off at a dead run.

"If the pay was fair. Too many want you to work yourself to death for nothing, then they hang you anyway when you poach a few rabbits."

"I make good money at the bank," Ellie said, "and I don't have to cheat anybody or lie about who I am to earn it."

"You lie to yourself, Ellie, my love. That's worse than lying to all the banks in England. I'll give Mick your regards when he lets me know where he's landed."

She walked away without looking back, and Jack apparently had the good sense not to follow her—this time.

* * *

"We can move on from your aunties' pin money to your London household accounts," Mrs. Hatfield said. "You dwell in Town now, and you can compare my findings with what's before your eyes. Then too, fraud anywhere in your books must eventually find its way to the London ledgers."

Rex paced her small parlor, while outside, a light snow was coating the walkways and streets. "You use the word *fraud* now."

"The ledgers suggest willful mishandling of your funds, not simple miscalculations, though I see some evidence of that as well."

The theater had run late the previous night, with Mama, the cousins, and the sisters chattering merrily the entire time. James and Eddie had joined the party at the interval, bringing several of their friends, all of them prone to uproarious laughter.

"My butler—"

Mrs. Hatfield held up a hand. She wore her version of battle attire today: fingerless gloves and a gray shawl, and she'd again turned back the cuff on her right sleeve. Her dress was dark gray wool, probably chosen because it wouldn't show ink stains. All she needed was a witch's hat and a cauldron to complete the portrait of the alchemist at her dark arts.

"Your butler," she said, "has too much to do and must rely on his station to effect discipline in the ranks. What he gets is the appearance of compliance with his orders and sloppy books."

The cat watched Rex from a perch on the windowsill. Her expression suggested that sloppy books should be added to England's long list of capital offenses.

"And my housekeeper?"

Mrs. Hatfield rose from her desk and swung the kettle over the coals on the hearth. "She's actually your mother's housekeeper, isn't she?"

My own mother…"You are working up to another revelation. Who is in the dock this time? My mother? My aunts? My house steward?"

"Come here," Mrs. Hatfield said, taking one of the two chairs before her desk. "I'll show you."

Rex hated that she had to instruct him on the topic of managing his dukedom, but he liked sitting beside her. Eleanora Hatfield had a sense of calm competence that soothed his temper, and just as she was unraveling his books, he enjoyed unraveling her.

The rose scent she wore was fine quality. Perhaps not Parisian, but not cheap shop goods either. She had apparently washed her hair recently, for her usual ruthless bun was looser today and less orderly. She wasn't wearing shoes but, rather, thick, scuffed slippers over black wool stockings.

Eleanora Hatfield was susceptible to creature comforts.

She opened a ledger from last spring. "Look here. Do you see any patterns?"

Rex saw a progression of numbers, each entry neatly labeled and dated. Coal, candles, paper, a set of livery for a new footman, boot black…

"I see a typical ledger."

"Exactly what you're supposed to see, and if you merely checked this or that column, probably fairly accurate. But look at my totals versus the ones your steward, secretary, or under-butler did."

She had penciled tiny figures at the foot of each column. For the most part, the totals were the same, occasionally they were off by a couple of pounds.

"Always a two-pound variance," he said.

"Which suggests somebody is working the three-for-five substitution."

"You call these frauds by name, like old friends." While she referred to Rex as Your Grace. Always, Your Grace, with an occasional prim little *sir* tossed in for reinforcement. Nearly everybody called Rex *sir* or *Your Grace*, so why did it bother him that Eleanora Hatfield did as well?

"Old enemies," she said. "I have a theory that most dishonest schemes started off as honest mistakes. Somebody mistakes a three for a five—it's easy to do. Then they realize that they've overstated the total owed by two pounds, and nobody has questioned that figure. The merchant is paid in full according to the merchant's books, and the two pounds finds an appreciative home in the pocket of a thief."

"I detest where this is leading."

She set the ledger on the desk. "My audits lead to the truth, Your Grace. Be glad whoever did this accounting didn't try to work the seven-for-one substitution. Those totals add up faster. I happen to know what coal and candles cost last spring because I keep Lord Stephen's books for this building. The only other way to spot the problem is to compare the exact figures entered with what was on the merchant's invoice."

She recalled the price of coal and candles—to the penny—from six months ago. "First my womenfolk are trafficking in dresses, now my secretaries—or somebody on my payroll—is fleecing me. I have the sense worse news lies ahead."

The kettle began to whistle, provoking the cat to scowling and switching its tail.

Mrs. Hatfield was out of her chair, swinging the kettle off the coals in the next instant. "Voltaire, you are a fraud. This kettle whistles at least twice a day, and only for the duke do you affect these histrionics."

Mrs. Hatfield certainly didn't bother with any histrionics, which was a pleasant change. "Are you hungry?" Rex asked. "I missed luncheon and could do with a sandwich or two. I could pop across the street in a trice."

He expected her to demure out of perpetual self-sufficiency, but instead she went to the window. "This snow might mean business. I love a snowy Sunday."

Had she ever before used the verb *to love* in his hearing? "What else do you love? Books that balance to the penny?"

She picked up the cat, and it occurred to him that her dark wool dress would also not show cat hair.

"I enjoy bookkeeping, Your Grace, and I'm good at it. My talent lies there. I need to make an honest living, so that's what I do. Maybe you feel the same way about being a duke?"

The question was posed casually, and yet, in her studied attention to the cat, in her half-turned posture, Rex caught a hint of genuine interest.

"Precisely. The title is my lot, to complain would be ridiculous, and I'm honor-bound to make the best of it. Will sandwiches do?"

She nuzzled the cat, who nuzzled her back. Was this how the aunties had started down the path of eccentricity? Only a cat to keep them company?

"If the shop has a good soup—pepper pot, fish chowder, beef and barley—I'd like some of that as well."

Rex shrugged into his coat and left the buttons undone. "And another bottle of wine. The last vintage was surprisingly good. Can you answer a question for me?"

"Of course, Your Grace."

"Why did you kiss me?" Despite getting to bed well past a decent hour, despite the eternities of socializing

Rex's evening had demanded, that question had robbed him of sleep.

"You kissed me first, sir."

A gratifyingly nonsensical answer. "I kissed you because a gesture of affection under the circumstances seemed appropriate. I hope I did not offend."

The ever articulate, always competent, not-to-be-daunted Mrs. Hatfield looked away. "You did not, and I hope I did not presume."

"You rather did," he said, tossing his scarf around his neck. "I adore you for it. Feel free to presume again whenever the mood strikes you."

He left her by the window, looking once again quite self-possessed. She was doubtless deciding how to explain to him that yet another trusted hireling was plundering the ducal coffers. So why was Rex's imagination fixed instead on images of Eleanora Hatfield plundering the ducal person?

* * *

Lord Stephen Wentworth's first toy had been a wooden duck on a string. He'd acquired this treasure at the age of eight, far too old for such a nursery diversion. His father had been dead for a month, and thus—for the first time in Stephen's life—personal possessions had become possible. He'd been too lame to do more than jerk the duck two feet at one go as he'd hobbled from chair to chair.

Then he'd used his bootlaces to extend the duck's leash—what need had a crippled boy for boots when he was barely able to walk?—and angled the leash around a table leg. He'd observed the duck's progress by the hour, until his curiosity overcame his good sense, and he'd dismantled the toy in an effort to understand its workings.

The inner mechanisms of that childish amusement—pulleys, weights, levers, wires—had formed the basis for the first lift he'd designed and for a crane the Navy had commissioned for its shipyards. He'd been figuratively dismantling ducks ever since.

And now, a ducal duck was quacking about in Stephen's building, a situation that demanded investigation.

"I can understand that Elsmore needs to tidy up his books," Stephen said, "but what specifically about that exercise requires him to roost in Mrs. Hatfield's rooms by the hour?"

Quinn took his time cutting a piece of steak, which Stephen had learned was not a tactic intended to control the conversation but, rather, the focus a man needed when polite manners had been learned later in life. Here at Quinn's club, if his etiquette should falter, the lapse would be remarked.

"Eleanora is going through the dukedom's estate books, property by property," Quinn said. "I'm sure she has questions. Unless Elsmore wants to announce to all of London that his staff and womenfolk are robbing him blind, she can only put those questions to him in person. Pass the salt."

Stephen first salted his own steak, then passed over the cellar. "Do these questions require regular infusions of hot soup, fresh bread, and roasted beef taken tête-à-tête with Elsmore?"

Quinn set down his knife and fork. "If you are spying, I will inform Jane."

Stephen held two people in limitless respect. The first was his cousin Duncan Wentworth, who'd been his tutor and traveling companion through Stephen's self-destructive adolescent years. Duncan had recently abandoned bachelorhood for the charms of the married state, and Stephen was happy for him.

Overjoyed, in fact. Very damned happy, indeed.

The other person whom Stephen held in unreserved esteem was Jane, Duchess of Walden. She'd married Quinn when he'd been a plain mister come to a very bad pass, and rescued not only Quinn but also his siblings in ways Stephen still had not dismantled to his own satisfaction.

"You'd tattle to Jane because I merely note the comings and goings outside my window?"

"You sit up in your apartment like an eagle in his eyrie, spinning tales about all the mice on the street below. Jane would be disappointed in you if you intruded on Mrs. Hatfield's privacy."

Jane's disappointment was nothing short of a curse. She'd been the first person to hold Stephen accountable without respect to his disabilities. He'd never thanked her for that and wasn't sure he ever would, because how could words convey gratitude that surpassed all understanding?

"What do we know about Mrs. Hatfield, Quinn? Who are her people? She never has callers, but she goes out every other week or so and doesn't return with any packages. She sometimes departs with a package or two, or with a particularly bulky reticule. I assume she's paying social calls."

"Stephen, leave it alone. Design something clever. Translate more Catullus. Devise a new cannon for the Army that actually hits what it's aimed at. Nobody appreciates a meddler."

The steak was overcooked. Stephen couldn't ignore that any more than Quinn could chase the last of the Yorkshire growl from his speech.

"Catullus is for naughty boys. Have you ever wondered why Eleanora isn't married?" Stephen had, and not simply because she was comely. Eleanora Hatfield would keep a man on his toes.

"Some women prefer independence to the married state, particularly when contemplating the perils of childbearing. She has the lot of us at the bank for company, and I believe some family accompanied her when she moved south. Cousins, siblings, I'm not sure which, and it's *none of my business*."

Meaning Quinn carried some secret or suspicion he wasn't willing to share with his only brother.

"Quinn, for pity's sake, *think*. Mrs. Hatfield goes about her duties at the bank, setting a sterling example of integrity and devotion to duty. She's not one of the clerks or tellers, and she prefers it that way. She never puts a foot wrong, and now she's rescuing Elsmore from potential scandal. Have you considered that he might steal her away from us?"

Quinn split his baked potato open and forked three pats of butter into the steaming middle. Eating like this—from most expensive item to least costly—was an artifact of poverty. Stephen made it a point to do otherwise.

"Elsmore is honorable. He won't poach."

"Elsmore is single, wealthy, spending substantial time alone with our Eleanora, and seeing firsthand what a treasure she is. I don't mean steal exclusively in the business sense." Though losing her as an auditor would be a blow.

"You mean steal, as in steal her heart?"

The Quinn of old would have found that notion laughable, but then Jane had stolen *his* heart. Stephen was quite willing to be victimized by similar larceny where his own organ of sensibility was concerned, but apparently no lady was sufficiently interested—or courageous—to attempt the theft.

"I mean precisely that," Stephen said. "Eleanora's wages are generous, but Elsmore can set her up for life."

Quinn mashed melted butter into his potato, then took a sip of his wine. "If that's what makes the lady happy, then we wish her the best and hire a replacement."

"You won't find her like again, Quinn. She takes apart ledgers like I take apart clocks. And you said Elsmore is cleaning up his accounts in anticipation of offering for a duchess. Where will Eleanora be when Elsmore ruins her good name, interferes with her livelihood, and then goes prancing on his way with a new duchess? Does that sound to you like a recipe for happiness? No other bank will hire a disgraced female as an auditor, and we owe that woman much more than her wages reflect."

"Have some more wine."

"I don't care for port. I don't care for the Duke of Elsmore, and right now, I don't care very much for the Duke of Walden, either." Wentworths were honest with each other, though the intensity of Stephen's sentiments came as something of a surprise even to himself.

"Are you in love with our auditor, Stephen?"

Oh, perhaps. Stephen did still fall in love, but he'd learned to watch his own periodic descents into infatuation with a sort of fatalistic amusement. His passions eventually passed, nobody the wiser, and he went back to designing cannon and dismantling watches.

"I am in love with anybody who defends the integrity of your bank, Quinn. You and Penrose opened for business with nothing more than audacity and ambition to your names. Eleanora Hatfield spared you from even a hint of scandal, sorted the honest clerks from the dishonest, and is the reason you have the cleanest books in London. She was instrumental in setting your dukedom to rights, but she's only human. If Elsmore waltzes into her bedroom and anybody gets wind of that, the blot on her escutcheon can't be repaired with a monthly reconciliation."

"Stephen, she is an adult. She is free to conduct her private life as she sees fit."

Was that Jane talking, or Quinn? Something about the way Quinn studied his wineglass wasn't characteristic of his usual forthright manner.

"You are unwilling to remind Elsmore of his manners," Stephen said, "because you don't want to offend a bloody duke. You have become a moral invertebrate like the rest of the bedamned peerage."

"That is quite enough, Stephen. Perhaps I don't want to offend Eleanora. She toils away at the bank year after year. If she takes leave, it's only to attend a sister in childbed. Should she decide to sample Elsmore's charms, that is her affair."

"And when the gossips and tattlers spread word that His Grace of E has been seen with a new fancy piece on his arm? What then?"

"Stephen, you grow tiresome. Will you have some trifle, or must I finish my meal alone?"

Stephen pushed his plate aside, though the steak was all but untouched—that much more for the kitchen staff.

"You must enjoy your trifle in solitude, not because I suspect you of abandoning your principles, though I do, but because the damned snow is making travel on foot treacherous. The sooner I'm back in my eyrie the better."

"Do you know how badly I long to beat the hell out of you?"

"The sentiment is mutual, dear brother, but Jane would

never forgive me for taking advantage of an old man's slower reflexes." Stephen arranged his canes and pushed to his feet. "My love to Jane and the girls."

"Jane and I have had this discussion, Stephen, about Elsmore."

Quinn's marriage was a clock Stephen could not take apart. The mechanisms were mysterious and invisible, and a prudent sibling didn't pry.

"And?"

"Jane is of the opinion that Elsmore's discretion is to be trusted."

"His discretion—which means the discretion of fourteen footmen, three coachies, eight grooms, a legion of personal secretaries, a valet and under-valet, three chambermaids, and a housekeeper, not to mention his own mother, from whom Jane herself has collected a store of interesting rumors. All that discretion is very reassuring indeed, but what of Elsmore's honor?"

"Elsmore's honor is to be trusted, and yet, it's my own darling brother bruiting the lady's business about in a club."

"In the deserted dining room of a private club." And if the discretion of a gentlemen's club could not be trusted, civilization was at an end.

"Besides," Quinn said, "Eleanora's discretion is to be trusted as well. She has never been careless of her reputation before."

Spare me from happily married older brothers. "Quinn, Elsmore enters the building at a pace that can only be described as eager, and two hours later, he slouches out into the elements, head down, scarf drawn up, not even watching where he's going."

"Then perhaps it's Elsmore who's headed for trouble, and not our Mrs. Hatfield, hmm?"

Chapter Seven

His Grace of Elsmore was becoming troublesome.

With each little scheme and device Ellie uncovered, she expected him to thank her kindly and send her packing. All the arrows pointed in the wrong directions, and his whole financial landscape was beclouded by poor accounting.

"And it is a vast landscape," she informed the cat. On the street below, Elsmore disappeared into the chop shop, his head bare, his scarf flapping about his neck. "A landscape on which I can leave no footprints."

Ellie wanted to. She liked his humor, his energy, his honesty. He considered her findings, grumbled, and then accepted what she showed him as trustworthy.

In other words, he accorded her respect.

"That's not the worst of it," she murmured, curling up with the cat in the reading chair. "The fellows at the bank respect me, the same way they respect the flu and lung fever—with a side helping of dread. Elsmore's respect is personal."

And he'd kissed her, which raised the real problem with Wrexham, Duke of Elsmore.

"I am attracted to him, not like a giddy girl is attracted to any flirt, but..." Ellie fell silent, because her attraction to Elsmore was irksomely complicated. She wasn't a blushing virgin, hadn't been for years. Poor girls grew up early, and their neighbors didn't judge them for it.

Elsmore was different. In a society where few people admitted that a woman could handle extensive figures with authority, he'd trusted her as an equal.

"Heady business, trust." Dangerous business. Grandpapa Naylor had trusted the Earl of Winston, and that had led to tragedy upon tragedy.

A sharp rap on the door had the cat bolting from the chair. Ellie admitted Elsmore, who set paper-wrapped parcels on the desk.

"Why haven't you a table?" he asked. "To partake of sustenance in the same place where you toil away by the hour seems wrong."

"The table is in the other room." The bedroom. For grand ladies, bedrooms could be social spaces. They received early callers there, chatting away the morning during the pleasant business of hair dressing and wardrobe selection.

Ellie was not a grand lady.

"You are blushing," Elsmore said. "Are the end times nigh?"

Oh, possibly. Ellie slid his coat from his shoulders. She'd done the same for Walden and Joshua Penrose, but she did not remark the breadth of the gentleman's shoulders on those occasions, did not treasure the feel of his body heat on expensive wool.

"Have you considered that another auditor might be a more prudent choice, Your Grace?"

"Getting cold feet over a pair of harmless kisses, Mrs. Hatfield?"

"Yes."

He took his coat from her and hung it on a peg, then he collected the parcels of food with one hand and took Eleanora by the wrist with the other.

"The soup is best consumed hot," he said, leading her into the bedroom. "You might be surprised to know that I can come within sight of a bed and remain on good behavior. That wasn't always the case. Once upon a time, I was a randy imbecile, but regretted folly, and the passing years have worked their sobering magic. You are entirely safe with me, madam."

"I never doubted that, but you beg the question: Are you safe with me?"

She expected a jaunty retort—Elsmore was nothing if not self-possessed. Society expected men of his station to deal openly with the masculine appetites, and Elsmore was a good-looking devil. He'd have plenty of offers, and his overtures—if ever he had to make any—would rarely be rejected.

He set the food on the table by the bedroom window and kept a grip on Ellie's wrist. "I am safe with you," he said. "I have pondered why that should be and whether it's to my liking."

"And?"

He drew her near, carefully, giving her every opportunity to pull away. Ellie stood in his embrace, torn between the longing to wrap her arms around him and the certain knowledge that to do so was errant foolishness. She averaged the difference between prudence and impulse by allowing the intimacy to go on, relishing the feel of his body against hers, and saving for later the regret that must follow.

"We have no pretenses between us," Elsmore said. "You are honest with me. You don't expect me to bring good cheer and ducal beneficence to every exchange. You skewer me if I toss out too much small talk, and I adore you for that. You do me the very great honor of dealing with me as if I am capable of grasping a significant problem and perhaps even solving it. To you, I am more than a prize to be hauled onto the dance floor." He kissed her temple. "You scold me."

"Somebody should scold the pair of us." Instead, Ellie's arms, which had been obediently at her sides, wound around his waist, inside his morning coat, where all was warmth and intimacy. He was lean, muscular, and tall enough that Ellie could rest her full weight against him, like a woman overcome with fatigue.

Or loneliness.

"If you scold me," he said, "I will apologize sincerely, and assure you that I won't presume again." He rested his cheek against Ellie's crown, and she stole another moment of forbidden pleasure.

This mutual interest in each other had no future. Not because he was a duke—dukes took mistresses, they had liaisons, they seldom made the most faithful of husbands.

Ellie had no future in any intimate capacity with Elsmore precisely because she was *not* honest with him and never could be.

"If you apologize," Ellie said, stepping back, "then I must do likewise. I am disinclined to apologize for harmless familiarities enjoyed when we are in private. Those familiarities, though, are a distraction from my appointed task. We'd best eschew them going forward."

He cradled her jaw against the warmth of his palm. "Mightn't you leaven that damned sensible pronouncement with a bit of reluctance, Eleanora?"

Nobody, nobody ever, had spoken her name before with

that combination of tenderness, desire, humor, and regret. A blow to the head would have been easier to withstand than Elsmore's hand, gently touching her cheek.

Ellie was ambushed by yearning and regret, a pair of emotions that could bring any woman low before she even knew she was under siege. What would it be like, to cast prudence out the window, and seize the duke?

I am an idiot. But was she an idiot for declining what Elsmore offered or for craving it? Ellie stepped closer, pressed her mouth to his, and took one kiss to save against all the damned sensible pronouncements by which she was doomed to live.

* * *

"Our Eleanora knew Mick had played the Old Man at Dorset and Becker's bank," Jack said, bouncing the baby on his knee. The little bugger was quite solid, much to Jack's relief. "Mick cashed out that account only last week, Pammie. He left town less than three days ago, and Ellie already has the details."

"Give me that child." Pamela plucked the infant into her arms, just as the little varmint began squalling. "You are an idiot, Jack Naylor. A purblind idiot."

She put the baby to her shoulder and began a slow circuit of the little parlor. Elsewhere in the building, a talented tenor sang about wild geese who would never fly home.

Damn the Irish and their penchant for despair anyway. "Ellie knew the name of the old gent Mick impersonated, his first and last name. How does an auditor for Wentworth and Penrose know the details of a rig at a rival establishment? The old man tried to cash out just yesterday afternoon, and yet, she knew all about it this morning."

The baby quieted, thank God. Jack could not abide a crying child. The lyrical Irishman wasn't much more tolerable.

"Clerks and tellers doubtless gossip," Pamela said. "They probably all drink at the same pubs and live in the same boardinghouses. When a bank is out two hundred pounds, word spreads."

"Our Ellie doesn't drink at those pubs or live in those boardinghouses." She had a cozy two-room apartment in a handsome building right on the edge of a wealthy neighborhood.

"But she works with the clerks and tellers, and they go to the pubs. Maybe the bank suspected something before the old man came in yesterday."

Jack was hungry and thirsty—cold weather always made him famished—but he wouldn't ask for food or drink when Pamela and Clyde had three little mouths to feed.

"Mick was careful," he retorted. Be careful or swing, that was Grandpapa's first commandment. "He figured out which teller was most recently hired, he picked a wet, raw day to go to the bank, and he cashed out the smallest of Butterfield's holdings. Ellie must be listening at keyholes."

Pamela resumed her seat at the battered table. "She's not like that—not like you. She notices details is all. We were all trained to notice details, and she remembers everything."

Did Eleanora remember how to smile? Remember that her family had always kept her safe? "I know my own cousin, Pammie. We were close once." They were actually cousins at some remove—first cousins twice removed or second cousins. Jack had never been sure which.

The fire on the grate was all but out, though Jack left

it for Pamela to decide when fresh coals were needed. The older children were off with their father, and she was likely conserving heat until they returned.

"You and Ellie were never close," Pamela said. "She was infatuated and you were an idiot. That was a lifetime ago."

"We were young and in love." Saying that sounded sweet, though Ellie would probably smack him for uttering the words. Jack had ended things with Ellie precisely because she hadn't even been infatuated. She'd been weary, lonely, scared, and willing to settle for the devil she knew and sometimes regarded with affection.

She had deserved better, even though to hear her tell it, she'd achieved a dream come true in her musty old bank.

"If Ellie feels anything toward you," Pamela said, "it's exasperation and maybe some misplaced shame. Leave her alone."

Jack rose, moving closer to the feeble heat of the hearth. "I got sacked, Pammie. Damned sodding squire is off to the family seat until the first of the year. Thanked me kindly for my service, passed me a three-sentence character and a few coins, and heigh-ho, Jack Naylor is out of work again. He wished me luck, which means I'm not to expect my job back if he ever returns to London."

"He didn't even warn you?"

"His kind don't. They just pike off, like you were a dog they no longer fancied. I'm supposed to slink back to the agencies and hope another position opens up, though half of London is leaving for the countryside, just when the coal man wants his tithe."

"Mick left us a bit of the ready. I'll say something to Clyde."

This was the worst of it. Not the loss of the job, but

the worry and pity from the family. "Don't you dare. I'll manage. I always do." Though lately, the managing was harder. Jack had left Mick's little scheme alone, because honest work and schemes didn't mix well.

Neither did honest work and regular meals.

"You know what I think?" Pamela said, taking a loaf of bread from the window box and producing a knife from the dry sink. "I think you should nip up to York. Look in on the elders. They miss you, and you've been gone long enough."

Even with the baby perched on her hip, she managed to slice the bread with the efficient movements of a woman inured to motherhood.

"The elders haven't invited me, Pammie. I'd be another mouth to feed, and I refuse to burden them like that. They looked after the lot of us, good times and bad. I should be looking after them."

The loaf went back into the window box. Pamela fetched butter and jam in separate trips and liberally slathered three slices with both.

"Don't be ridiculous, Jackson Naylor. Home is home. You go there when you please. London isn't home. Clyde has been talking about moving up to Edinburgh. He knows people there, and the port is booming. They don't mind if a man has a bit of a burr, provided he works hard."

She made a sandwich of two slices and passed it to Jack. Her own portion was the single piece made into a half sandwich.

"Maybe I should go north with you. Mick could join us when he's done larking about." English laws didn't reach across the Scottish border, which was ever a source of comfort when a man contemplated travel.

Pamela resumed her seat and took a bite of her bread and jam. "Talk to Clyde."

In other words, maybe Jack should stay in London, while his family scattered to the four winds. "Mick was thinking about going someplace warm."

"He'll end up someplace very warm, if he doesn't watch his step."

Jack wanted to wash his hands before he ate, a clerk's habit. An honest clerk. "You agree with Ellie, then. Work yourself to death for a pittance, go to church for a weekly scolding, die sober and broke with a sore back."

"Ellie isn't broke, she's not working for a pittance, and I'm fairly certain she doesn't bother with services or disdain good liquor. Eat your bread."

"Ellie was lucky, Pamela. How many times do I have to say it? She was living hand to mouth along with the rest of us, and then she got lucky."

Pamela took another bite of her sandwich, chewed slowly, and set the remaining portion on the bare table.

"You are lucky too, Jack. You are a handsome man and a quick study. You could do what Ellie does—the fancy bookkeeping. You know all the rigs, you see what others miss, but you're always on the lookout for the easy swindle. You could paint portraits, do sketches, teach the young ladies their watercolors. All of that comes naturally to you."

I want to wash my hands. I want to wash my damned hands so everything I eat doesn't taste like coal. "I wasn't swindling the sodding squire."

"Not yet, you weren't."

"Six months I worked for him, Pamela. Kept his books, told him when Cook was helping herself to the sherry and padding the marketing. For that I get three sentences and good luck."

"This baby is falling asleep," Pamela said, which

probably meant Jack should shut his gob. "Will you go to the agencies?"

I want a family. I want people who are glad to see me when I walk in the door. That was the part of Ellie's situation that bewildered Jack. How did she carry on year after year with no people to call her own? No mates, no sisters to gabble with once the children were all asleep? She spent maybe two hours a month in Pammie's parlor, coming to call like some representative from the visiting charities.

"I'll go to the agencies," Jack said, "but I'll also keep an eye on our Ellie. She knows things she shouldn't, and she's not keeping her regular hours at the bank."

"Mind your own business, Jack."

He picked up his bread and jam, probably the last decent food he'd have for a while. "Ellie has had a lot of good luck, but luck can change. Ask Grandpapa how that works. When her luck turns sour, we will still be her family."

Pamela remained at the table, the baby cradled against her shoulder. "Just make sure you aren't the reason her luck turns, Jack Naylor. Ellie has toiled too long and too hard for you to wreck everything with one of your schemes."

* * *

Eleanora Hatfield is kissing me.

That dazzling reality landed in Rex's awareness like a match struck in stygian darkness, which made no sense. He'd kissed dozens of women—scores, rather—from his sisters and aunties and dear Mama, to opera soloists with a Continental view of intimate recreation, to the occasional frolicsome widow, and the even rarer courtesan.

He knew the difference between a friendly peck on the

cheek, a cheerfully naughty buss, a prelude to copulation, and the many gradations in between.

Knew them and enjoyed them all.

Eleanora Hatfield's kiss wasn't sorting itself into any tidy column. She pressed her mouth to his and her body to his in a lusciously erotic manner. Her hands those marvelously competent, usually ink-stained hands—wandered his chest, ribs, and back as if she were wrapping arrows of desire around his entire person. Then she sank her fingers into his hair, angled her head, and gentled her kiss from plundering to wondering.

Two minutes ago she'd told him they would focus strictly on business. All Rex could focus on now was *her*.

He kissed her back, accepting her invitation to taste and touch. She was more slender than he'd thought, her clothes bulkier. Petticoats and corsetry frustrated the craving to touch her bare skin. He settled for stroking her hands and face, especially the tender join of her neck and shoulder and the soft flesh of her bare wrist.

She turned her head as if to listen to the caress of his thumb against her palm and he dared to gather her closer lest she mistake the impact she was having on him. Rex had learned years ago to control his urges. There was no controlling his reactions, though, not to her, not this time.

And what a relief that was, what a pleasure and a joy to be simply a man in good health enjoying a kiss with a woman who desired him for his own sake.

Eleanora eased back and pressed her forehead to his chest. "The soup will get cold."

So plaintive and paltry, that display of common sense, so dear. "While everything else threatens to go up in flames."

"I hadn't planned on..." She gave him a squeeze, then

stepped away. "I miscalculated." She patted his cravat, which was doubtless thoroughly wrinkled.

For her to admit a miscalculation probably took as much fortitude as for Rex to admit his ledgers were a disgrace. He wanted desperately to kiss her again, to toss her on the bed and romp away the rest of this cold, snowy day.

Even more than that, he wanted to banish the uncertainty from her gaze. She had for once allowed herself to indulge in a pleasurable impulse and her usual self-possession had deserted her. He could not allow her to doubt herself, could not be the reason Eleanora Hatfield's composure faltered.

"If you miscalculated," he said, "the error was harmless and of no moment. I brought you pepper pot soup with fresh bread and butter, a few slices of cheese and two apples. A pair of French chocolates might have stowed away among the offerings. For the cat, there's a bit of gammon."

Only a man who'd complimented clumsy young women on their dancing and clapped heartily at botched sonatas by the dozen could have offered that speech with such breezy—and false—good cheer.

Eleanora began to unpack their meal. "The cutlery is in the top drawer of the sideboard. Now that the food is here, I'm famished."

She was also blinking as if cinders afflicted both eyes.

"Eleanora?"

"Mrs. Hatfield, please. You even brought more wine. Very generous of you, Your Grace."

Your Grace. How he hated that appellation from her now, but he was beginning to understand the paths her arrows of emotion traveled and how to dodge their flights. She needed her dignity, her sense of order and predictability just as he needed to nip out to Ambledown, go for mad gallops, and wear boots to a solitary dinner in the library from time to time.

"Give me the gammon," he said. "I'll feed the tiger lest she disturb our feast with her growling."

A single tear slid down Eleanora's cheek. She caught it on the back of her wrist. "Voltaire loves gammon."

And I could love Eleanora Hatfield. What a bloody inconvenient revelation for all concerned. Rex took the wrapped meat from the table and left the lady some privacy. He could not bear that he'd made her cry, but he withdrew to feed the cat, because he too had miscalculated.

Badly.

* * *

"I know something you don't know."

The old taunt shouldn't have bothered Howell, but lately, everything bothered him. "Indeed, Eddie. you know how to arrive late to the bank without getting sacked. You know how to chew enough parsley to choke a horse, a skill I have yet to acquire. You know how to cozen old Ballentyre into joining you for a pint at noon while the rest of us remain at our desks, ciphering by the hour. You still haven't learned to dress with quite the understated good taste Elsmore displays, but I have faith in your aspirations."

Eddie leaned over Howell's desk. "The skill you have yet to acquire is the ability to enjoy yourself." His breath bore the foul under-note of one dedicated to over-imbibing.

"While you lack discretion, among other virtues."

The clerks across the room pretended to ignore this exchange. On Saturdays, the bank closed two hours early, and the clerks were dismissed while the supervisors did weekly tallies. Howell liked those two hours best—or he had—because of the peace and quiet, and also because with the clerks away, he needn't guard every word.

Lately though, James and Eddie had been leaving the bank together more and more often, and the sense of rejection stung. They'd always been a trio—two brothers who got along better when James's mild temperament and good humor buffered fraternal competition. The aunties and cousins referred to them as the beautiful bachelors, because all three had a fair complement of Dorset good looks.

Eddie brought a bit of flair to his wardrobe—probably trying to outshine Elsmore, which was hopeless—while James had enough dry wit and flirtation to make Byron envious. The pair of them could make a hardworking fellow not given to fashion feel more than a tad overlooked, except that had never been the case previously. Howell had flattered himself that he was the sensible one, the one making slow and steady progress in the right direction.

His confidence in that conclusion had wavered lately.

"All right, lads," Ballentyre called from his desk at the front of the room. "Be off with you, and we'll have a look at those books. Enjoy your Sabbath rest, and we'll see you back here Monday morning at eight of the clock sharpish."

The clerks, a good lot of fellows, were off their stools and piling ledgers on Ballentyre's desk in the next instant. Amid a general chorus of "See you Monday," and "Regards to the missus," the room emptied out.

"I am always astounded at how quickly those scamps can move when they travel in the direction of the nearest pub," Ballentyre said, his standard observation on a Saturday afternoon. "Shall we to the books, gentlemen?"

Eddie sorted through the stack of ledgers and chose two. His specialty, other than looking dapper and dashing, was commercial and agricultural real estate. He passed Howell two other ledgers having to do with general business accounts—butchers, bakers, and the like.

"Where is James?" Howell asked, taking the ledgers to a clerk's desk.

"He went home hours ago," Ballentyre said. "Poor fellow was done in with an ague. Dashed weather makes my gout act up abominably."

Eddie returned to Ballentyre's desk and sorted two more ledgers from the pile. "I can review his share of the books."

When did Eddie ever volunteer for extra work?

"Good of you, young Edward," Ballentyre replied. "Always said the Dorsets were a hardworking bunch."

Howell plucked one of the account books from his brother's hands. "No reason you should have to do all the extra work. Damned snow is starting to pile up, and the sooner we finish here, the sooner we'll be home before a warm fire with a tot of grog."

"Grog's the thing," Ballentyre muttered. "Nothing like a toddy to ward off the chill. I believe Mr. Bitzer's handwriting becomes more crabbed by the week."

Another frequent rejoinder from Ballentyre. Howell brought two lamps over from the vacated desks.

"Maybe that will help. Gloomy weather never did make close work easier."

Ballentyre's desk was beside the parlor stove, meaning he had less natural light to illuminate his labors. Not that he labored long or hard. Within minutes, he was snoring contently, a ledger open before him, his hands folded across his belly.

"Such a dear old thing," Eddie said. "Once he's planted himself on that cushion of a morning, I don't believe he moves until noon. How he becomes fatigued enough to nap is a mystery."

Howell slid onto a hard stool at a desk by the windows. "He's getting worse, but then, you probably share more than a pint with him at your Saturday luncheons." Those luncheons had become a regular habit, now that Howell thought about it.

"If you look over old Ballie's ledgers, I'll do James's," Eddie said.

"Fair enough." Howell eased the open account book from beneath Mr. Ballentyre's hands, which provoked a few peaceful snuffles, but did not rouse the dreamer.

"Will you apply for Ballie's job when he retires?" Eddie asked, running a pencil down a column of figures.

"I didn't realize Ballie was going out to pasture." Howell started on the weekly totals, and right off, found an error.

"You should apply," Eddie said, turning a page. "Let Elsmore know you're interested, and the job is as good as yours."

"Somebody was having an off week," Howell muttered, noting the volume number of the ledger before him. "I've found three errors in five minutes. Aren't you interested in Ballie's job?"

Another page turned. "Me? I'm quite happy with my land accounts. Land is still the most respectable form of wealth for an Englishman, and I do favor the company of those with means. Elsmore would enjoy doing you a good turn, if you chose to supervise the clerks."

Eddie's pomade, a citrus and musk scent perceptible even across the room, made Howell's nose run.

"It shouldn't be like that, Eddie. I should be promoted on the basis of merit, not because my cousin is a director."

And a duke. And the major shareholder. The bank was inordinately pleased to enjoy that association.

"You always were overly burdened with scruples." Eddie set aside the first ledger and reached for a second. "Believe I'll take the rest of these back to my office. It's warmer, and nobody is snoring."

No invitation to walk back to their rooms together, no invitation to join him in that warmer space, but then, Eddie's office likely reeked of oranges.

"I suspect I'll be a bit late leaving," Howell said, "if the first few columns are any indication. This volume wants a close look." And how did Eddie review an entire ledger in less than ten minutes?

"Gout, ague, and inaccuracies. Must be the full moon." Eddie collected his remaining ledgers and rose. "Do you ever wonder if we'll be doing this twenty years from now? Staying late on Saturday, toting up the same dreary columns, listening to Ballie's tired jokes?"

"The work is honorable and spares us from the military and the church." The church wouldn't have been awful, but the military? Howell had no wish to be blown to bits for the glory of old England.

Eddie leaned on the door jamb. "But what of your future, Howell? Will you ever be able to afford a wife? To send your sons to private school and university? Elsmore is our first cousin, and the old duke did right by us. Our sons will grow up at a further remove from the title, and are less likely to benefit from a ducal connection."

For Eddie that observation bordered on solemn reflection.

"If that's your concern, *young Edward*, then stop spending your wages on expensive tailoring, a horse you seldom ride, and gentlemen's clubs where you lose more at cards than I earn in a week." Howell put a bit by with every fortnight's wages. The sum was invested in funds that provided a steady return, and the principal was growing at a modest rate. More than that was nobody's business but his own.

"Howell, she doesn't even see you." That remark was offered gently. "Lady Joanna might be able to overlook your lack of a title, but you have neither fortune nor prospects beyond a career waiting for old Ballie to go to his reward. She will never see you."

Was Lady Joanna Peabody the cause of the distance Howell felt from his brother? "Her ladyship doesn't see you either, brother, despite your fine wardrobe and witty banter." None of the respectable ladies took Eddie or Howell seriously, not when Elsmore was running around unmarried. The other kind of women were too busy fawning over James, not that *paying* for a woman's attentions appealed to Howell.

"And the sheer hell of it," Eddie said, shoving away from the door, "is that Elsmore sees all the hopeful ladies as so many pretty duties he must stand up with."

Howell returned to checking figures, which he could do with one part of his attention while mulling over Eddie's strange mood with another. Ballentyre occasionally roused, but mostly napped, while Howell reviewed ledgers—Eddie had left him one of James's in addition to all of Ballie's— and contemplated another twenty years of tidy columns and small errors.

Ballentyre's clerks were going to pot, that became plain before Howell had finished the first ledger. Eddie was unhappy, that was also obvious and puzzling, and as for Lady Joanna...

Maybe someday, but today was not that day.

Chapter Eight

Pepper pot was Ellie's favorite soup, and yet, she'd barely tasted her serving. Elsmore had taken leave of her after they'd eaten, a bit of gallantry she'd appreciated. For her to have kissed him and then all but burst into tears had to have been as bewildering to him as it was to Ellie.

Voltaire sat on the mantel looking peevish, as if she blamed Ellie for chasing away the person who brought the lovely gammon.

"I kissed him," Ellie said, dashing away another stupid tear. "I should have known better."

Voltaire closed her cat eyes and flicked her tail.

The tears were because the duke had kissed Ellie back. Gently, then passionately *and* gently, and oh...ye angelic choruses, he knew more about kissing than Ellie had ever known about anything. She'd been a fool to yield to impulse with him, but his savoir faire had been equal to the occasion. He was a virtuoso kisser, having so much ability to stir both sensation and emotion—yearning was an emotion, wasn't it?—that Ellie wanted to simply be still and recall every instant of Elsmore's embrace.

And then—the most sophisticated kindnesses—he'd agreed that such a glorious intimacy was "of no moment."

A sharp rap on Ellie's door nearly startled her out of her chair. "Coming."

"Don't open the damned door until you know who is calling," came an annoyed male voice.

The apartment doors in Lord Stephen's building were equipped with spy-holes. The opening was covered with a pear-shaped metal flap on the apartment side, so that the occupant could peer into the corridor, but not conversely.

"I recognize your voice," Ellie said, opening the door. "Come in, my lord."

Stephen Wentworth made Ellie uneasy, and she suspected he liked it that way. She liked making everybody at the bank uneasy, after all. He wheeled his Bath chair through the door and over to the fireplace.

"Are you religiously opposed to heating your dwelling?" he asked. "I understand Laplanders thrive in caves of ice, but I had taken you for an Englishwoman."

"I am an Englishwoman, meaning I conserve coal."

Without rising from his wheeled chair, his lordship pushed the fire screen aside, dumped half a bucket of coal onto the flames, and poked it about so the blaze doubled in size.

"I'm considering installing a furnace," he said. "The difficulty is controlling the dissipation of the heat. If the fire in the basement is roaring and you take a notion to freeze, then you close your vents, and the fire stops drawing. When I want my rooms as toasty as the tropics, you will have all but put out my fire. The design wants further study. I could maintain the furnace exclusively for my own use or create a separate furnace for each apartment." He shoved the screen back against the hearth. "Have you been crying?"

Lord Stephen was not a bank employee or a duke to be put in his place with a firm *none of your business*. He was neither and a little of both.

"Women do," Ellie said. "Men do as well."

"If you are crying because your female humors are in an uproar, I know better than to offer any comment, lest even my blighted existence be brought to a period. If you are crying because Elsmore misbehaved, I will hold him accountable."

Lord Stephen maneuvered his Bath chair like a chariot-eer in battle. He was nimble and decisive in his navigations, and they took him to the window box.

"He plied you with wine." His lordship held up the last of the bottle of claret. "Not enough to get you drunk, assuming he drank a portion, but enough to make you tipsy."

Ellie resumed her seat rather than stand higher than her visitor. "My lord, did you call for a particular purpose?"

"Yes and no." He opened the bottle of wine, sniffed the cork, and then put it back. "I wanted to let you know that I'll be making modifications to the lift next week. You might have to use the steps, so best do the big marketing on Monday. At least Elsmore plied you with a decent vintage."

"Nobody plied anybody." *More's the pity.* "We enjoyed an informal meal, not the first or the last." Lord Stephen in his present mood reminded Ellie of her nieces and nephews, a one-person swarm of intrusion. "If you are hungry, I can offer bread and butter, leftover soup, and the last of the wine."

"I would never impose," he said, apparently in all

seriousness. "Tomorrow is my day to review the bank books, my feeble effort to compensate for your absence at Wentworth and Penrose. Have you any guidance for me?"

Ellie knew his lordship well enough to see the distraction in that question. She would focus on the topic he raised— the bank ledgers, her favorite subject in the world—while he circled around to pounce on the information he was truly interested in.

"If I provide you warnings," she said, "such as that Mr. Cummings tends to argue with his wife on Thursday night, which is skittles night at his favorite pub, so his accounts are slightly the worse on Friday mornings, or that all the clerks bear closer scrutiny on Friday morning, then you will not see the errors Cummings makes on Tuesday, or the rest of them make on Saturday."

He wheeled over to position his chair opposite Ellie's near the hearth. "You think me incompetent?"

That possibility amused him. "I think you human. We all have a tendency, once our vigilance is rewarded, to relax our guard. When I find an error in one column, I often miss the error in the very next one, but am back on my mettle by the time I turn the page. Sophisticated crooks know this, so they leave small errors in plain sight, the better to hide the large deceptions lurking nearby."

"Do you trust me, Mrs. Hatfield?"

And there was the Congreve rocket aimed at Ellie's self-possession, fired from a harmless thicket of nosiness and shop talk.

"In some capacities, of course."

"Fair enough. Have I ever given you reason to doubt my honor?"

Ellie reviewed what she knew of him and what she knew of his ledgers. "I trusted you with the Wentworth and

Penrose books, so I would say my opinion of your honor is positive."

"I am gratified rather than insulted that you had to think about that answer. One likes to be considered a bit menacing when one cannot cross a room without stumbling."

"You menace my peace, your lordship. If you have any other questions regarding the bank accounting, I am happy to answer them." Happy was an overstatement.

"My sisters bide in the north for much of the year," he said. "You've seen their estate books."

Ladies Althea and Constance had the same fierce quality Lord Stephen did, though their acumen expressed itself more subtly. Ellie liked them, in part because neither woman was the least bit intimidated by their ducal brother's consequence or Lord Stephen's intellect.

"I review your sisters' books quarterly, now that the properties are in hand." A few years ago, the picture had been very different.

"They have nothing better to do for much of the time than take an interest in their neighbors and the local society, such as York boasts of society. I correspond with them as a dutiful brother should."

Unease joined the general misery of Ellie's day. "Say your piece, my lord."

"Lady Althea has a particular ear for scandal, and she has heard mention of a decent family brought low by a talented painter's attempts to dabble in forgeries. What had been a gentlemanly reputation was ruined overnight."

He recited Grandfather's history, but not the whole of that history. Very few people knew the whole of it.

"What has this to do with me?"

"I recall your family dimly from my tragically blighted boyhood. Your grandfather could sketch anything."

Grandpapa had done so to amuse the neighborhood children, and he'd also sat in the local pubs doing caricatures and portraits in pencil for small change.

"Many people have artistic talent." Jack certainly did, not that he'd put it to any useful purpose.

"I don't. I see how things operate, like you see how finances work, but I can't make art."

You can make me anxious. Ellie held her peace rather than admit as much. The dratted man probably enjoyed making her worry. If his objective was blackmail, she hadn't much personal wealth to give him. Though she did have access to the bank books, and now to Elsmore's books.

Oh, dear. "Earning a living as an artist is difficult," Ellie said. "You have other talents."

"Talents like wasting your afternoon when you'd rather be snuggled up with Elsmore's books?"

His lordship's smile put her in mind of a wolf contemplating a fricassee of lamb. "My lord, I do have work to be about, as do you."

"Jane adores you," he said, "and I adore Jane. I do not always adore Jane's husband."

The last squabble Ellie would involve herself in was sibling rivalry in a ducal family. "His Grace employs me at generous wages. Discredit him at your peril."

Lord Stephen shifted his chair back, farther from the hearth. "Oh, for God's sake, settle your feathers. I don't always like Quinn, nor is he unrelentingly fond of me, but we are loyal to each other. The point of this digression is to make you aware of several facts."

Don't tell me to settle my feathers, you arrogant popinjay. "I do enjoy being lectured, my lord, particularly in my own home by a man who knows me but little. One might even say the trait is amusing."

"There is my dear Mrs. Hatfield, sporting her true colors. I blame Elsmore for your temporary docility. Your family is steeped in scandal. Your grandfather was utterly ruined and should probably have swung for his crimes, but some wealthy patron or other hushed the whole business up, and Jacob Erasmus Naylor was permitted to slink off into penurious obscurity."

With numerous dependents and a wife to feed. "Mr. Penrose and His Grace of Walden are acquainted with my family history."

"No, they are not. They are acquainted with your grandfather's history. I'm sure there's much more to the story, Eleanora, and you can either tell me that tale, or allow me the pleasure of discovering it through my own means, for I will."

Ellie had known this day would come, when somebody—it would be a titled, wealthy, male somebody, of course—unveiled a past she'd worked so hard to leave behind. She had the means to move to the Continent. She had skills that the more enlightened French would likely pay her for, and she even had a few words of French.

But she did not want to go, not in disgrace, not on terms dictated by this preening meddler, not before she'd untangled the web of incompetence and deceit wrapped around Elsmore's finances.

I will kill Mick if I ever see him again. "Why?" she said, rising. "Why destroy my life simply because you can? Is that your idea of amusement? Will your lofty brother thank you for running off the single greatest claim to integrity Wentworth and Penrose has?"

"The greatest claim to integrity the bank has is my brother's damned honor. You are the greatest claim it has to trustworthiness, though you mistake my motives entirely."

"Then for the sake of all that tallies accurately, tell me your perishing motives before I pitch you out the window, my lord. I am not my grandfather. I am not my cousins. I have done nothing to earn anybody's distrust, and you are no gentleman to imply otherwise."

Ellie paced, battling back more angry words. For years, she'd kept her temper in check, but what was the point, if all that self-restraint was to be rewarded with another aristocrat playing God with a commoner's life?

Lord Stephen turned his chair to face her. "You daft, demented woman, I am not your enemy. You are without allies, you hold a position of immense trust, you've taken on the thankless business of laundering Elsmore's financial linen, and you do this while balancing on a tightrope over a flaming pit of family scandal. I thought you could use a friend."

He held out a white square of linen with a crest and initials embroidered on one corner.

Ellie snatched the handkerchief from him and wiped her eyes. "Do you always make your lady friends cry, my lord?"

"Never having had a lady friend before—in the sense you intend—I cannot answer that query. Sit down and let me know how I can help."

"Stop telling me what to do." Outside the snow had gone from pretty to purposeful. For the first time, the prospect of a snowy Sunday on the morrow struck Ellie as dreary rather than cozy. She sank into the chair by the fire and forced her mind to focus.

Lord Stephen was right: She was without allies and she was balanced over a flaming pit of scandal. He had no reason to blackmail anybody—he was wealthy in his own right and his brother's heir.

"Shall I get the wine?" he asked.

"Please." She began arranging the story in her head, which details to include, in what order to present them. "You can do nothing to help, by the way. Matters as they stand are quite acceptable. I'm gainfully employed and respected by those whose opinions matter."

He retrieved the wine bottle from the window and two glasses from the sideboard, putting the lot in his lap so he could use both hands to wheel his chair about.

"Respect can be lost in an instant," he said, "as can employment. Friends, I'm told, are more durable."

Ellie accepted a glass of wine rather than point out that he'd apparently not spoken from experience. Maybe she wasn't the only person to regard the first snowfall bleakly.

"My grandfather never set out to be a forger," she said. "Circumstances not of his making controlled his fate, but once ruined, an artist cannot be un-ruined." That much was true. That was the old scandal. Ellie sipped her wine and promised herself the Naylor family's more recent tribulations could remain private, at least until she'd finished repairing Elsmore's accounting.

* * *

Rex enjoyed the Sabbath in part because Sunday socializing was limited to the churchyard and those friends who merited an invitation to supper. The churchyard had been filling with yet more snow, which curtailed that penance.

For the Sunday meal, Lord Jeremy Bledsoe and the Honorable Phineas Hornby graced the table. Rex's sisters kept the conversational shuttlecock aloft, leaving Rex free to smile graciously while he brooded over one luscious, ill-advised kiss.

Eleanora Hatfield kissed with her whole body. She'd wrapped Rex in her arms and in her rosy scent and plundered his every asset, from his reason to his restraint, until he'd been roaringly aware of the bed and of the manly humors he'd been neglecting for too long.

"Elsmore, haven't you anything to add to this discussion?" Lord Jeremy inquired.

Rachel, who was wearing a blue walking dress sprigged with gold embroidered fleur-de-lis, sent his lordship a toothy smile. "Elsmore is being diplomatically silent, as a good brother will be when the topic of ladies wearing trousers is aired on the Sabbath."

Mama held her wineglass up for Mr. Hornby to refill. "Such a topic ought not be aired on any day of the week. My guests will think I've reared a trio of hoydens."

Mr. Hornby next offered the wine to Samantha, Rex's middle sister. "I have always preferred the company of ladies who can speak their minds," Hornby opined. "One needn't be as cautious with one's own words in their company."

Samantha saluted him with her refilled wineglass. "Precisely, Mr. Hornby. What is the purpose of spending time in company if all we're to do is prose on about the weather—which is obvious to all—and the health of one's elders, which topic the elders happily broach at any gathering?"

Samantha—green ensemble with gold piping—punctuated her observation with a sidelong glance at Rex.

"Do I qualify for elder status?" he asked. And why was Hornby aiming such a calf-eyed smile at Samantha?

"Of course you do," Rachel replied. "You are the oldest sibling, the head of the family, and your well-being is of great interest to all of polite society."

"Not all," Kathleen, the youngest, replied from Rex's right hand. "I've heard a bachelor or two wish our dear brother to the Pit, and the concern mentioned most often among the ladies is a great worry that Elsmore might be lonely." She drew out that last word for the sake of melodrama, and provoked a round of laughter. Her attire today was cream linen with fanciful flowers embroidered on the bodice and cuffs. She'd made her come-out the previous spring, which had left Rex feeling ancient and protective.

Had even Kathleen learned to return her dresses for coin?

Mama rose, wineglass in her hand. "Let's do our part to lend credence to the concern regarding Elsmore's loneliness, ladies. It's time we abandoned the menfolk while we enjoy a respite in the drawing room."

The ladies rustled out on a cloud of silk and laughter, Hornby offering them escort.

"I asked Hornby to give us a moment," Lord Jeremy said. "Seemed more discreet than trying to find you at your clubs."

Rex left off wondering about ledgers, kisses, and returned dresses. "You have the look of a man with something to say, my lord. Speak your piece. If you need a second, I can be counted on to serve with discretion, though I insist on an attempt at reconciliation before battle is joined."

"Oh, my goodness me, not at all. On an occasion such as the one I contemplate, one is supposed to make an appointment with the head of the lady's family." Lord Jeremy had become fascinated with the half serving of trifle that remained in a bowl before him. "Except that my family will know if I make any such appointments, and I haven't mentioned my ambitions to the lady, and one wants to be spared unnecessary humiliation."

Blooming, blasted hell. "You aspire to court Lady Rachel."

Rachel was entirely deserving of courtship. She was gracious, kind, well read, dear, and also patient with her siblings and mama. Rex could thus not explain the impulse to grab Lord Jeremy by the lapels and heave him out the window, for Rachel was more than of age to marry.

"I seek permission to ask the lady if I might pay my addresses. I realize some fellows start by presuming to approach the lady herself, but Lady Rachel's rank is superior to my own. I am a younger son, and she can afford to be exceedingly particular in her choice of husband."

"My lord," Rex said gently, "the daughter of a duke can afford to be exceedingly particular regarding *everything*." Just how particular, he'd only lately come to realize.

Lord Jeremy was the third son of a marquess, and Rex knew nothing unflattering regarding the would-be suitor or his family. Before giving his lordship permission to court Rachel—assuming she approved—Rex ought to make financial inquiries. Shortly thereafter, financial inquiries would also be made of him.

"What makes you think Lady Rachel will look with favor upon your suit?"

Rachel's swain was a pleasant-looking fellow. Sandy-brown hair, friendly blue eyes, a ready smile. His complexion was ruddy, his build muscular. On a football team, Rex would have played him as a goalie or defensive back, where minding one's post and quiet, vigilant courage could win the day.

Not bad qualifications for a man who sought the hand of Rex's sister.

"When I am with Lady Rachel," his lordship said, "the time passes as if on wings. I forget what day it is,

I forget where I am to be that evening. We talk about everything—books, sports, the proper rearing of children, favorite memories, and difficult memories. I have never encountered her like, and I know, Elsmore, I know in the tenderest and most private part of my heart, that I will never encounter her like again."

Ye flaming arrows from Cupid's bow. What was a conscientious brother to say to such twaddle?

"I will confer with Lady Rachel before you and I explore this topic further. You do understand that the solicitors will make both of our lives merry hell over the settlements, should the matter progress that far?"

Lord Jeremy's smile was high summer on a dreary winter afternoon. "You aren't saying no."

"I'm not saying yes, either, my lord. I'm saying, I will confer with her ladyship and give the matter some thought." *Though I would rather toss you out the window headfirst into the snow.* His lordship's timing was awful, dangling a sword of urgency over the whole accounting mess, which was growing more complicated the longer Rex and Mrs. Hatfield explored it.

"My parents just fired off both of my younger sisters," Lord Jeremy said, downing half his wine. "The finances will present no difficulties on our end. Hornby said I should approach you directly, but then, Hornby is hardly disinterested."

Hornby was a popinjay, a flirt, an heir waiting to inherit his papa's considerable wealth. He was from an old and respected family, but not exactly...

"Hornby is *hardly disinterested*?"

Lord Jeremy studied a heaping spoonful of trifle. "He gets on rather well with Lady Samantha, wouldn't you say? Should Lady Rachel accept a proposal, then Ladies

Samantha and Kathleen would doubtless follow her up the church aisle in short order."

The prospect of three sets of solicitors pawing through the ducal books had Rex's digestion turning queasy.

"One doting hopeful at a time, my lord. I will find a moment to have a private discussion with Lady Rachel. Until I do—and my schedule is quite full—you are to make no assumptions."

Lord Jeremy slurped up his trifle. "Wouldn't dream of assuming. Your mama would box my ears from here to Brighton. Rachel will be every bit as formidable, I'm sure."

That's Lady *Rachel to you, puppy.* "I don't suppose you know of any gentlemen who might have caught Lady Kathleen's fancy?"

"She's such a fetching little thing. Half the bachelors still in Town seem happy to stand up with her. The gents are probably waiting for the older sisters to find matches, lest you take exception to their aspirations."

Half the bachelors in Mayfair...Kathleen was pretty and diminutive, with an impish sense of humor, and ferocious skill with the violin. She was also wickedly accurate with a bow and arrow.

"Get your sisters launched," Lord Jeremy went on, "and your mama can devote herself to the happy task of finding you a duchess. What more could a duke ask for?"

A man longing for holy matrimony was not a creature in possession of all of his wits, apparently. "I can think of a few things I might enjoy more than having my mother turn her matrimonial gunsights in my direction."

Hornby rejoined them before Rex could elaborate, as did a pair of footmen, who began clearing the table.

"Her Grace told me that we gentlemen are not to linger

overlong in here," Hornby said. "I do believe the ladies are intent on making some music later on, and I volunteered to turn pages for Lady Samantha."

He looked more pleased to contemplate that honor than he had been at any point during the previous two hours of good food and witty conversation.

"Splendid," Lord Jeremy said. "And I will perform the same office for Lady Rachel."

The beaming bachelors finished off the last of the wine and the last of the trifle, while Rex contemplated schemes by which he might leave London before the course of true love revealed to half the realm's solicitors the scandalous state of the Dorset family finances.

* * *

"What in fourteen purgatories is Lord Stephen doing with that lift?" Elsmore asked over the incessant pounding reverberating through Ellie's dwelling.

"He warned me that he'd be making some modifications," she replied, tossing down her pencil. "He failed to point out that the entire building would be subject to an unrelenting din."

Elsmore paced Ellie's parlor, a sheaf of papers in his hand. "How can you work with all this noise?"

The pounding grew louder, which ought not to have been possible.

"I can't. I made an error this morning. Added 263 and 432 and got 795. If Voltaire hadn't tried to climb into my lap I might not have caught it."

Though if Elsmore hadn't been prowling about in the back of Ellie's mind, she probably wouldn't have made the error in the first place. He'd kept her awake last night—

again—and he'd rendered her day of rest more of a day of moping.

Him and his kisses.

And his scent.

And the feel of his embrace.

All of which had been *of no moment*.

"How much longer will this racket go on?" Elsmore asked, tossing himself into Ellie's reading chair. "I cannot think amid such noise."

"Installing the lift took weeks. Lord Stephen doesn't do things by half measures."

Somebody started singing in rhythm with the hammers, two somebodies, judging from the wretched attempt at harmony.

"Bedlam would be a more productive environment than this," Elsmore muttered. "And now is no time for Lord Stephen's queer start to be..."

He fell silent. Today's version of His Grace was not the charming aristocrat with a few inconsequential peas tucked under his downy financial mattress. Elsmore hadn't smiled once, hadn't assayed a single flirtatious aside.

Ellie should have been relieved. Instead she was hard put not to stare at his mouth, or his hands, or the breadth of his shoulders beneath his exquisitely tailored maroon morning coat.

"We need to get out of here," he said, rising and gathering up the ledgers strewn about the room. "How soon can you pack a few frocks?"

"My entire wardrobe consists of only a few frocks. What are you going on about?"

"I will commit acts of violence to the premises if we remain here much longer. Now, when I need for this audit to forge ahead with all due speed, Lord Stephen

Went-to-Blazes has sabotaged even your formidable accuracy with figures. I won't have it, Mrs. Hatfield. We're for Ambledown, where a man can hear himself think and a woman can have peace and quiet."

"Leave Town? *With you?*"

The notion terrified Ellie even as it tempted her. She knew everybody in the building, even the carpenters and engineers Lord Stephen hired for his renovations. She knew the owners of the chop shop across the street and all of their employees. She knew the street urchins, the bank clerks...

She was safe in her London world. Safe from the unknown and, more importantly, safe from foolishness.

"You insist that I be available for regular interrogation," Elsmore said, stacking the last of a dozen ledgers on the desk. "That means whither thou goest and so forth. We cannot work here, we cannot work at the bank, and you have refused the unoccupied dwelling I offered you earlier. Ambledown is less than two hours away, boasts every amenity, and above all, *it is quiet*."

Above all, Ambledown was beyond the notice of Jack, Lord Stephen, and polite society.

Don't do this. The voice in the back of Ellie's mind sounded very like Grandmama, whose proper upbringing had never become reconciled to the exigencies of life as a disgraced portraitist's wife. Ellie might ride about Town in the Walden ducal conveyance when the weather was inclement and attract only passing notice. Leaving London with Elsmore was another proposition entirely.

"You are concerned about the appearances," he said, "though Lord Stephen's porte cochere assures that nobody will see you climbing into my coach. The crests can be turned, the shades drawn, and your privacy assured. My sanity, however, is imperiled every moment that we remain in this pounding purgatory."

The clerks were like this. Some could work in dim lighting, but not amid noise. Others needed the desk closest to the window, but could focus on their task despite riots in progress on the street below. This one had a messy desk, while that one could not work until he'd sharpened every pencil in his tray, set a cup of tea at his left elbow, and positioned the standish just so.

"I must have clean blotters," Ellie said.

Elsmore stepped closer. "I beg your pardon?"

"Clean blotters," Ellie said, more loudly. "I cannot work at a desk if somebody has covered the blotter with figures, doodles, and random scribbling."

She could smell the fragrance of Elsmore's shaving soap, a whiff of springtime amid coal smoke and sawdust. He, by contrast, apparently took no notice of proximity to her. He'd been a more than perfect gentleman today. He'd been preoccupied, answering her questions without any questions of his own, falling silent once he'd replied to Ellie's inquiries.

In fact, he'd been *indifferent* to her, proof positive that for His Grace, a kiss truly could be *of no moment*.

"You require clean blotters," he said, "because a blotter covered with jottings would be a puzzle-scape for you. A compilation of conundrums and riddles, the ultimate distraction. If I promise you clean blotters will you please accompany me to Ambledown?"

She wanted to smooth her fingers over his lapel—his boutonniere was an orange blossom today—and to lean against him as she had once before, a moment of complete rest and surrender. Resenting his focus on completing the audit was irrational of her, when only a fool would try to work with figures while hammers literally pounded the walls.

Did the bank clerks feel similar exasperation regarding Ellie's own obsession with figures? When she nattered on about quarterly reports while the clerks simply wanted a fresh pot of tea?

"Yes, I will go to Ambledown with you, for a day or two. If you make yourself available to me without interruption, I can accomplish much in a short amount of time."

He murmured something she didn't quite catch.

"I beg your pardon, sir?"

"Do we take the cat with us or abandon her to the fare available in the alley?"

Elsmore thought of the cat, but he could ignore the most passionate kiss Ellie had known. Soon, she'd be able to hate him, a vast improvement over pining for him.

"I'll leave a note for Lord Stephen's cook, and Voltaire will feast on cream and cutlets. When shall we leave?"

"How soon can you be packed?"

"Ten minutes."

Chapter Nine

Belonging to three exclusive clubs was both a pleasure and a necessity for Eddie the Elegant Dorset. His place of business was the bank, which would hardly do as a venue for a man gaining a reputation for brokering discreet financial transactions. Membership in the best clubs was within reach only because Eddie had ducal connections, but he wanted those memberships assured for his sons as well.

For his daughters, vouchers to Almack's were the sine qua non of gentility, while for his wife...

No need to travel down that path yet. Madam Bisset was far too interesting a companion for the nonce.

Lord Bartleby, by contrast, was as dull as day-old pudding. He was a reliable customer though, never needing too much money for too long, and usually repaying promptly.

"How was your steak?" Eddie asked. "Done to a turn, I do hope?"

"Quite good," his lordship replied, pouring the last of the port into his glass. "Unlike the present state of my finances."

"Oh, dear," Eddie murmured. "Speaking as one who has experienced the occasional run of bad luck, you have my sincere sympathies. Is there anything I might do to help?"

A burst of laughter came from a table across the club's dining room. The Thomlinson heir was doing homage to his third bottle of claret in little over an hour. He was abetted by two of his cronies, though their drinking was more moderate than his.

Perhaps Thomlinson was working up his nerve to approach Eddie for a loan. He had the look—anxious, hearty, drunk at midday. The poor lad was newly down from university and likely playing too deeply. All the lordlings and cits-in-waiting did, and Eddie the Elegant was ever so willing to help.

"One doesn't like to impose," Bartleby said, keeping his voice down, "but two thousand on the usual terms would be much appreciated."

The usual terms—never reduced to writing—were fifteen percent interest for ninety days. Five percent found its way into Eddie's pocket as broker at the time the balance was lent, ten percent went to the lender, who was happy to earn in ninety days twice what the usury laws permitted for a year's interest.

While Bartleby was happy to have his little problem solved for a mere fifteen percent. All quite civilized, and only outside the bounds of decency in the opinion of high sticklers and solicitors, who were denied any revenue from such arrangements.

"I'm delighted to be of service," Eddie said. "Is the need urgent?"

"Not yet. By this time next week it will be."

"Never let it be said that I allowed such a vexation to trouble you for an entire week, my lord. Let's meet for lunch again on Friday, and I'm sure I'll be able to alleviate your present inconvenience."

Bartleby finished his wine and rose, extending a soft, manicured hand. "You are a proper brick of a fellow, Eddie Dorset. Much obliged."

Eddie got to his feet and shook hands, mentally sorting through his list of potential lenders. A half dozen titled ladies came to mind. God knew the lot of them had the blunt, but then so did Madam Bisset. He considered the advantages of connecting his current fancy piece with the lucrative business of informal lending. Madam understood money as only a working woman could, and she would one day need more than wit, charm, and loose morals to keep her in coal and candles.

"You are contemplating a scheme," James said, sliding into the chair Bartleby had vacated. "Based on your smile, the scheme has the potential to be profitable."

Eddie kept his expression genial, because one did when in public. "I fear young Mr. Thomlinson is only now realizing that a quarterly allowance is supposed to last three long, dreary months. I'm sitting here looking helpful and harmless."

"He gambles." James set Lord Bartleby's plate aside. "I thought we avoided the gamblers if at all possible."

"Everybody gambles. You yourself took an enormous risk by dodging work on Saturday. If I hadn't collected your ledgers from beneath Ballentyre's nose, Howell might have found a deal of irregularities in your accounts." Howell had, in fact, reviewed one of James's ledgers, apparently one of the tidier ones.

James signaled the waiter for another bottle of wine. "Rounding errors, possibly, or an occasional mistranscription. What are supervisory reviews for, if not an acknowledgment that no man's math is infallible? We are Dorsets, after all, and bothering our handsome heads with ciphering the livelong day runs counter to our blue blood."

"Precisely. We are not clerks." Clerks were never born to a ducal family headed by a fellow who was very good at being a duke, but too busy squiring the ladies about to trouble much over figures, poor sod. "Were you truly under the weather?"

James remained silent until the waiter had removed the empty plate and observed the little ritual of offering the next bottle of wine. Eddie took the first taste, pronounced it exquisite, and poured James a glass.

"I confess I was more nearly under the hatches," James said. "You heard about that business with the Butterfield account?"

"Belatedly. Howell and old Ballie had a chinwag once the books were done on Saturday. Howell shared what he knew over supper. Very bad business and I gather it's being kept quiet. The likes of thee, me, and Howell aren't even to know of it. I gather the teller might lose his post."

"And he is one of the honest ones," James said, sampling the wine.

Eddie needed the honest clerks and the conscientious tellers. No scheme of any duration could go forward profitably unless the bank operated on assumptions of trustworthiness and competence.

"Whoever impersonated Mr. Butterfield invested a deal of effort into the ruse," Eddie observed. "One must commend hard work and diligence wherever one finds them."

"I met the teller involved at the pub after the bank closed on Friday. The poor man was distraught, and all too willing to let me stand him to a pint or six."

At the back of Eddie's mind, where interest calculations purred along without him expending mental effort, where memories of the fair Madam Bisset sat side by side with musings about her potential as a lender, he felt a stirring.

"James, what scheme are *you* contemplating?"

James was by nature moderate. He neither flew into a passion over trivialities nor mourned missed opportunity at any length. His quips were humorous without quite shading into sarcasm. His pragmatism was a comfortable counterweight to Eddie's ambition—most of the time.

"What if Butterfield himself sent a trusted emissary to the bank to close that account?" James asked.

Eddie mentally collected the scraps of information Howell had passed along. "You mean, he sent a supernumerary to the bank in the first instance to close the account, and then he appeared at the bank, claiming fraud? He'd double his money and at no risk to him whatsoever. If the first man is found out, Butterfield can claim he simply didn't care to brave the elements himself."

"And the bank would never breathe a word of it, beyond the grumblings among the directors. It could work."

Doubling one's money was a lovely prospect, particularly when accompanied by the words *at no risk*. "Whoever attempted this plan would have to choose his bank carefully. He would need an institution with a spotless reputation."

"Purer than the driven snow and determined to remain that way."

James was choosing his mark, in other words, and he wasn't about to share the details with Eddie, which was for the best. Handling a few private loans outside of business hours was one thing; defrauding another institution ventured beyond the risks Eddie was willing to take.

The conversation drifted to James's recent trip to Peebleshire—why Elsmore hung on to a drafty Scottish castle was a mystery—and Cousin Rachel's possible interest in Lord Jeremy Bledsoe.

"You don't suppose Bledsoe will come up to scratch, do you?" Eddie asked as they finished the bottle.

"Her followers never do," James said. "A pity, that." Bland, smiling James was looking entirely too pleased with himself.

"James, what aren't you telling me?" Eddie trusted James, more or less, but he also did not take James entirely into his confidence.

"Would I keep secrets from my favorite cousin?"

"Yes."

"Exactly," James replied, "and I don't inquire too closely into your affairs either. Best for all concerned that way, don't you agree?" He helped himself to more wine that Eddie would pay for, lifted his glass a few inches, and smiled. "To the Dorset family fortunes, long may they thrive."

Eddie joined the toast, because in all sincerity, thriving family fortunes were good for business, and good for Eddie the Elegant too.

* * *

A peer of the realm should not feel that a temporary remove ten miles into the countryside was a narrow escape from hostile forces, but Rex certainly did. He'd commandeered the traveling coach that morning because the heavier vehicle was preferable for navigating London streets muddy with melting snow.

The choice was fortuitous, given that Mrs. Hatfield—he must not think of her as Eleanora—had agreed to spend a few days at Ambledown. Her acquiescence to an arguably improper excursion was either a testament to her common sense—nobody could do accurate work amid pounding hammers—or proof that she wanted to finish Rex's audit as quickly as possible.

"Your coach is even more splendid than His Grace of Walden's," Mrs. Hatfield said. "I am tempted to open a ledger and get back to work."

Rex did not tell her that a lap desk folded down on her side of the forward-facing seat.

"You can surround yourself with ledgers when we reach Ambledown. For now, explain to me that business about the larcenous rounding."

"Compound rounding, which is only productive when accounts are handled in quantity. I rarely see compound rounding schemes in domestic books, but it's a common ploy with commercial ventures."

"Are you cold?" She wore a scarf and gloves in addition to her cape, and remained swaddled in the lot of it.

"It's winter, Your Grace, and we are traveling. Ergo, I am cold."

Rex hadn't stopped by Dorset House to procure a brazier of coals, nor had he had the bricks fitted into the floor heated. Daylight was precious, and his need to vacate London urgent, once he'd made the decision to bolt.

"You are traveling with a duke of some means," he said, lifting the seat of the opposite bench. "We do not like to be cold. Share a lap robe with me."

She gave him a look presaging the predictable arguments.

Rex extracted a wool blanket of blue and black plaid from the chest built into the coach seat. "Do you choose lung fever over pride, Mrs. Hatfield? I'd thought you more sensible than that."

"Are there two blankets?"

"Yes, and if you are under both of them, sitting next to me, you will be warmer than if you try to make do with one. Honestly, madam, what do you think I'll attempt in a moving coach with a woman whose financial expertise is all that stands between me and impending scandal? You could ruin me with a word."

Rex reminded himself of that fact regularly, though it did nothing to drum the memory of her kisses out of his idiot mind. In a curious reversal of status, she had the power to ruin him every bit as effectively as he could ruin her.

Not that he would. Ever. For any reason.

She scooted two feet to the right, so she was sitting next to Rex but not touching him.

"Your imagination is prodigiously overactive," she said, as Rex draped the first blanket over their knees. "Minor irregularities with your books won't occasion scandal."

"Last week it was fraud and embezzlement. Now it's minor irregularities?"

He draped the second blanket atop the first, the wool carrying the scent of the cedar panels lining the chest in which it had been stored.

"I tell you in strictest confidence, Your Grace, that the Walden ducal finances were in a state of utter chaos when the current titleholder inherited. Nary a property was managed honestly. Those not plundered outright were being slowly bled to death by the crooks and charlatans in His Grace's employ. We will set your situation to rights with nobody the wiser, but you must be patient."

"I cannot afford to be patient."

The coach halted at one of the many turnpike gates encircling London. Rex pulled down the shade on his side of the vehicle, Mrs. Hatfield having already done so on hers.

"I'm glad you understand that time is of the essence, Your Grace. The longer you turn a blind eye to the swindlers picking your pocket, the bolder they become. That a fraud was perpetrated on your bank is most discouraging."

She left off fussing the blankets and scooting about, like a cat circling on a bed before choosing where to curl up.

"You equate the problem at the bank with the irregularities in my books?" Rex surely hadn't. One was neglect, the other bad luck, and ne'er the twain should meet.

"The coincidence is troubling."

God save me. If Eleanora Hatfield was troubled over a coincidence, it wasn't a coincidence. "I'll tell you what's troubling. Lord Jeremy Bledsoe seeking to pay my sister his addresses is troubling."

"He's not suitable?"

"He *is* suitable. My sensible, prudent sister has likely fallen for his lordship, and once they've shared a few waltzes—a few more waltzes—the solicitors will begin the negotiations. The dower properties will be examined under multiple quizzing glasses, and the only estate I can honestly vouch for is Ambledown."

Which Rex had promised to the lady sharing a coach with him. She'd brushed his offer aside, though for salvaging a dukedom, Eleanora Hatfield deserved more than a few pounds and ink-stained fingers.

"Impending negotiations do present a challenge."

"What a gift for understatement you have developed. The honorable Mr. Hornby is making calf eyes at my sister

Lady Samantha, and even Lady Kathleen is apparently inspiring bad sonnets."

"All three at once, Your Grace?"

"So it would appear. Tell me about compound rounding."

She rustled about some more. "The concept is straightforward. If you invest a hundred pounds at five percent, then calculating the interest is simple."

"Five pounds," Rex said, as the coach picked up speed.

"But what if the sum invested is an odd number? Say, eleven pounds and five pence?"

"You deal in farthings."

"Or, if I end up with an odd number of farthings, I must eventually deal in decimals and rounding. If I consistently round down, while keeping a tally of all the pennies that result, the cash drawer will eventually have a greater sum than the ledger sheet reflects."

"But one doesn't round downward unless the figure is below five. Otherwise, one rounds upward, and the two exercises eventually cancel each other out."

Perhaps Mrs. Hatfield was less self-conscious when discussing embezzlement, perhaps she yielded to the animal temptation to draw nearer to warmth, but draw nearer to Rex, she did.

"To detect a scheme of this nature," she went on, "you'd have to double-check every calculation and every rounding. To be productive, a compound rounding rig should be spread over many active accounts, at least hundreds."

What sort of mind devised these schemes? "The bank has thousands of accounts."

Mrs. Hatfield yawned behind her hand. "I beg your pardon. I was up late last night."

"Working on ledgers? I thought you took the Sabbath off."

"I could not resist the lure of your family seat, Your Grace. You will be relieved to know the books are holding up to scrutiny."

Meaning the fraud was happening elsewhere, probably on the properties Rex was most likely to choose as his sisters' dower portions.

Splendid. "The same person would have to be overseeing many accounts for this rounding business to be lucrative."

"A bank manager can supervise five hundred minor commercial accounts, if he's conscientious and has good clerks. If compound rounding nets him a penny a week per account, that's more than two pounds per week total, or a hundred pounds a year. Run the rig over a thousand accounts, and you can begin to live on the proceeds of your rig while investing your wages. Over ten thousand accounts—"

"And the customers would never notice."

"Nor would most supervisors, managers, or directors. How many times have you seen a minor discrepancy, then shrugged and attributed it to rounding?"

Many times. Too many times. "You are giving me dyspepsia."

"Perhaps it's the movement of the coach, though I have never traveled this comfortably before."

The coach was well-sprung and luxuriously upholstered, true enough. "You're no longer cold?"

Nor was she making any pretense of keeping a distance between them. As Town gave way to winter-bleak fields, shaggy cattle, and wooly sheep, Mrs. Hatfield gradually listed against Rex's left side.

She prattled on about some mercer's counting house, where the clerks had all been told to round down by the manager overseeing the accounts, until the manager had absconded with hundreds of pounds.

When Mrs. Hatfield concluded that cheering recitation she fell silent, her breathing slowed, and she became a warm, comfortable weight against Rex's side.

"I begin to fear that my finances are not suffering as a result of haphazard practices or the occasional blunder," Rex said, "but rather, as a town suffers under siege. The stores gradually diminish, morale erodes, betrayal from within becomes more and more likely."

For once, Rex got no argument from his auditor. She was snoring softly, her head on his shoulder, her hand casually resting on his thigh.

"Mrs. Hatfield?"

Nothing.

"Eleanora?"

A soft sigh.

Rex curled an arm around her lest she be bounced off the seat by some disobliging rut. She knew every clever device for stealing coin from a legitimate enterprise, but he would not have predicted that she also had the knack of sleeping in a moving vehicle.

"I've worn you out," he murmured.

The miles rolled by, Eleanora slept, and Rex contemplated why it should be that the farther they trotted from London, the more peaceful and content he became, and the more pleased to be traveling to Ambledown with her.

* * *

Ambledown exuded the cozy rural domesticity Ellie had known in early childhood. The dwelling itself was a modest three stories at the end of a circular drive. Woods lined one side of the drive and climbed the hill behind the house, and rolling pastures fell away from the other. The manor was a sparkling white Tudor half-timbered structure, complete with mullioned windows, green shutters, and a bright red front door.

Merry Olde England at its finest. Ellie was glad this place belonged to Elsmore, and pleased for his sake that its books were as spotless as its windows. She had not been pleased to find herself all but cuddled in his lap as the coach had rocked to a halt before the house.

For him, the familiarity had likely been *of no moment*.

He'd escorted her into the house, directed a smiling footman to convey the ledgers to the estate office, and commended Ellie into the keeping of the housekeeper. That good soul had been stout, friendly, and not quite able to hide her curiosity regarding the duke's guest as she had provided a tour of the premises.

Ellie had been an object of curiosity at every one of the Walden holdings, and had found that the most effective response to veiled glances and subtle hints was to ignore them. When a footman summoned her away from her ledgers mid-tally, she could not ignore the grumblings of her empty belly.

"You might have told me I'm to take supper with you," she said, once the footman had quit the dining parlor.

His Grace of Elsmore stood at the head of the table, quietly resplendent in country attire. "Where else would you dine?" he asked.

"At the second table, with the housekeeper, the butler, and the senior staff." Remonstrating with him for holding her chair would have felt ridiculous.

"You literally fell asleep on me on the drive out here," he said, "and now you'd leave me to dine by myself. Is my company so objectionable, madam?"

His company was becoming too interesting. At his Hampshire estate, he'd taken on the living for the local vicarage at the same time he'd rented an unused chapel to a Quaker gathering, charging them one shilling a year. What sort of man did that?

"I apologize for my lapse in manners earlier." Ellie whisked a monogrammed table napkin across her lap. "One moment, I was regaling you with some tale about compound rounding, and the next I was waking up to the sight of this charming estate."

He gestured with the wine bottle. Ellie nodded, because once the bottle had been opened, the spirits should be consumed.

"And the moment we arrived," Elsmore said, "you closeted yourself with the blasted ledgers."

"That was rather the point of the excursion, sir." Then too, her nap, or perhaps the crisp country air, had left her refreshed and motivated. "Tell me about your extended family."

She'd amused him with that clumsy change of subject.

He ladled out a portion of soup that smelled divine. "Why?"

"Because they are involved in both your commercial and domestic affairs. In the alternative, we could assess the potential dower holdings and choose the three most likely to withstand close financial scrutiny. This soup is delicious." The base might have been potatoes, but quantities of cream, cheddar, winter vegetables, and a dash of spirits made the fare rich and savory.

Best of all, the course was served at the almost-too-hot temperature that made good soup on a cold day a taste of heaven.

Elsmore buttered a slice of bread and dipped it into his

soup, yeoman fashion. "If you allowed yourself the occasional respite from your labors, you wouldn't fall asleep in moving coaches, Eleanora."

She ignored his use of her given name, though it pleased her all the more for being in that chiding tone. "If you paid more attention to your ledgers, you would not need to haul a busy auditor off to the countryside for the sole purpose of straightening out your books, Elsmore."

He laughed and passed Ellie the butter. "Good God, you are as relentless as Wellington's infantry. I like your idea about sorting the dower properties, I loathe that you are so fatigued you can sleep for nearly two hours at midday."

Not much more than an hour, by Ellie's reckoning. "I loathe that your dukedom is being plundered. Who among your relations works at the bank, and do you trust them?"

He dipped his bread again, and Ellie regretted the question. She could not afford to trust her family, but they were crooks, albeit crooks by necessity. They grasped that she'd crossed a divide that did not allow for her to trust them.

Elsmore's nature was to attribute to others the same honor he expected of himself. Grandpapa, unfortunately, had had the same decent outlook on his fellow man and that had not ended well at all.

"Must we have this discussion now?" Elsmore said.

"We must have it soon. Please give some thought to who might be motivated to steal from you. Who has excessive debts, a spouse unable to control her expenditures, too many daughters to launch, an inability to refrain from wagering?"

"Half of London?"

"Elsmore, this is not charm. This is evasion. What is amiss?"

He set aside his empty soup bowl and took up the carving

knife. "What if you are right?" he asked, starting on the joint of beef. "What if the domestic irregularities signal worse trouble at the bank? Scandal tarnishes a personal reputation, but for a family engaged in banking, scandal can also cause financial ruin. Generations of probity and hard work out the window like a pail of slops tossed on the midden."

He set a slice of perfectly done beef on Ellie's plate.

"The Butterfield business has you concerned," Ellie said. "Good. If you're concerned, you will be thorough in your examination of the books. Right now, your bank is solvent, the merchants are willing to extend you personal credit. Now is exactly when you should be quietly putting your house in order."

He served himself a greater portion of the roast, which the enterprising cook had produced without any warning that the master would be on hand to consume it.

"I hope you send your compliments to the kitchen," Ellie said. "This meat so far exceeds my usual chop shop fare that to discuss embezzlement in the same room is sacrilegious."

"I'm glad you're enjoying it. You can say no, you know."

"I beg your pardon?"

"You can refuse the wine, the roast, the invitation to dinner. The kitchen had a tray ready in case you decided to remain with your ledgers. I had meant to discuss dinner with you, but my land steward got word I was on the premises."

"And you did not refuse his summons, did you?"

"Touché, Mrs. Hatfield. Tell me how to spot an embezzler."

Ellie would rather not. She would rather enjoy the food and pretend, for once, that she and Elsmore were simply socializing for the pleasure of each other's company.

Foolish, foolish, foolish. Besides, needs must when the duke had nobody else to guide him.

"Embezzlers come in two varieties," she began, "the desperate and the greedy. The desperate are in perilous need of blunt. They might be involved with the moneylenders, who can turn a debt of five pounds into an obligation of two hundred pounds. You will know a desperate embezzler by his worn attire, especially his footwear. He might have only one coat decent enough to wear in public.

"You casually note that he's appropriately attired," she continued, "and only realize that he's always in the exact same coat when your sister mentions it. He wears no chain on his watch, having pawned that along with most of his rings, cravat pins, and sleeve buttons. He might instead wear a chain that has no watch attached to it. His person will never bear the fragrance of scented soaps or pomades, but you might detect a whiff of tallow or ale on him."

Elsmore set another half slice of beef on her plate, then added a serving of mashed potatoes. "Go on."

"A greedy embezzler, by contrast, has tastes that exceed his or her means. He might dress a little better than his station. He indulges in scents, new boots, a splendid mount, monogrammed linen, beeswax candles, good wine. When he gives a gift, it might be a touch too extravagant for good taste. His domicile will be a shade too commodious compared to others similarly situated."

"We are back to your talent for spotting what doesn't fit a pattern."

Elsmore looked more at home in this relatively rustic setting than he had amid the splendor of Wentworth and Penrose's business offices. The ceiling here was a mere eight feet, both hearths held roaring fires, a rosy-cheeked young couple in powdered wigs smiled down from the portrait over the sideboard.

He also looked pensive.

"Something troubles you," Ellie said. "Something beyond untidy books."

He crossed his knife and fork over a half-empty plate. "All three of my sisters are now apparently keeping company with doting swains, two of them in contemplation of courtship. After years of being received everywhere but having few creditable offers, my womenfolk are now besieged. Why now? The Little Season is hardly when most matches are made, and I can think of nothing in the family circumstances that has altered to make the ladies more attractive to lonely bachelors."

"You are correct that a pattern has abruptly changed, but I am hardly an authority on the passions of the human heart. Aren't you having any potatoes?"

He served himself, and he obliged Ellie's demand to discuss his extended family. She and Elsmore took their raspberry fool with them to the estate office, where Ellie drew the Dorset family tree, from the elders right down to the latest arrivals.

"How does your family tree compare to mine?" Elsmore asked, finishing his sweet. "Can you claim eleven male cousins? A trio of aunties named for famous battles?"

He clearly loved those aunties and was fiercely protective of his cousins. "My family is smaller," Ellie said, trying to make her dessert last. "We aren't as close-knit as your family is." Grandmother kept track of everybody, passing along news in her tidy script. A pang of homesickness assailed Ellie, though surely not homesickness for godforsaken Yorkshire?

"What of parents?" Elsmore asked. "Do they post

regular lectures to you about the perils of life in wicked old Londontowne?"

The homesickness became old, brittle sorrow. Dry as dust, sharp as glass. "Let us attend to the task at hand, Elsmore, rather than wander off into irrelevancies. Do not think to steal the last of my fool, either, or I will deal severely with you."

"I live in hope. Did I mention a pair of elderly bachelor uncles? One suspects them of peculiar inclinations, but one doesn't pry." He cherished those eccentric uncles, clearly, just as he valued everybody from the current duchess down to the latest arrival born to a young cousin who held the living near Elsmore's estate in Shropshire.

All of these people, several dozen in number, looked to Elsmore for support, security, and influence. And he never refused them, apparently, which only made the state of his accounts that much harder to explain.

Chapter Ten

While Eleanora studied the plethora of family relation-ships that formed the fabric of Rex's life, he thought back over the day. For the duration of ten rutted, slushy country miles, he had wallowed in the pleasure of having Eleanora snoring against his side. She'd slept deeply, necessitating his arm around her shoulders as her hair had tickled his chin.

He'd let his imagination roam, as if having her next to him anchored him bodily in a way that permitted mental flights of fancy.

Details about her were becoming so much treasure: Her valise had a Parisian maker's mark and hadn't been used much. She'd also brought a lap desk with her, an antique with intricate carving adorning both sides. The quality of that article bespoke an eye for finer things or perhaps a lady fallen on hard times.

Her departure from her cat had been a series of

instructions: *No dead mice upon my carpet, please. You will not consort with ruffians of any species in any alley.* Then a cuddle—which the cat tolerated—and a kiss to her furry head.

Be here when I come home. You are my sole companion, and I would worry endlessly should you abandon me.

Rex had ignored that last admission, which he hadn't been meant to overhear in any case, but it troubled him. Why would an intelligent, interesting, attractive female be without even a companion? He grasped that some women chose not to marry, but to be entirely alone? Where were her parents as she toiled year after year in London? What about siblings or cousins?

He occasionally resented his family's hovering, but to have no family at all? He would not wish that fate upon his sworn foe.

"You are falling into a brown study," Eleanora said, setting aside the family tree that traced maternal cousins and aunts. "Or I have bored you witless with my maunderings. I'm like a vicar with a sermon on my favorite obscure passage. The congregation has no choice but to indulge me."

She seemed so *happy* here among the ledger books, her feet curled beneath her in the reading chair, while Rex was increasingly discontent. For all that he had little solitude in Town, he was also without a companion, not even a cat. Nonetheless, he was prodigiously attracted to a prim auditor whose coiffure was for once slipping free of its pins.

"Are we making any progress, Eleanora?"

She tucked her skirts over her toes and sent him a glance. She had not commented on his use of her given name at dinner, and she was not commenting on it now—not verbally.

"This is how an audit proceeds," she said. "You feel as if you have all this wet laundry and nowhere to hang it, but you forge ahead, wringing pillowcase after sheet after tablecloth, and then, when you think the ordeal will have no end, the bottom of the basket comes into view. Based on this afternoon's work, I can tell you that your four northern properties are in good order."

That was not necessarily good news. "I have no family at the northern properties."

"None?"

"James recently visited the castle in Peebleshire, but no family resides there, and the accountings come straight to me, not through any London steward or manager at the bank."

She rearranged the pillow at her back. "You will sleep much better when you disentangle your family's finances from your bank. I understand the temptation to lump them together for the sake of efficiency and generosity, but it's not a sound practice."

Meaning the Duke of Walden, arbiter of all things financially prudent, doubtless ordered his finances so his bank and his family holdings never touched, like a toddler with his vegetables.

"Such an adjustment would require significant changes."

"Make them," Eleanora retorted. "The bank's loyalty should be, in theory, to its customers. Your loyalty should be to your family, but as a director, you must also prioritize the welfare of the bank's customers. Those loyalties are more likely to conflict, the more you entangle your family with your business, and then you will have no good choices when a problem arises."

"And my family employed at the bank?"

"Ideally, they would work elsewhere. Most of the

aristocracy adheres to the convenient rather than the ideal, however."

"Where do you bank?" The question felt intimate, but then, the fire was burning low in the grate, the household was largely abed, and darkness had fallen hours ago.

"I don't, precisely. When I was employed as a mercer's clerk, I kept an account at Wentworth and Penrose. Now, I have a sum invested in the cent-per-cents, but when I amass coin of a certain value, I buy silver goods."

"Your teapot." The little vessel sat in pride of place on her mantel, and he'd never seen her use it.

"I have a porringer, some spoons, a vase. Silver is portable and can be engraved with marks of ownership that are not easily altered."

"How do you know these things?" The itch to unravel her secrets was approaching a compulsion. Where had she learned her skills, why was her sole confidant a semi-reformed alley cat?

"Most people with few means know the value of silver," she said, pausing to yawn behind her hand. "Silver can withstand proximity to fire, serve a purpose, and be easily stuffed into a traveling bag should a swift departure be necessary."

Silver could also be melted down and recast for myriad purposes, though in all of creation there was only one Eleanora Hatfield. "You need to depart this office for your bed, madam. I'll light you to your room." Rex stood and offered her his hand.

"Coming out here was a fine idea, Elsmore," she said, grasping his fingers and rising. "I'd forgotten how much more clearly one thinks when breathing fresh country air. How the mind settles when nature is always in sight just beyond the window."

She'd known that once. When and what had obscured the knowledge?

"I love it here," Rex said, a prosaic admission, also a confidence. "I love the quiet and the privacy. I can ramble in my woods for an entire afternoon with no company but a curious rabbit or a lazy pheasant."

He took up a carrying candle and led her through the chilly corridors. No wind set the old house to creaking or groaning, no footman stayed awake anticipating a late night summons. Ambledown was a functioning estate, not a duke's elegant showpiece.

"Your affection for this property is evident," Eleanora said as they mounted the steps. "But I suspect all of your holdings are well maintained. Do you visit them regularly?"

"I either visit or I send a cousin to show the colors." He paused outside her room. "I might not find another time to say this, so I will say it now: Thank you." Gratitude was not all he wanted to express to her, but it seemed a good place to start.

"I'm merely performing a service, Your Grace, one I enjoy providing."

Your Grace. His thanks apparently embarrassed her. Rex opened her bedroom door, letting a warm draft into the corridor.

"I'll light your candles," he said, gesturing her to precede him into her sitting room. "You are doing more than performing a service, Eleanora. You allow me to raise difficult questions with absolute faith that my confidences will not be betrayed. You take my interests to heart. You instruct me on matters nobody has seen fit to include in my ducal education. I am indebted to you."

He was also attracted to her, and not in the casual sense he was attracted to any comely female. He liked watching her mind work. He liked *arguing* with her. He liked hearing the click of the abacus beads because she moved them around with the brisk speed of a sharpshooter wielding a favorite weapon.

She closed the door, plunging the room into deep gloom.

"Somebody kept my fires built up," she said. "You cannot imagine what a luxury that is for me."

She wore a plain wool shawl when he wanted to wrap her in cashmere and silk. Her bun was drooping, and he yearned to unravel the lot and learn how long her hair was, learn the feel of it in his hands.

He wanted...her. To cherish, explore, appreciate, and indulge.

"The bedroom candles, if you please, Elsmore. I'll not be using the parlor tonight."

A man intent on observing propriety would pass her the candle, bow, and wish her sound slumbers. Rex thought back over the day, when Eleanora had slept so trustingly against his side in the coach. She'd come to dinner with the barest minimum of a fuss.

She'd patted his hand.

She'd toed off her house slippers in his presence.

She'd taken his arm as she'd traversed the steps.

Now, she was inviting him into her bedroom on the most mundane of pretexts.

"Eleanora, are you flirting with me?" *Please say yes. Please, please, please.*

"If you must ask, then the venture isn't being very competently executed, is it?"

"Why?"

She stepped closer, took the candle from him, and put her arms around him. "Because I'm an idiot. I'd like to kiss you."

"I'd like to kiss you too." The words of a fellow-idiot, but Rex meant them from the bottom of his heart.

* * *

Ellie had not always been honest with Elsmore, but she'd told him the truth about the progress of the audit: The end was approaching, and the findings looked to be fairly predictable. The people closest to the duke, most familiar with him and most secure in his affections, were the least conscientious about keeping his books and the most likely to dip their fingers into his pockets.

With a little oversight, some changes of procedure and changes of staff, his personal accounts would withstand prenuptial scrutiny from any quarter. Ellie had misgivings about matters at his bank, but auditing Dorset and Becker would be a massive undertaking that could put her loyalties in conflict.

Her common sense and a mad impulse to share more than a kiss with Elsmore were already waging a war.

"An interlude can't mean anything," she said.

Elsmore took her by the hand and led her not to the bedroom, but to the sofa. "I'm to be a lady's passing fancy? How novel." He had the grace to sound both amused and chagrined.

"You are a director of an institution that competes with my employer. I should not allow you even passing fancy status." How her family would crow, to see her ethics wavering for the sake of pleasure.

"Eleanora, no less person than His Grace of Walden has given his blessing to your review of my personal books. If you wanted to ruin me, my bank, and my family, you have the means. I'm willing to take that risk. Can't you trust me to be even a fleeting indulgence?"

He was making a sort of sense, but Ellie could not follow his logic when distracted by the pleasure of watching his mouth.

"I am about to be horrendously foolish," she said. Also daring and, for once, even a little selfish.

Elsmore enfolded her hand in both of his and kissed her fingers. "I rejoice that I have the honor to be the object of your foolishness."

The gesture was both courtly and intimate, and Ellie's last hope of reversing course sank beneath a tide of anticipation. Elsmore would not bungle these intimacies. If she permitted herself one spectacular lapse of judgment, he'd make the experience more than worth the regrets.

"I'm not chaste," Ellie said. "You needn't worry that my feminine sensibilities are overly delicate."

"I'm not chaste either," Elsmore replied. "Feel free to indulge your every fantasy and whim with me."

That would take far more than the few days they had. "You also aren't in any great hurry, apparently."

Another kiss, this one to her wrist. "Does one swill the finest vintage like cheap ale?"

Clearly not, if one was the Duke of Elsmore. Whatever parts of his business education had been neglected, he knew how to thoroughly please a lover. He brought to life in Ellie the long dormant glory of being a female in contemplation of intimate congress with a man she desired.

His lips wandering from her wrist to her elbow conjured heat and longing. When he shifted to kneel over her on the sofa, she relaxed into the pleasurable posture of a woman who need only enjoy being kissed, caressed, and cherished.

She endured tenderness upon tenderness. Elsmore's thumb brushing the inside of her elbow, his fingers teasing the pins from her hair, his heat and scent enveloping her in warmth and a promise of pleasures to come.

He gently removed her spectacles, which Ellie allowed, a much greater gesture of trust than he knew.

Long-held tension unraveled as Elsmore wrapped her in an embrace, her face pressed to his chest, her jaw cradled against his palm. The moment was ineffably sweet. Whatever else came after—passion, pleasure, repletion—Ellie would recall those few instants of peace and closeness.

"You won't regret this?" Elsmore asked, sitting back.

I will regret so much, but never this. "No more than you will."

He rose and when Ellie would have taken his hand, he instead scooped her against his chest. A reflexive inclination to protest slipped away on a sigh, for to be carried in Elsmore's arms was lovely. The bedroom was as well heated as the sitting room, meaning several degrees above chilly. Elsmore was a toasty male brick and Ellie curled into his warmth.

He deposited her in the reading chair by the hearth and knelt to remove her slippers.

"I haven't a sheath with me," he said. "I want your promise, Eleanora, that if our passion has consequences, you will notify me."

"I can make that promise." She'd notify him, though she would first quit London if she so much as suspected she'd conceived. The notion was sobering, but then, Ellie knew all the tisanes to bring on menses, and she—like most women of modest station—kept at least two of them on hand.

Elsmore shrugged out of his jacket and draped it across the back of Ellie's chair. He dispensed with her stockings next and when she stood, he undid the hooks at the back of her dress.

"Shall I brush out your hair?" He kissed her nape and wrapped his arms about her middle. "I want to see it down, I want to know what the prim Eleanora Hatfield looks like all undone and eager."

Ellie turned and looped her arms around his neck. "I look forward to seeing His Grace of Elsmore winded and satisfied, not a flowery compliment or pithy insight to his name. I want him panting and dazed, his only thought an incoherent sense of gratitude and joy."

She was already panting and dazed.

"I want you to forget what an abacus is."

"I want you to forget your own title."

They shared a smile, for their discourse was becoming silly and, clearly, neither of them cared. Ellie would not forget Elsmore's title or his station—not ever—and neither would she forget that once upon a time, he'd been her lover.

She allowed him to wield the brush on her unbound hair, then re-braided it while he undressed. He was un-self-conscious of his nudity, using the bed warmer while Ellie dodged behind the privacy screen to change into a nightgown and dressing robe.

"You are modest," he said, propping an elbow along the top of the wooden screen. "I would not have anticipated that in such a practical woman. I like it."

Ellie tossed her dress at him. "You are naked. I like that."

"A duke is always appropriately attired for the occasion."

"You are awful." Awfully dear, drat him.

"Come to bed, Eleanora, and I'll improve your opinion of me."

And there was the problem no amount of tallying or rounding could solve. Ellie not only desired Elsmore, she respected him and *liked* him. She was truly enamored of him, which meant, when her audit was concluded in another few days, her path and his would diverge, permanently and absolutely.

As she settled onto the warmed mattress, and Elsmore drew the covers up over her, she admitted a quiet, devastating truth: This was how it should be between a woman and the man with whom she chose to share intimacies—comfortable, pleasurable, and so very special.

Nonetheless, she would enjoy her passing fancy, and then slip away to her safe, predictable life, there to remain in obscurity as long as she possibly could.

* * *

Rex paraded around in the altogether because a quantity of cold air was one sure way to take the edge off his passion. Nothing would entirely defeat nascent desire when Eleanora Hatfield, now swaddled in exactly one layer of soft white cotton, had given him permission to become her lover.

But this occasion was more than a casual coupling.

He dithered at the hearth, arranging coals, trying to assemble an erotic strategy, because his objective was more than a few minutes of shared pleasure. He wanted to *be with Eleanora* well beyond a stolen interlude and even past the duration of a discreet liaison.

Rex's conviction in this regard had been building since the moment she had first bickered with him over the privilege of holding her chair. To her, he was not a lofty aristocrat owed deference as a result of an accident of birth.

Her esteem was earned, her favors given or withheld based on her honest regard.

This was not, of course, how it should be. A duke did not fall in love with anybody excepting perhaps himself. He might humor an infatuation with this or that temporary partner. Affection for a lady was within permissible bounds, and he owed his duchess proper respect.

A duke did not become attached to a party far beneath his station.

Except...he did. British history was rife with examples of mésalliances between the blue-blooded and the common, and whatever Eleanora's antecedents were, she herself was unassailably decent. She was also nestled amid the quilts like a contented cat, while Rex wasted precious moments deciding between lovemaking and proposing.

"Are you joining me under these covers or pondering the fate of the realm?" she asked, tossing a pillow to the foot of the bed.

A little of both. Rex fished in the pockets of the breeches he'd draped over the back of the reading chair and found a wrinkled handkerchief.

"Stay right where you are," he said, putting the linen onto the bedside table and pouring a glass of water from the carafe on the windowsill. "I'm plotting my course."

"I will plot your course, lest you catch your death. You climb into bed, we make passionate love, then we fall asleep on a cloud of contentment. You will not apply your cold feet to my person at any time, and you will discreetly take yourself off in the small hours, lest there be awkwardness in the morning for the chambermaid."

He sauntered to the bed. "I like the part about passionate lovemaking and the clouds of contentment. I'm increasingly displeased with that nightgown." Though if he was about to propose, she might rather be wearing at least one article of clothing when he did.

"Too bad, Elsmore, because you won't get it off me until the candles are blown out."

She was serious. "You are the pocket Venus who has haunted my dreams since the day we met, and now you— Eleanora, have you borne a child? Is that what prompts this excess of modesty?" Where was that child, and who was the father? Rex sat on the edge of the bed, his conscience at war with his body, because he did not approve of dueling in the general case. "*Is* there a Mr. Hatfield? Please be honest with me."

She thrashed free of the covers and knelt up to wrap him in a hug from behind. "Mr. Hatfield is a figment of my craving for propriety. I have never married, and I have no children. I am also not like you—casually naked, confident in my appeal. I haven't…"

She buried a cold nose against Rex's neck, a peculiar sensation when her cheeks were so warm.

He kissed her forearm, the part of her that happened to be closest to his lips. "You haven't taken many lovers?"

"I have not, and I haven't taken any in recent years. You have confidence I lack."

"If you were any more confident, you'd hold a Cabinet post and the realm would be better for it. Turn loose of me, and I'll blow out the candles."

She kissed his nape, an odd, tender gesture, then let him go.

Rex made a circuit of the room, gratified to note that Eleanora watched him, and her gaze was frankly appreciative.

"Like what you see?" *Like it enough to marry me?*

"I like *who* I see, though I will doubtless regret that admission. Come to bed, Elsmore."

Yes, ma'am. He paused on the step beside the bed, one

knee on the mattress. "My given name is Wrexham, though under the circumstances, Rex will do." *We are to be married, after all.* His allegedly abundant confidence did not allow him to assay that observation, for with Eleanora, he dare not make any assumptions.

She held up the covers, he lay down beside her, and she drew the quilts over him. "Now what?"

He adored the disgruntled edge to her question. "You ravish me within an inch of my sanity."

She curled up along his side and wrapped her fingers around his arousal. "That shouldn't take long at all."

"For you, the work of a moment, but Eleanora, might we discuss—*Eleanora*?"

Her head disappeared under the covers, and Rex's sanity—along with any comprehensible offers of marriage—vanished as well. He barely had a moment to grip the spindles of the headboard before she put her mouth to an intimate location. By the time she emerged from her mission of mischief, Rex was in a state of uproarious desire, Eleanora was clearly pleased with herself, and one of the spindles had come loose from its moorings.

"I like to start out on top," she said, straddling him. "What have you to say to that?"

"A gentleman never argues with a lady, and I like for you to be happy." He would also like to burn the damned nightgown, but settled for bunching it up around her waist.

"I'm not a lady." She curled down onto his chest and mashed her nose—no longer cold—against his throat.

"You are a lady. *My* lady, and my lover." *Won't you be my wife?* That was what made Eleanora so precious. She would be not only Rex's duchess, appearing on his arm for the requisite social occasions, managing his households, and guarding his interests. She would also be his *wife*, his ally, his confidante, his lover. The safe haven for his soul, the intimate delight of his heart.

She kissed him on the mouth, then sat up, whisked off the damned nightgown, and aimed it over her shoulder. "You say the most outlandish things."

For the next little while, Rex said nothing with words, but with his caresses and kisses, he tried to communicate to her that she was infinitely dear, that his yearning for her went well beyond mere erotic fixation.

Perhaps Eleanora understood, for her touch became lyrical and sweet, until they were joined and moving as one.

As a younger man, Rex had indulged in the usual excesses, or perhaps more than usual, given the privileges of his station. Making love with Eleanora was new, though. Intimacy built on aspirations of a shared lifetime imbued the experience with something approaching reverence. When Eleanora at last came undone in his arms, he followed her into a completion so limitless that for a moment, there was no Rex or Eleanora, there was only surrender and joy.

She sighed against his neck, the sigh of a well-pleasured lady. "We'll make a mess," she murmured.

The nature of the undertaking meant . . . Rex's rosy mental peregrinations came up against a rock wall of chagrin. He hadn't withdrawn. Great God Jehovah have mercy on a miserable duke, *he hadn't withdrawn*.

"Eleanora, I am so—"

She pushed herself off his chest, yawned and stretched, and reached for the linen cloth on the night table. "I'm not much of a talker in these situations."

The handkerchief disappeared beneath the covers, and Eleanora arranged herself along Rex's side.

She did not seem upset—far from it, which boded well

for Rex's ambitions. Time enough in the morning to offer matrimony, and really, Rex ought to begin by asking to pay his addresses, just as he would with any woman whom he aspired to marry.

And he'd need a ring. Flowers, French chocolates, bended knee, the whole production, which he would happily plan down to the last detail tomorrow.

Now, Eleanora's breath fanned across his chest and her knee rested against his thigh.

"Did I acquit myself adequately?" he asked, freeing her braid from between the pillows.

"If you had acquitted yourself any more adequately, I would have expired from a surfeit of pleasure. A woman underestimates you at her peril."

He gathered her near, loving the feel of her warm and naked next to him. Perhaps he could broach the topic of marriage preliminarily, in a general sort of way.

"I look forward to the day when such pleasures are a regular aspect of my situation. Domestic bliss and all that."

She said nothing, but then, he'd probably been *too* general.

"Do you ever contemplate marriage, Eleanora? Speculate about what benefits it might offer with the right fellow?"

Rex waited, mapping the curve of her hip and the turn of her waist in slow strokes. She was small but sturdy and ye gods, she was passionate. "Eleanora?" He seized all of his courage and whispered, "Will you marry me?"

The fire crackled softly in the hearth. Somewhere on the floor below, a longcase clock bonged the quarter hour.

Rex knew the feel of Eleanora in slumber, knew the peaceful weight of her in his embrace. He'd loved her within an inch of her sanity, apparently, all the way to a sound sleep.

He kissed her temple and drew the covers up over her shoulder.

"Tomorrow, then, or certainly before we return to London, we will embark on that conversation. I look forward to being your doting duke, if you'll have me."

* * *

"So where is she?" Jack asked, accepting the slice of buttered bread Pamela passed him. He had to let the brat on his knee have a bite first, and wee Mickey—named for his cousin—knew to take as much at one go as he could manage.

"Down with you," Jack said, putting the boy on the floor. "If you keep eating like that you'll soon be eight feet tall."

The lad grinned around a mouthful of bread—no manners whatsoever—and skipped off.

"Go tell your sister to stop pestering Mrs. Hilton," Pamela said. "The girl's been up there for half the day."

Jack had, to his shame, timed this call for noon, when food might be in evidence. Waiting around in doorways was hungry work this time of year.

"Ellie hasn't gone to the chop house," he said. "Not since Saturday. It's Tuesday noon, and no Ellie. What if she's ill?"

As far as Jack knew, no Naylor kin had ever set foot on the premises of Ellie's fine lodgings, nor had they darkened the door of the Wentworth and Penrose bank. Never let it be said Ellie's family had betrayed her before her betters. Kept a watchful eye on her, of course, but nothing more.

Pamela passed him the baby and rose to pour him a cup

of tea from a pot swaddled in a towel in the dry sink. The towel was dingy, but the tea was steaming hot.

"Ellie has the constitution of a horse," she said. "You are simply out of work and looking for inspiration. You won't find it spying on her."

"She could have been set upon by thieves, be lying in a ditch somewhere unshriven, and all you can think to do is scold me for caring about her."

The tea was actual tea, not some imitation concocted of meadow weeds and the orts and leavings of a tea chest. Mick's generosity was being put to good use.

"You care about yourself," Pamela said, taking the other chair at the table and situating the baby in her lap. "Not that I blame you for it. The agencies aren't hiring?"

"The better families are leaving for their Yuletide holidays in the country, while half the yeomanry has come to Town looking for work now that the harvest is in. Any merchant will hire his cousin's neighbor's niece's boy from Greater Sheepshite before he'll turn to the agencies."

The baby reached for Jack's teacup, which was still half full of hot drink. Jack moved it aside and offered the child his hand, for his pockets were empty of all treasure.

"Do you think Ellie can find you a job?" Pamela asked.

The question was merely curious rather than derisive. Jack took encouragement from that. "I'm almost as good with numbers as Ellie is, and as you said, I know all the rigs and schemes even better than she does. I can keep honest books, and I often have."

Once, he'd even alerted an employer to a valet padding his accounts. Two weeks later, the mistress's nacre-handled penknife had been "found" by a housemaid among Jack's effects, and he had learned a valuable lesson. *If you're not working a rig, somebody else in the household likely is.*

"Clerks don't earn much," Pamela said. "Not at first. You could ask Ellie if any of the banks are hiring."

"I can't ask her if I can't find her."

"Ask among the clerks from Wentworth and Penrose," Pamela said. "They doubtless have their favorite pubs and chop shops, the same as all of London. The City thrives on the custom of the counting house clerks."

The City of London, which encompassed the walled bounds of old Roman Londinium, had traditionally been the safest place for merchants to transact business. As Britain's trading empire had grown, the heart of English finance had remained within and near those walls even as the metropolis had sprawled to the west along the Thames.

The infant seized Jack's thumb and, like every healthy baby, tried to put what he grasped into his mouth.

"Ask where my own cousin has got off to?" Jack mused around a mouthful of bread. If Ellie had spun some yarn for the bank about influenza or lung fever, nosy questions could undermine that story.

"Ask if they're hiring, if they've heard of any work for a man who's good with numbers. I'd like to know that you have a job before Clyde and I head north."

"You're definitely leaving Town?" Clyde had still said nothing to Jack about this decision.

"Clyde wants to be back in Scotland by New Year's. I'll let Ellie know the next time she comes calling."

Mick was off to Antwerp, Ellie nowhere to be found, and now Pamela was leaving for bloody Scotland? "I don't like this, Pammie. We do better when we stick together."

"I married Clyde more than five years ago. His family is in Scotland, and Mick shouldn't come back this way for some time, if ever."

True enough. "Then I'll wish you well, and thanks for the tea and sympathy." Jack finished his bread, the first food he'd had since yesterday, and would have risen, except the baby bit him hard on thumb. "You wretched little rascal!"

Pamela smacked the infant gently on the nose. "For shame, Mickey mine. You'll get food poisoning snacking on our Jackie."

Jack shook his abused hand—the rascal had exactly four tiny teeth—and downed the last drops of the tea. "I might come to Scotland with you. No sense biding here if Ellie's going to ignore her own family."

"Talk to Clyde," Pamela said, positioning the baby on her hip. "I have all I can do to keep track of the children."

Pamela wasn't prepared to argue for Jack to join the caravan to Edinburgh, in other words. Nothing like family loyalty when a man was down on his luck.

"I'll do that. Stay warm, and mind the weather. Looks like we're in for more snow."

"Winter has arrived," Pamela said. "Can the head colds and lung fevers be far behind?"

Jack had been fed, he'd been fortified by a cup of tea, and Pamela was right: Ellie had found a job at a bank, and she was female. A man equally versed in ciphering might be able to do likewise.

Chapter Eleven

I will look back on this week and recall that once, I was happy.

That refrain had run through Ellie's mind for the past two days, as Elsmore had shared quiet meals with her, asked her opinion on what to do with this or that farm, and told her stories of his boyhood escapades.

He had not—thank heavens—renewed his inquiries about Ellie's family.

Elsmore, to Ellie's surprise and delight, was an affectionate man. When he held her cloak, he patted her shoulders. If they wandered arm in arm down a row of stalls in the stable, his hand rested over hers. When he wanted to point out a portrait of him with a trio of blond, smiling boy cousins, he took her hand simply to guide her along the gallery.

He never presumed or gave the servants reason to gawk, but he let Ellie know that he enjoyed touching her and being with her, whatever the reason.

When they piled into a sleigh to admire the view from the belvedere, he tucked in right beside her and gave her a turn at the reins, a pleasure she hadn't known since childhood. He kissed her at the top of the tower's steps, a stolen pleasure where nobody could see them and nothing more than a kiss could transpire.

"That's the home farm," he said, leading Ellie to the railing and pointing to a plume of smoke drifting up through the trees to the east. "There and there are two of the tenancies."

A tidy estate village huddled at the foot of a rise to the west, and to the northeast, a gray pall gathered on the horizon.

"London," Elsmore said, wrapping his arms around Ellie from behind. "That it should wear a mantle of darkness seems appropriate."

Ellie was comforted to think he'd be sad to leave the next day. "But now you know where the boggy ground is with your account books. I hope that makes the darkness less oppressive."

Unfortunately, the boggy ground lay mostly with his London household. A steward in Northamptonshire was sloppy, perhaps a matter of needing spectacles, for the mistakes went in all directions. Elsmore's aunties were overstating expenses, and a widowed cousin was engaged in the occasional 3-for-5 swap, but the other holdings were reasonably well accounted for.

"Actually, no," Elsmore said, turning loose of her and propping his elbows on the balustrade. "I must confront four female family members and ask them why they have been dishonest with me. My cousin in particular bothers me, because I'm putting two of her boys through Oxford, and I increased her quarterly remittance only last year."

"Ask for receipts," Ellie said. "Tell them you are check-ing up on your accountants and ask for receipts."

"They can falsify those too, can't they? You accurately stated some time ago that as long as I am not doing business directly with the person supplying the invoices, I am to some degree at the mercy of whoever is incurring the cost."

This apparently bothered him, but for the first time in her life, Ellie did not want to discuss figures, ciphers, or account books. The insight was...daunting, for all too often, she'd insisted that a conversation remain rooted in numbers, when the other party had tired of the subject.

She and her duke had so little time left, though, and she did not want to spend the waning hours discussing two pounds here and a shilling there.

"Hold me," she said, moving into Elsmore's embrace.

His arms came around her securely, no need to ask again. "We have reached the end of our task, have we not?"

"We have. I will send you a summary of my findings next week." Ellie had suspicions about the goings-on at his bank, but those concerns were beyond her marching orders. "I will miss you, Elsmore. I had become a walking abacus, nothing to occupy me but the next report or statement, as a starving cat thinks only of mice. Nobody sees me as anything else, and I convinced myself that was for the best."

"I see you as much more than that."

She knew he did. He asked her opinion about whether to offer a tenant's son articles for a clerkship, and then he *listened* to her reply. He grumbled about his sisters' pro-spective beaus, as he'd grumble to a friend. He braided her hair, then unbraided it, all the while discussing the Irish question with her.

In the evening, he sat patiently with Ellie, reading

while she worked at her accounting, occasionally reciting a humorous passage for her, quibbling with the author's turn of phrase.

"I saw you as merely a duke," Ellie said. "Those words should not make sense in the English language—merely a duke—for what status could be more intriguing than that of a man who ranks below a king and often has more power than one?"

The sun was traveling the inevitable journey to the horizon, the temperature dropping. The gray haze over London had acquired a fiery red underbelly, and Ellie's heart was breaking.

"How do you see me now, Eleanora?"

You are the man I love, the man I must leave. "You have become a friend, Elsmore. An intimate friend. I will always treasure the time spent with you."

Even as the countryside settled in for another frigid night, Ellie was warm in her lover's embrace. He sheltered her from the elements and from a loneliness so crushing she dreaded her return to it, but he could not shelter her from the reality that they must part.

"I would like to be more than a friend, Eleanora. Much more."

If she'd been any other woman besides Eleanora Naylor, granddaughter of the disgraced Jacob Naylor, sister and cousin and—most damning of all—*daughter* to ne'er-do-wells and criminals, she would have accepted his offer.

Her own cousin had very likely stolen from him, though. Her mother lived an isolated life under an assumed name in France. Her grandparents didn't dare even write to her. And as for poor Papa…

"I cannot be your mistress, Elsmore. You would grow tired of me, and I would miss my ledgers."

He rested his cheek against her temple. "You daft woman, I am asking you to be my wife."

Ellie first heard the affection in his endearment—*you daft woman*—then the sense of his words cut through the fog of sorrow and longing in her heart. She wiggled away, though she had to be insistent about leaving his embrace.

"Your wife? I do not understand. *You are a duke.* You do not marry a bank auditor."

"His Grace of Chandos married a hostler's castoff wife. Bought her at a wife sale, in fact. His Grace of Devonshire married the mistress with whom he and his first duchess had lived in an open arrangement for years. He did so with his late duchess's blessing and nobody dared refuse to receive any of them. John of Gaunt, a royal duke, married his children's governess after having four illegitimate children with her. This fiction that a duke cannot marry where he pleases is a recent invention designed to serve everybody's interests but the duke's."

Ellie's grasp of the aristocracy's history was shaky, but she was absolutely certain that she and Elsmore could not marry.

"I don't know how to waltz." A stupid fact to seize on, but a lack she was acutely aware of. Only women with wealth, free time, and social ambitions learned how to waltz.

"I'll teach you."

"I have no money."

"I have more than I need, and you are eminently capable of showing me how to be a better steward of it."

"Elsmore, I am *not* suitable. I will *never* be suitable, and I *cannot* marry you."

He took a step closer, and again, Ellie was reminded that she dealt with a powerful man, one who had the means to get what he wanted usually on the terms that suited him.

"You *can* marry me. You deal with me honestly. You take my interests to heart when you could have easily led me in a dance about my own accounts. You make love with me as if I matter to you."

Oh, he did matter. He did, he did. But even Elsmore could not forgive a duchess whose associations would drag his name through the gutters and expose his bank to scandal. If Mick's role in the Butterfield scheme ever came to light, the bank would fail in a week flat.

And this marriage Elsmore proposed would fail even more quickly.

"My antecedents are not proper," Ellie said, a vast and fraught understatement. "You must take my word for that. I am not a lady, as Devonshire's mistress was. I am not good *ton* and I never will be. I care for you, Elsmore, more than I can say, and because I care for you, I cannot be your duchess."

He was half a step away, and the compulsion to seek his embrace was a physical pain. Ellie stood her ground and saw the battle in his eyes. Elsmore could harangue her and browbeat her, he could interrogate her and wear her down...or he could respect her decision.

Argue with me, Ellie silently pleaded. *Bicker and fume and give me the smallest pretext for turning my heartache into anger and resentment.*

He kissed her forehead, a brush of warmth in the growing chill. "I will never love another as I love you, Eleanora, and I will not pretend otherwise to spare your sensibilities. We are honest with each other. Your candor is an attribute I have always treasured about you."

She could never be honest with him. "I am sorry, Elsmore. We would not suit."

He stepped away, his gaze going to the snowy expanse

spreading out from the manor house below. He owned a small kingdom, but more than that, he carried responsibility for a kingdom's worth of souls. Above all else, Ellie regretted leaving him alone with that burden.

"We should be going," she said. "Cook will expect us back in time for dinner."

Elsmore offered his arm, and they descended into the gloom of the stairway without another word.

* * *

Rex wasn't giving up without a fight, and he had Eleanora Hatfield to thank for igniting his willingness to join battle. For too long, he'd been the doting brother, the indulgent cousin, the dutiful nephew. His largesse was so taken for granted that petty thievery had sprung up among his nearest and dearest.

He'd deal with that affront upon his return to London. For now, he had one more night with Eleanora, and he would use it to give her every possible doubt about her rejection of his suit.

"How did you come to be an auditor?" he asked, tossing another log onto the fire in her sitting room.

"By merest chance."

She'd been quiet all through dinner, and when Rex would have taken himself off to the solitary splendor of the ducal bed, she'd clasped his hand and led him to her quarters.

"I cannot believe chance alone resulted in your expertise, Eleanora." He sat beside her on the sofa and draped an arm around her shoulders. She cuddled up as if this had become their routine, which in a very few days, it had.

"I was without means," she said, "my family having

come into some bad luck. My cousins and I were loose on the streets for most of the day, and because dressing as a boy was safer, that's how I went about. I was slight and easily hid my gender."

Rex *hated* that she'd been left to fend for herself, that she'd known poverty and danger. "Go on."

"I took any odd job, of course. Crossing sweeper, errand boy, porter, links boy. I was loitering outside a haberdasher's, hoping for some packages to carry, when a gentleman emerged, his footman trailing behind and laden with parcels."

Rex saw those children every day, cluttering up London's streets, scavenging its alleys. He'd never considered that some of the destitute were girls whose very gender made them even less safe than the boys.

"Tell me the rest, Eleanora. If I have to call out some old blighter because he disrespected you, I will."

She kissed his cheek. "You will do no such thing. The gentleman had dropped his receipt. I handed it back to him and pointed out that the total was off by one shilling and tuppence. He asked me how I'd seen that mistake at a glance, and I hadn't an answer for him."

"You thought everybody did math without thinking about it."

"Most of my family can, and they'd certainly never seen my ability as remarkable. Numbers behave in a predictable and orderly fashion, and I grasped those rules without much effort."

While life on the street was predictable only insofar as it involved suffering. The sitting room was toasty, but Rex draped a crocheted afghan around Eleanora's shoulders.

"He spotted your talent, this gentleman?"

"He spotted the talent of a grubby boy and offered to article me as a clerk. For the first year, I had to maintain the fiction of boyhood."

And thus did a girl learn to spot every detail of dress, every nuance of gait and expression. "You were able to shed that fiction?"

"I was lucky. My employer was both kind and shrewd. He realized within a month that I did not need instruction regarding the keeping of books or the management of accounts. He was a cloth merchant who also owned mills, and he caught me one day with the silk inventory."

"Caught you?" Not stealing. Eleanora would no more steal from an employer than Rex would get roaring drunk in the middle of a Mayfair avenue.

"I had never touched silk before, and the feel of it was magic. Nothing is as soft, as smooth and warm, and the way silk loves the light...I was enraptured, and my mannerisms gave me away."

After a year, in an unguarded moment, she'd faltered in her disguise. "Did he keep you on anyway?"

"I was indispensable by then, and hiding my gender was becoming more and more difficult. He told me to stay home for two weeks, then to apply as a girl for work at his offices. On the Continent, women can be clerks, and my employer traveled back to Hanover frequently. He explained hiring me to his junior managers as a favor he must do for a fellow merchant, and besides, that unreliable Naylor boy had run off, hadn't he?"

Naylor. Her family name was Naylor. Mr. Hatfield had been a fiction in more than one sense of the word.

"You were soon running his business."

"I had already been running his business, but in the two weeks that I'd been absent, one of the other clerks had instituted a three-for-five scheme. That was my first audit, and I've been auditing ever since."

This recitation left enormous gaps in Eleanora's history, but it also explained how she'd climbed from destitution into a relatively comfortable profession.

"And Wentworth and Penrose has no idea what a treasure they have in you." She was so much more than an auditor. She should have been a bank director, if not manager of the whole enterprise.

"My wages are generous, Elsmore. Wentworth and Penrose treats me well, and I manage my money carefully."

By purchasing portable items of silver, like an itinerant peddler never welcome anywhere for long. The notion made Rex demented with worry for her.

"Do you fear Penrose and Walden will learn of your humble origins, Eleanora?"

"His Grace of Walden knows something of my past," she said. "He respects my privacy."

Well, hell. "Does your privacy require that you sleep alone tonight?"

She rustled about until she was straddling Rex's lap. "My privacy requires no such thing. I will have my bed to myself for the rest of my days, I'd like to spend this last night with you."

Even as she commenced kissing him and casting his wits to the night wind, he gathered a scintilla of comfort from what she'd admitted: She did not foresee another man taking his place in her bed, and that was fitting, because he'd never love another as he loved her.

* * *

Ellie's tale about the great good fortune that had befallen her outside the haberdashery all those years ago was the truth. She could disclose that much of her past only because she and her duke would say farewell on the morrow, likely never to see each other again.

That should have been a relief, should have been a burden lifted, to think of parting from a man who saw her too clearly and cared for her too dearly.

Ellie had cried for days when her mother had moved to France. She'd cried for two hundred miles when she had left her grandparents in York. She'd told herself then that attachments came at too high a cost, and had kept her distance since that day from even her own sister.

The prospect of parting from Elsmore multiplied her capacity for regret by ten, but then, he'd increased her capacity for joy a hundredfold.

"You'll stay with me tonight?" she asked, curling down against his shoulder.

His arms came around her, so welcoming and sheltering. "Of course, if you want me to, Eleanora. That you find me acceptable for a dalliance but not as a suitor is puzzling." His tone balanced humor and genuine bewilderment. His touch on her back was beguilingly gentle.

My cousin stole from your bank and put your whole family at risk of ruin. A hanging felony, and probably the least impediment to further dealings with Elsmore. *My other cousin has worked every rig and scheme known to the criminal mind, and my father taught them everything they know.* Instead, she kissed Elsmore with all the regret in her, for the time they could not have together, for the truths she could never share with him.

She kissed him for joy too, though. For parts of herself reclaimed from banishment, for physical pleasures she'd never thought to experience again. She kissed him for being an honorable man whom privilege might have made a lesser creature by far.

"Eleanora, if we don't remove to the bed now, I will soon be naked in your sitting room."

She loved seeing him naked. "Talk," she said, drawing the pin from his cravat. "Idle male boasting, which never did win fair maid."

He rose with her wrapped around his waist. "Indifference," he said. "Grand, impenetrable female indifference, which has prompted more male foolishness than drink and arrogance combined. Do you truly want me to share your bed tonight, Eleanora? I will not take offense regardless of your answer."

Guilt singed the edges of the emotional riot in Ellie's heart. She was being greedy, demanding another night with him and then abandoning him.

"Elsmore, if I could have the rest of my life with you, as your mistress, your paramour, your wife, your steward—anything—I'd like nothing better. Our stations are too different, and you'd come to regret our association. You must believe me when I say that—"

He braced her back against the door jamb and kissed her. "You believe this drivel you're spouting. Pray do me the courtesy of not telling *me* what to believe, for I know my own heart, Eleanora." He'd spoken gently, but his kiss was ferocious, unlike any of his previous overtures. When he carried Ellie to the bed, his embrace spoke of determination and primal desire, not of courtship or ducal affection.

And that unfettered male need freed Ellie to match him passion for passion. That they should part was necessary—and wrong, so very wrong. That she could love him and know that her regard was returned was right and true and *good*.

Clothing became a foe to be vanquished. His coat went sailing to the reading chair, her dress was flung over the vanity. Breeches ended up draped over the privacy screen, stays fell to the floor. Before Ellie could untie the garters holding up her stockings, Elsmore had her on the bed, more than six feet of aroused duke pinning her to the mattress.

"Please, Elsmore. Don't make me—"

Then he was inside her in one unerring, glorious thrust, and Ellie's body took flight. He laughed, redoubling her pleasure, then went still, nuzzling her neck.

"Elsmore, I will have my revenge for that." She'd meant to sound authoritative, not as if she'd just won the local hill race.

He wrapped her close. "Do you promise, Eleanora? Will you take your revenge until we are the most sated and spent pair of lovers this side of myth?"

"I will give it my very best effort, you varlet."

He began to move, slowly, and she did give it her very best effort, but before the cold winter dawn arrived, she also gave in to silent, wrenching tears.

* * *

Low ceilings, roaring fires, and bodies densely packed on settles and benches ensured that the average London tavern was warm even on a winter evening. Jack Naylor found that loitering at the Bull and Baron was still a challenge for a man with a functional nose.

The stink of wet wool, mud, sweat, and worse filled the pub's air. As long as Jack nursed a pint—and a lady's pint at that—the innkeeper said nothing, though his wife cast Jack many a chiding glance. She was small, dark-haired, and nondescript, also as quick as a bullwhip with a hard word for an overly flirtatious tavern maid.

Jack would have found friendlier surrounds, but this was one of several pubs catering to the clerks and accountants employed at the nearby banks and counting houses. He sat at the end of a long communal table and listened for word of anybody getting ready to quit his post or any business that might be hiring.

So far, the effort had been fruitless. The Bull and Baron was his last stop, the taverns closer to the City having been a waste of coin and time.

"Mind if I join you?"

The gent was too well dressed to be a clerk. His gray wool greatcoat had three capes, and his walking stick looked to be carved mahogany with a silver handle and a brass—not gold—ferrule. His attire spoke of prosperity and good taste, rather than great wealth.

A manager then, or investor of some sort.

"Please have a seat," Jack said, opting for public school accents. He was in his accountant's attire, shabby around the edges but proper enough.

"You've been working on that pint for nearly an hour," the gent said. "Might I buy you another?"

Another pint was good, failing to notice an observant stranger was bad; but then, Jack had been focused on the clerks and working men, not the occasional swell.

"Thank you kindly," Jack said, extending a hand. "Jason Tolliver, at your service."

"Mr. Tolliver, good evening. You may call me Mr. Edwards."

A lie for a lie. A promising start to a conversation. "Evening, Mr. Edwards. Beastly cold out."

Edwards signaled for a waitress and ordered two pints and a plate of toasted ham and cheese sandwiches.

The hour was growing late by the standards of working-men, which meant Jack and Mr. Edwards had their end of the table to themselves.

"Are you in the banking line, Mr. Tolliver?"

"As it happens, I am an accountant, sir."

Edwards put a pair of fur-lined black gloves on the table. "Do you perchance work for Dorset and Becker? I am new to London, but have heard good things about them."

This man was no more new to London than Jack was in line for the throne. The cut of his coat alone testified to Bond Street tailoring, and his gloves hadn't been stitched by any provincial seamstress.

"Dorset and Becker is a venerable institution, sir, though their clerks prefer the Handy Harper, two streets to the east. The fellows enjoying a pint here are mostly employed by Wentworth and Penrose, while I am not at present affiliated with any specific bank."

The tavern maid came over with two pints and a plate heaped with toasted sandwiches. Jack's mouth watered at the scent of the hot ham and cheese, though he focused on draining the last of his lady's pint before accepting the larger drink.

"This is too much for one person," Edwards said. "You must help me with it, lest I commit the cardinal transgression of wasting good food."

The charm fell flat, but Jack wasn't in a position to quibble. "Generous of you, Mr. Edwards. Where do you hail from?"

"Lately, I've been sojourning in the north. Peebleshire was my most recent billet before traveling south."

He wasn't *from* Peebleshire, unless Peebles had started producing English toffs with Eton diction and Oxford vocabularies.

"Pretty up that way, I hear." Jack waited until Edwards had chosen a sandwich, then selected the smallest of the lot. "Cold though, I imagine."

Now came the interesting part of the discussion, when somebody made an offer, and somebody else considered that offer. Jack could casually comment that it was a hard time of year to be out of work, or he might intimate that it was too bad the banks weren't hiring—for they apparently weren't. Instead, he focused on appreciating some of the best food to be had anywhere in the realm, good old English pub fare.

"Cold doesn't begin to describe the Borders this time of year," Edwards said, tearing off a corner of his sandwich and popping it into his mouth. "As one familiar with the local financial community, Mr. Tolliver, where would you put your trust, if you had to choose a bank? I'm looking for an institution of spotless character, one that puts reputation before any other consideration."

So great was Jack's pleasure at good, hot food and a fresh pint that he answered with only half a thought.

"Dorset and Becker goes back for centuries and caters to the nobs. Schilling's is Quaker-owned, and they tend to be cautious with their coin. Wentworth and Penrose isn't so high in the instep, but some say that makes them ferociously careful with their customers' money."

Ellie, at least, was unfailingly cautious when it came to Wentworth and Penrose accounts, and that doubtless kept the whole place on the proper side of prudent.

"Wentworth and Penrose, you say?" Edwards took out a silk handkerchief bearing a coat of arms monogrammed in gold and red. He patted his lips, his display of breaking bread apparently concluded, and laid the handkerchief next to his gloves.

"Wentworth's is a fine bank," Jack said, "though of recent origin. One of the owners has come up in the world in the past few years, but I've never heard a breath of scandal associated with the place. Schilling's is equally respected and has been around decades longer."

Jack did not want Edwards sniffing about Ellie's bank, particularly when Ellie had yet to return from wherever she'd got off to.

"You don't particularly trust Dorset and Becker?" Edwards asked.

Jack helped himself to a larger half sandwich. "I don't know them well, sir."

"So you haven't heard anything unflattering about Dorset's. You're simply unable to venture an opinion?"

This quibbling was most odd. "I did hear that Dorset and Becker had a recent spot of trouble, sir. Nothing major, just an older client being a bit forgetful. The unfortunate thing is, when there's a problem with an account or a ledger and that problem is resolved, we tend to go on our way thinking we're immune to further difficulties."

"Like putting a coin in the poor box absolves us of charitable obligations for the week?"

Was *that* how the wealthy so easily ignored the suffering of their neighbors? No wonder the church poor boxes were so small.

"Something like that, sir. Find one error, and you can miss three others."

"Then you're saying Dorset and Becker might have let down their guard?"

The conversation wasn't going where Jack had thought it would, but ye gods, the food was wonderful. "To some extent. They might be on the lookout for another crochety old gent, but they wouldn't see a poor widow standing before them with larceny in her heart."

And whatever else was true, Jack suspected Mr. Edwards—who was not Mr. Edwards—had larceny in *his* heart. He'd barely touched the food and drink, and any man wiping his mouth on monogrammed silk was hardly the sort to frequent the Bull and Baron.

"Eve did hoodwink Adam into tasting that apple, didn't she?" Edwards mused.

"Wasn't it more a matter of the serpent doing the hoodwinking?"

Edwards regarded him for a long moment, his air distracted. "Mr. Tolliver, you have given me much to think about. I'll wish you good day."

He set a few coins on the table, gathered up his effects, and sauntered out into the frigid darkness. He'd overpaid by more than a few pennies, but Jack left the money on the table. The food and drink he'd enjoy, while Edwards's coin bore a hint of ill-gotten means.

Ellie was living a decent life, Clyde and Pammie were after honest work up north, and Mick wasn't likely to return to London for some time. Jack picked up the plate of sandwiches and Edwards's nearly full glass of ale and moved to the table closest to the fire.

He had a full belly, he was warm, and he'd not put a foot on the far side of the law for nearly half a year. The months of not watching every step, not living like a crook, not avoiding Ellie's pointed questions and fulminating looks had been dull.

Blessedly, wonderfully dull.

Chapter Twelve

Rex walked into the Dorset and Becker lobby, for once using the front door rather than the private entrance favored by the bank employees.

How would Eleanora see this place?

He'd parted from her a week ago, bowing over her hand in the corridor outside of her rooms because he had not trusted himself to see her into her apartment. His final moments with her had been free of begging, pleading, and idiot declarations only because Lord Stephen Wentworth might have overheard any conversation that took place at Eleanora's door.

Rex stood for a moment in a corner of the bank lobby, an oppressive gloom affording him anonymity. The skylights hadn't been cleaned within his memory. The clerestory windows, so necessary to ventilation in the warmer months, were all but covered with soot. The walls behind the sconces needed a good scrubbing, and half the candles in the chandelier were guttered.

This was all doubtless excused under the heading of economies, though Eleanora had pointed out that clerks could hardly keep accurate tallies of ledgers they couldn't see.

The lobby smelled of coal smoke—all of London smelled of coal smoke—with an under-note of muddy boots, damp leather, and ink lending a cramped and tired air to what should have been a dignified and businesslike enterprise.

"Your Grace." Old Mr. Ballentyre smiled up at him owlishly. "Good day. Might I help you with something?"

Ballentyre had been on his way out the door, though by Rex's reckoning, the lunch hour was still twenty minutes off.

"Ballentyre, when did our establishment become so dingy?"

"Dingy, Your Grace?"

Rex took him by the elbow and steered him to the door that separated the bank's public and private spaces.

"Dingy, dank, and uninviting. No wonder Mr. Butterfield was so easily impersonated. It's a miracle the tellers can see their own accountings."

For a week, Rex had avoided Dorset and Becker, focusing instead on settlements to propose for his sisters should the bachelors find their courage. In the back of his mind, Eleanora's memory had chided him for not confronting what could be more complicated problems at Dorset and Becker.

"Perhaps Your Grace would like to join me for a bite to eat," Ballentyre said, stumping along beside Rex. "We're always pleased to see our directors on the premises, of course, and Your Grace especially, but one does grow peckish."

When had Ballentyre become so rotund and so lame?

"Elsmore." Cousin Howell stood in the doorway to an office, a ledger book clutched to his middle as if it protected his modesty. "Good day."

"Howell, good day."

Ballentyre was eating too well, while Howell looked skinny and anxious. Rex noticed these attributes and saw them as reasons for suspicion, which was more of Eleanora's influence. Howell's wages were generous. Why shouldn't he be eating well and dressing a bit more fashionably? Ballentyre's means weren't that lavish. Why would he be in a position to indulge gluttony?

"Was there something you wanted, Elsmore?" Howell asked, setting his ledger aside. "I'm not aware of any directors' meetings today." He fluffed his cravat and shot his cuffs, neither of which sported any lace.

"I *want* to see how my bank is doing, Howell." *I want to get off my ducal backside and notice what's right in front of my face, lest Eleanora be ashamed of me.*

Ballentyre stared at the worn carpet.

Howell looked past Elsmore's shoulder. "Well, you do have an office here. Don't let me stop you from occupying it."

James happened by, also attired for the elements. Did a bank manager really need a silver-handled walking stick?

"Are we having a meeting?" he asked. "Elsmore, will you join Ballie and me for lunch? Howell, you should come along as well, and I'll see if Eddie is free."

I did not come here to socialize or be press-ganged into another family gathering. "I must decline, but please enjoy your meal."

"Ballie?" James gestured with his walking stick. "Shall we?"

"'Deed we shall, sir. 'Deed we shall. Your Grace, good day." He toddled off, James at his side.

"Do they take lunch together frequently?" Rex asked Howell. Not a pairing he would have anticipated.

"Mostly on Saturdays. Eddie sometimes goes with them."

"And where is dear Edward?"

Howell sidled back into his office. "Why all the questions, Elsmore?"

Rex followed him, because a man's professional space could say a lot about him. Eleanora would have read Howell's office like a theater program—who mattered to him, what mattered, his aspirations and frustrations...

Howell took the seat behind the desk. Correspondence was neatly stacked on the blotter, the ink was capped, the pens trimmed and laid tidily in their tray.

"Rachel and Samantha have attracted the notice of potential suitors," Rex said.

"My cousins are lovely women," Howell replied. "Of course they have devoted followers. What has that to do with you lurking in corridors and interrogating me about Eddie?"

"Where is he?"

Howell twisted a signet ring on his smallest finger. "I'm not sure. The tailor's, the bootmaker's. On sale days he sometimes wanders by Tatts. He frequently lunches at one of his clubs."

Look for patterns, Eleanora had said, and Eddie was creating a pattern of inattention to his work. "He already has a matched pair of chestnuts and a riding horse. Why attend the sales at Tatts?"

Howell took off the ring and slipped it into his pocket. "You'll have to ask him that. I am not my brother's governess."

The same unease Rex had felt when he'd poked his nose into the ducal accounts crept down his spine.

"I did not mean to imply that you were anybody's governess." Rex closed the door and took the chair opposite Howell's desk. "Have you had occasion to stop by Wentworth and Penrose's establishment lately?"

"I have not. Gentlemen don't spy on other gentlemen."

"I don't propose that you spy, Howell. I propose that you remain alert to your surroundings, that you watch and you see, you listen and you *hear*...I've given the ducal estate books a good going over, because as soon as my sisters bring some hopeful swain up to scratch, the solicitors will descend like starlings on a crust of bread. I was not pleased at what I found."

Howell took out his penknife—plain, no engraving on the handle—and put a finer point on a goose quill that hadn't needed trimming. "What did you find?"

"I found a duke who is never too busy to stand up with one of the aunties' regiment of goddaughters but who hasn't a clue about the price of coal. That same duke squires his sisters about wherever they please to go but hadn't realized the steward in Northumberland has all but gone blind. I have become complacent, Howell. I'm a titled footman ordered here and there by my family while I neglect the financial duties I have been charged to execute since my birth."

Howell, rather than provide Rex with excuses and remonstrations, looked thoughtful. "You are somewhat under petticoat government, true enough."

"And I love the ladies dearly, but if the family is to thrive, I also need to attend to my ledgers."

Howell swept the trimmings into his palm and dumped them in the dustbin. "That is a bloody lot of ledgers, Elsmore."

"The sooner I begin, the sooner I'll know where we stand. Any recommendations for where I should start?"

"With mine," Howell said, going to a cabinet beside the window. "I don't mind telling you that Ballentyre has grown a bit lax, and I'm as prone to mistakes as any man." He took out a pair of volumes bound in green leather. "I suspect we'd get better results from old Ballie if the review happened prior to his daily pilgrimage to the pub rather than after."

"Ballentyre always reviews your weekly tallies?"

"And I review his, which is becoming a thankless task."

"What about Eddie and James?"

"They trade ledgers, as Ballentyre and I do."

The family swell and the family man-about-town traded ledgers. A month ago, Rex would have shrugged and gone whistling on his way. He could hear Eleanora Hatfield warning him that shrugs goeth before a fall.

"If you would be good enough to have your ledgers brought to my office, I'll begin there."

Howell piled a third volume on top of the first two. "Elsmore, you might not like what you find here at the bank either."

"I don't expect perfection, Howell, but I do expect us to uphold the trust our customers place in us, and they are not paying me to waltz."

* * *

"Eleanora, *êtes-vous en bonne santé*?" The Duchess of Walden held out a plate of cinnamon biscuits to go with her polite question.

"I am in good health, thank you, Your Grace. No sweets for me."

The duchess sat back and stroked the ears of the hound seated at her knee. "No sweets, two sips of tea, longing glances at the window, and you haven't attempted a word of French since you arrived. I have never before seen you daunted, Eleanora. Not when your sister nearly died in childbed, not when you had to battle Lord Stephen for a peek at his estate ledgers, not when His Grace demanded you travel about the realm as his personal avenger of financial sloth and inaccuracy."

I was daunted. I am almost always daunted, but I could admit that only to Elsmore. "Perhaps a megrim or a head cold stalks me."

"Or a broken heart?"

The dog, an enormous black hellbeast, came over to Ellie's chair, sat, and put its chin on her knee.

"I never cry."

The dog gazed up at her, and that—kindness, even from a dumb animal—had a tear slipping down her cheek.

"I hate this."

"But you love Wrexham, Duke of Elsmore." The duchess spoke gently, which only sent a second tear following in the path of the first.

"His familiars call him Rex. It suits him. I must never see him again." Ellie fished out the handkerchief he'd given her, the one she took with her everywhere. She didn't use it to wipe her eyes—her tea napkin served for that purpose. Instead, she traced the crowned unicorn rampant on his coat of arms.

"Did *he* tell you that you must never see him again?"

Oh, this hurt. This gentle peeling away of layers of heartache hurt and hurt and hurt. "He did not. I'm thinking of moving to France or at least of returning to York."

"You aren't thinking at all." The duchess handed Ellie

the half-finished cup of tea, and Ellie drank, not because her hostess was a duchess, but because she was Jane, wife of Quinn Wentworth, and the mother of his three daughters.

"I feel as if I have lost every whit of sense and direction I ever had," Ellie said, folding Elsmore's handkerchief in careful eighths. "My sums no longer interest me. My work has become boring." She tucked the handkerchief away and stroked the dog's head.

He scooted closer, as if he'd climb into her lap on the least provocation.

"Perhaps your work has served its purpose," the duchess said. "His Grace was able to step back from the bank once the children came along, though until that point, he struggled to keep up with the bank, the estates, his siblings, *me*."

"The Duke of Walden *struggled*?" The only struggle Ellie had seen her employer endure was the struggle not to thump the heads of any who brought waste, inefficiency, or sloth to their work.

"My husband knows exactly how to go on in business," the duchess said. "Exactly, precisely. His sense of true north is unwavering. He doesn't lie, cheat, steal, go back on his word, or—to hear him tell it—make exceptions. A bargain is a bargain, his word is his bond, and all that other huffing and puffing. A two-year-old is a very different article from a mortgage agreement."

"You're saying His Grace could not distinguish between family and business?"

The dog settled at Ellie's feet, his chin on the toe of her boot.

"Walden could not distinguish between life and business. He knew great poverty as a child, and no safety whatsoever. For him, safety boiled down to having so much money that nobody could jeopardize the welfare of those he loved." The duchess took a sip of her tea, looking elegant even in so mundane a gesture. "I do believe my darling puppy has fallen in love."

I have fallen in love. As true, lamentable, and wonderful as that sentiment was, something in the duchess's words tickled the edge of Ellie's mind.

"I haven't delivered my final notes to Elsmore yet," she said. "I have most of my report written, and it's all very tidy, but I read over it, and feel I'm missing something." Ellie was missing *him*, of course, but she was also failing to see a pattern that should be obvious. An important pattern that hovered just beyond her awareness.

"Elsmore's sister, Lady Rachel, appears to have attached the affections of a suitor," the duchess said. "Lord Jeremy Bledsoe. Excellent lineage, sweet young man. Elsmore will soon have more family, and he's already awash in relatives."

"He puts the male cousins without other prospects to work at the bank," Ellie said. "I know the head of the family is expected to use his influence for the benefit of his relations, but..."

The dog sat up.

"But?" the duchess echoed, a cinnamon biscuit halfway to her mouth.

"But all of the family accounts..." Ellie could not disclose Elsmore's financial arrangements to anybody. "There is a common thread, and I missed it."

All of the family accounts were handled, ultimately, through the bank, where more family was employed. Ellie had pointed fingers at Elsmore's sisters, aunts, mama, and widowed cousin when, in fact, they were very likely not the issue.

"Your Grace, please excuse me. An urgent matter of business requires my attention."

The duchess set down her biscuit untasted. "I'll have the coach brought around for you."

"I haven't time to wait for the coach, ma'am. I'll just be leaving."

"Take the dog," the duchess said, rising. "Lord Stephen can send him back with a footman. The poor pup hasn't been getting enough exercise because the weather has been so disobliging, but today is at least sunny."

The dog was on his feet, looking toothy and hopeful.

"Very well, I'll take Wodin, but I really must be on my way."

* * *

"Elsmore, a pleasure." Lord Jeremy bowed, shook hands, and took the seat opposite Rex at the table for two. Rex had asked the waiter for a spot in the corner where a man could see who else was in the room without half of them eavesdropping on his conversation.

"My lord, the pleasure is mine." Rex had nearly declined the invitation, because what mattered this empty ritual, when the outcome for his lordship and Lady Rachel was all but assured? And yet, Rachel mattered to Rex very much, and being seen to share a meal with Lord Jeremy was a step in a dance that led to Rachel's wishes coming true.

If ever a fellow had enthusiastically embarked on a courtship, Lord Jeremy was that man. He'd driven out with Rachel, waltzed with her, and walked home from services with her. She beamed at him, played duets with him, and lingered on his arm after the one dance they shared at each gathering.

Having not only seen some of this billing and cooing, but also having heard about it at length from his mother and sisters, Rex was struck by how badly he'd bungled anything resembling a courtship with Eleanora.

"I've taken the liberty of ordering the wine," Rex said, "though we can add to the selection depending on your preferences."

This meal had been at his lordship's invitation, and Rex had come straight from the bank, after an afternoon spent poring over Howell's books. Lord Jeremy was a convivial dinner companion, regaling Rex with family anecdotes and holiday stories.

This too was part of a well-planned courtship, familiarizing the head of the lady's family with the suitor's estates, connections by marriage, and other assets. Why hadn't Rex bothered with these courtesies where Ellie was concerned? His sisters would love her, and she and his mother would be a wicked pair to oppose at whist.

Lord Jeremy ordered beefsteak, which Rex would have predicted, and he drank only sparingly, as did Rex.

"You seem a bit pre-occupied, Elsmore. Will the rest of your evening be spent in more interesting pursuits?"

"I am doubtless expected at the theater later this evening. You are more than welcome to join the party if you'd like."

"Lady Rachel extended an invitation, but you might prefer not to catch sight of me for a bit after I air the next topic."

Rex signaled the waiter to clear their plates.

"Will you gentlemen be having a sweet?" the waiter asked. "Our rum cream cake is not to be missed."

"None for me," Rex said. Of all things, he wanted to return to the bank. Howell's books had been respectably accurate. Occasional errors had been crossed out and corrected rather than carried forward from week to week. Howell, at least, was minding his p's and q's.

A niggling splinter of unease told Rex that Howell might be the exception among the bank's managers.

"Another time for the cream cake, then," Lord Jeremy said.

The waiter cleared the table, leaving the wine and wineglasses, while Rex wondered what Eleanora was having for dinner. Was her cat growling in the corner over a nibble of fish? Had the lady indulged in any wine since returning from Surrey?

"Your Grace is welcome to call me out for the subject I'm about to raise," Lord Jeremy said, "but I feel something must be said."

"Calling suitors out is beneath my dignity, my lord. My sisters and my mother have all had occasion to assure me of this."

His lordship's brows rose, but he acquired the look of a man determined to soldier on. "I am in love with Lady Rachel. I admit this proudly, knowing she might yet decline me with the dreaded speech about we-would-not-suit."

I've heard that speech, and it is to be dreaded. "Go on."

"Her ladyship has recently favored me with her attentions, and my good fortune has been remarked by others."

"If you make my sister the object of gossip, Bledsoe, no power on earth—"

His lordship held up a hand. "Not gossip, Your Grace. Angels defend me, never that. I ran into Lord Norcross at Tatts this week."

Every idle gentleman in London milled around Tattersalls on sale days. Cold weather only meant they stood about nipping from flasks rather than miss a chance to enjoy a parade of good horseflesh and better gossip.

"I hope you found his lordship well." Norcross was another eligible, and last year, Rachel had seemed to favor him.

"He asked me a very curious question, Your Grace. He asked if Lady Rachel had won free of her little attachment to the poppy. He seemed quite concerned for her, else I would have drawn his cork on the spot."

Rex pulled his attention away from Eleanora's cat, Howell's ledgers, and the sheer stupidity of sitting in a theater box week after week when nobody could hear what was said on stage.

"I beg your pardon?"

"Well you might, but I am telling you the truth. Norcross was most confident in his assertion that Lady Rachel is afflicted with a penchant for laudanum. I asked him who would propound such a falsehood and he grew defensive."

"While I am growing furious. Lady Rachel enjoys one of the least excitable dispositions ever bestowed upon woman. She has no need of nerve tonics or laudanum."

"Which is what I told Norcross, though of course, I have never raised the subject with her ladyship."

A delicate and fair question lay in his lordship's rejoinder.

"I have reviewed my family accounts in detail, Bledsoe. No unusual expenditures at the apothecary or herbalist's blight my books." What a pleasure to know that was true.

"Just so, Your Grace, but I thought you should be aware of the exchange."

"I commend your loyalty to the lady. Did Norcross say where he'd heard this rumor?"

Lord Jeremy found it necessary to study the label on the wine bottle. "He wouldn't say, but intimated that somebody of unimpeachable veracity had put a word in his ear last spring. Norcross hinted that it might have been you or a person equally close to her ladyship."

What would Eleanora have made of this development? "Shall I interview Norcross myself?"

"You can't. He caught last night's packet for Calais. I gather he'll spend the holidays there rather than endure Yuletide at his family seat. Do I conclude, Your Grace, that I might mention my aspirations to Lady Rachel in the near future?"

"You may."

Lord Jeremy poured himself the rest of the wine. "A toast, then, to her ladyship's continued good health."

Rex obliged, but then rose. "The matter now lies between the two of you, at least until the solicitors wreak their havoc. Best of luck."

Lord Jeremy stood as well. "Will I see you at the theater, Your Grace?"

The weight of duty pressed down on Rex, another evening spent greeting acquaintances, bantering, pretending he was enjoying himself. Not too much for family to ask, but tonight, that was more than he had to give.

"Not this week," he said. "I am required elsewhere."

Lord Jeremy bowed, then resumed his seat and commenced beaming fatuously at his glass of wine. Rex left him to it, and retrieved his hat and coat from the doorman.

"There you are." The speaker, a young man, started forward from the porter's nook. "I've been looking all over London for you, Your Grace."

The fellow was dark-haired, dark-eyed, and vaguely familiar. "Do I know you?"

"My name is not important. I come bearing a note from Mr. Patrick Entwhistle."

Patrick Entwhistle had been Rex's first tutor...? Which was why he'd given that name to Eleanora to use if she needed to arrange an urgent meeting.

"Not here," Rex said, taking the man by the arm. "Whatever you have to say, it can be said where we have more privacy."

"I have nothing to say." He shoved a note at Rex, folded and sealed. "You don't put hands on Ned Wentworth no matter how many titles you have."

The wording was general, as Rex had once told Eleanora it should be. *The favor of an interview would be appreciated at Your Grace's earliest convenience.*

"Is Mr. Entwhistle well?" Rex asked, jamming his hat onto his head.

"Seems right enough to me, though I keep a safe distance from that personage. Lord Stephen said I wasn't to cease looking until I found you though."

"You've found me, and the requested meeting is convenient for me at this very moment."

Chapter Thirteen

"If you're besotted with Elsmore, you should tell him," Lord Stephen said, leaning against Ellie's doorjamb, cane in hand. "He'll go mad thinking you don't care for him, and while I am ignorant of the particulars, I know a smitten man when I see one."

"Please do come in," Ellie snapped. "Or lounge there at your lordship's leisure, letting out all the warm air while you expound on topics that are none of your concern."

His lordship lurched into the room, closing the door behind himself by virtue of shoving it with his cane.

"You come to my apartment," he said, "demanding that I find you a discreet messenger not in Wentworth livery. You confide the purpose of the errand only to Ned's discretion—the most dubious variety of discretion known to the realm—and then you whirl off, clearly on the verge of strong hysterics. Have a nip."

He held out a silver flask embossed with the Wentworth crest.

"No, thank you. Taking spirits will solve nothing."

"Strong hysterics solve nothing, but I've been known to indulge on many an occasion." He waggled the flask, and Ellie took it mostly to forestall further lecturing.

"What the hell is wrong, madam? If Ned can't find your pet duke, I might be able to help."

Ellie opened the flask and took a sniff. The brandy had an excellent nose, but it wasn't the same as the spirits she'd taken with Elsmore. Even so, the scent brought back memories of snuggling before a wood fire, a country house gone quiet in evening darkness, and a contentment as precious as it was temporary.

"You cannot help, my lord. On second thought, you can, by taking yourself off and forgetting that I prevailed upon Ned to deliver a message. Forget that immediately and entirely."

"Alas, dear lady, an excellent memory is among my greatest failings." Lord Stephen propped himself against the arm of Ellie's reading chair, his bad left leg on the side facing the fire. "I have made further inquiries of my sisters Althea and Constance in the north, for example, and what they had to say was most distressing."

Ellie was desperate to see Elsmore, desperate to convey her suspicions to him. After that…France was looking better and better.

"You can talk to your sisters until the King stops overspending his funds, my lord. I've told you more of my situation than I should have, you are bluffing, and you are prying where—"

A hard rap on the door saved Ellie from hurling his lordship's flask at his head.

"Mrs. Hatfield, it's Ned."

"And Elsmore." This second voice was louder than the first.

"Come in."

And there he was, Elsmore in the flesh, looking a bit tired, a bit worried, and perilously dear. He was still in morning attire, his boots were damp, and his greatcoat was only half-buttoned.

"Your Grace." Ellie curtseyed, mindful of Lord Sticks-His-Nose-Everywhere Wentworth watching this exchange. "Thank you for coming."

"What's *he* doing here?" Elsmore asked, lifting his chin in Lord Stephen's direction.

"I'm engaged in my usual occupation," Lord Stephen said, shoving to his feet. "Trying to talk sense into a rock. You'd think she was a Wentworth, as stubborn as she is. Come along, Ned. Designing incendiary devices is more entertaining than waiting for Eleanora Hatfield to explain that her grandfather got caught on the wrong side of a few rumors, and decades later, she's still afraid of the scandal."

"I am not afraid of a few rumors," Ellie retorted. She was terrified of hanging felonies, charges of accessory after the fact, and a broken heart, not in that order.

"That will be enough, my lord," Elsmore said softly. "I'll bid you and Wentworth good evening."

Ned obligingly marched out the door, while Lord Stephen lingered, leaning on his cane. "Tell the poor man what he needs to know, Eleanora, because as a brilliant auditor has often declared, we cannot solve problems we refuse to face." He offered a slight bow and left with the immense dignity of a man whose every step brought pain.

"I cannot plant him a facer," Elsmore said, unbuttoning his coat, "though somebody dearly needs to."

"Many somebodies already have," Ellie said. "I'm sorry to bother you, but I've been thinking about my final report to you, going over my notes."

"What the hell is that?" Elsmore's gaze was aimed at the hearth.

"That is Wodin, on loan from Her Grace of Walden."

Voltaire was curled up next to the dog, who panted gently and regarded the humans as if surely every sensible canine had a soft, warm, furry little feline companion. Voltaire was purring audibly, nose covered by the tip of her tail.

"What sort of self-respecting pedigreed canine befriends an alley cat?" Elsmore finished undoing his coat, and Ellie let him slip it from his own shoulders and hang it on a peg near the door.

If she touched his coat, she'd want to touch him. If she hung up his coat for him, she'd sniff the wool and brush it against her cheek. If she started crying, she'd never stop.

"A dog raised with cats should be more tolerant of them. What I have to say won't take long, Your Grace, but it strikes me as urgent."

Elsmore ran his hands through his hair and looked around the apartment. "I don't see any ledgers, Eleanora. You always surround yourself with ledgers."

"Might we attend the topic at hand?"

He approached her, looking vexed and determined. "First, tell me what Lord Stephen was babbling about. What happened with your grandfather?"

Ellie whirled away from him, lest he touch her and destroy the last shred of her composure. "Grandfather's circumstances are not relevant to the present inquiry."

Elsmore remained where he was, near the fire. Why must he be so attractive, why must he look at her with such concern?

"When you turn up all duchess-y and impatient, you are nervous," he said. "You have no ink stains on your fingers, Eleanora. Your watch is affixed nowhere on your person.

You are upset. I hope we are friends enough to confide our upsets to each other, for I have a few matters to discuss with you as well."

"I am moving to France." The decision was made on the spot, having seen Elsmore again, having exercised the monumental effort not to lash her arms around him and never let go.

"Does this have to do with your grandfather, the victim of rumors?"

Ellie turned, finding herself face-to-face with the chill coming off her front window. Below her, the street was dark and deserted, the occasional porch light illuminating icy mud and dirty snow.

"He was rumored to be a forger of paintings. He was not a forger."

"Then what was he?" Elsmore's voice came from just behind Ellie.

She could feel him near, feel his curiosity, also his great patience. This man had spent years reconciling himself to obligations he did not enjoy; he'd wait an eternity for Ellie to share the truth with him.

"Grandfather was a fool, a trusting, talented fool, and that is by far a greater offense than copying a few paintings." She sneaked a glance over her shoulder, expecting to see Elsmore's expression go politely blank. Expecting him to step back, to fetch his coat.

"Go on." His eyes held concern and maybe a little surprise. No judgment, no shock. *No betrayal of Ellie's trust in him.*

In for the proverbial penny... She faced Elsmore squarely. "An earl hired my grandfather as a portraitist. Grandfather was—is—very good. He was so good that when the earl asked him to provide copies of a few famous paintings, purely for the earl's private enjoyment, Grandfather easily obliged. He'd made a grand tour in his youth, he had sketchbooks upon sketchbooks filled with likenesses of the great works. Many wealthy families enjoy copies of famous paintings."

"The earl sold the likenesses as the genuine articles."

In one sentence, Elsmore summed up facts that had nearly seen Grandfather's days ended on the gallows.

"Without Grandfather's permission, without his knowledge. While Grandfather was delighted to have a supportive patron of such impressive rank, the earl was sending the paintings to the lesser capitals, claiming the artwork was for sale to discreet private collectors to liquidate the true owners' debts. This went on for two years before anybody realized what was afoot. Back then, marching armies made travel more difficult, and those private collectors had been carefully chosen for reclusive qualities and obscure addresses."

Elsmore stood right before her at the window. A month ago, Ellie would have worried about being seen with a man in her quarters after dark, but the street was empty, not even the chop shop had any customers.

And she was—truly—moving to France.

"What happened when the paintings were discovered to be copies?" Elsmore asked.

"The earl feigned dismay, but he declined to press charges. He made the purchasers whole—I gather two years had seen improvement in his finances—and the duped customers also declined to press charges rather than admit they'd been taken for fools. Grandfather never had another legitimate commission."

The ensuing silence was awkward, though Ellie honestly could not say if she was more sad to share Grandpapa's fate or angry that all these years later, Lord Winston's wrongdoing still hadn't been punished.

"You look pale," Elsmore said, which had nothing to do with anything. "Shall I get us something to eat? Something hot from across the street?"

What mattered food when a family's ruin was under discussion? "No, thank you. I suspect you have a problem at your bank, Your Grace, and that is a more pressing matter than my next bowl of soup."

"Not to me it isn't."

Ellie closed her eyes. "Please don't."

"Don't care about you? Even you, Eleanora, cannot audit genuine regard away from my heart. Shall I fetch us soup, or would you rather have some roast and potatoes?"

"Soup will do." Ellie wasn't hungry, but she needed food. She'd eaten little in the past few days, and still had no appetite.

The duke went to the door, bellowed for "Mr. Wentworth," held a short conversation with somebody in the corridor, and came back to Ellie's side.

"You suspect the author of all my irregular books is employed at the bank, don't you?" he asked, leading Ellie to the sofa.

He spoke so calmly, the import of his words took a moment to penetrate Ellie's misery—and her pleasure at holding his hand.

"I fear that very possibility. All of the family accounts ultimately run through the bank. If you ask your aunties, they will probably tell you they don't total those ledgers— whoever you've assigned to the accounts at the bank does the actual bookkeeping for them after they make the entries. The same will pertain with your widowed cousin and with your sisters' pin money. The common factor is not that your womenfolk are cheating you. It's that their accounting is actually done at the bank."

Elsmore came down beside her, his hand still in hers. "How did you come to this conclusion?"

"I should have spotted it straight off. Who keeps the actual books is not a detail. I was distracted with my money maps, my schemes, my sums." *With you.* She'd missed one of the first aspects of the accountability that made auditing a useful undertaking. She'd tracked who bought the market vegetables, who had pin money, where the duchess's dresses were made, all while she'd neglected to note *who tallied the ledger entries.*

"You are not distracted now. Something caught your eye."

"The handwriting. Numbers are as distinctive to me as literary penmanship when numbers are all I see, and yet…I didn't see it. All of the entries *for the totals* in the various accounts—for your sisters, your aunts, your cousins at university, the widows—are made in the same hand. I've stared at those ledgers for weeks, and not seen what was in front of my face."

"You were too busy plotting your escape to France, and over a few old paintings nobody cares two figs about."

Ellie extricated her hand from Elsmore's, because apparently she needed to instruct a duke on the realities of scandal for the lower orders.

"What fate do you suppose a disgraced painter faces, Your Grace?" *What fate do you suppose awaits that painter's family?* Ellie did not want to embark on this recitation, but neither could she stand the thought that Elsmore would hear the details elsewhere.

"A disgraced painter likely has to travel on the Continent for a time, take lesser work, maybe change his name and produce landscapes or casual art."

The cat stirred, getting up to stretch with the thorough leisure at which cats excelled. The fire gave out good heat, and the moment would have been cozy except that Ellie's heart was breaking all over again.

"That scenario would have been a romp, compared to what Grandfather endured. Bear in mind that the Corsican made travel on the Continent perilous, especially for an Englishman with a family. The earl blackened Jacob Naylor's name, making it obvious that no scoundrel ever deserved hanging more than Naylor had, and only exceptional honor—and concern for Naylor's children—stayed the earl's hand. He told all and sundry that as a well-educated gentleman, he should have known the paintings Naylor found for him were forgeries, and his lordship's humility—his admission of fault—made that Banbury tale convincing."

"Did you ever meet this earl?"

"I saw him, but a painter's young granddaughter is not introduced to a peer."

"How did your family survive?"

"You know the answer to that: We survived any way we could. Grandfather did penny sketches in the pubs. His sons and daughters did anything to bring in a little coin. One aunt became a courtesan of some renown, and that wasn't the worst heartbreak my grandparents had to endure."

"Do you believe I would not marry you just because your aunt became a courtesan before I was even sent off to public school?"

The cat leapt into Ellie's lap and began circling. "You would not marry a courtesan's niece and a disgraced painter's granddaughter. You cannot. You have too much regard for your sisters, for your family, and your bank. Had I only a single wayward aunt, that would be one thing, but a wayward aunt, a forger for a grandfather...I am the last person you can marry."

To say nothing of Mr. Butterfield, and, and, and...

The cat settled in just as a knock on the door had the dog looking up.

"Food," Elsmore said, going to the door. "I am famished. I worked through lunch and did not do justice to my supper. Half the bank came by to gawk at me this afternoon, my sleeves rolled up, ledgers all around me. I don't know whether they were amused or horrified to see a duke wielding an abacus."

Ellie was enchanted with the image his words conjured. She'd seen both the Duke of Walden and Mr. Joshua Penrose immersed in such tasks often, and to her, their attention to detail, their conscientious accounting, was the epitome of masculine appeal.

The dog rose, perhaps inspired by the scent of food.

"I told Wentworth to procure a bone for your wolf," Elsmore said. "Scraps of fish for the tiger. Shall we eat in the other room?"

Not the bedroom, please merciful angels, not the bedroom. "At the desk," Ellie said, "and then you must be going."

"So you can move to France, covered in the shame of a scandal that had nothing to do with you and was forgotten before you were born?"

"Not before I was born. I was ten years old when the earl ruined us, and I recall our fall from grace well. One day I was a happy girl living on a pleasant property at the edge of town. The next, everything was being sold, except my favorite doll. I do not relish the thought of a similar fate befalling the Dorset family."

The duke set a crock of soup on the blotter and removed

the lid, sending savory steam wafting to Ellie's nose. Pepper pot, her favorite.

"I'll fetch the butter," she said, for Ned Wentworth had purchased bread and cheese to go with the soup.

Also a bottle of wine.

* * *

If the public learned that a bank employee—doubtless one of Rex's own cousins—was embezzling from the Dorset family, the bank would be ruined. Rex's womenfolk would be dragged into that affray and his own name blackened, but all he could think about, all he could see, was that Eleanora was miserable.

She hadn't been sleeping well, clearly, and she probably wasn't eating regularly. Lord Stephen might be able to confirm that last suspicion, but Rex wasn't about to give his lordship another opportunity to spread innuendo in Eleanora's direction.

She's still afraid of the scandal...

"Why France?" Rex asked, as he ladled servings of soup into two bowls. "Why not Scotland, Ireland, Italy? Why France?"

"I've always wanted to go," Eleanora replied, helping herself to one of the bowls. "The Duchess of Walden has been teaching me a little parlor French. I'm told one can live very economically there."

Rex took the chair opposite the desk and sampled his soup. Not quite as hot as he liked it, but tolerable.

"*One* can hide in France," he said. "Are you hiding from me, Eleanora?" Or was she hiding from the law, another victim of some scoundrel with more consequence than conscience? The question destroyed his appetite.

"Your sisters will soon be settled, Your Grace. They will doubtless turn their attention to seeing *you* settled then, and your account books—all of them—will be subjected to a most thorough examination. Perhaps you should focus your energies on the challenge of enduring that ordeal."

In theory, she raised a daunting prospect: How would Rex find a duchess if his bank was sunk in ruin and his family no longer received? Polite society could be that vindictive, and his ducal rank would only make the retribution of the club gossips and hostesses more gleeful.

But then, *he had found his duchess.* She was sitting across from him, nibbling buttered bread, looking preoccupied and disgruntled.

"I can weather old scandal, Eleanora. Hell, I'm about to weather new scandal, if I can't figure out who among my cousins, uncles, family friends, and my mother's godsons has stolen from the family accounts."

She put down her bread. "That only makes the whole business worse. You are correct that old scandal is bad enough—very bad—but add to that Mr. Butterfield, add to that an embezzler, add to that a duchess of dubious antecedents...even you, Elsmore, can't charm your way past that much wrongdoing."

He'd forgotten about Butterfield. "What aren't you telling me, Eleanora?"

She resumed eating, but Rex doubted she was tasting her meal any more than he was tasting his.

"What is the point in telling you anything, Elsmore? You go on your way, doing as you please, ducal consequence ensuring that what *you* please is what everybody pleases. My life has been the opposite. What I wanted, what I longed for, was held away from me by every agent of Providence I encountered."

She got up to pace, the dog pausing in his devotions to the ham bone, the cat hovering over her fish in the corner.

"I was born the wrong gender for my profession," Eleanora went on. "I was born to the wrong family for a girl who desired above all things to be respectable. I was sent to London in the wrong company at the wrong age for the wrong reasons." She fetched up against the hearth, her back to Rex as she stared into the flames. "I fell in love with the wrong man at the wrong time."

The look she sent him over her shoulder—bewildered, impatient—confirmed that Rex was that man.

How could such a joyous revelation result in such misery?

"I fell in love with the right woman," Rex said, rising. "I can finally see the right way to go on with my family. I am at last in possession of the means and motivation to run my bank properly. I need only hurl a few thunderbolts, banish a knave or two, and earn your trust and I can share my life with the right duchess—the only duchess—for me. If she will have me."

"And you think you can hurl those thunderbolts and banish those knaves with nobody the wiser?" Eleanora asked as Rex stalked across the room. She watched his approach, her mouth pressed into a bitter line.

"I will for damned sure try, Eleanora. My happiness has lately come to matter to me, as has yours."

They were within kissing distance, close enough that Rex caught a whiff of roses. Close enough that desire was trying to crowd out rational thought and largely succeeding.

Eleanora took a taste of him, her kiss flavored with butter.

Rational thought galloped off the field. "Do that again. Please."

"That was my farewell kiss," she said, patting his chest once. "Mr. Butterfield's impersonator was my cousin. The scheme he ran was one my family has perfected through long practice. My own cousin stole from your bank, Elsmore, and if that doesn't render me ineligible to be your duchess, somebody should appoint a guardian to see to your affairs."

The words were simple enough: Mr. Butterfield...my cousin. Rex grasped their import with the part of his mind that could plan crop rotations for his Surrey property while he endured a minuet in a Mayfair ballroom.

"Did you know your cousin was planning to steal from my bank?"

Eleanora backed up a step, her bum hitting the edge of the reading chair. "I *should* have known, but I've tried to distance myself from that branch of the family. The Old Man is a long game, taking weeks or months to do well. Mick had first to earn Mr. Butterfield's confidence and learn his accounting habits. Then he had to wait for inclement weather to render the ruse convincing. We are crooks, Your Grace, but we have learned to be competent crooks."

"You did not know of this plan?"

"I did not, not specifically."

"Where is Mick now?" Rex was asking questions because he ought to, because his obligations to his bank required it of him.

"Out of the country, possibly in Scotland, now that I think on it. I was told the Low Countries, but that was likely to throw me off the scent."

Rex advanced until he and Eleanora were toe to toe. "Who else knows of your connection to Butterfield?"

"Some of my family members, but as I said, I keep my

distance from them and they keep their distance from me. They would never approach Wentworth and Penrose, for example, because they know I work there."

"I don't care that"—Rex snapped his fingers—"for your cousin's schemes, Eleanora. He's banished himself, and very few at the bank even know of the problem. What is the real reason you are fleeing to France?"

She had a reason, Rex was as certain of that as he was that two plus two equaled four.

"Take me to bed," Eleanora said. "Time enough to discuss looming scandal later, but right now, all I know is that I want you to take me to bed."

She was distracting him, luring him away from answers she did not want to give, answers that were somehow worse than a grandfather sunk in ruin and a cousin who'd stolen from Rex's bank in broad daylight.

"You will tell me, Eleanora. If you truly wish to leave the country, I won't stop you, but at least do me the courtesy of explaining why being my duchess is such an awful prospect."

"The prospect is wonderful," she said, "but I would make an awful duchess." She took him by the hand and led him into the bedroom.

* * *

"Who knew how much there was to move?" Pammie said, looking around her little parlor.

She'd taken down Jack's sketches from the walls, packed up her crockery, and untied the bundles of dried herbs that had hung from the rafters.

To Jack's eye, the parlor had gone from humble to bleak. "Why not wait until spring?" he asked, taking the larger of the two chairs before the hearth. "Why go north now, when it's too bloody cold and dark even here in London?" Jack would have put that question to Clyde, but Pammie's husband was apparently avoiding him.

"Clyde's cousin has some work," Pammie said, extracting two cups from a wooden crate and swinging the kettle over the coals on the hearth. "Loading ships or unloading them, probably both. It's good work for a man like my Clyde. The harder the work, the better he likes it."

Clyde did prefer manual labor, which made no sense to Jack at all. "Where is Clyde?"

"Doubtless having a pint or two." Pammie fished a tea strainer out of another box. "He unpacks a box as fast as I pack it, and then the children get involved. We'll arrive in Scotland with neither quilt nor thimble to our names."

The children were asleep in the other room, darkness having fallen some hours ago. Jack would miss the little beggars, which was proof he'd lost his wits.

"You'll stop in York?"

"I'd like to bide there for Christmas," Pammie said, as the kettle began to whistle. "Clyde wants us in Scotland for the New Year, so we'll have to get right back on the packet come Boxing Day." She used the edge of her shawl as a potholder and took the kettle from the coals to pour boiling water into the two cups. She set the strainer over the larger mug. "Grandmother always had the best plum pudding."

To mention that plum pudding to a man who hadn't eaten for two days was cruel. "Don't suppose you have some shortbread to go with this tea?"

The tea was again real China black, the scent hitting Jack like the music of a skilled violinist gusting up a cold, dark alley—beautiful and bittersweet.

Pammie went to the window box and produced a pitcher of milk. "What will you do with yourself, Jack?"

"I could go north with you."

She set a single square of shortbread before him. "Clyde said you'd best wait until we're settled. We'll be staying with his cousins at first. When we have our own place, you can visit."

Visit, not join them. Jack took the strainer from his tea and set it in Pammie's cup. "I might look Mick up."

"You haven't heard from him, have you?"

Jack shook his head. "Better if we don't, for a time. You aren't having any shortbread?"

Pammie took the other seat, settling into her chair and wrapping her shawl about her. "I had some earlier."

"I could pop up to York with you, look in on the elders."

"They'd tell you to bide here, so Ellie's not all alone."

Not what she'd said the last time they'd conversed. Jack took a sip of tea, the heat alone a benediction. "Ellie wants no parts of me."

"She wants no parts of your schemes, no parts of you trying to get under her skirts."

Jack leaned his head back and closed his eyes. His feet were thawing for a change, he had a hot cup of tea, he was out of the elements. Sleep dragged at him, as did a weariness of the heart. He'd seen the gin-drunks snoring their last in the city streets. At the end, there was no shivering, no cold, nothing but peace.

"I am not trying to get under her damned skirts. I am trying to make her smile. Those bloody nobs she works for have starched all the joy from her. She used to laugh with us, Pammie. Now, she acts as if we're not fit to touch her hem."

"That is not fair, Jackson Naylor, and you know it. She calls on me and the brats regularly, but she can't afford to risk her job for scapegrace ne'er-do-wells like you and Mick."

Old ground, which they'd plowed before. "I have looked for work with every agency and service in London. I have worn my bum numb in the taverns by the City, listening for word of an opening, a new venture, anybody who would take on a man who can keep honest books. Nobody wants that kind of help, not from me, not at any price."

Jack had returned to the Bull and Baron in hopes of sharing another pint with Mr. Edwards, but to no avail. The publican reported that Edwards had been in again twice, but had left in the company of Beveridge Larson, a fellow of less than sterling reputation.

"You sit about in pubs because you like to swill ale," Pammie said. "If you were truly interested in finding honest work, you'd do the obvious."

Jack had to eat the shortbread. He'd asked for it, and to slip it into his pocket would be pathetic. He bit the sweet in half and chewed slowly, the buttery texture as much a pleasure as the sweetness.

"What's the obvious?" Jack could find work in the brothels—he wasn't bad-looking—but it wasn't in him to put up with what a molly boy did to earn his keep.

"Ask Ellie for help," Pammie said, tapping the tea strainer against the lip of her cup. She let the strainer drip for a few moments, then set it aside on the hearthstones. The leaves would doubtless be used again, probably for the children.

"Ellie has nothing to do with the hiring and firing at her bank." Various Wentworth and Penrose clerks and tellers had made that plain to Jack in casual conversation.

"Bankers gossip like laundry maids, to hear her tell it. Can't hurt to ask her, Jack."

Asking Ellie for help would hurt, but would it hurt worse than being a molly boy for nasty old men with a fondness for the birch rod? Would it hurt worse than coming down with the French pox?

Worse than the shame of dying on the end of a rope when some scheme or rig went sour?

"This is good shortbread, Pamela. I will miss your shortbread." Would she miss him? Would anybody miss him?

She went to the window box and passed him two more squares. "Call on Ellie. She'll be home at this hour, and if you're honest with her, she'll help you."

Jack took the shortbread and finished his tea, though it pained him to swill what should have been savored until the cup itself had no more warmth to give. "I'll stop by again before you leave town, and I want your direction in Scotland, Pamela. Family stays in touch."

"Family that's not in trouble stays in touch. Go see Ellie, and do it now, before you talk yourself into more time wasted in the pubs."

She was right. The hour wasn't that late, and two pieces of shortbread wouldn't last Jack another day. He donned his coat, kissed Pamela's cheek, and made his way back to the frigid darkness of the street.

Chapter Fourteen

Nothing added up for Ellie as it should, nothing remained in its assigned column or on the proper row. She stopped with Elsmore at the foot of the bed, though the bedroom was colder than the parlor.

"Eleanora, you will regret this," Elsmore said, a hand on each of her shoulders. "A passionate interlude solves nothing."

How that note of patient reason in his voice grated. "I am not trying to solve anything. I am trying to for once have what I want, even if only for a short time."

"We already did that," he said, wrapping her in his arms. "The experience was lovely and heartbreaking. In hindsight, the selfishness was not well done of me. I should have courted you properly and at length. Why don't you trust me?"

Heartbreaking? He called the greatest intimacy she'd ever known *heartbreaking*? "I have confessed to you my grandfather's scandal and my cousin's crimes. How can you say I don't trust you?"

He rubbed her back in slow circles, and more than kisses or passion, that sweet, intimate touch hurt her heart. *I can never have this again. I can never know his embrace again.*

"You would rather subject yourself to my company in that bed than explain to me the real battle we face. I can't slay a dragon I can't see, Eleanora, but neither can I make love with a woman who will run from me in the morning. Old scandal, your ne'er-do-well cousin, my own problems at the bank can all be dealt with. You are keeping something from me."

Ellie could feel the determination in him, the bone-deep certainty and steadfastness. He was not to be swayed, manipulated, inveigled, or cajoled past this point.

She rested her forehead against his chest. "You pick a fine time to turn up ducal."

"If I care for you, and I very much do, then I cannot bend to temptation when an enemy threatens our future."

Where was the man who'd ignored his own accounts for years? The man who sat through evening after evening of society gossip, the man who waltzed on command simply to placate his family?

"It's Friday," Ellie said. "You should be at the theater."

"Not unless you allow me to escort you."

She slipped from his embrace. "I cannot show my face in public like that. Some dowager viscountess will whisper that I remind her of somebody—I look very much like my grandmother, and she was one of Grandpapa's favorite models. Because I am on your arm, the gossips won't rest until my past has been exhumed. You have an embezzler to catch. Perhaps we ought to concentrate on that?"

She stalked from the bedroom, angry to have been rejected, though a small serving of rejection from Elsmore reminded her of the much worse rejections he and his family would face if she became his duchess.

"I suspect I have more than one embezzler to catch," Elsmore said, following her back into the sitting room. "Were I to hire a competent auditor to examine my bank, she'd likely find all manner of rounding errors, transcriptions, incompetence, inflated invoices, and just enough accurate bookkeeping to make the lot of it harder to decipher."

Elsmore was angry. Not merely annoyed, irritated, or ducally impatient, but quietly furious.

"Why do you say that? A smart embezzler cloaks himself in the respectability of the institution from which he's stealing. He wants as much probity and rectitude around him as he can summon."

"Or she does." Elsmore considered Ellie, his gaze unreadable. "Is that why you're determined to elope, Eleanora? You've been made to take responsibility for somebody else's wrongdoing and you fear the noose?"

She feared the noose. She absolutely feared the noose. "And if that were the case? If I myself had committed crimes?"

He tore off a bite of her buttered bread and offered her the rest of the slice. "You are incapable of breaking the law, excepting possibly to rescue your damned almighty employer. You'd likely do the same for his duchess, maybe for your dodgy family members or your cat. If that's the case, Eleanora—you were backed into a corner and exigencies arose—then we will sort them out."

Ellie took the bread and stuffed it into her mouth, because she did not know what to say. He'd face even criminal wrongdoing for her?

The man was flat barmy. "You don't know how impossible it is to do as you suggest, Your Grace."

"I can't know. You won't tell me what the difficulty is. I have had warrants quashed before, Eleanora—though granted, they were old warrants resulting from boyhood pranks gone wrong. Shall I provide you the details?"

"You shall take your leave of me," Ellie said.

The cat had apparently finished her meal for she stropped herself against Elsmore's boots. He picked her up, and cat and duke turned upon Ellie gazes that both looked pitying.

"I won't take you to bed, so you turn me out into the street," Elsmore said, petting the cat. "What of my failing bank, Eleanora? Can you resist that lure?"

No, she could not. "You likely have not a failing bank, but an ailing bank. Hire your own auditor—quietly, discreetly—and have him go department by department. As the auditor makes his way from innocuous peripheral measures to those closer to the seat of the problem, whoever is guilty of wrongdoing will slip away, probably with his pockets full. You will avoid scandal and clean house, though it will take weeks if done carefully."

"That's how you began at Wentworth and Penrose?"

"I liked you better when you were lazy and charming."

"I was never lazy," Elsmore said, setting the cat down in the reading chair. "I was simply misguided." He crossed the room to don his coat. "I wish you would help me, Eleanora, but I mean to put my bank on solid footing with or without your aid. I also wish you'd allow me to help *you.* Your grandfather sank the whole family in scandal, and your cousins threaten your livelihood. If you have a brother or a father, you'd likely have to disown them on general principles, but I am not those men. I am the man asking for your hand in marriage."

Ellie did not have a brother and she no longer had a father. "You are the man whose proposal I have refused. One day you'll—"

He put a finger to her lips. "I will not thank you. Don't turn up arrogant on me now, Eleanora. You insisted I look where I didn't want to look, and now you keep me in the dark. I will never thank you for that. I appreciate the warning regarding my bookkeeping, but I was already stumbling to the same conclusion. The books at the bank are far from pristine."

He was leaving, and if Ellie were smart, she'd wish him farewell and be on tomorrow's packet for Calais.

"You think there's more than embezzlement going on at the bank?"

Elsmore left his coat unbuttoned and whipped his scarf over his shoulder. "I suspect there's every sort of graft and mayhem neatly obscured by the sort of accuracy to which you have devoted yourself. The issue isn't whether somebody is embezzling, it's how many of my relations are either stealing from the bank or ignoring those who do."

And he apparently had no idea who, no idea which smiles were false, which were genuine—if any.

"You will be dragged down with them," Ellie said. "If the problem is that extensive, you will be accused of turning a blind eye to it, profiting from it. You cannot charge into the middle of this and expect to emerge unscathed."

He kissed her cheek. "A token, as I ride into battle. Wish me luck, Eleanora. I'll need it."

She wanted him to stay, to explain to her every shred of evidence he'd collected from his bank ledgers, and she wanted him to go to the theater, there to be handsome and charming for the rest of his evening, and the rest of his life.

"Do you want to see your family members hanged?"

she asked, as Elsmore strode for the door. "They will be. Murderers get transportation, but English judges take a very dim view of those who mishandle money."

She'd said too much, but at least she had his attention.

"People put their life savings into my bank, Eleanora. They entrust their entire security to me. I turn a blind eye to this pilfering and I become as reprehensible as the embezzlers and cheats."

"Elsmore—Wrexham—what about the duty you owe your family? When you are tried in the Lords for fraud and misfeasance, what about your sisters and widowed cousins? What about the boys at university who will no longer have your consequence to open doors for them?"

His scowl suggested he hadn't followed the path of righteousness to its logical conclusion, straight into a briar patch of conflicting loyalties.

"I must go," Elsmore said. "The sooner I identify the swindlers, the sooner they can be dealt with. Goodnight, Eleanora. Safe journey."

Two words, and they hurt, though they weren't meant to. "Good luck, Your Grace. Be careful."

He pulled on his gloves and again, the cat stropped herself against his boots, the traitor.

Elsmore picked Voltaire up and passed her to Eleanora. He turned to go, and a knock sounded on the door.

"Are you expecting company?" he asked.

"At this hour? Of course not." Ellie brushed past him and moved the little pear-shaped metal flap to peer into the corridor.

Jack stood on the other side of the door, staring straight at the spy-hole. He was bare-headed, meaning he'd pawned his hat, and he was alone. He was also family, and he wouldn't be here if he had anywhere else to go.

Ellie opened the door. "Jack, this is unexpected." She purposely stood in the doorway lest Jack see that she had company.

"Pammie and Clyde don't want me going north with them. My landlord cut me loose a week ago. I have two pieces of shortbread to my name, and nobody is hiring a bookkeeper, accountant, clerk, or porter answering to my description. I'm desperate, Ellie, and unless you are willing to help me, my options are to starve or go back to picking pockets."

Oh, Jack. Why now? Why offer that confession when Elsmore could hear every word?

The door opened wide enough to reveal Elsmore at Ellie's side. "You understand bookkeeping?" the duke asked.

"I do."

"Eleanora?"

"Your Grace, may I introduce to you my cousin Jackson Naylor, part-time scapegrace. Jack, Wrexham, His Grace of Elsmore, full-time nuisance. Jack has an excellent eye for numbers, but he's also a competent sneak thief, housebreaker, confidence trickster, and a fair hand cheating at cards. Oh, and he's as talented an artist as Grandfather ever was. Elsmore is as smart as he is well mannered, Jack, so don't think to run a rig on him."

Jack stepped into the parlor. "You'd kill me if I tried to run a rig on him."

I won't be here to kill you. I'll be in France. Wodin stood, gaze alert and fixed on Jack. "I'd kill you," Ellie said, "and feed the pieces to my four-legged friends."

"What if he ran a rig for me?" Elsmore asked. "Or did a little discreet reconnoitering on my behalf?"

"No." Ellie nearly shouted, which had all the occupants in the room—dog, cat, and both men—regarding her quizzically. "You will not involve my cousin in arguably illegal schemes to extricate your family from impending ruin. I won't have it."

"What does it pay?" Jack asked.

"Jack, no," Ellie said, lowering her voice by dint of sheer will. "You could swing for it. Breaking and entering, attempted theft, trespass. You know what can happen. Transportation would be the most you could hope for, and claiming you were on some errand for a duke would not save you."

Jack was gaunt. His clothing hadn't been pressed in ages. He didn't stink yet, but Ellie knew intimately the progression from respectability to desperation, and Jack was one step away from wild schemes and criminal misconduct.

"I can swing for a little nosing about on His Grace's behalf," Jack said, "or I can be found frozen to death in some church doorway, my clothing stolen before I breathed my last. Forgive me, Ellie, if I at least hear what your duke has to say."

He sauntered across the room and took the chair behind the desk, while Elsmore closed the door.

* * *

"Why aren't you at the theater?" Eddie asked, for James wasn't dressed to attend the theater, and James did very much like to be seen on Drury Lane. He usually flirted the evening away with his mistress, whose box was opposite Elsmore's. Now he stood in the doorway to Eddie's office, a ledger tucked against his hip.

"Why are you still here?" James settled into the chair across from Eddie's desk and set the ledger on a corner of the blotter. "You are hardly what I'd call a dedicated bank employee, my boy, and the hour grows late."

That was the point—for the hour to be so late that nobody else was on the bank premises. An old watchman snored his nights away in a chair by the hearth in the lobby, periodically rousing himself to trim a few wicks or take a piss in the alley. Other than that, the bank should be deserted this late on a Friday evening.

"I am better able to concentrate when the place is quiet," Eddie replied. "I have considered the possibility you've raised that Ballentyre will retire or be rendered too infirm by gout to do his job. When that happens, a fresh set of eyes might be looking over our books, James, and my ledgers need some attention."

A lot of attention. Eddie had nearly finished tidying up the past year, but that left four previous years in disarray.

"I thought you or I would get Ballentyre's post," James said, crossing an ankle over one knee. "You're welcome to it, by the way. I'm content with my lot for now." He spoke as if the bank belonged to him, and any post he pleased to have could be his.

"I am not content. My books are in order, more or less, but your haphazard review of them has left every inaccuracy and error in plain view. Howell says yours are in worse condition yet."

James sat up. "When the hell did Howell go poking his nose into my ledgers?"

"When you were indisposed a few Saturdays ago. I gathered up your account books, but Howell apparently got his mitts on the one dealing with the Oxford allowances. I don't know as he suspects anything more than sloppiness, but—"

"You are only telling me this now? Plodding, dull, dear Howell has had a thorough look at one of my accountings, and you didn't think to mention this to me?"

"If he hasn't said anything to you, then he likely corrected your errors and went on to the next set of figures. Not like Ballentyre's clerks are models of accuracy and diligence these days." Though Eddie's books were increasingly in order, and that felt oddly satisfying.

James rose and dumped half a bucket of coal onto the hearth, an extravagance, for Eddie did not intend to tarry much longer.

"Our lady cousins are likely to marry this spring," James said, stirring the coals to stoke the flames. "My days as keeper of the family exchequer are coming to an end."

"I'd hardly say that. The aunties, the widows, the college boys, the pensioners...there's much more than their ladyships' pin money to oversee."

James straightened, the poker in his hand. For a moment, illuminated by the rising flames, with the length of wrought iron in his grip, he bore little resemblance to a duke's heir preparing for an evening of cards with his friends.

"That's not the point, Eddie. The point is, you have allowed Howell the Hopeless to sniff at my books. The cousins are soon to be married. Elsmore will likely start hunting a bride after that, and with the joys of family life could well come an increased interest in the bank. I do believe it's time I saw more of the Continent."

"You just returned from Scotland."

"If you are smart, which you believe yourself to be, you might consider a repairing lease in the north yourself."

What nonsense was this? "I thought you were about to double your money with some scheme directed at our competitors? The Butterfield trick played on the unsuspecting?"

James lounged against the mantel. "That was before you told me Howell has had a go at my books, before dear cousin Samantha told me she has every confidence of following Rachel to the altar. The situation here is changing, and a prudent man doesn't wait for change to overtake him."

Eddie closed his account book and locked it into a desk drawer. "Elsmore was on the premises for most of the afternoon. Planted the ducal backside in his office and didn't stir except to have a clerk bring him more ledgers. Very odd business."

Very odd, unnerving business, which had inspired Eddie into occupying the seat behind his desk well past dark.

"I don't like it," James said, staring into the flames. "I most assuredly do not care for Elsmore nosing about the bank. Why didn't you tell me this sooner?"

"You were out." And Eddie had had work to do. "You are frequently out. Ballentyre has developed the ability to waste three hours at lunch and an hour at each of his tea breaks. Elsmore will notice that, if he hasn't already."

Footsteps shuffled past Eddie's closed door, the watchman stretching his legs no doubt.

"Do you mind if I use this office for a bit?" James asked. "My own is lamentably chilly and I find I'm in the mood to think bankerly thoughts for a bit."

Eddie rose. "Never let it be said I denied you an opportunity to indulge a bankerly impulse. I expect I'll be here again tomorrow."

James studied him. "Will you? Getting ready to bolt, Eddie?"

And if I am? "My work for the bank is above reproach, James. That I occasionally facilitate relations between a borrower and a lender beyond what the bank can accommodate is certainly no cause for alarm. Many bankers do likewise."

And were careful never to document any of it, because the law did so frown on usury.

"Of course they do," James said. "I'll see you Monday, assuming we aren't dragooned into Sunday dinner with the ducal relations." He slid his sleeve buttons free, turned back his cuffs, and reached for the ledger he'd brought with him.

Eddie itched to know what was in the account book. Whatever it was, it had the power to keep James at the bank well after dark, his handsome nose buried in figures for the first time in all the years Eddie had worked with him.

Perhaps Elsmore should be alerted to this development. On that thought, Eddie turned to leave.

"Eddie, before you go, one other thing."

Eddie pretended a concern he didn't feel. "If you need some blunt—"

"Hardly, but thank you. I've had occasion lately to rub shoulders with some of the clerks and tellers from other institutions."

The institutions James was planning to fleece, no doubt. "If I'm the object of gossip, I'd rather you just say so."

James lounged back in the chair and propped his boots on Eddie's desk. "Don't flatter yourself. The gossip had to do with Elsmore."

"Doesn't it always? He would do us all a favor if he got leg-shackled." Though then, a direct heir was likely to appear in short order, and James would be demoted to spare. What a pity *that* would be.

James dragged the ledger into his lap. "The talk had to do with Elsmore and the auditor at Wentworth and Penrose, a female. He's been seen sharing a coach with her, and the clerks at Wentworth's say a couple weeks back he met with her for most of two afternoons. They are petrified of the woman. They claim she can find a missing farthing in pitch darkness amid gale-force winds."

Eddie's desire to leave became urgent. Leave the bank, leave London, perhaps even leave England. "I can't say I'd care for such a woman."

"She took a holiday from Wentworth's at the same time my eyes and ears at Dorset House claim His Grace collected all the ducal ledgers for his personal review."

"But those ledgers..."

"Are brought to me at the bank to be tallied at the end of every month. I thought it only fair to warn you. By this time next week, I will be enjoying a change of air. If this auditor is halfway competent, she'll advise Elsmore to turn the bank inside out once she's wreaked havoc on the personal accounts. Sooner or later, awkward questions will be asked. I don't intend to be here when that happens."

How delicately a ducal heir referred to utter ruin. "I will wish you safe travels, James. If there's anything I can do to help, you have only to let me know."

Elsmore would be at the theater tonight, but tomorrow morning, Eddie intended to have a very pointed discussion with His Grace. James had taken calculated risks and enjoyed copious rewards. His run of good luck had come to an end, but even that might be turned to an enterprising fellow's advantage.

Eddie closed the office door softly and made his way down the corridor as quietly as possible. No need to wake the watchman. The night was young, and Eddie had time to go home, change, and be at the theater in time to join Madam Bisset for the second act.

"Eddie the Enterprising," he murmured. "I like it."

* * *

Eleanora's cousin started on a bowl of cold soup while Rex sorted options and considered Eleanora. She cared for her cousin Jack, but she regarded him with a despair that echoed Rex's sentiments about his own family.

"If Jack is knowledgeable about ledgers and a competent sneak thief," Rex said, "he's exactly the man for a quiet investigation of the bank after hours."

Eleanora flopped into the reading chair, whereupon the cat leapt into her lap. "Elsmore, do you think embezzlers leave trails of bread crumbs pointing to where piles of cash have been stowed? Do you suppose they simply twist a lock and go about their business, confident that nobody ever comes looking for a spare quill or is curious about what's kept in a consistently locked drawer?"

Jack paused with a spoon halfway to his mouth. "If there's cash on the premises where it ought not to be, I'll find it. I have a nose for cash."

Eleanora put the cat to her shoulder, like a nursemaid with a baby. "And what if the cash isn't on the bank premises? Only a fool would store it there when safer locations are available."

"The bank is the safest possible location," Rex said. "The windows are stoutly barred, the locks secure, and a watchman stands guard all night."

"A watchman," Eleanora muttered. "You expect Jack to elude the vigilance of a man who's paid to do nothing but deter intruders. Do you want me to hate you, Elsmore?"

Jack started on the second bowl. "Do you want me to starve, Ellie? This is work, one old man with a feeble lantern isn't that hard to dodge, and putting me in the dock when I'll be in the bank on the duke's say-so will be a lot harder than if I'm there for my own purposes."

Ellie closed her eyes as the cat skittered from her

shoulder, up over the back of the reading chair and thence to the floor.

"If you are caught," she said, voice tight, "with money in your pockets, or a ledger written in some bank employee's hand, you will be hanged on Monday next."

Jack sat back, a piece of bread in his hand. "I won't be caught, I won't nip anything, and it won't be like that."

He and Eleanora exchanged a look, pleading on his part, furious on hers. A silent conversation ensued, one Rex was not meant to understand. The duel ended when Eleanora sneezed.

Rex passed her a handkerchief, which she glared at before taking out her own handkerchief.

"I despair of you, Jackson Naylor," she said. "If you want coin, I'll give you coin. My lease here is paid up for the rest of the month, and I doubt Lord Stephen will turn you out without warning. He's more charitable than he lets on. Please tell Cook the cat will need a new owner, for I refuse to bide in England while..."

Her glower should have cindered Jack on the spot.

Jack had apparently weathered that fire before, because he sopped his bread in the soup as casually as any drover at his evening meal. "Something about His Grace's linen looks familiar."

"What the devil does that matter?" Rex asked. "I'm properly attired for daytime, and most men wear a neck-cloth."

Jack gestured with his bread. "Not that linen—your fancy little kercher. Has a unicorn on it. Don't see many unicorns in my parts of London."

"My family crest," Rex said. "The sixth countess brought Scottish wealth to her marriage. When the family was elevated to ducal honors, the unicorn was a nod to her antecedents. You've probably seen the crest on my town coach."

Eleanora left her chair. "Did you see this exact crest, Jack, or one like it?"

He studied his bread. "That one, on a handkerchief, and I recall thinking, 'Only a fool would flash that bit of fancy about in a place like this.'"

"Where were you?" Eleanora asked, crossing to the desk. "Who was the fool?" She gazed at her cousin with the same focus she turned on a fresh set of figures. "Think, Jack, because if a member of Elsmore's family has been haunting low places, that's relevant."

Jack tore off another bite of bread and chewed. "Not low places. I've been looking for honest work, Ellie. Haven't run a rig or picked a pocket in months. I've been over by the City, where the clerks and counting-house bookkeepers stop for their pint."

"Not high places," Rex said. "By the standards of a ducal cousin or uncle, those would be unusual haunts."

"He talked like you," Jack said, cocking his head. "But where…?"

"Concentrate," Eleanora said. "See him in your mind's eye, Jack, like Grandpapa would. Note the details that a portrait would include. What color were his gloves?"

"Black, kid, lined, very fine. No mending," Jack said. "A touch of lace at his cuffs, but just a touch. Three capes on his greatcoat. Looked like a Schweitzer and Davidson cut."

"Snuff box?" Eleanora asked.

"Didn't see one."

"What about a hat?"

"Lock, or similar quality," Jack replied. "He was a fine gent."

Rex listened to this exchange with growing dismay. "Did the fine gent give you a name?"

"Edwards," Jack replied around the last mouthful of bread. "But that wasn't his name."

Edwards? Would Eddie have used that name as an alias? "Did he have a walking stick?" Rex asked. "A cane, anything of that nature?"

Eleanora put her palms on the blotter and leaned across the desk. "Think, Jackson. You took note of this man for a reason. Amid the noise and stink and crowding of some pub or tavern, this fellow sat down and made an impression on you. You took in the details, because we were taught to look carefully. Fancy beaver hat, touches of lace, fine tailoring...what was in his hands when he took a place at your table?"

"Walking stick," Jack said. "Silver handle, dark wood. Might have been mahogany because it held a nice, high shine. Brass ferrule rather than gold. He hooked it on the edge of the table, set his gloves next to it, his handkerchief atop his gloves. We talked about the little problem His Grace's bank recently had with a certain Mr. Butterfield. Mr. Edwards was familiar with that situation."

Eleanora straightened, her gaze swinging to Rex. "You know this man. You know which of your managers or cousins has been chatting up out-of-work pickpockets and swindlers."

"Ellie," Jack began, "I'm not a swindler these days. I'm going honest, or I would if anybody would hire me. The fancy gent apparently has taken up with Beveridge Larson, and that association recommends him to no one." Jack took the lid off the crock of soup and poured the remaining contents into an empty bowl.

"It does cross my mind," he went on, "that if the fancy

gent intends to play the Old Man on some unsuspecting bank, then Larson resembles him more nearly than I do. They are of a height and built the same, while I have been missing the regular occasion of nutrition lately."

The dog rose from the hearthrug and pressed against the side of Rex's leg. The weight was comforting, an anchor against a reeling sense of betrayal.

"The fancy gent is my heir apparent," Rex said. "The fancy gent trolling for the next Mr. Butterfield is my cousin James. My friend, the closest thing I have to a brother."

"Enterprising fellow," Jack said, spoon scraping the last of the soup from the crock. "Give him that, but stupid."

"Greedy," Eleanora said. "The greedy ones eventually get caught. Now that you know where the problem is, nobody need break into any banks." Her smile was overly bright and false.

"Now that I know at least one of the cheaters," Rex replied, "I have more need than ever for a look around the premises after hours before anybody has reason to get nervous."

Eleanora's smile disappeared. "You are not putting my cousin at risk, Your Grace. Once the authorities get hold of someone, no amount of consequence can overcome the corruption of the thief-takers, magistrates, and beadles. There is no justice for one such as Jack, and even you can't change that."

Eleanora's gaze promised slow death to any duke who'd gainsay her. She'd find a way to destroy him if any harm came to Jack, and make charges of embezzlement a mere nuisance by comparison. With the backing of the Duke of Walden, Lord Stephen, and Wentworth and Penrose as an institution—to say nothing of Walden's duchess—she could do it.

"I'll be careful," Jack said, picking up his bowl and slurping the soup directly from it. "I'm always careful, Ellie. You know that."

"Careful isn't good enough," Eleanora snapped. "Careful never earned a man a pardon or a commutation. Jack Naylor, I will disown you and tell the rest of the family to do likewise if you attempt this foolish errand."

Rex shoved aside his fury at dear cousin James—who dressed to the nines, worked when he pleased to, and stole from widows—to focus on the argument between Eleanora and her cousin.

"I've been disowned before," Jack said, setting aside the empty bowl. "Don't much care for it, but I'm surviving. If His Grace pays me to sneak about the bank after hours, then he'll have to give me an honest job, won't he? I'll know his secrets, and he'll want me to keep them to myself."

"You cannot blackmail your way into an honest job," Eleanora retorted. "And you aren't breaking into any bank if I can help it."

This argument was not about an evening of peering in dark corners at Dorset and Becker, though Rex wasn't sure what the true issue was.

"Eleanora is correct, Naylor. You cannot blackmail your way into an honest job, but neither will you know any dirty little secrets if the evening goes as planned."

"He is not trespassing on bank grounds," Eleanora said, folding her arms. "I will not have it."

"You are leaving for France, madam," Rex said, gently, lest she lay into him with her fists. "But as it happens, nobody need trespass anywhere. I have a key to the bank, I am a director, and a major shareholder. If I choose to take a prospective employee on a discreet tour of the premises, that is entirely within my purview."

Eleanora sank onto the sofa. "I give up. I wash my hands of the both of you. Break into as many banks as you please and take yourselves on an uninvited tour of Carlton House while you're about it. This is madness, and will profit you nothing. Jack, you are putting your trust in a duke who will be ruined by scandal should a word of any of this become known. Tread lightly."

"We're doomed, Your Grace," Jack said, dusting crumbs into his soup bowl. "When Eleanora gets all chilly and polite, there's no talking sense to her. We might as well drop by your bank and have a look about."

Chapter Fifteen

"My problem," James informed the empty room, "is that I lack a ruthless streak."

Eddie's office was cozy, the appointments tasteful. The watchman had come by once, and James had waved him off with assurances that he need not look in again. The old fellow had shuffled back to his brazier, happy to commune with his flask rather than traverse chilly corridors.

A sketch hung on the wall opposite the desk, though in the dim light of sconces and candles, the youths portrayed by the artist were more shadow than form. Elsmore had been caught with the three bachelor cousins, lounging about on a picnic blanket after a cricket match.

A foursome of good-looking young men, though the image somehow managed to portray that Elsmore's team had won. The duke half-reclined on his side, like a Roman statesman, a plate of grapes before him. The other cousins sat in equally relaxed postures, but they lacked Elsmore's sense of...

Something. Self-possession, self-assurance. Something unfairly denied the duke's cousins, and most especially denied his heir.

A noise down the corridor disturbed James's musings, which was fortunate. He had put right what he could in the family ledgers and had only to collect his funds and his personal account book, and then he could be on his way.

Dover by morning was too much to hope for on winter roads, but Dover by noon was entirely possible. The tides and winds might leave him kicking his heels for a day or two if he was unlucky, and few boats would sail on the Sabbath under even favorable conditions. Money could solve that problem, if the weather was obliging.

James banked the fire in the hearth, blew out the candles, and bid a silent farewell to Cousin Edward and to all the cousins. He'd hoped to play out the game a little longer, but a smart man knew to put safety ahead of wealth. He donned his coat and hat, took up his walking stick, and made his way down the corridor, past the snoring watchman, and into his own office.

He had no warning that anything was amiss—and why should it be? The moment he opened the door, he perceived that a room that ought to have been in pitch darkness was illuminated by a pair of carrying candles on the mantel. His first thought was that a charwoman had carelessly left lamps behind, but then a movement caught his eye.

"I know you." The man at James's desk was vaguely familiar, though not a bank employee. "What the hell are you doing in *my office* plundering bank records after hours, trespassing, sneaking about, and doubtless thieving from your betters?"

A memory came to James of a pub, a fellow down on his luck who knew a bit too much about the bank's troubles. Instinct had warned James away from that man—he'd been too honest, too knowledgeable about criminal logic, as a thief-taker would be—and here he was.

Where he should have never been.

"Mr. Edwards." The fellow rose. "Jackson Naylor at your service. What a strange hour for you to be attending to bank business. Perhaps you can explain why the false bottom in your desk drawer conceals nearly two thousand pounds in banknotes?"

"*Naylor*, is it now?" James spat. "This is a bank, exactly where most prudent people choose to store their money, myself included. The more pertinent inquiry is whether your affairs are in order, because I will most assuredly be summoning the watch and informing the authorities of your criminal activities. Bank robbery is a capital offense."

Naylor lounged back on the cushioned seat. "You won't find a bent copper in my pockets, *Mr. Edwards*, but His Grace of Elsmore will be very interested in your little personal account book. You should never have kept it here, but then, you should not have been stealing from family."

"His Grace of Elsmore will see you hanged," James said, taking a firm grip of his walking stick. Naylor appeared unarmed, but a knife was always a possibility. "And don't think he can't see it done quietly. A duke's consequence is vast, and even Newgate will respect his wishes when it comes to ending your existence."

Naylor peered upward, at the shadows dancing on the ceiling. "*You* steal from family, but *I* am to be hanged, and Elsmore is to bribe the magistrates to see it done—do I have that right?"

"Elsmore will protect the reputation of this bank," James said, "and if that means spreading a bit of coin around to keep lips buttoned, he'll see it done. I know him well, and I know how precarious a bank's reputation is. You chose the wrong business to rob, Naylor."

"Except," a quiet voice said behind James, "he's not robbing anybody. Why are you here at this late hour, James?"

Elsmore had silently closed the door behind James, though this was not a version of Elsmore James had seen before. His Grace wore no hint of lace or finery. He was attired all in black, even to his shirt and neckcloth. His head was bare, no watch chain, rings, or cravat pin lightened his attire. He was darkness made human, the opposite of the charming, sociable aristocrat James called cousin.

"Elsmore, I've caught a thief in the very act of robbery. I know this fellow. He's doubtless traveling under false colors again. When last I met him he went by the name of Tolliver. Lurks in unsavory taverns, and I have reason to know he's been keeping a close eye on this very bank. He knew of the Butterfield matter. Every measure was taken to keep that incident from becoming public, and yet, he knew. That alone should incriminate him."

Elsmore advanced and James took a step back. James's walking stick went sailing through the air, caught one-handed by the man still seated at the desk.

"You have been stealing from the aunties," Elsmore said, almost pleasantly. "Stealing from the widows and school-boys, even stealing from my sisters. I can only conclude you've also been stealing from the bank customers. Doing a little three-for-five transcribing in the ten-pound column, James? Indulging in some creative rounding where the interest-bearing accounts are concerned?"

Elsmore should not even know those terms. "You are mad. I make the occasional mistake, as anybody does when handling figures all day. If I've erred, I am happy to reimburse the bank from personal funds."

Naylor, or whoever he was, snorted. "I suspect the other side of this handsome desk also has a drawer with a false bottom, Your Grace, but I've yet to pick that lock."

"He admits to picking locks," James said. "That man should be arrested."

Elsmore remained between James and the door. "You will be arrested. You will be tried for stealing, possibly for embezzling, and the court will pass sentence on you without any attempt on my part to keep the matter quiet."

"Elsmore, *I am your heir*. I am a manager at this bank, and if I am disgraced then you, the family, the bank...think, man. Do you really begrudge me the fruits of a little enterprise so much that you'll bring ruin down on every employee and customer of this bank?"

Naylor rose. "He has a point, Elsmore. I could quietly dispatch him for you. Solve a lot of problems and provide me with enough entertainment to last half the night."

Naylor's dead-cold gaze unnerved James, but Elsmore's silence turned worry into panic. "Elsmore, you will not ruin this bank simply to punish me. You aren't a murderer."

The next silence was hellish.

"You can't let him be publicly hanged," Naylor mused. "The scandal would pass, but a certain party isn't keen on hangings of any sort. Won't serve, Your Grace."

That got Elsmore's attention. "No public hanging?"

Naylor shook his head. "Our mutual acquaintance has strong feelings on that topic."

"Interesting." Elsmore plucked the walking stick from Naylor's grasp and tossed it at James. "You can pawn that in Dover for passage to someplace I won't think to find you. Your greatcoat will bring some coin, as will your gloves and waistcoat. Rings, watch, sleeve buttons, and cravat pin all have value, as does the education I paid for. One question before you go."

He will allow me to live. Later James would puzzle out how to get to Dover without any funds. "Ask."

"Why slander my sister? Why spread lies about Rachel when she's never done anything to hurt you?"

"Because as soon as she marries, Samantha and Kathleen will each bring some bachelor up to scratch. I'll lose access to their accounts, and their accounts are lucrative. You never begrudged them anything, never questioned their expenses no matter how extravagant. A few very discreet rumors in the ears of would-be suitors hardly amounted to slander. The aunties are getting old, the boy cousins only spend a few years at university, but a spinster sister or two... You would have bought them the stars if they'd asked it of you."

"While you, poor thing, had to pretend to work," Elsmore said. "Is Edward part of your scheme?"

"No. Nor is Howell. Howell is too decent, Edward is too careful. He does some lucrative brokering, but that's the extent of his misconduct that I know of."

Naylor came around the desk and held out some banknotes. "Elsmore is also afflicted with decency. He doesn't grasp that if you're to slink off to some stinking hole in Amsterdam, you need the means to slink there. We can't have you kicking your heels in Dover or Portsmouth causing embarrassment when the authorities find you. You don't dare go to Paris, where familiar faces will ask awkward questions, and passage to Rome is too costly."

"I'll go," James said, eyeing the banknotes. "I'll go and I'll stay gone. I was planning on leaving soon anyway, and there's no need to alert the authorities."

"The molly houses pay something," Naylor said. "For a while. Then your looks begin to go, and the patrons aren't as generous. Bon voyage." He smiled and waved the money before James's nose.

Elsmore said nothing to that horrific taunt, so James snatched the banknotes and fled.

* * *

Rex spent the night wandering the streets of London. He avoided the worst neighborhoods, but he would have welcomed an opportunity to pummel a foolhardy footpad or two. None had obliged him, more's the pity.

His bank was riddled with problems. His close relatives had betrayed him, and the one person whose welfare most concerned him was probably not speaking to him.

As the first glimmers of light streaked the eastern sky, he found himself at his own front door, though he didn't particularly want to go inside. He did anyway, because all the problems he faced affected his family, and it was with them he proposed to embark on a few solutions.

"Mama. Good morning. Couldn't you sleep?" He'd come directly to the breakfast parlor from the front door. A few cups of hot tea were in order—or a few pots. A yawning maid was only beginning to lay out the buffet on the sideboard, but she took one look at Rex and slipped away.

The duchess wore a dressing gown and shawl, her silver hair hung in a single, thick braid. The hour was early enough that candles were lit on the sideboard, while the sun had yet to break the horizon.

"I missed you at the theater last night," she said. "Your sisters are so much better behaved when you escort us.

Are you only now finding your way home, Elsmore?" She perused his attire, the dark, nondescript ensemble Jackson Naylor had insisted upon.

"Is this place home?" Rex asked, pouring a cup of tea from the silver pot on the sideboard. The sole purpose of the silver was to keep the tea hot longer than a ceramic pot would have. Had Eleanora ever used her silver teapot for that reason? He put a currant bun on a plate and looked around for the butter because Eleanora did love her butter.

"I don't know if this is home, but we certainly spend a fair amount of time here," Mama said, taking up the cup and the currant bun. "Do your sisters' situations have you considering taking a bride?"

"Yes and no." Rex braced himself for one of Mama's usual homilies. Lady Joanna Peabody was gracious, tolerant, and pretty. Miss Nehring was only the daughter of a viscount, but her family's lineage went back to the Conqueror himself, and their resources were impressive. Then too, she was an only child, *poor dear*, Mama's genteel reminder that Miss Nehring was an heiress.

"Shall we sit?" Mama asked. "You can tell me about the yes part."

She took her customary seat at the foot of the table, and Rex assumed what was usually Kathleen's place at Mama's left hand.

"Yes, I am thinking of marrying," he said. "No, the recent tide of adoring bachelors has nothing to do with that."

"A lady has caught your eye?" Oh, the hope in her question. The pure, human hope. "I do think you and Lady Francesca Honeycutt would suit. She's a bit of an original, but not too original. Aren't you having any tea?"

He'd poured the cup she held for himself, and Mama

had assumed it was for her—an easy mistake to make when one was half asleep.

"I'll have a tray when I go up to my room. Lady Francesca is all that is lovely, but she and I would not suit. I can barely call her to mind, though I'm sure when she happened purely by chance to come upon me in the park—again—I would recognize her easily enough."

"You're peckish," Mama said, patting his hand. "Grab a cinnamon bun before you go upstairs, and please don't let your sisters know you've been out prowling. That will not comport with the image they hold of you as the perfect fellow, though I do know a man has needs. Lady Francesca or Lady Joanna would be understanding about that. They grasp that perfection in a spouse is a hopeless objective."

"No, it is not."

Mama set down her currant bun. "You are now an authority on the married state?"

"I am an authority on who and what could make me happy. The women you mention are all lovely, and they deserve adoring swains of their own, but they will never interrupt me. They won't call me to account when I'm being ridiculously ducal. They won't tell me the truth when flattery is the easier course. They will play games with their pin money rather than admit to me when they are short of funds. If a duke is to have only one honest ally in life, one person with whom he can absolutely be himself, shouldn't that person be his duchess?"

In the gloomy pre-dawn light, Mama's expression became as wistful as a bride's. "I was such a duchess once. Everybody was aghast that your papa married a mere baron's daughter, everybody but the dowager duchess. She said new blood enlivens the line, and if you and your sisters are any indication, she was right. Her grandfather was a brewer."

Rex had forgotten this aspect of his own heritage, but then, polite society didn't exactly fling it in his face. They doubtless whispered about it behind his back.

"You would not object if I became engaged to a woman of questionable antecedents?" he asked.

Mama set the teacup before him. "You should drink that. I don't care for my tea piping hot. A woman cannot help her antecedents, Wrexham."

Not what he'd expected to hear. "Do you ever consider remarrying?"

She shook her head. "To say that your father was the love of my life sounds trite. He could infuriate me like no other and make me laugh in a most unladylike fashion. We were friends, my boy. Best friends, which the poets don't much mention, though that sort of love between spouses is precious and rare. I loved him—the man—and I will miss him until my dying day."

Rex took a taste of the tea, which was plain. The way he drank it when a headache was bearing down.

"Mama, the lady doesn't always make me laugh, but she makes me *think*. About how I manage my dukedom, about whether I'm happy, about where my duty truly lies."

"And she interrupts you and doesn't mince her words with you?"

"She doesn't know how to mince words, and she's a demon with ledger books and hidden patterns. She's shy, though, and fierce. Life hasn't been kind to her."

Mama took Rex's hand. "Then for God's sake, you should marry her. Snatch her up before some other duke sweeps her into his arms. We make poor decisions when we're lonely, and if she's missing you, she'll be very lonely indeed."

Lonely enough to hide in France for the rest of her life?

The tea was good and strong, also the way Rex liked it. "I'll be making some changes at the bank."

"Change at the bank is overdue. Lady Jersey doesn't say much, but in the occasional aside, I gather in her opinion our institution has grown a bit behindhand."

And Lady Jersey was herself a very experienced banker. "Do you mind if I abandon you to your breakfast? I have a few calls to pay."

"Looking like that?"

Eleanora doesn't care how I dress. "The matters I need to tend to are urgent." Rex rose and kissed his mother's cheek. "Thank you, Mama. I love you."

She waved her currant bun. "For God's sake shave before you go out, and of course, the feeling is mutual. Tell the maid to bring up a pot of chocolate if you see her."

"Yes, ma'am." Rex left his mother munching her currant bun and smiling, while he took the stairs to his rooms two at a time.

* * *

"Elsmore was ready to see his own cousin hanged," Jack said around a mouthful of omelet. "You would not have recognized your pet duke, Ellie. He was a whisker away from summoning the watch. Pour me a spot more tea, would you, love?"

Jack had been eating steadily since retrieving breakfast from the chop house. In the light of a cold morning, he was gaunt and tired, no longer a charming schemer.

Maybe he never would be again.

"You expect me to believe that Elsmore would turn a family member over to the magistrate, bring scandal down on the bank, and ruin his own name over a few quid?" Ellie asked, pouring the tea. "He's not stupid, Jack."

"He's also not the Earl of Winston, Ellie, and thousands of pounds is not a few quid. Moreover, even Winston didn't prey on his own family. You should have some eggs. You're peaky and cross."

She'd waited up until Jack had come strolling back from his midnight errand, and then she'd tossed in her bed until sunrise. Where was Elsmore, and what would he do about an embezzling ducal heir?

Ellie buttered a slice of toast. "How did His Grace leave matters?"

"You should ask him. When I left the bank, he was going through Mr. James Dorset's desk drawer by drawer. His Grace paid me handsomely from the small fortune we'd unearthed from one false bottom alone."

"A small fortune?"

"We found two thousand pounds, Ellie, and that was simply the ready money Dorset stored on the premises in one drawer. My guess is, a safe in the man's apartments will hold five times that amount. His jewelry box will bear investigation, as will his snuff boxes, wardrobe, mews...He could not have taken all of that with him. He and I were of a height. I'm tempted to have a look."

The toast was good, probably made from bread baked fresh that morning. "What about turning honest, Jack?"

He took another bite of eggs. "Put in a word for me with your duke, Ellie. Another cousin was apparently brokering loans, and who's to say additional mischief isn't afoot?"

"Elsmore will blame himself. That's why he's not turning James over to the authorities." Ellie added a drizzle of honey to her toast and missed the cinnamon she'd enjoyed at Ambledown.

She missed Elsmore, too, desperately. No need to state the obvious.

"If your duke hasn't laid information against Dorset yet," Jack said. "I suspect he still might, though I told him you don't favor hangings."

A toast crumb caught in Ellie's throat. "Why would you tell him that?"

"Because it's the truth," Jack said, thumping her on the back. "It will always be the truth. This is excellent bacon, but then, I haven't had bacon since Michaelmas. Are you really determined to pike off to France?"

"I miss Mama, Jack. I miss her every day, and my bank runs like a top now. I have some money put by, and she's apparently never going to leave France. I will write to our grandparents and ask them to visit me there."

"Stubborn," Jack said. "The Naylor womenfolk should be in Dr. Johnson's lexicon under the definition of stubborn. Grandmama has threatened to travel to France on her own, you know. That dog would fancy a nibble of bacon. I suspect he'd fancy a nibble of me as well."

Wodin had kept Ellie and Voltaire company in the small hours of the night. "I'll take him back to the duchess today. The sun's out, and I could use some fresh air."

"You don't mind if I bide here for a bit?" Jack asked, tearing a strip of bacon in half and tossing a portion to the dog.

Wodin caught the treat with a snap of his teeth.

"Stay as long as you like," Ellie said. "I really am leaving for France."

"Then, Eleanora, you really are a fool. Your duke will tidy up his accounts at the bank whether you move to France or not, but what happens after that depends on you. You've spent your life looking for schemes before the schemers could take advantage, but that man's only aim is to cherish you."

He's not my duke. He will never be my duke. "Hush, you."

Jack tossed Wodin another bite of bacon. "I've said my piece. I can take the dog to the duchess for you."

Jackson Naylor offering to do favors was unnerving. "Wodin prefers my company. If you leave, lock up before you go."

Ellie wanted time to think, and rambling around London was good for that. She also wanted to say farewell to a duchess who'd never planned to wear a tiara. Perhaps Ellie should have a word with His Grace of Walden too.

A word of thanks, offered in parting.

* * *

"You are certain?" Walden asked. "You don't want time to consider?"

Rex was far from certain, but the decision he'd made felt both liberating and terrifying, suggesting the choice was sound.

"The solicitors will take forever to draw up the documents," he said, surveying the volumes of poetry assembled in Walden's library. When was the last time Rex had taken an hour to enjoy good verse? "The lawyers' deliberations will give me ample time for second thoughts."

Walden was attired for an outing, though a tiny stain that looked like jam marred his linen. Rex, by contrast, was still wearing the ensemble Jackson Naylor had recommended for an evening of catching thieves.

Plural. After that enlightening chat with Mama, Rex had called on Eddie and confirmed that illegal brokering had paid for Eddie's matched team, his mistress, and his well-appointed apartment. The brokering was likely impossible to prove, which left banishment to Peebleshire as Eddie's fate.

"Are you angry?" Walden asked. "Finding out that your relatives have been stabbing you in the back must have been an unpleasant revelation."

"Come here," Rex said, waggling his fingers. "You cannot go out in public with jam on your neck cloth."

"I'm a papa," Walden said. "I can go out in public in any state I please. As long as one of my daughters is grinning at my side, clutching me by the hand, I will be forgiven any number of minor imperfections in my wardrobe."

"This imperfection is a jam stain," Rex said, "not a badge of honor." He retied Walden's cravat so the stain wasn't visible.

"It's both," Walden said, using his reflection in a glass breakfront to survey Rex's handiwork. "I hope you learn that one day soon. My solicitors, unlike the leeches you employ, can have the documents drawn up within the week."

"I won't be here."

Walden fluffed the cravat, so the jam stain peeked out from beneath his lace. "Running off to brood?"

"We're peers," Rex said. "I am among the very few men who can call you out, Walden. I'm running off to France."

"Licking your wounds? Do you think you're the only duke who's had a rotter or two among his relations?"

Rex stalked across the room, forcing Walden to stop preening and to instead look at him. "Where would you be without an auditor who could spot larcenous thoughts as they formed in the heads of your clerks, tellers, and customers? Where would you be without a woman quietly toiling away out of sight, a lady who knows every rig and scheme ever attempted at a financial institution? You have built a reputation for scrupulously fair dealing, Walden, but you've maintained that reputation in part because Eleanora Hatfield has been patrolling your bank's ramparts."

"She was born to perform that office," Walden said. "She thrives on it. I gather you seek to steal her away?"

"I seek to offer her a real option."

Walden consulted a gold watch, though the mantel had an eight-day clock that looked to be keeping good time. The duke was stalling, then, considering options of his own.

"Eleanora likes to remain beyond the notice of the customers and managers," Walden said. "She wanted a post answering directly to the partners, and she's done well with that arrangement."

"Do you know why she sought such anonymity?"

"I have my suspicions."

Rex silently commended Walden for guarding a lady's secrets, but that very display of caution confirmed that Eleanora's problems extended beyond a grandparent ruined by scandal and a cousin absconding with two hundred pounds. Lord Stephen had all but said as much over a morning cup of chocolate, but he too had refused to provide details.

"I will leave you to flaunt your finery," Rex said. "I suspect a certain young lady is packing for a voyage, and I do not intend to let her sail alone."

Walden had somehow positioned himself between Rex and the door, though Rex hadn't noticed him doing it.

"You ruin her at your peril, Elsmore. I value my association with you, but a duke is as a duke does. Eleanora has worked for years to establish herself as a decent woman. You take that away from her, and I will remind you that I am one of the few men who can *and will* call you out."

"Will you stand up with me when I speak my vows? Will you welcome my wife and me under your roof when I marry a duchess polite society shuns? Will you offer hospitality to Eleanora when she's no longer an employee who serves you well?"

Rex was gratified to see he'd caught the almighty Duke of Walden by surprise, though His Grace recovered quickly, and his smile put Rex in mind of the duchess's hound.

"Of course you and your duchess will be welcome under this roof. Her Grace of Walden wouldn't have it any other way, and she counts many other well-born ladies among her acquaintances. I sincerely hope you have the chance to enlist their aid."

That was the second ray of sunshine to penetrate Rex's day, the chat with Mama having been the first. "Then I'm off to France."

Walden resumed his preening before the glass breakfront. "Try Dieppe," he said. "If you've no other place to start."

"Why?"

"Just a suggestion. Dieppe is a quiet town but not too far from Paris. Mail and English travelers reach it quickly."

"Thank you." Rex strode for the door but had to leap back as a blond footman opened it from the corridor.

"Mrs. Eleanora Hatfield to see Her Grace," the footman said. "Excuse me, Your Graces. I thought the lady would like to wait in here for the duchess to come down. I did not know the library was in use."

He had a slight accent, Scandinavian or German, and Eleanora stood behind him with the hellhound panting at her side.

"Take Wodin," Walden said to the footman. "I'll leave Elsmore to keep the lady company, and I'll be across the corridor should anybody have need of me."

Walden paused to whisper something in Eleanora's ear before pulling the door closed, and then Rex was alone with his beloved. All the flowery speeches he'd spent half the night rehearsing, all the clever arguments he'd concocted, flew out of his head at the sight of Eleanora looking pale and for once, uncertain.

"If you want to move to France," he said, "we'll move to France. I'd rather your parents move here to England instead, but even more than that, I need to know that you're safe and happy. Tell me how to make that happen, and if it's within my power to bring it about, I'll do it."

Eleanora stalked past Rex, whirling only when she reached the poetry shelved across the room. "Who told you about my parents?"

"Nobody has told me, but an exceedingly clever auditor taught me to notice what's in front of me. You mentioned cousins, siblings, grandparents, all manner of family, but you never once brought up your parents. You do, though, threaten to abandon me for the shores of blasted France. Why is that, I asked myself, and then the answer presented itself.

"Will you do as I've been doing," he went on, "and sacrifice your happiness for the sake of familial duty, Eleanora? Are you truly determined to rejoin your exiled parents rather than reach for the joy that's standing before you, or will you find the courage to be my duchess?"

Chapter Sixteen

Ellie cowered by the books lining the walls of the Walden library and tried to think. Elsmore looked very, very determined and willing to fight dirty to get what he wanted. Every duke should know how to fight dirty, though she didn't want him resorting to such measures on her account.

"You cannot live in France," she said, grasping at the nearest spar of reason floating among the wreckage of her morning. "You are an English duke."

"I'm also a Scottish earl, but I don't dwell in Peebleshire, do I?" He came closer, step by measured step. "I am a Surrey farmer, though I spend only a small portion of my time there where I'm happiest. I'm your lover—or I was—and I claim that identity on the strength of only a precious few hours that sparkle in my memory like every wish ever granted to a despairing man."

"I cannot marry you." Ellie had spent hopeless dark eternities telling herself that. "I cannot. You'd hate me."

"Would I?" Elsmore came to a halt before her, a solid wall of black-clad man who looked more like a minion of darkness than a duke. "My cousin and heir has been embezzling not only from my bank customers, but also from my own sisters, aunts, and dependents. I am furious with him, but I do not hate him. James seized opportunities I put under his very nose. When he exploited those opportunities, I was too busy being bored witless at the theater to curb his greed."

Do not touch Elsmore. Do not put your hand on his dear, handsome, fierce person. For if Ellie touched Elsmore, she'd want to cling to him.

"You blame yourself," she said.

"In part, I do, and what I have allowed to go wrong, I must put right. James deserves hanging. Naylor forbid that course. He said you'd disapprove."

Elsmore bore his signature beguiling scent, and his cheeks were freshly shaved. Ellie put her hands behind her back.

"Jack had no right to tell you what to do," she said. "When a man commits multiple felonies and betrays the trust of family and customers alike, his fate should not be decided by my fancies."

"I'm selling most of my shares in the bank, Eleanora."

Ellie left off staring at Elsmore's chest. "You're *what*?"

"I am selling most of my shares in Dorset and Becker. I've explained to Walden exactly what has transpired with James, and His Grace is willing to take on the thankless task of putting the place in order. He has the means and temperament to do it. I lack both, and more to the point, I could not be both the head of my family and hold a controlling interest in an institution that employs family members. Cousin Howell needs his job, ergo, I will relinquish a controlling interest in the bank."

Ellie sidled away, down the bookcase, around Elsmore. She put an enormous globe between them, a fitting metaphor for their situation.

"Walden will sort out Dorset and Becker," she said, "but you should not have given up your shares. Land rents have done nothing but drop since the war ended, you have few truly commercial ventures compared to many other peers, and your estates are flung all over the realm, making them harder to manage."

Elsmore wandered off to an orrery positioned before a large window. The planets and their satellites circled the sun in endless orbits, set in motion by a winding mechanism that the duke cranked a few turns.

"And you still think you are not suited to be my duchess," he said. "Tell me about your parents."

Why must he seize on that detail now? "I had one of each, a father and a mother. Mama dwells in Normandy, and I'd like to visit her."

"We can visit her together. Tell me about your father." Elsmore spoke both gently and implacably.

"You will not let this go."

"I've learned to *listen*, Eleanora. You taught me that. Tell me the tale, and I'll listen to every word."

"I don't want to say those words." Didn't want to think them or acknowledge that they existed. "I want only to balance ledger books and make accounts come right. I am good at it."

He stood on the other side of the known universe and held out a hand. "Tell me. I love you, and wherever the story leads, you will not journey there alone."

She wrapped her arms around her middle and kept her

gaze on the golden sun at the center of the complicated model. *I love you.* The last man to make that declaration had come to a very bad end.

I love you, my little Ellie. Be a good girl for Papa. Make me proud of my best girl. Not poetry, not much more than a father's platitudes, but they'd been his final words to her.

The universe wound to a halt, and still Elsmore stood with his hand outstretched. "Tell me, Eleanora. I'm listening."

Ellie withstood a drowning tide of pain, until Elsmore's fingers closed around hers. If he let her go, she'd sink and never surface. And for what? Ledgers and accounts? Years toiling over books that any half-awake clerk could put to rights? Family that had never needed her in any real sense?

"We'll go to France," Elsmore said, stepping closer, "if that's what you want. We'll live in obscurity at Amble-down. I'll deed it to you and we'll live there in sin. We'll set up a household in York, but twelve estates, thirty-two near relations, a ducal title, a bloody box in Drury Lane, and shares in a damned bank mean nothing, Eleanora, if you force me to muddle on without you. *I love you.*"

He enfolded her in a careful embrace that by degrees became more secure. In Elsmore's arms, Ellie found every comfort she'd ever needed, every joy she'd aspired to, every dream she'd cherished in secret.

Also the courage to say the hard words.

"Papa was a counterfeiter. He was hanged before a jeering mob on a pretty Monday morning." And then, at long last, she began to cry.

* * *

"Somebody is upset," Jane, Duchess of Walden, muttered, pacing before the door of the family parlor. Across the corridor, the door to the library stood closed.

"Somebody is probably crying her heart out," Walden replied. "We'll be late for our outing if we eavesdrop much longer."

"We are not eavesdropping. We are concerned for our guests. Was Eleanora angry?"

Walden took his duchess gently by the elbow and stilled her pacing. "I suspect she has been angry for much of her life."

He and Jane wore the finery appropriate for strolling in the park. To appearances they would be very much the duke and duchess on display with their darling daughters in tow. Quinn liked parading about at Jane's side, liked seeing polite society brought to heel by a poor minister's daughter and a guttersnipe from York.

Arrogant of him, but a duke was expected to be a bit arrogant.

"Why would Eleanora be angry?" Jane asked. "She has an excellent post, one suited to her abilities, one very few women could hope for. Her wages are ample, and you and Joshua respect her for the asset she is."

The weeping from the library grew softer.

Quinn recalled the day Eleanora Hatfield had marched into his bank, prepared to turn the place upside down over tuppence. "Anger can sit atop a world of hurt."

Jane gave him the look, the one that said she was sparing him verbal acknowledgment of what he'd just admitted—about his own anger, about the world of hurt he'd been raised in.

"Eleanora's path has been difficult," she said, worrying a fingernail. "One doesn't learn to spot every patch of boggy ground and every inaccurate sum while embroidering samplers in a rose garden."

A thunder of small feet on the floor above suggested the nursery contingent was about to interrupt the proceedings. "Shall we leave our guests in peace, Your Grace?"

"If he breaks her heart, Quinn, I will ruin him."

So fierce. "Of course. And if she breaks his?"

"We will intervene. A moping duke, above all things, is not to be contemplated. Come along. I know you like to show off your ladies in the park, and we like to show you off as well."

Quiet voices murmured behind the library door.

Quinn offered Jane his arm as the two oldest girls slid down the bannister and the third churned down the steps pulling her nurse by the hand. God willing, Elsmore would soon know the joy of being taken captive by his womenfolk, or at least by one woman in particular.

* * *

"Grandpapa claimed his son was the greater artistic talent," Eleanora said, "but he had no money to give Papa a proper education."

Rex was indulging in the pleasure of holding Eleanora in his lap, stroking her hair, and rubbing her back. She was still sniffly, still taking the occasional shuddery breath, but a long overdue storm was moving out to sea.

"So your papa received an improper education?"

Eleanora folded Rex's handkerchief, which had become hopelessly wrinkled in her clutches. "We were in Birmingham at the time. Every metal trade in the realm is pursued there, and Grandpapa thought engraving would provide Papa a steady, honest living. Then some war or other ended, the gunsmiths and artificers took up engraving, and the newest employees were let go. My aunt did what she could to survive, and Papa…"

"He did what he could, in hopes of retrieving his sister from a dubious profession." What a damned muddle. What an unfair, sad, stupid muddle.

"There's no retrieving a woman *or a family* from ruin."

Rex kissed Eleanora's temple. The sofa was commodious, but he propped a pillow at Eleanora's back in hopes of making her more comfortable still.

"A family cannot be retrieved from ruin easily, I agree, but it can be done."

Eleanora glared at him, her lashes still spikey with tears. "This is England, and not even a duke can erase an executed felon from the family escutcheon."

"Did you know that the Eighth Earl of Argyll was executed for treason, his lands and titles forfeited? Two years later all was restored to his son, who became the ninth earl. Matters went along smoothly until the ninth earl had the bad judgment to participate in the Monmouth Rebellion, so alas, he was done away with as well."

"My papa was not an earl."

"The tenth earl—the son and grandson of traitors—was raised to a dukedom. I could list you any number of similar tales, from a foreign secretary in this century married to a legendary courtesan, to a duke's daughter who waited all of two days after her divorce to marry her lover, then two of her children when grown, though half siblings…" Eleanora was regarding him as if he'd begun discoursing in Mandarin. "Society gossiped and whispered, but nobody refused their invitations."

"And none of that is relevant because I am an auditor, not a duke's anything." Eleanora scooted away and took the place beside him. "The situation is hopeless, Elsmore. You mean well, but you cannot marry a woman bound to be a disgraced duchess."

How obstinate she was, and how wrong. "When you took a look at my books, I was certain you'd fuss, shake your head, and tell me the situation was too complicated to be set to rights."

Eleanora smoothed her skirts. "I wanted to. Your ledgers were a mare's nest of inaccuracies, schemes, and incompetence, but numbers can be made to come right. They behave in a predictable fashion."

"*So does polite society, Eleanora*, and I am as competent at tallying those books as you are at auditing bank records. I know which hostesses to charm, which charities to support, which MPs to flatter. I know whose daughter to stand up with. I know whose son needs a good word put in with a Cabinet minister. I know exactly which people to invite to the theater or to a dinner party, and I know how to quell gossip with a raised eyebrow."

She smoothed an index finger along that portion of his anatomy. "You sound so confident."

Was that relenting he heard in her voice? Hope? "I am very confident. I was not brought up to manage a complicated financial institution, but I was trained to be a duke. Acceptance of our union will take time and there will be talk, but it will be quiet talk. You will dance with me at Almack's, we will enlist the aid of Walden and his duchess, and they will recruit others to our cause. My entire family will rally to our side, and we will be so very publicly besotted that everybody will know we are a love match."

He could see the arrows and connections flying across the pages of Debrett's. The aunties knew everybody, including the dowagers and hostesses who held the real social power in London. Mama had already promised her support, and even allowed that a *soupçon* of notoriety enlivened all the best family histories.

"We will hint that your grandfather was duped by a scheming wastrel," he went on, pausing to kiss Eleanora's hand. "A subtle reference to the truth never hurt the course of true love."

"And what of my mother?" Eleanora asked. "She is the widow of a felon, living in self-imposed exile."

"While my very heir is a felon, and his excuse is what? An inability to survive without a mahogany walking stick? A pressing need for more gold sleeve buttons? Your mother has committed no crimes, while my cousins—note the plural—have, and yet you think she should be banished to France?"

"What I think doesn't matter."

"What you think is all that matters," Rex retorted. "Dealing with polite society will be messy and tedious, Eleanora, just as putting my accounts in order was messy and tedious. We'll think we've laid the gossip to rest only to hear another nasty rumor. We'll see glances exchanged when we're announced and know damned well we're being slandered purely for spite until some other couple stumbles into society's gunsights. I don't care, as long as you'll marry me and be the woman I cleave to for the rest of my earthly days."

She was quiet for so long Rex nearly resorted to begging on bended knee.

"I have no abacus for this, this proposal you put before me," she said slowly. "I don't understand the columns and figures."

Rex's heart sank straight to his toes, and he resigned himself to a lengthy courtship in blasted France.

"But you know what you're about," Eleanora went on, "and you love me."

"I most assuredly do and always will."

She clasped his hand in both of hers. No ink stains on her hands today, maybe no ink stains ever again.

"I love you too, Wrexham, Duke of Elsmore, and if love demands anything from us, it's courage. You trusted me with your wretched bookkeeping. If you say a marriage between us will work, I am insufficiently unselfish to argue with you."

Insufficiently unselfish meant...*yes*. "You already talk like a duchess."

"I will be your wife, and if that means I must also be a duchess, then I will rise to that challenge to the best of my ability. I do wish though..."

He kissed her. "What do you wish?"

"Why did you sell Walden your bank shares, Elsmore? Your bank is on solid footing, though in another two years who's to say where it might have tottered."

"Eddie was brokering usurious loans. James embezzled outright. My head clerk, Ballentyre, was literally asleep at his post, and nobody—not a teller, not a manager, not a well-meaning fellow at the clubs where I've been playing cards for the past ten years, not my own cousin Howell— said a word. I kept a significant interest in the institution, which I expect to prosper under Walden's watchful eye, and I will hold a seat on the board, even if Walden chooses to combine the two banks."

Eleanora climbed back into his lap. "A seat on the board of directors?"

"I was hoping you'd attend the meetings with me." He wrapped his arms around her and she sighed.

"We will cause talk, won't we?"

"A love match usually does." He kissed her again, and she kissed him back, and while they did cause talk—a lot of talk—it's also true that the marriage of Eleanora and Elsmore resulted in the addition of one plus one totaling not two, but rather…seven, and every one of them was both ferociously good with numbers *and* ferociously charming.

Keep reading for a peek at Althea Wentworth's story in

A DUKE BY ANY OTHER NAME

Coming in Spring 2020

Chapter One

"Lady Althea Wentworth is, without doubt, the most vexatious, bothersome, *pestilential* female I have ever had the misfortune to encounter." Nathaniel Rothmere was prevented from pacing and shouting by the sow sniffing at his boots, but his store of pejoratives concerning Lady Althea was bottomless.

The sow was a mere four-hundred-pound sylph compared to the rest of the herd milling about Nathaniel's orchard, though when she flopped to the grass, the ground shook.

"Have you?" Treegum asked with characteristic delicacy. "Encountered the lady, that is?"

"No." *Nor do I wish to.*

Another swine, this one on the scale of a seventy-four gun ship of the line, settled in beside her sister and several others followed.

"They seem quite happy here," Treegum observed. "Perhaps we ought to simply keep them."

"Then her ladyship will have an excuse to come around again, banging on the door, cutting up my peace, and disturbing the tranquility of my estate."

Two more pigs chose grassy napping places. Their march across the pastures had apparently tired them out, which was just too damned bad.

"Has the time come for a Stinging Rebuke, sir?" Treegum asked, as a particularly grand specimen rubbed up against him and nearly knocked the old fellow off his feet. Treegum was the butler-cum-house steward. Swineherding was not in his gift.

"I've already sent her ladyship two Stinging Rebukes. She probably has them displayed over her mantel like a privateer's letters of marque and reprisal." Nathaniel shoved at the hog milling before him, but he might as well have shoved at one of the boulders dotting his fields. "Her ladyship apparently longs to boast that she's made the acquaintance of the master of Rothhaven Hall. I will gratify her wish, in the spirit of true gentlemanly consideration."

"Mind you don't give her a fright," Treegum muttered, wading around swine to accompany Nathaniel to the gate. "We can't have you responsible for any more swoons."

"Yes, we can. If enough ladies swoon at the mere sight of me, then I will continue to enjoy the privacy due the neighborhood eccentric. I'm considering having Granny Dewar curse me on market day. I could gallop past the village just as some foul weather moves in, and she could consign me to the devil."

Treegum opened the gate, setting off a squeak loud enough to rouse the napping hogs. "Granny will want a fair bit of coin for a public curse, sir."

"She's partial to my elderberry cordial." Nathaniel vaulted the wall one-handed. "Maybe we should leave the gate open." The entire herd had settled on the grass and damned if the largest of the lot—a vast expanse of pink pork—appeared to smile at him.

"They won't find their way home, sir. Pigs like to wander, and sows that size go where they please."

Running pigs through an orchard was an old Yorkshire custom, one usually reserved for autumn rather than the brisk, sunny days of early spring. The hogs consumed the dropped fruit, fertilized the soil, and with their rooting, helped the ground absorb water for the next growing season.

"Perhaps I should saddle up that fine beast on the end," Nathaniel said, considering a quarter ton of livestock where livestock ought not to be. "Give the village something truly worth gossiping about."

Treegum closed and latched the gate. "Hard to steer though, sir, and you do so pride yourself on being an intimidating sort of eccentric rather than the other kind."

"Apparently not intimidating enough. Don't wait supper for me and be sure the hogs of hell have a good supply of water. They have to be thirsty after coming such a distance, and even the neighborhood recluse ought to offer some hospitality to ladies who've wandered so far from home."

* * *

Althea Wentworth heard her guest before she saw him. Rothhaven's arrival was presaged by a rapid beat of hooves pounding not up her drive, but rather, directly across the park that surrounded Lynley Vale manor.

A large horse created that kind of thunder, one disdaining the genteel canter for a hellbent gallop. She could see its approach from her parlor window, and her first thought was that only a terrified animal traveled at such a speed.

But no. Horse and rider cleared the wall beside the drive in perfect rhythm, swerved onto the verge, and continued right up—good God, they aimed straight for the fountain. Althea looked on in horror as the black horse drew closer and closer to unforgiving marble and splashing water.

"Mary Mother of God."

Another smooth leap—the fountain was five feet if it was an inch—and a foot perfect landing, followed by an immediate check of the horse's speed. The gelding came down to a frisking, capering trot, clearly proud of itself and ready for even greater challenges.

The rider stroked the horse's neck, and the beast calmed and hung its head, sides heaving. A treat was offered and another pat, before one of Althea's grooms bestirred himself to take the horse. Rothhaven—for that could only be the dread duke himself—paused on the front steps long enough to remove his spurs, whip off his hat, and run a black-gloved hand through hair as dark as hell's tarpit.

"The rumors are true," Althea murmured. Rothhaven was built on the proportions of the Vikings of old, but their fair coloring had been denied him. He glanced up, as if he knew Althea would be spying, and she drew back.

His gaze was colder than a Yorkshire night in January, which fit exactly with what Althea had heard of him.

She moved from the window and took the nearest wing chair, opening a book chosen for this singular occasion. She had dressed carefully—elegantly but without too much fuss—and styled her hair with similar consideration. Rothhaven gave very few people the chance to make even a first impression on him, a feat Althea admired.

Voices drifted up from the foyer, then the tread of boots

sounded on the stair. Rothhaven moved lightly for such a grand specimen, and his voice rumbled like distant cannon. A soft tap on the door preceded Strensall announcing Nathaniel, His Grace of Rothhaven. The duke did not have to duck his head to come through the doorway, but it was a near thing.

Althea set aside her book, rose, and curtseyed to a precisely deferential depth and not one inch lower. "Welcome to Lynley Vale, Your Grace. A pleasure to meet you. Strensall, the tea, and don't spare the trimmings."

Strensall bolted for the door.

"I do not break bread with mine enemy." Rothhaven stalked over to Althea and swept her with a glower. "No damned tea."

His eyes were a startling green, set against swooping dark brows and features as angular as the crags and tors of Yorkshire's moors. He brought with him the scents of heather and horse, a lovely combination. His cravat remained neatly pinned with a single bar of gleaming gold, despite his mad dash across the countryside.

He was precisely as his reputation had foretold, from the fierce dignity of his bearing, to the perfect details of his appearance, to a disregard for decorum that made him all the more imposing.

Althea could barely contain her glee, for he was all she'd hoped for and more. "I will attribute Your Grace's lack of manners to the peckishness that can follow exertion. A tray, Strensall."

The duke leaned nearer. "Shall I threaten to curse poor Strensall with nightmares, should he bring a tray?"

"That would be unsporting." Althea sent her goggling butler a glance and he withdrew. "You are reputed to have a temper, but then, if folk claimed that my mere passing caused milk to curdle and babies to colic, I'd be a tad testy too. No one has ever accused you of dishonorable behavior."

"Nor will they, while you, my lady, have stooped so low as to unleash the hogs of war upon my private property." He backed away not one inch, and this close Althea caught a more subtle fragrance. Lily of the valley or jasmine. Very faint, elegant, and unexpected, like the moss green of his eyes.

"You cannot read, perhaps," he went on, "else you'd grasp that 'we will not be entertaining for the foreseeable future' means neither you nor your livestock are welcome at Rothhaven."

"A neighborly call is hardly entertaining," Althea countered. "Shall we be seated?"

Lynley Vale had come into her possession when the Wentworth family had acquired a ducal title several years past. Althea's brother Quinn, the present duke, had entrusted an estate to each of his three siblings, and Althea had done her best to kit out Lynley Vale as befit a ducal residence. When Quinn visited, he and his duchess seemed comfortable enough amid the portraits, frescoed ceilings, and gilt-framed pier glasses.

Rothhaven was a different sort of duke, one whose presence made pastel carpets and flocked wallpaper appear fussy and overdone. Althea had been so curious about Rothhaven Hall she'd nearly peered through the windows, but His Grace had threatened even children with charges of trespassing. A grown woman would get no quarter from a duke who cursed and issued threats on first acquaintance.

"I will not be seated," he retorted. "Retrieve your damned pigs from my orchard, madam, or I will send them all to slaughter before the week is out."

"Is that where my naughty ladies got off to?" Althea took her wing chair. "They haven't been on an outing in ages. I suppose the spring air provoked them to seeing the sights. Last autumn they took a notion to inspect the market. In spring they decided to attend Sunday services. Most of my neighbors find my herd's social inclinations amusing."

"I might be amused, were your herd not at the moment rooting through my orchard uninvited. To allow stock of those dimensions to wander is irresponsible, and why a duke's sister is raising hogs entirely defeats my powers of imagination."

Because he had never been destitute and never would be. "Do have a seat. I'm told only the ill-mannered pace the parlor like a house tabby who needs to visit the garden."

He turned his back to Althea—very rude of him— though he appeared to require a moment to marshal his composure. She counted that a small victory, for she had needed many such moments since acquiring a title, and her composure yet remained as unruly as her sows on a pretty spring day.

Though truth be told, the ladies had had some *encouragement* regarding the direction of their latest outing.

Rothhaven turned to face her, the fire in his gaze banked to burning disdain. "Will you or will you not retrieve your wayward pigs from my land?"

"I refuse to discuss this with a man who cannot observe the simplest conversational courtesy." She waved a hand at the opposite wing chair, and when that provoked a drawing up of the magnificent ducal height, she feared he'd stalk from the room.

Instead he took the chair, whipping out the tails of his riding jacket like Lucifer arranging his coronation robes.

"Thank you," Althea said. "When you march about like

that you give a lady a crick in her neck. Your orchard is at least a mile from my home farm."

"And downwind, more's the pity. Do you raise pigs to perfume the neighborhood with their scent?"

"No more than you keep horses, sheep, or cows for the same purpose, Your Grace. Or maybe your livestock covers up the pervasive odor of brimstone hanging about Rothhaven Hall?"

A muscle twitched in His Grace's jaw.

Althea had been raised by a man who regarded displays of violence to be all in a day's parenting. Her instinct for survival had been honed early and well, and had she found Rothhaven frightening, she would not have been alone with him.

She was considered a spinster, while he was a confirmed eccentric. He was intimidating—impressively so—but she had bet her future on his basic decency. He patted his horse, he fed the beast treats, he took off his spurs before calling on a lady, and his retainers were all so venerable they could nearly recall when York was a Viking capital.

A truly dishonorable peer would discard elderly servants, abuse his cattle, and ignore basic manners, wouldn't he?

The tea tray arrived before Althea could doubt herself further, and in keeping with standing instructions, the kitchen had exerted itself to the utmost. Strensall placed an enormous silver tray before Althea—the good silver, not the fancy silver—bowed, and withdrew.

"How do you take your tea, Your Grace?"

"Plain, except I won't be staying for tea. Assure me that you'll send your swineherd over to collect your sows in the next twenty-four hours and I will take my leave of you."

Not so fast. Having coaxed Rothhaven into making a call, Althea wasn't about to let him win free that easily.

"I cannot give you those assurances, much as I'd like to. I'm very fond of those ladies, and they are quite valuable. They are also particular."

Rothhaven straightened a crease in his breeches. They fit him exquisitely, though Althea had never before seen black riding attire.

"The whims of your livestock are no affair of mine, Lady Althea." His tone said that Althea's whims were a matter of equal indifference to him. "You either retrieve them or the entire shire will be redolent of smoking bacon."

He was bluffing. Nobody butchered hogs in the spring, for any number of reasons. "Do you know what those sows are worth, sir?"

He quoted a price per pound for pork on the hoof that was accurate to the shilling.

"Wrong," Althea said, pouring him a cup of tea, and holding it out to him. "Those are my best breeders. I chose their grandmamas and mamas for size and the ability to produce large, healthy litters. A pig in the garden can be the difference between a family surviving winter or starving, if that pig can also produce large, healthy litters. She can live on scraps, she needs very little care, and she will see a dozen piglets raised to weaning twice a year without putting any additional strain on her upkeep."

The duke looked at the steaming cup of tea, then at Althea, then back at the cup. This was the best China black she could offer, served on the good porcelain in her formal parlor. If he disdained her hospitality now, she might...cry?

He would not be swayed by tears, though he apparently could be tempted by a perfect cup of tea.

"You raise hogs as a charitable undertaking?" he asked, accepting the cup and saucer.

"I raise them for all sorts of reasons." Not the least of which was to donate many to the poor of the parish.

He took a cautious sip of his tea. "What must I do to inspire you to come get your sows? I have my own swineherd, you know. A capable old fellow who has been wrangling hogs more than half a century. He can move your livestock to the King's highway."

Althea hadn't considered this possibility, but she dared not give quarter when she'd finally flushed Rothhaven from his covert. She put three sandwiches on a plate and passed it to him.

"My sows are partial to their own swineherd," she said. "They'll follow him anywhere, though after rioting about the neighborhood on their own, they will require time to recover. They've been out dancing all night, so to speak, and must have a lie-in."

Althea could not fathom why any sensible female would comport herself thus, but every spring she dragged herself south, and subjected herself to the same inanity for the duration of the London Season.

This year would be different.

"So send your swineherd to fetch them tomorrow," Rothhaven said, taking a bite of a chicken sandwich. "My swineherd will assist, and I need never darken your door again—nor you, mine." He sent her a pointed look, one that scolded without saying a word.

Althea's brother Quinn had learned to deliver such looks, and his duchess had perfected the raised eyebrow to an art more delicate than that of the fan or glove.

While I am a laughingstock. A memory came to Althea, of turning down the room with a peer's heir, a handsome, well-mannered man tall enough to look past her shoulder. The entire time they'd been waltzing, he'd been rolling his eyes at his friends, affecting looks of long-suffering martyrdom, and holding Althea up as an object of ridicule, even as he'd stalked her fortune and made remarks intended to flatter.

She had been blind to his game until her own sister had reported it to her in the carriage on the way home. The hostess had not intervened, no chaperone or gentleman had called the young dandy to account. He had thanked Althea for the dance and escorted her to her next partner with all the courtesy due the sister of a duke, and she'd been the butt of another joke.

"I cannot oblige you with an immediate removal of my sows, Your Grace," Althea said. "My swineherd is visiting his sister in York, and won't be back until week's end. I do apologize for the delay, though if turning my pigs loose in your orchard has occasioned this introduction then I'm glad for it. I value my privacy too, but I am at my wit's end, and must consult you on a matter of some delicacy."

He gestured with half a sandwich. "All the way at your wit's end? What has caused you to travel that long and arduous trail?"

Polite society. Wealth. Standing. All the great boons Althea had once envied and had so little ability to manage.

"I want a baby," she said, not at all how she'd planned to state her situation.

Rothhaven put down his plate slowly, as if a wild creature had come snorting and snapping into the parlor. "Are you utterly demented? One doesn't announce such a thing, and I am in no position to..." He stood, his height once again creating an impression of towering disdain. "I will see myself out."

Althea rose as well, and though Rothhaven could toss her behind the sofa one-handed, she made her words count.

"Do not flatter yourself, Your Grace. Only a fool would seek to procreate with a petulant, moody, withdrawn, arrogant specimen such as you. I want a family. There's nothing shameful or inappropriate about that. Until I learn to comport myself as the sister of a duke ought, I have no hope of making an acceptable match. You are a duke. If anybody understands the challenge I face, you do. You have five hundred years of breeding and family history to call upon, while I..."

Oh, this was not at all the soliloquy she'd rehearsed, and Rothhaven's expression had become unreadable.

He gestured with a large hand. "While you...?"

Althea had tried inviting him to tea, then to dinner. She'd tried calling upon him. She'd ridden the bridle paths for hours in hopes of meeting him by chance, only to see him galloping over the moors at breakneck speed, heedless of anything so tame as a bridle path.

She'd called on him twice only to be turned away at the door and twice chided by letter for even presuming that much.

Althea had only a single weapon left in her arsenal, a lone arrow in her quiver of strategies, the one least likely to yield the desired result.

She had the truth. "While I need your help," she said. "I haven't anywhere else to turn, and I am tired of being a laughingstock, an outcast who's nonetheless greeted cordially at every door. I need your assistance if I'm ever to comport myself in a manner appropriate for a lady of my station."

Copyright © 2019 by Grace Burrowes

About the Author

Grace Burrowes grew up in central Pennsylvania and is the sixth of seven children. She discovered romance novels in junior high and has been reading them voraciously ever since. Grace has a bachelor's degree in political science, a bachelor of music in music history (both from the Pennsylvania State University), a master's degree in conflict transformation from Eastern Mennonite University, and a juris doctor from the National Law Center at George Washington University.

Grace is a *New York Times* and *USA Today* bestselling author who writes Georgian, Regency, Scottish Victorian, and contemporary romances in both novella and novel lengths. She's a member of Romance Writers of America and Novelist, Inc., and enjoys giving workshops and speaking at writers' conferences.

You can learn more at:
GraceBurrowes.com
Twitter @GraceBurrowes
Facebook.com/Grace.Burrowes

A lady with secrets, a man with a burning desire, a love that breaks all the rules...

Lady Charlotte Beaumont has spent her whole life being ignored, even though she possesses artistic talent that well exceeds the Royal Academy's standards of admission. When she gets a chance at her dream commission, she'll do whatever it takes to make it work, including disguising herself as "Charlie" and fighting an attraction for her classmate, the inspiring and charming Flynn Rutledge.

Please turn the page for a bonus novella,

THE LADY IN RED

by RITA award-winning author Kelly Bowen.

For my readers.

Chapter 1

London, 1818

The forgery was flawless.

Or at least Charlotte hoped it was. It would need to be to fool the man currently examining the painting. From the canvas, a young girl clutched a fan and gazed back at her with an enigmatic look far beyond her years, offering no reassurances.

A bead of icy sweat slid down Charlotte's spine.

"Van Dyck did not paint many children," the man said, straightening slightly, his fingers drumming against the silver head of his ebony walking stick. He turned his unsettling pale blue eyes back in Charlotte's direction.

"He did not," Charlotte agreed smoothly, relieved her voice didn't shake.

"That fact would make this painting very valuable."

"It would."

"And where did you say you acquired it?"

"I didn't say." Charlotte was treading carefully. It had taken all her courage to request an audience with this man, known only by the name of King. A man whose origins were murky at best, though there were rumors that his control of the underworld stretched far beyond the limits of London. A man whose knowledge of fine art was eclipsed only by his reputation for being able to secure anything. For a price.

And Charlotte had come to bargain.

King tipped his head slightly, and had his gaze not been so remote, Charlotte would have believed the man had almost smiled. "What is it, exactly, that you wish to do with this painting?" he asked.

And there was the crux of this entire matter. "I was told that you were a purveyor of fine art," she said slowly. "The best in England. I wish to... sell it." Not entirely true, but a starting point.

"Ah." The man wandered to the far side of his desk, and Charlotte was once again struck by the stealthy grace in which he moved. He had red-gold hair and aristocratic, austere features, and if she were to paint the most infamous Tudor king, before age and excess had ravaged his appearance, this is how she imagined he would have looked. This man was almost too beautiful to possess the dark reputation that cloaked him.

King was examining a painting that dominated the wall behind his desk. "*Judith Beheading Holofernes*," he said, and Charlotte wasn't sure if he was talking to her or himself. "A woman driven to extreme measures." He gestured at the maiden, her wickedly curved blade buried deep in the neck of a man whose eyes bulged in terror. "Tell me, what do you see in her expression?" King asked.

Charlotte hesitated, looking for pitfalls to his question but unable to find any. "Determination," she finally answered. "Maybe a small measure of desperation."

"Indeed." He turned around again, and now his cool eyes were fixed firmly on hers. "Similar to what I see on your face. So I must ask what extreme measures have driven you to try and sell me a forgery."

Charlotte felt her stomach plummet to her toes and bile rise in her throat. She focused on keeping her breathing even. "How can you be so sure that it's a forgery?" she asked with every ounce of bravado she still clung to.

King's lips twisted, and his eyes became positively glacial. "I would advise you not to insult me further. Just answer my question."

"Perhaps I should go," Charlotte murmured, chilled to the bone. "Perhaps we're done here." She had risked everything coming to see this man. No one knew she was here. Only the bored hackney driver she had paid to bring her here, who had agreed to wait for twenty minutes and no longer. She was utterly on her own, and if she were to disappear, there would be no trail to follow. Which was probably just as well. At least they wouldn't carve *fool* on her headstone.

"I think not, Lady Charlotte," he said, moving with a lethal grace to block the door. "For I am not done with you at all."

Charlotte's heart stopped before it resumed again. "How do you know my name?" she whispered. She had not given it to King. Only identified herself as Miss Hawkins, using the surname of one of the kitchen maids. She didn't look like a refined lady—she was too tall to be elegant, too broad shouldered to be sophisticated. And she had twisted her plain brown hair into a forgettable plait. Left every trapping of wealth at home in favor of homespun wool and worn leather purchased in Petticoat Lane to cover her unremarkable figure.

"I asked you not to insult me further," King repeated coldly. Which told Charlotte nothing. But then, that was probably the idea. "The forgery," he said, leaning over his walking stick. "Tell me who painted it."

Charlotte swallowed hard. Should she lie? Tell the truth? Would it matter at this point, or would she simply become a footnote in history either way? A woman who had badly underestimated a very dangerous man and didn't survive to tell the tale. "Me," she finally said. He wouldn't believe her, but at least she wouldn't meet her demise as a liar.

"Good." King nodded like she had just passed some sort of test. "And the original? Where is it?"

Charlotte blinked, trying to find her voice. The sneering censure and mocking disbelief she'd expected at her declaration were absent. "Um..."

"The original," King repeated as though he were talking to a half-wit or a panicked filly. "It must be somewhere where you had access to it to execute a forgery of this quality. Where is it?"

"Jasper House," Charlotte blurted. "In Aysgarth. North of York." One of the many estates that her father, the Earl of Edgerton, owned. Her solitary prison every summer and every winter for as long as she could remember. And one that she would be returning to within a fortnight unless she did something drastic. Like this.

"I know where Aysgarth is, Lady Charlotte," King replied, sounding pleased. "Can you be more specific?"

"Specific?"

"Where is the painting? In a drawing room? A ballroom? A gallery—"

"The attics."

King's expression flattened. "The attics," he repeated, his lip curling.

"It's been there for generations. No one in my family has ever believed that portraits of children are worthy of wall space. Or have any value at all, really."

"Except you."

"It's a Van Dyck, for pity's sake," Charlotte retorted, forgetting herself.

"It is indeed." King took two steps closer to her.

Charlotte steeled herself against the urge to take two steps back. If these were her last moments, she would live them no more a coward than she would a liar. King had been right. Extreme measures had brought her here, and determination and desperation would see this out, come what may.

"Tell me, Lady Charlotte, why not just bring me the original?"

Because here in London, she didn't have access to it. Because time had been of the essence and a lengthy journey up to Aysgarth and back would have taken too long. "This was in my possession," she said honestly. "The original was not."

This time, the beautiful man smiled, though it fell short of his eyes. "And what, exactly, is it that you need money for so desperately that it would be worth your attempt to defraud me?"

And now they had come full circle. Because this wasn't about money. It never had been. It was about her life and the way she was watching it crawl by from the confines of the empty, gilded cage she resided in.

She raised her chin a notch and met his gaze directly. "I don't want money."

Something shifted in his pale eyes. "Indeed? Well, you certainly have my attention, Lady Charlotte."

She wiped her damp palms on her plain skirts. "I want a job. St. Michael's. Coventry. The Renaissance-styled murals that have been commissioned for the church."

King regarded her coolly. "Hmm." He turned abruptly and wandered back behind his desk. "I've always felt a rather odd affinity toward that particular saint. A great warrior, vanquishing those who deserve it. Yet descending at the hour of death to offer each soul a chance to redeem itself." He stopped. "Redemption is highly underrated, don't you think, Lady Charlotte?"

She gazed back, feeling the perspiration trapped against her skin. "Yes."

"I am familiar with the project. I understand that there are two artists to be hired for the work. I also understand that the architect overseeing the project has already selected one."

"Yes. And I would like to be the other. My work is as good as or better than anything currently on display at the Royal Academy. But—"

"You are a woman," he finished for her.

"Yes." A woman and a lady. Slowly suffocating under the crushing limitations that both imposed.

He turned from her to study the painting, his elegant fingers drumming slowly on the head of his walking stick again. "I would agree with you, you know. That your work is better. This copy really is quite astounding," he said. "There are very, very few in the world who would notice the minute technical discrepancies between this and a true Van Dyck." He paused. "It must have taken you some time to paint."

"Yes." But time she had in spades. Months and months of exile to the countryside every year assured that. Yet each of those months was time that she was left alone with her pigments and oils, her turpentine and canvases. Months every year in which she continued to be ignored and was allowed to covertly perfect her craft and proficiency.

"Your application of asphaltum is masterful," King murmured. "So few forgers can get that last step right." His eyes drifted back from the painting toward her, and he fell silent.

Somewhere in the room, a clock ticked into the quiet, small noises marking the passage of time as more of Charlotte's life slipped by her.

"I'll have the original," King said suddenly as if coming to a decision. "Because I do not sell forgeries."

Charlotte felt a tiny ember of hope ignite amid all the trepidation. "I can get it—"

"I don't need you to fetch it for me, Lady Charlotte. I employ professionals for such menial tasks." He smiled another empty smile. "You can keep your copy."

"Then you'll help me in exchange for the painting?"

"My assistance will cost you more than a single painting, Lady Charlotte." He set his walking stick against the side of the desk.

The tiny hairs on the back of her neck rose. She forced herself to remain still, even as she wondered just how far she would be willing to go. Just how much she would be willing to sacrifice for the opportunity to escape—

"You look pale, my lady." The bastard sounded like he was enjoying this.

Charlotte forced herself to hold his gaze. "A mere trick of the light, I assure you," she replied steadily.

King moved silently out from behind the desk to stop before Charlotte. He raised his hand, his fingers stopping a breath away from her face. Charlotte could feel every muscle in her body go rigid. Yet she didn't move. His fingertips descended, grazing the sharp edge of her cheekbone, a gesture that was terrifying for all its gentleness.

"I am not for sale," she said, her words sounding like they were coming from a great distance.

King's lips curled, as if he found her defiance amusing. "Everyone is for sale, my lady. For the right price." His hand dropped, and he turned away from her.

Charlotte remembered to breathe as King returned to the other side of his desk. He once again stopped, the fingers that had caressed her face now sliding over the top of a gilded box set on the edge of his desk. The ruby ring on his little finger glinted a macabre bloodred. "Consider my assistance a retainer for your future services, my lady. Your artistic services," he clarified silkily. "A painting of my choosing to be executed to my satisfaction. Skilled forgers are far more difficult to procure than skilled whores."

Charlotte felt suddenly weak, as though she had just emerged unscathed from a reckless, dangerous battle she hadn't been sure she would survive.

"Do you agree to the terms, Lady Charlotte?"

The hope that had been snuffed suddenly flared again. "Yes, of course. Whatever you need. I promise."

A red-gold brow rose slowly, as if measuring the sincerity of her response. "Be careful what you promise, my lady. Circumstances can change and make promises difficult to keep."

Charlotte swallowed hard. "Of course."

"I do not tolerate disloyalty. Nor do I suffer fools, or those who possess loose lips and wagging tongues. Such individuals are invariably silenced at the bottom of the Thames, and neither your gender nor your title will offer you protection."

"I understand." And she did. It should horrify her, this entire conversation and her willingness to embrace the shadows of a world where she understood little. And perhaps she was selling her soul to the very devil, but it was better than continuing on the way she had been for the past twenty-three years of her life. She needed to do this. Break herself out of her cage. There was no white knight thundering to her rescue, ready to sweep her away and make her dreams come true. That was on her. And no matter the cost, it would be worth it, ten times over.

"For your sake, I hope so." King pulled a desk drawer open and withdrew a sheet of paper. "You've heard of the Haverhall School for Young Ladies?" he asked without looking up.

"Yes," Charlotte replied. Everyone had heard of Haverhall. The most exclusive finishing school for young ladies in all of Britain. A place where only the most elite and most wealthy of families sent their daughters to prepare them for a life as a society wife. A school that had been deemed a waste of time and money for Charlotte by her parents, given her dismal prospects.

"Then you will be familiar with the school's headmistress? Baron Strathmore's sister, Miss Clara Hayward?"

"I've never met her." Charlotte had only heard all the rumors that everyone else had about the obscenely wealthy Hayward family. That Clara Hayward, a woman of stunning beauty and flawless deportment, had had any chance of a good marriage destroyed by her excessive and unconventional education. That her younger sister, Rose, a gifted artist, had similarly been compromised. Though Rose had been, for a brief time, improbably engaged to the son of a viscount until he was killed at Waterloo, and Rose all but disappeared from the public eye. The baron himself, Harland Hayward, had married, though his unorthodox insistence to continue working as a physician had angered his highborn wife until the day she had met her own scandalous demise.

Though what the Haywards or a ladies' finishing school could do for Charlotte was beyond her comprehension.

"Your unfamiliarity will be remedied shortly." King finished writing after a few minutes and set his quill aside. "The baron, or more likely, Miss Hayward, will call upon you." He folded the paper and reached for the wax. "I can't imagine it will take longer than a few days. They will have instructions for you then, and I suggest that you go along with whatever it is that will be presented to you."

Charlotte frowned. "I don't understand."

King sealed the letter and reached for his quill again. "The baron is not everything he seems. And he owes me a significant favor, though that bit of information will stay between us if this is to work. At no point in time should my name ever come up in conversation outside this room. You may consider that your first test of loyalty, understood?"

Charlotte nodded.

"Very good." With precise movements, King wrote *Dr. Hayward* across the front. He reached back and pulled on a tasseled rope hanging near the wall behind the desk. In moments, a man the size of a gorilla materialized, and King handed him the letter. "Have this delivered to the good doctor, please."

The gorilla nodded and vanished with disconcerting speed.

Charlotte frowned. "If the doctor—baron is to assist, won't he need to see my work? A portfolio? How will he know that—"

King folded his hands on the desk and fixed his pale,

icy gaze on her once more. "One, the baron is only a single cog in this wheel that has now been set in motion. Second, my endorsement of you and your work will be sufficient. Unless, of course, you give me a reason to withdraw it."

Charlotte nodded, biting her lip.

"I hope you never give me that reason, Lady Charlotte. For I believe this arrangement has the potential to be mutually beneficial."

"I understand. You have my word," she replied, ignoring the small voice in her head that was demanding her to acknowledge the enormity of what she had just done. "And my thanks," she said instead. "For your assistance."

King sat back in his chair, his face expressionless. "Do not make me regret it."

Chapter 2

"Lady Charlotte? Are you here?"

The question came from somewhere behind the towering rose trellises, the blooms, along with the warmth that had sustained them, now faded in the grip of fall. Charlotte shot to her feet, pulling her cloak tightly around her against the chill in the air. She'd come out to the deserted gardens in the watery sunshine because she couldn't stand to be trapped in the house any longer, pacing and waiting and pacing some more. Three days had passed since she'd returned from her clandestine visit to King and she'd been on tenterhooks ever since, waiting for a visit she wasn't sure would ever come from a woman she didn't know.

"I'm here," she replied, trying her best to arrange her features into normalcy.

The housekeeper rounded the garden path, her usually pinched face looking unusually befuddled, her arms wrapped around her middle against the cold. "You have a caller," the woman said, sounding perplexed. "She's been shown into the orange drawing room. Your aunt is already there."

Charlotte felt her heart skip, and she willed her expression to remain serene, as though callers for her were regular fixtures. In truth, the housekeeper had every right to be perplexed. Charlotte never had callers. Of any sort. The only time that she supposed there were visitors to their London home was when her parents were in residence, and Charlotte hadn't seen her parents in almost three years. They never came to Aysgarth and spent little time in London. Currently, they were wintering somewhere on the sunny shores of Spain, leaving Charlotte in the temporary company of an aunt who rarely left her rooms and never had even a passing interest in her niece.

Charlotte spun and hurried through the gardens and into the house, tossing her cloak aside and stopping just outside the door to the drawing room. She could see her aunt installed on the orange-and-yellow settee, the lace trim of her cap drooping over her gaunt face, a woolen blanket folded over her lap.

A soft, melodic voice that Charlotte didn't recognize drifted from the room, but from her vantage, she could not see the owner. She smoothed the flyaway hair back from her face as best she could and brushed a dead leaf from her skirts. She squared her shoulders and stepped through the doorway.

Her aunt gazed up at her and blinked, as though she couldn't understand where Charlotte had come from or why she was here. "I thought you were already gone to Aysgarth," she said, and it sounded more like an accusation, as though she found Charlotte's continued presence offensive.

"Not yet, Aunt," Charlotte replied absently, her attention already fixed on the other woman in the room.

She was clad in a simple day dress the color of claret, which made her flawless skin glow. She had rich mahogany hair and dark eyes that met Charlotte's with frank directness. Confidence and poise positively radiated from her, transforming her classical beauty into something far more striking.

Clara Hayward. Baron Strathmore's sister and headmistress of Haverhall. She could be no other.

Excitement crackled through her.

"Lady Charlotte, it is lovely to see you again," Miss Hayward greeted with an ease that made it sound like they were old acquaintances, simply picking up a conversation that they had failed to finish earlier that morning.

"Indeed," Charlotte offered, a polite smile plastered on her face.

"I knew nothing about these plans of yours, Charlotte," her aunt warbled from where she sat, sounding grieved. "Someone should have told me. Nobody tells me anything."

"My plans?" she asked carefully.

"Don't be coy, Charlotte. It's not attractive." Her aunt sniffed. "I was not advised that you had applied to Haverhall. Your parents mentioned nothing of this to me before they left me here."

Charlotte gazed at her aunt. "An unfortunate oversight, I'm sure," she murmured.

"I must take the blame for any confusion," Miss Hayward interrupted smoothly. "For it was I who belatedly recommended that Lady Charlotte apply to our program."

"Isn't she a little long in the tooth for a finishing school?" her aunt muttered waspishly, the lace on her cap drooping farther over her eyes.

"Not at all," Miss Hayward replied, her pleasant smile not wavering. "Lady Charlotte's artistic skill is highly regarded. She has come recommended to us through numerous society channels as a young lady who possesses the maturity and poise to act as a mentor of sorts to our younger students. A very enviable position, I assure you."

Charlotte blinked at her polished delivery. Her aunt seemed unsure what to do.

"This specialized term will run over the next twelve weeks," Miss Hayward had continued, without giving anyone a chance to respond. "It is, of course, similar to our exclusive summer program. And like our summer program, it will also be hosted in Dover, at Avondale House. Aside from art, our curriculum will further develop skills that are equally as refined as the young ladies who take part." Miss Hayward directed another smile at her aunt. "These specialized terms get so many worthy applicants, and as such, we must take great care to select only those most suitable." She paused. "In fact, earlier today, I explained the exact same thing to the Duke of Holloway's sister, Lady Anne."

"The Duke of Holloway?" Her aunt sat up a little straighter, and Charlotte shot Miss Hayward a surreptitious glance from under her lashes. Had the baron's sister done that on purpose? she wondered. Dropped the Holloway name because the bachelor duke had become a symbol of the sort of wealth and power that was coveted in all corners of Britain?

"Indeed. The Lady Anne has expressed interest in our Dover programs. As have the daughters of both the Marquess of Pevendel and the Earl of Marchant. An illustrious group of young women, one in which the Edgerton name fits well, don't you agree?"

"Yes," her aunt managed, looking a little overwhelmed.

"We are holding the last spot in this upcoming term for Lady Charlotte," Miss Hayward said briskly. "If she wants it. But I must have a decision, for we will be departing almost immediately. And there are dozens of other young ladies vying for—"

"Of course she wants it." Her aunt stopped, her colorless lips thinning, a look of utter distaste crossing her face. "Wait. Do I have to go with her?"

"No. Haverhall's students are, as always, impeccably chaperoned. We also employ skilled lady's maids to assist the students, and Avondale House has a sterling staff at our disposal."

"Well, I suppose that's something then." Charlotte's aunt sat back against the settee, looking appeased. "I despise traveling, you know." She smoothed the wool over her legs and glanced sourly at Charlotte.

Miss Hayward stood. "Can you be ready to depart to Dover this afternoon, Lady Charlotte?"

Charlotte recognized that it wasn't really a question, even though Dover was nowhere close to where she needed to be.

Go along with whatever it is that will be presented to you, King's voice echoed in her head. "Yes."

"Very good." Miss Hayward nodded. "You may bring a single trunk of clothing and toiletries. I would strongly suggest that you pack any and all art supplies that you feel you may need in another."

"I understand," Charlotte replied, not really understanding anything.

"Please present yourself at Haverhall by three o'clock, Lady Charlotte," Miss Hayward said, moving past her. "We will travel to Dover from there. I do hope you will enjoy your experience with us."

* * *

Haverhall School for Young Ladies had once been a grand manor home before it had been converted into a school. It sat on a lush parcel of land just beyond the northwest corner of London, complete with gently rolling hills, fish-filled ponds, expansive gardens, and a handful of cottages. Charlotte looked around her at the pretty blue drawing room she had been deposited in, holding on to the pretty rose-patterned teacup a pretty maid had provided her with, and wondered how any of this prettiness fit into what she was about to undertake.

"Lady Charlotte."

Charlotte started, almost splashing tea over the edge of her cup. She set the cup aside and looked up to find Clara Hayward standing just inside the door, a petite, copper-haired woman at her side, a leather-wrapped bundle in her arms.

"Welcome to Haverhall," Miss Hayward said. "Allow me to introduce my sister, Rose. Rose, this is Lady Charlotte. Rose will be helping you with your transformation. She's got quite the eye for... appearances, shall we say."

Charlotte scrambled to her feet, stepping around her trunk and feeling like a bloody Amazon warrior next to the slight form of Rose Hayward. And a dull witted one at that. For nothing that had come out of Clara Hayward's mouth after her introduction had made any sense.

Rose was studying Charlotte thoughtfully with the same dark eyes that her sibling possessed. "My brother tells me you're a very accomplished artist. A Renaissance special-ist, as it were."

"Yes," Charlotte replied simply, remembering that this was the Hayward sister known for her own artistic ability.

"You must be for him to go to such lengths on your behalf. There was no lack of competition for the

St. Michael's commission." Rose's eyes lingered on her, considering, though not unkind. "I would like to see your work sometime," she said.

"I would like that, Miss Hayward."

"Call me Rose." She tipped her head toward her sister. "And you can call her Clara. You'll quickly learn titles have little value here."

Charlotte stared. "Forgive my...indelicacy, but I was under the impression that when it comes to Haverhall and its clientele, titles are almost as important as the money that stands behind them."

Rose made a decidedly unladylike noise. "For our regular fall and spring terms, they are," she said.

Charlotte tried to make sense of that and failed. Regular terms? "I'm still not entirely sure what it is I'm doing here," she said, ignoring that unanswered question and focusing on the one that impacted her the most.

Clara cleared her throat. "Yes, my apologies for that. I would have given you some warning prior to our unexpected visit earlier, had my brother given me the time. However, he brought this—and you—to my attention only late last night, and he was rather cryptic in his urgency and his request for my assistance." She strode into the room, her skirts swirling gracefully. "My presentation to your aunt was somewhat crude and shamelessly transparent, but we can't have anyone believing you've been kidnapped for the next twelve weeks, can we?"

Charlotte shook her head, still at a loss. Somewhere, she'd missed something important.

Rose followed her into the room and settled herself on a brocaded chair near the hearth. "I understand that the position that Harland secured for you working in Coventry on the St. Michael's commission will start immediately."

Charlotte blinked, shocked excitement suddenly bursting through her confusion. The position that was secured? It couldn't be that easy. Could it? "So I'm not going to Dover?"

Rose and Clara exchanged a glance, and Clara sighed. "Of course not. That is just a cover. My brother did not confirm this with you before he disappeared again, did he?"

"No?" Charlotte felt like she was feeling her way around in the dark. Should she admit that she had never actually met the baron? "I'm afraid it was all very...last-minute."

"Ah. Only our two medical students are heading to Dover. You will be traveling directly to Coventry. Mr. Henry Lisbon, the architect overseeing the St. Michael's project, was a classmate of Harland's and remains a close friend. He specializes in cathedrals, churches, that sort of thing. We've used him before to place our architecture and art students, and even an aspiring mason once."

Charlotte stared at Clara. "Architecture and art students?" *Medical students? Aspiring mason?*

Clara's eyes narrowed. "Exactly how last-minute was this all?"

"Very?"

"And how was it that you came to the attention of my brother?"

"A mutual friend?" Charlotte tried, not sure what alternate explanation she could offer.

"I see. And what details did my brother give you about your placement with us, exactly? Or Haverhall, for that matter?"

"Not much?" Charlotte winced. It seemed every one of her answers came out a question.

"Hmph. Well then, allow me to explain." Clara clasped her hands behind her back. "The students that are part of Haverhall's exclusive programs, such as this one and the one we run in the summer, are not chosen based on their position in Debrett's or the amount of coin in their family's coffers. They are chosen for their ambition and their willingness to defy every preordained expectation put upon them by a society who most often measures their value by their title and their looks. They are selected because they dare to disregard the conventional and possess the courage to do more. To become more." Miss Hayward was watching her. "To do things denied to them, not by ability or acumen but by gender. Architects. Doctors. Solicitors. Artists." She paused. "And we help them do it."

Charlotte stared at Clara, at a loss for words. Her throat felt unusually tight and her heart was racing. For the first time, she understood that she wasn't alone. That there were others who had circumvented the condescending attitude that had labeled women like her as unnatural. That there were others who had broken themselves out of the cages constructed for them by antiquated attitudes and intransigent expectations.

"Are you all right, Lady Charlotte?" Rose asked from her chair.

"Yes." She'd never been more all right in her life.

"And you are sure that this is something that you still wish to do?"

"God, yes," Charlotte croaked.

"Good. Though I warn you, there are conditions that come with this placement you should be aware of before you fully commit." It was Clara who tapped the toe of her half boot against the side of Charlotte's trunk that contained her clothes. "You won't need anything in here.

You will travel not as Lady Charlotte, but as Charlie, to facilitate your ability to freely focus on your work and not the reaction or biases of those who may be working with you. Your appearance, like your identity, will be drastically altered. We—and Mr. Lisbon—have learned from experience that these measures, as unfortunate as they are, work best when we have students who are placed directly in their chosen field. Not everyone is...open-minded enough to see your value. I'm sure you can understand that."

"You have no idea," Charlotte said harshly, the frustration that had festered for so long igniting. Her brothers and parents had never regarded her as anything more than a decoration when she was a child, though not pretty or witty enough to display. As a debutante, she'd been called an epic failure. Now, as a woman, she was considered as nothing more than an embarrassing duty. From the time she'd been small, Aysgarth had always been her parents' solution to her shortcomings. Out of sight, out of mind.

Charlotte was done with being invisible.

Miss Hayward arched an elegant brow. "Should you go through with this, you cannot reveal your identity to anyone, Lady Charlotte. You need to be aware of your conduct, your mannerisms, and even your knowledge of certain matters. It won't always be easy."

"No, I don't expect it to be," Charlotte replied, the frustration that had risen fading fast amid her growing excitement. No, excitement was too pale. What she was feeling now had crystalized into something more pure. Joy. Anticipation. Determination to succeed.

"How dependent are you upon servants?" Clara asked. "Can you make your own pot of tea? Boil an egg? Lay a fire?"

"Yes to all of those," Charlotte said. All those years she'd been ignored and left to her own devices, free to range over the dales of Aysgarth and the empty rooms of Jasper House, had suddenly become not a penance but priceless.

"Good." Rose stood and approached Charlotte, untying the bundle she still had in her hands and rolling it out over the top of Charlotte's trunk. A comb, a razor, and a pair of shears glinted in the light, and she gestured to the chair that Charlotte had vacated. "I'll start with your hair. It will grow back, of course, and upon your return, we have an entire host of excuses you may use for the alteration."

I doubt anyone will notice, Charlotte thought to herself.

"We'll move on to your clothing and your mannerisms," Rose continued. "You'll need to look—"

"Mannish," Charlotte supplied. "I've heard that word already applied to my appearance more times than I can count. My jaw is too square, my face too wide. My height too cumbersome, my figure too sparse. Your task should not be difficult."

"Predictable fools," Rose hissed under her breath, and Charlotte was momentarily taken aback at her venom.

"It's never bothered me," Charlotte murmured.

Rose impaled her with a long look.

"That much," she added more truthfully.

Rose looked as though she wanted to say something further though her sister interrupted.

"Perhaps you should get started," Clara suggested tactfully.

"Yes," her sister agreed, making a visible effort to temper her animosity on Charlotte's behalf. Rose reached out and fingered a long strand of hair that had come loose from its pins. "Are you ready to be introduced to a new Charlotte?"

Charlotte took a deep breath, the prospect of that freedom positively intoxicating. "I've been ready my whole life."

Chapter 3

Flynn Rutledge shifted on the uncomfortable pew and gazed up at the massive windows that soared up into the heavens. His eyes roamed the colored glass, windows crafted with a delicate detail that artisans centuries ago had perfected. It was almost dizzying, the way the brilliant morning light streamed through the collage of color, dappling everything around him like a field of wildflowers. He let his head fall back, the sheer grandeur and size of what had been built by human hands so long ago almost as humbling as the skill in which it had been done.

Flynn sighed and straightened, glancing down at the sketchbook he held in his hands, frowning at the empty pages. Amid all this majesty, he was going to have to come up with something magnificent if he was going to accomplish anything over the next months. God knew it would be up to him to save this damn project. The corners of his mouth drew down farther.

Charlie Beaumont. The name of the man Lisbon had

given him as the other artist Flynn would be working with. He'd never heard of him. Nor had any member of the Royal Academy he'd questioned, though there was no way to tell if any of those sanctimonious blackguards were being honest with him. But the apprentices Flynn had asked had offered the same answer, and none of them had any reason to lie. This Beaumont had seemingly appeared out of thin air, unknown. And if Flynn had never heard of him, how was he supposed to believe that this man had sufficient talent for this commission?

Flynn needed this project to go right. His eyes wandered to the framed canvas that was set on the dais of the apse. It was an image of Mary, her expression soft and serene, the baby Jesus settled in her arms. When Flynn had painted it five years prior, he'd had the copy he'd seen of Raphael's painting of the *Madonna del Granduca* in his mind, the brilliant colors and beautiful lines providing all the inspiration he'd needed.

And he'd executed that portrait extraordinarily well, Flynn thought, feeling another wash of the aching, angry sadness that festered every time he looked at it now. That portrait had earned him a place on this commission, but all the enthusiasm and ambition that he had possessed five years ago had since been lost. Destroyed, perhaps, would be a better word. And now he found himself adrift and jaded, cynicism replacing the joy he had once—

"It's exquisite."

"What?" Flynn started, realizing that he was no longer alone. There was someone standing in front of him, his form and features half obscured by the light behind him.

"The portrait of the Madonna and her child. You captured her inner peace with incredible skill. Raphael would have approved."

Flynn scowled, shifting and squinting against the light to better see the person who seemed as familiar with his previous work here as he was with a Renaissance master. He sounded young, whoever he was.

"My apologies if I've intruded. Mr. Lisbon indicated that I could find you here. I wanted to take the chance to introduce myself."

Flynn pushed himself out of the pew and stared at the youth before him. He had a bulky canvas bag slung over one shoulder and a long, leather-covered tube for rolled canvases strapped across his back. Dammit, had Lisbon gone against his wishes and hired him an apprentice? Did he think Flynn had the time for such foolery? His scowl deepened. "Who are you, exactly?"

There was an uncomfortable pause. And then, "I'm Charlie Beaumont."

Flynn goggled at the boy. He was tall and lanky, with short brown hair that fell carelessly around his ears and over his forehead. Eyes the color of warm caramel matched the hue of the baggy, slightly rumpled coat and trousers he was wearing. His voice was soft and raspy, his cheeks smooth above his bright red scarf, and Flynn wondered if the boy even shaved. *This* was Charlie Beaumont?

Jesus Christ.

"You can't be serious," Flynn snarled. This was the last thing he needed. His own twenty-nine years had been questioned as being inadequate to execute a project of this magnitude, so to have a...a *child* as a partner was ridiculous.

"I can assure you, Mr. Rutledge, I am quite serious." The boy simply gazed at him with steady eyes, shifting his bag on his shoulder. If Flynn's manner fazed this boy, he wasn't showing it.

"How old are you?" Flynn demanded.

"You first." The response was cool.

God help him, the whelp had an insolent tongue to boot. If he didn't need this commission, if he hadn't been forced to— Flynn stopped before his mind could go down that pointless path. Again.

The boy cleared his throat. "Look, Mr. Rutledge, it seems we got off on the wrong foot. I only wished to introduce myself and say that I am looking forward to working with an accomplished artist such as yourself—"

"Where is Lisbon?" Flattery would get this pup nowhere. And nowhere was exactly where Beaumont would be going once he got to the bottom of this.

"I believe he is still working at the rear of the nave."

Flynn stalked by the boy, the soles of his boots echoing on the stone floor. This was not the nursery of some country house that they were painting with bunnies and birds. This was a work that would be judged by those who had the means and the power to offer him a key to their world. A world where he could stop struggling and have access to everything that artists like Thomas Lawrence or John Crome did.

"Lisbon." Flynn spotted the architect leaning over a set of schematic drawings that had been laid out across a narrow table just inside the wide doors. Behind him, a handful of masons were working to prepare the area where the painted panels would be mounted.

Henry Lisbon looked up, his expression of slight distraction giving way to a frown when he saw Flynn approaching. "Rutledge." Lisbon's green eyes skipped past his shoulder, and Flynn glanced back to find that Beaumont had followed him. Of course. Because that is what puppies did.

"I see you've met Mr. Beaumont," Lisbon said. "Please

tell me you've come to share your design ideas with me." There was an edge to his words. "The bishop has been asking for more detailed drawings."

"May I have a word?" Flynn tried to arrange his face into what he hoped was composed reason.

Lisbon glanced down at the drawings. "Go ahead."

"In private?"

The architect's frown deepened, and he made a noise of impatience. "You have two minutes."

Fine. This wouldn't take one. Flynn followed Lisbon's substantial frame back down the aisle until they reached the first transept pillar.

"Is there a problem, Rutledge?" he asked, pushing dark hair in need of a barber from his face with irritation. He couldn't be more than five or six years older than Flynn, but silver had started to streak his temples.

"Charlie Beaumont."

The architect dropped his hand. "What about him?"

"Who is he? Where did he come from?"

Lisbon put his hands on his hips. "This isn't Almack's, Rutledge, and I am not your damn chaperone. I thought I'd leave the introductions and the getting-to-know-you part to the two of you."

"I've not heard of him."

"So?"

Flynn took a deep breath. "Is he any good?"

Two dark brows shot up. "You're questioning my judgment now?"

"Of course not." Flynn pinched the bridge of his nose. "But this work has to be spectacular. My name is going to be on this."

Lisbon's expression darkened. "So is mine. And as such, I've hired the best. But if you are reconsidering—"

"No. That's not— I'm not reconsidering anything."

"Good. I'm glad we had this talk." Lisbon brushed by him.

"But Beaumont is a mere *boy*."

"He's an artist."

"At the very least I think I should take a look at some of his—"

The architect spun. "Listen carefully, Rutledge. I did not hire you because you went to the right schools or studied in the right countries or exhibited your work in the right places. I hired you because of your skill. What makes you think I hired Beaumont for anything less?"

Flynn could feel his teeth clench. Why did this man have to sound so reasonable?

"The next time you have something to share with me, Rutledge, I am confident that it will be on paper. Now go do your job, or I will find someone who will."

Flynn watched the architect retreat, trying, with effort, to relax his jaw. He took a deep breath and turned to stare sightlessly in the direction of the apse. He needed to relax. Getting frustrated with fate was one thing. Taking that frustration out on Lisbon or Beaumont or anyone else in the chain of events that had deposited him here was not helpful.

"I believe this is yours."

Flynn jumped. Dammit, the boy moved like a cat. "What?"

"Your sketchbook." Beaumont was holding out the heavy book of pressed paper to him. "You left it on the pew."

Flynn took it from the boy's hands. Delicate hands, he couldn't help but notice. Long, tapered fingers that had not suffered manual labor but were stained with colorful pigments in the crevices of his nail beds. Flynn supposed he should find that somewhat reassuring. "Thank you," he said gruffly, wondering how much Beaumont had overheard.

"I'd enjoy seeing any sketches that you might have for the panels," Beaumont offered, sounding hopeful.

Flynn scowled. He couldn't show the boy sketches because he didn't have one he was happy with. Everything that he had done so far seemed…less than impressive, even the rough preliminary drawings that he had submitted months ago to Lisbon. They were missing a dimension, as though the soul of each was absent. And that terrified him to no end. Because no matter how many drawings he did or how many sketches he started, he couldn't seem to reclaim something that had once come so easy to him.

There were two panels to be completed—each as tall as two men and as wide as one, both to be mounted on either side of the interior doors of the church. They would be highly visible, and they would be the last thing people would see as they left. And Flynn intended to make them memorable. He just wasn't entirely sure how.

"Perhaps a little later." He tried to relax his expression. "Would you like to see where we will be living and working? The panels that have been prepared?" There, that was something that existed that he could show Beaumont. And the offer sounded professional. Accommodating, even. And perhaps another look at the panels would inspire something within him.

"I would. Thank you." Beaumont was watching him, an unreadable expression on his face.

"This way then." He didn't wait to see if Beaumont was following but simply spun and headed toward the north transept, slipping through the heavy door at the end. He felt the cool air cut into his skin as he made his way along the edge of the building, though it abated as he entered what had been a sizable outbuilding at one time. Lisbon had claimed it and converted it into a live-in studio of sorts, the tall windows on the north side offering a consistent light and the hearth on the south end offering a consistent warmth against the drafts and damp. Someone had put a wide, blue rug in front of the hearth in what Flynn supposed was an attempt to make the space seem more homey, though the effort fell short. This wasn't his home any more than any other temporary place he had ever stayed in his travels.

There were two meager rooms off to the side that had been cleared out and furnished with a bed and a washstand each. Flynn had already claimed the one with the bigger bed, and now, given Beaumont's youth, he felt perfectly justified.

He glanced back to find that the boy had followed him as soundlessly as ever. "You can put your things in there," Flynn said, gesturing at the remaining empty room. He saw Beaumont hesitate briefly before complying and reemerging. "Coal for the hearth can be taken from the church. There is a pail just outside. Meals can be taken anywhere you please. If my door is closed, I do not wish to be disturbed. Refrain from doing so." Flynn wondered if that had come out somewhat rude, but he refused to be reduced to a nanny. "And if you have a pretty mot who catches your eye, please be so kind as to use her bed. Or a barn. Or anywhere else where I don't need to endure the racket of a banging headboard. I will return the favor. Understood?"

"Of course." The boy had flushed a shade of crimson so intense it suggested that banging headboards would not ever disturb his sleep. Just as well.

"Any other questions?"

"Not at the moment, no," Beaumont replied, his color slowly returning to normal as he looked past Flynn at the wood panels that had been secured against the far wall. Twin scaffolds had been assembled in preparation for the work, and long tables awaited supplies. The murals would be painted here, away from prying eyes, and then moved into position once they were complete.

Flynn considered the towering blank surfaces before him. "Have you painted on wood before, Mr. Beaumont?"

"I have," came the polite reply. "Many times. Canvas was not always...available when I was learning."

Flynn eyed the boy as he moved forward past the scaffolding, running his hand over the smooth, sealed surface. Properly prepared canvas had rarely been available when Flynn was learning either. Paint had generally been begged, borrowed, or stolen. At least until his craft had managed to pay for itself.

"Sealed oak," Beaumont said without looking back.

Flynn wasn't sure if that was a question or not. "Yes," he answered anyway.

"Sufficiently aged?"

"Yes. There is little chance of them warping." At least the boy was asking the right questions. Perhaps he wasn't completely clueless.

Beaumont's hand dropped, and he gazed upward, toward the rounded edges of the upper portion. "Soldier or savior?" he asked suddenly.

"I beg your pardon?" Flynn moved a step closer.

"St. Michael. Soldier or savior?"

"I suppose it depends on the individual," Flynn replied slowly. He saw Beaumont smile briefly as though he had found something amusing in his answer. "Why do you ask?" he demanded.

"These panels will tell a story. I'm curious which one it is you intend to tell."

Flynn's fingers tightened around the edges of his book. He had no idea. Which, he realized, was exactly the problem. Leave it to a bloody boy to put into words so succinctly what Flynn had been unable to. "I am assuming the clergy and the parishioners would like to see the savior."

"Hmm."

"You disagree."

"I didn't say that."

"But nor did you agree."

Beaumont turned from the panels and jammed his hands into the pockets of his baggy coat. "I think St. Michael is both. And should be painted as such."

Flynn's lips thinned. "That sounds...cluttered."

"Cluttered?" Now it was Beaumont who looked unimpressed.

"Yes, cluttered. Chaotic, slovenly, disorderly. Too much going on in a single space. These panels are meant to inspire. Not give the viewer a headache."

"Funny. I suspect someone said that to Michelangelo when he painted the Sistine Chapel," Beaumont retorted. "Yet I might argue that it is that aspect which makes it inspiring. Every time you gaze upward, there is something new to be discovered."

Flynn felt the breath punched from his lungs and his jaw slacken. "You've been inside the Sistine Chapel."

He saw Beaumont still, something shifting warily behind those caramel eyes. "Yes."

"You studied in Italy?" Jealousy was turning like a double-bladed knife in his gut, and he hated himself for the reaction. He had never had a chance to escape the borders of England. See the works of the great Renaissance masters in all their glory—the Sistine Chapel in particular. It had been one of Flynn's most desperate wishes since the day he had been told about it.

"Not exactly."

"What does that mean?"

"It means I was there." Beaumont was being deliberately evasive.

"Why?" Flynn closed the gap between them.

"I was traveling with an aristocratic family," the boy said after a long pause. "Italy was one of their annual destinations, and they had accompanied their son on a leg of his grand tour. I recorded their adventures. Places they went, things they did."

Flynn had never heard of the like. "What do you mean, recorded their adventures?"

"A series of sketches, featuring each of them. Watercolors. Some more substantial paintings when we returned to England." His eyes slid away.

"Bloody hell." Flynn knew the ridiculous excesses of the nobility, but this was beyond the pale. To pay to have an artist trail one around the Continent, sketching portraits and pictures all the while, was the height of narcissistic idiocy.

And Flynn would have jumped at the chance to do it. A thousand times over, if it had meant he could see what Beaumont had.

"I would paint them as opposites."

It took Flynn a moment to realize that Beaumont was talking about the panels again, deliberately changing the subject. "I beg your pardon?"

"Opposites. Hope and despair. Love and hate." The boy was watching him from beneath his tousled hair. "What do you think?"

Flynn once again found himself scowling. "I don't know. But what I do know is that this work must be compelling. Inspiring. Resplendent."

Charlie Beaumont sighed. "And what I'm telling you, Mr. Rutledge, is that to evoke emotion, an artist must paint emotion. Real sentiments and passions that others can relate to." He paused. "Like your Madonna. Your use of color and perspective is lovely, the way you've mastered the light is impressive, but it is not those things that make that painting so riveting. Your Madonna positively radiates the unconditional love a mother might have for her child. She glows with the peace she has found in stopping time long enough to simply hold her son in her arms, safe and protected in that moment."

With horror, Flynn felt his throat suddenly thicken. Because when he'd created that portrait, it had been his mother's face he had painted. A woman who had raised Flynn on her own, who had done what she had to so that they both might survive. A woman who had loved Flynn unconditionally until the day she had died, even though he hadn't been able to give her her greatest wish.

"Are you really lecturing me on how to paint, Beaumont?" Flynn barked roughly because he couldn't say any of that to this boy. Wouldn't say any of that to Beaumont or anyone else for that matter. Ever. He could feel the weight of the boy's gaze on him, and he resisted the urge to fidget. Dammit, what was wrong with him?

"I'm not lecturing you on anything, Mr. Rutledge," Beaumont finally said. "I'm...envying you, I think."

Rutledge made a rude noise. "For what?" he demanded. "You envy me that commission? I did it five years ago, and—"

"I'm envying you that love. Whoever it was in your life

who possessed a generous heart like that and allowed you to see what unconditional love truly looks like."

Flynn found himself staring at Beaumont, utterly unnerved and unable to find words. What the hell was happening? In a handful of sentences, Charlie Beaumont had obliterated the fortifications he had constructed between Flynn Rutledge the professional artist and Flynn Rutledge the man. Seen right through him with a terrifying accuracy. Seen parts of his past that no one else had.

Beaumont abruptly turned. "I'm sorry if I've made you uncomfortable, Mr. Rutledge," he said. "That was not my intention."

"I'm not uncomfortable," Flynn snapped, lying through his teeth.

"Oh. Then I'm glad." Beaumont disappeared into his room and reemerged with his sketchbook.

"Where are you going now, Mr. Beaumont?" Flynn asked with an edge to his voice.

"To compose some ideas," Beaumont replied politely.

"And to capture buckets of *emotion* on those pages, I'm sure." He was behaving like an ass but he couldn't seem to find his equilibrium.

Beaumont paused, silhouetted in the door frame against the winter-dulled grounds. "I certainly hope so, Mr. Rutledge," he said, before closing the door behind him.

Chapter 4

W hen she first saw Flynn Rutledge with the light streaming through the windows turning his rich skin gold and his grey eyes silver, she had wondered if perhaps she had stumbled across the archangel she'd been charged to paint.

He'd stood, unfolding his long limbs, and Charlotte had had to look up at him, half-expecting a pair of wings to unfold as well. He had a face of the sort that ancient artists had fawned over—a straight nose balanced by a strong jaw, a wide forehead over thick brows and deep-set eyes. He seemed impervious to the chilled air, his rough shirt sleeves shoved up to his elbows, revealing sandy-blond hair on lean, muscular forearms. The same shade of sandy hair fell over his forehead and ears in thick, careless waves. He was, quite possibly, the most handsome man Charlotte had ever seen in her life.

And possibly, the most angry.

She had known that her youthful appearance was bound to raise brows, and she had been prepared for the inevitable questions and doubt. What she hadn't expected was the resentment and bitterness that seemed to roll off Rutledge in dark waves. If Charlotte had painted him as a color, he would be a ragged black slash across the canvas, crimson seeping from beneath the unhappy darkness. For a man who looked like an archangel on the outside, it seemed that he harbored more than a few demons within.

Not that it was any of her business. This was a professional partnership, and she would work within its confines. His prickly, defensive response to her more personal comments had been noted. She would keep her distance and do absolutely nothing that might put this precious opportunity in peril. She didn't need to be his friend; she didn't need to be his confessor; she didn't need to be anything other than pleasant, regardless of how he chose to act.

In truth, it was probably best that Flynn Rutledge was so disagreeable. Not only because it made him less attractive, but because a disagreeable man could be handled. Managed. No differently than every other man in Charlotte's life who had spent the duration of it telling her what she couldn't do. What wasn't possible or acceptable or practical. That was nothing she wasn't used to.

Though the uncomfortably close quarters she found herself in with Rutledge would take a bit more acclimation. When she had arrived, Mr. Lisbon had apologized, but the living arrangements had been set long before he'd known that Miss Hayward was sending Charlotte to be placed with him. He offered to find an alternate solution but warned her that, in his experience, such actions raised slews of suspicious questions neither one of them would care to answer. Charlotte had agreed.

But the reality was far more intimidating. It had taken her a long time to fall asleep last night, something that she attributed to her new surroundings as much as she attributed it to the fact that she was cohabiting with an unfamiliar man.

She continually reminded herself that Charlie Beaumont would think nothing of it. It wasn't as though she were sharing a bunk with Rutledge. She was sharing a space with separate rooms and doors, and this would be perfectly acceptable—luxurious even—references to banging head-boards and all.

Before she'd emerged from her own room, she'd waited until she'd heard Rutledge leave. She'd made herself a cup of tea, wolfed down the remnants of last night's bread, and then set to work. Rutledge hadn't returned yet, and Charlotte found herself caught between a strange mix of impatience and unease. Perhaps he had—

A draft of cold air announced his return. "You've been busy."

Charlotte's hand froze over the last of her sketches before it continued, adjusting the paper to lie straight. "Good morning to you too, Mr. Rutledge." She heard him shove the door shut and move farther into the room, pacing slowly around the circle of drawings she'd laid out, each capturing a part of the vision that had been gathering force deep in her imagination.

"Soldier and savior," he muttered as he made another lap.

"Have I managed to convince you?" She kept her eyes on her sketches.

"I didn't say that."

"You didn't disagree either," Charlotte replied, hearing echoes of their conversation yesterday.

Rutledge suddenly stopped, dropping to crouch in front of her.

Charlotte glanced up at him and swallowed reflexively. He was wearing an overcoat today, the well-tailored fabric a snow-cloud grey, and she could feel the cold still clinging to it. His head was bent slightly, and Charlotte could see that his hair was damp from a recent wash, the ends plastered against his neck. The scent of his soap reached her, something that should be ordinary, but somehow, this unguarded closeness made it overwhelmingly intimate.

"Is St. Michael tending a cooking fire here?" Rutledge asked abruptly, stabbing a finger at her drawing. And just like that, the intimacy vanished.

"I beg your pardon?" Charlotte replied, taking care to keep her voice even.

"Your soldier, your defender of heaven, your all-powerful leader of God's army looks like he has no idea what to do with the sword in his grasp. He's holding it like a poker—the way one does to stir hot coals. I've seen children on the street wield blades to defend a crust of moldy bread with more authority."

Charlotte bit back the instant and defensive retort that rose. Instead, she leaned forward, peering at the drawing. She had sketched St. Michael, rising above the writhing form of a flame-engulfed serpent, his sword drawn in triumph. Or at least what she had thought was triumph. Her lack of expertise on the handling of weapons was somewhat evident, she admitted.

Rutledge stood, not waiting for her to respond. He moved to her other side and dropped into a crouch again, reaching for another drawing. This he held up, his eyes flinty in the light. It was her sketch of St. Michael descending toward a void of blackness, extending a hand to a soul reaching up. She'd spent a great deal of time on that one, feeling a deep kinship with both the angel and the soul being rescued. Proof that one could be reinvented. Saved from a prison of purgatory.

"He's not tending a fire in that one either," Charlotte said before she could think better of it. "Though I suppose one might argue that, if one were speaking in metaphors."

Grey eyes met hers over the top of the sketch. "This one is actually quite arresting."

"Oh." Charlotte could feel herself blush all the way down to her toes at the unexpected praise, and she averted her eyes, shying away from his assessing gaze. "Thank you."

"Don't thank me, Beaumont. Because while this one has merit, your other drawing is hopeless." Rutledge rose and set the purgatory sketch aside on a low table.

Charlotte scrambled to her feet. "You have something better then, Mr. Rutledge?" she asked, trying not to sound like a sulky child, but like a professional. Because in truth, she knew that her sketch of the avenging St. Michael had been less than inspiring.

"Of course I do." He retrieved a leather satchel from just inside the door and opened it, withdrawing what looked like his own bundle of sketches. He rifled through them until he found what he wanted. He set everything else aside on the end of the table except for a single drawing and then hesitated, a curious expression on his face.

"Are you going to show it to me?" Charlotte asked as pleasantly as possible.

"Yes." He made no move to hand the sketch over.

"Today? Or should I return next week?"

Rutledge seemed to start. He set the drawing beside Charlotte's purgatory sketch and stepped back. Charlotte eyed him, but he had turned his attention to the wood panels that still waited, silent and empty.

Charlotte approached the table, her eyes falling on the drawing. "Oh," she whispered. It had been executed in charcoal, the lines sure and deft as the image of an archangel rose up against a constellation of stars. This, however, was not the angel she had created, staring up at the heavens, clutching his sword. This seraph glared out from the page, his expression wild and fierce, convincing her he was prepared to fight to the death. He wielded a curved sword before him, raised in either defense or aggression—it was impossible to tell. A ragged cloth was draped over a shoulder and belted at the hips, displaying broad expanses of muscle, straining and flexing. It had elements that she had seen in works by Raphael and Reni, but the romanticism that softened the edges of those paintings was absent here. This was visceral and real and . . . violently emotional. And made her wonder just what Rutledge had drawn upon from within to create it.

I've seen children on the street wield blades to defend a crust of moldy bread with more authority.

Charlotte wondered if Flynn Rutledge had been one of them.

She ran the tip of her finger along the edge of the paper. She could almost feel the defiance and the determination emanate from the paper itself.

"You haven't said anything." Rutledge still hadn't looked at her.

"It's actually quite arresting," she said, taking the coward's way out and stealing his words.

He made an indecipherable noise.

"Why didn't you show this to me yesterday?" Charlotte asked.

"I didn't have it yesterday. I did that last night."

"Ah."

"I'm not saying you're right," he said, finally turning. "About depicting St. Michael as a savior and as a soldier."

"But you're not saying I'm wrong either." She hid a smile.

"I think there is room for both." He pinned her with a steely gaze. "Where are you from, Mr. Beaumont?"

"I'm sorry?" The question caught her off guard.

"Where are you from? Where did you study?"

Charlotte shifted uncomfortably. She'd practiced answers to these questions with Clara. Every answer was a version of the truth. Just like the story she had spun yesterday when she had slipped and made her thoughtless comment about the Sistine Chapel. It had been the only time she'd ever traveled with her family, grudgingly included for ten glorious weeks. And it had almost betrayed her here.

"Aysgarth," she said, answering his question. And hoping that Flynn Rutledge was not familiar with the tiny village. Or the fancy manor house that loomed on its outskirts.

A sandy-blond brow rose. "Yorkshire?"

"You've been?" Charlotte asked with trepidation.

"No. But I can read a map as well as the next man."

Relief trickled through her.

"You didn't tell me where you studied."

Charlotte shrugged. "Nowhere."

"Nowhere," Rutledge repeated with heavy skepticism. "You're telling me you are completely self-taught?"

"I suppose." She shrugged again. "I took a handful of lessons in watercolors." That was true. One of her early governesses had been enthusiastic if not overly talented. "But I've always preferred to work in oils." Which no governess would ever have taught. Oil paints were not a medium suitable for well-bred ladies.

"Have you publicly exhibited your work anywhere?"

Charlotte almost snorted at the utter absurdity of that question before reminding herself that Rutledge was asking Charlie, not Charlotte, that question. The number of women who had somehow managed to exhibit their work at a venue like the Royal Academy in the last fifty years could be counted on one hand. "I'm afraid not."

"How did Lisbon find you?"

Charlotte gazed at Rutledge, realizing he had been leading up to this question. "I did a piece for a mutual friend." That explanation had worked on the Haywards.

"What sort of piece?" Apparently, Rutledge was not so easily satisfied.

"A portrait."

"Of what?"

"A girl." Charlotte leaned back against the table and crossed her arms over her chest, feeling the bindings across her breasts pull beneath her baggy clothing. "Where are you from?"

He gave her a hard look, as if he was weighing the sincerity of her query.

"It's not a trick question, Mr. Rutledge."

"The art community is a small one. I would have thought..."

"Thought what? That you are that famous? Or that I am that ignorant?" She said it lightly.

"You knew I had painted the Madonna in the apse of the church."

"Because Mr. Lisbon pointed that out to me when I arrived."

He scowled. "London," he said after a moment, finally answering her original question. "I'm from London."

"Where?"

"Nowhere pleasant you'd want to hear about."

Charlotte couldn't say she was surprised, given her earlier suspicions. "Did you attend one of the academies?"

"I attended the same one as you, it would seem." Rutledge looked grim.

Charlotte tipped her head, trying not to look startled. Now that surprised her. No matter where he'd grown up, his skill should have gained him entry to a collection of academies and schools. "We have something in common then."

"I really doubt that." There was bitterness lacing his words, a sort of anguish that made Charlotte want to take his hand and ask what he meant by that. Ask what she could do to help. She jammed her fingers farther under her arms to prevent herself from doing anything so foolish.

"Tell me how you're going to paint your soldier," she said instead.

"My soldier?"

"You have captured the warrior in a way I could not. I think there is a great deal of you in this."

She could almost see Rutledge bristle. "What are you implying?"

"I'm not implying anything." Charlotte gazed at him. "I'm only suggesting that one paints what one knows," she said slowly. "It is impossible for our own experiences to not act as a filter through which we see the world. How we reproduce it here on these pages. It's what makes us unique. It's what gives our work life." She glanced down at the sketch, wondering again at the circumstances that had shaped this man's view.

Rutledge made an odd noise, somewhere between a sneer and a scoff. He advanced and reached past her, snatching her own sketch of St. Michael off the table and holding it up between them. "You are a savior and I am a soldier? Is that the light you see yourself in? How you see me?"

"I'm not anyone's savior," she said carefully. *Save, perhaps my own.* "And I don't know you well enough to see you in any sort of light." His eyes flickered down to the drawing again, and Charlotte cast about for words that would extricate herself from the dangerous undercurrents of his challenge. "I was only proposing that the juxtaposition of these sketches is what will make the completed work compelling," she said quietly. "That is what you wanted, isn't it? Something compelling?"

The scent of him enveloped her completely now, soap tinged with a hint of wood smoke and turpentine. She could see his chest rising and falling faster than normal, his features tight, his eyes stormy. The ridiculous urge to reach out and touch him again, to brush the hair from his troubled eyes, rose hard and fast. A longing to smooth the deep lines from his forehead, feel the roughness of the stubble that covered his rigid jaw.

He was still staring at her, and Charlotte shifted uneasily under his scrutiny, feeling suddenly and horribly exposed. She took a step back and then another.

"Fine," he said abruptly, before she could retreat farther.

"Fine?" she repeated, her voice wobbling a little.

"I will present these to Lisbon. See if he agrees with the idea."

"We should discuss other aspects of the composition first, don't you agree?" Charlotte said, desperately trying to distance herself from these dangerous feelings and yearnings with practical, safe subjects. "Background and balance. Proportion and the palette." She thought she might be babbling now, but she couldn't stop.

Rutledge didn't seem to notice. "And I suppose you have suggestions for those things as well."

Charlotte nodded. "Some." She shuffled back just a little farther for good measure. "Lisbon will want a detailed proposal."

Rutledge sighed but moved to extract a blank sheet of paper from the pile of drawings he had left on the end of the table. "Very well. Let's get this over with."

Chapter 5

The juxtaposition of these sketches is what will make the completed work compelling.

That was what Beaumont had said to Flynn in that quiet, utterly unflappable manner of his. But what Flynn was finding compelling was the juxtaposition that seemed to be Charlie Beaumont.

The eloquence of his words and the careful thought he seemed to give each sentence that came out of his mouth were not what he might have expected from a boy from Aysgarth. Though assumptions were rarely wise or valuable. Perhaps the time Beaumont had spent in the presence of rich, titled families, like the one he had traveled with to Italy, had educated him. Or perhaps his fine speech, like his artistic skill, had also been self-taught, to better appeal to his wealthy and elite clients.

Though if he was trying to appeal to wealthy clients, his appearance was an oddity. The baggy clothes that

Beaumont wore did nothing to make him look older, which is what Flynn guessed was his intent. In fact, the shapeless garments made him look even younger—like a boy playing dress up. Surely when Beaumont had traveled to Italy with his rich clients, he had not dressed like that, given the effort that he had put into his speech? Surely, somewhere, he had a coat and trousers that fit properly?

And surely Flynn had better things to be worried about than what Charlie Beaumont wore. Or how he spoke.

Or how his gentleness seemed to snuff every single fight that Flynn was spoiling for.

He groaned and rubbed his temples, staring up at the empty space at the end of the nave, the walls waiting for something that truly deserved his concern and attention. Something that really did need to be...compelling.

"Mr. Rutledge." Henry Lisbon jolted him out of his musings, and Flynn turned to find the architect walking toward him, looking somewhat harried as usual.

"Lisbon." Flynn pushed himself away from the back of the pew he had been leaning against.

The architect held out the drawings and detailed proposal Rutledge had submitted to him that morning. "Yes."

"Yes?"

"Yes to it all. Save for the gilding on the panel edges— no one wished to spend additional money. But the directors and the clergy, down to the last man, are thrilled with the concept. A brilliant idea."

Flynn felt a muscle in his jaw flex. Of course they were thrilled. "I must confess, the concept idea was Mr. Beaumont's."

"Indeed? Then I am pleased to hear that the two of you are working together so well." Lisbon was peering at him intently.

"Of course." What else was he going to say?

Lisbon was still studying him closely. "You see no problems moving forward with the work?" he asked. "With Mr. Beaumont?"

What kind of question was that? "No," Flynn said, trying to cover his irritation.

"I trust you've found his work to be...satisfactory?" It was said with a bit of an edge.

"Indeed."

"And he has, for all his youth, thus far conducted himself in a professional manner as I, and our clients, expect?"

His teeth clenched. "Yes."

"I'm glad to hear it." The architect pulled his coat closer around him. "You'll advise me when there is a preliminary mock-up of the panels?" he asked.

"Yes." Flynn tucked the drawings under his arm. "We'll get started immediately."

Flynn retreated from the church, his strides eating up the ground. Despite his initial discontent, a familiar feeling was starting to unfurl, one he hadn't felt in a long time. The thrill of a new project soared within him, accompanied by the anticipation of being able to do what he loved more than anything in the world. Confidence that he possessed all the skill to make it as incredible as he wished it to be. Eagerness to simply...create, now that he had a direction.

With a bit of a start, he realized that he was suddenly grinning like a fool.

Flynn shoved open the door of the makeshift studio. "Good news, Mr. Beaumont—" He stopped abruptly. "What the hell do you think you're doing?"

Charlie Beaumont jumped slightly though he didn't turn. He had a number of Flynn's sketches laid out before him, the sketches that Flynn had failed to put away earlier and had carelessly left on the end of the table.

"She's quite beautiful," Beaumont murmured quietly. "Who is she?"

Flynn stalked to the table and swept the sketches into his hands in a single movement. "None of your goddamn business," he snarled. He gathered the rest of his drawings and stuffed them back into his satchel. "You had no right to look at them. No right to touch them."

"You left them on the table," Beaumont pointed out mildly.

"That didn't give you leave to pry." He was almost shouting, even as he realized that his anger was aimed inwardly. Truth was, he should have burned those drawings long ago.

"My apologies, Mr. Rutledge." Beaumont retreated back toward the panels. "It was not my intent to cause you grief over so personal a matter."

"It's not personal, dammit," he snapped. At least, not anymore. Cecelia had made that abundantly clear. Belatedly, and with no little dismay, Flynn wondered if Beaumont's efforts to convince him he was a stranger had been a ploy. Wondered if the boy was already privy to the rumors that seemed to dog Flynn everywhere he went. If he already suspected who the woman in the drawings was and was merely baiting Flynn or seeking confirmation. "And it's none of your concern."

"Of course," Beaumont replied quietly. "Again, my apologies."

Flynn searched the boy's words for sarcasm or judgment but found only distant civility. Which made him feel even worse. He closed his eyes briefly. He was being absurd and had only succeeded in making an utter fool of himself. Even if Beaumont knew exactly who he was and had heard every scandalous, duplicitous detail, it was long in the past and irrelevant to the here and now. He needed to pull himself together.

"You will be pleased to hear that Lisbon has endorsed our proposal," Flynn said, trying for a more conciliatory manner. "All the detailed plans save for the gilding on the edges."

"That is indeed pleasing." Beaumont's voice was devoid of inflection.

"He is anxious for us to start."

The boy turned away from him. "As am I."

Chapter 6

Charlotte successfully avoided Flynn Rutledge for the next two days.

Well, perhaps *avoided* was a bit of an exaggeration for two people sharing the same space, but at no point in time did they trade any words other than a *good morning* and a *good night*. As it was, the days passed in a blur, Charlotte completely losing track of the time, as she was often wont to do when she became immersed in a project. Minutes and hours ceased to have meaning. She was aware of nothing save for the scratch of charcoal over the smooth oak surface, the crinkle of paper as she consulted her detailed sketches, and the soft creaking of the wooden boards on the scaffold as she moved across them.

It wasn't until her eyes started to ache at the end of the second day that she realized she had lost almost all of her natural light.

She sat back, balancing on the middle span of the scaffold, her cramped muscles protesting loudly. She winced, but even the discomfort couldn't diminish the rush of pleasure she felt as her eyes roamed over her work. The initial sketch across the panel was complete, black lines waiting to be brought to life by color. Her fingers, tired as they were, already itched for her brushes.

"Lady Cecelia Mountbatten."

Charlotte jerked, her pulse skipping. While she worked, she had mercifully forgotten about Flynn Rutledge and his mercurial temper. Had she known how defensive and furious he would get over those drawings, she wouldn't have come within ten feet of them. She hadn't had any interest in a confrontation then, and she certainly didn't want to confront him now. "I beg your pardon?"

"The woman in the drawings."

Charlotte turned carefully on the platform to find Rutledge looking up at her, holding two steaming mugs. With a start, she saw that at some point he must have fed the fire in the hearth and lit the lanterns hanging on the walls against the encroaching night. He'd shed his coat, and dark smudges marred the paleness of his shirt. Her eyes darted to his panel, but as usual, he had covered it with a long sheet. She had no idea why he insisted on hiding his work, but she was certainly not going to ask and risk another tirade.

She eyed him warily, making no move to descend.

His own gaze examined her work behind her. "An impressive start, Mr. Beaumont."

"Thank you." Still, Charlotte hesitated, unsure what he wanted from her. Unsure she wanted to engage in any sort of conversation about any part of his life that wasn't related to the panels behind her.

He held a mug out to her. "I come in peace." Charlotte supposed that was as close to an apology as she was going to get. Her stomach suddenly rumbled in hunger, and she realized she hadn't eaten anything all day, too absorbed in her work. She left her tins and charcoal on the scaffold and climbed down.

She accepted the mug from his hands, careful not to touch him, and let the warmth seep into her skin. She took a tentative sip of the steaming tea, closing her eyes briefly in appreciation. He had brewed it strong, exactly how she liked it.

"Lady Cecelia Mountbatten was my...lover." Rutledge said it flatly—how he might describe a pebble in his shoe that had been difficult to dislodge.

Charlotte studied him over the rim, trying to determine why he was telling her this and what it was he wanted her to say. *I'm sorry* seemed a possibility, given his tone. She didn't know Lady Cecelia Mountbatten personally, had never met her, but she'd overheard someone mention her many years prior. The widow of the Earl of Boyle was as famous for her dalliances with artists and actors as she was for her wealth. Though details of those dalliances had never interested Charlotte. Until now.

Now she found herself suddenly fascinated in a manner that was downright appalling.

"Did you love her?" Charlotte clamped her mouth shut too late. That had been a stupid question to ask. She refused to examine why she had asked it.

Rutledge looked at her sharply. "No. Though there was an unfortunate period of time in which I thought I did. And believed she loved me in return."

"And the two of you are no longer on...um...ah... intimate terms?" she ventured, trying to better imagine how Charlie Beaumont would respond while ignoring the heat that she could feel climbing into her cheeks.

"No." A shadow passed over his face. "We're not."

"Ah." Charlotte took another sip so that she didn't have to say anything else. What could she say? What did men say to each other in situations like this? Bloody hell, Charlotte didn't even know what women said to each other in situations like this.

"Are you a virgin, Beaumont?" Rutledge asked, his grey eyes almost silver in the low light.

"What?" The heat in her cheeks turned into an uncontrollable inferno, even as she tried to reason that Charlie Beaumont would probably not be embarrassed by the question. In the next heartbeat, Charlotte felt the color leach from her face as quickly as it had risen as a new possibility occurred to her. Holy gods above. Surely Rutledge was not going to propose a night of debauchery? A visit to a brothel? That aside from an apologetic cup of tea, he had taken it in his head to introduce Charlie Beaumont to the delights of the fairer sex while banishing the unpleasant memory of his mistress?

"No," she blurted before she caught herself. "No," she said again, this time trying to achieve the casual flippancy that she imagined Charlie Beaumont would display. Even as Charlotte Beaumont spoke a truth that, until this moment, no one else in the world knew. There was a liberating irony in that.

Though Charlotte wasn't entirely sure how much a single afternoon counted against Rutledge's apparent experience. An afternoon when Allan, the bookseller's son, had led her deep into the Aysgarth dales and, in the privacy of a sun-dappled clearing, kissed her until she was dizzy. And then his hands had come to rest nervously against the ties of her dress, asking permission. Young and drunk on the idea of love, she had nodded, undoing the first knot herself.

"You're not married, are you?" Rutledge asked, interrupting her reverie and looking as though he found that possibility absurd. He wouldn't be the first, Charlotte thought, though not for the reasons he thought. Allan had shyly asked her to wait for him to return from the wars, and Charlotte had agreed to that too. He'd been killed in Vitoria two months later.

No one had asked since then. For her hand in marriage or otherwise.

She shook her head. "No."

"You have a girl waiting on you somewhere?"

"No." She didn't have anyone waiting on her. Anywhere.

"You're better off, you know," Rutledge muttered. "Women can't be trusted."

Charlotte felt her brows shoot upward. "That's a little unfair, don't you think?"

"You're right." Rutledge stared darkly into his tea. "Rich, titled women can't be trusted," he amended. "For they are all conniving, duplicitous creatures."

Charlotte's fingers tightened on her mug. That was a little unfair too. But she bit her tongue on behalf of a boy from Aysgarth who would probably not have reason to have an opinion. She should go now. Nod and make some sort of noise that would neither agree nor disagree and then remove herself. She really didn't need to argue, and she certainly didn't need to know what lay between a capricious widow and a gifted artist to make him so bitter. What his rich, titled mistress had done to wound him so deeply was none of her business.

"I must assume it is the Lady Cecelia who has inspired such...umbrage?" Morbid curiosity triumphed over good sense.

"Of course it is." His eyes snapped up, narrowed and

mocking. "You really haven't heard the tales? About me? About us?"

Suddenly clouding her vision was an image of Rutledge in all his golden glory, reclining on satin sheets, the dark-haired Lady Cecelia peeling away his clothes as he kissed her senseless. The expected rush of horrified embarrassment that should have followed that was strangely absent. In its place was a feeling of...jealousy. A deep, inexplicable longing to know what it might feel like to be seduced by Flynn Rutledge. To be expertly kissed by a man capable of the deep, intense emotion that she had already glimpsed in his work. To be taken to bed and caressed by his clever hands, his long fingers gliding over her bare skin, toying and teasing, his body moving deep inside hers. To be tasted and touched and treasured and—

"I have not heard the tales," Charlotte said, realizing that her breathing wasn't entirely even. Her breasts ached beneath their bindings, and a pulsing need had settled deep at the juncture of her thighs. Good God, what was wrong with her? She squared her shoulders. "And I cannot imagine that it is either fair or reasonable to assume Lady Cecelia Mountbatten represents the...integrity or decency of all titled women. Or women of any sort, really." Charlotte wished those words back the second they escaped. She had promised herself that she would not pick a fight with this man. It was injudicious, and one wrong step could cost her everything. But combative was better than besotted. Besotted was beyond foolish.

Besotted was insane.

Rutledge was giving her a hard look. "Right."

Charlotte couldn't tell if he was being sarcastic or serious. But his belligerence and hostility were certainly back in full force. "Look, Mr. Rutledge, I am here to work. I am not your enemy. I am not here to judge you. For your past or anyone who may be a part of it. Your privacy, beyond what you wish to share, is just that. Yours."

He hadn't looked away from her but had gone eerily still. "I think you actually mean that."

"I am not in the habit of lying." Charlotte bit her lip against the jarring self-reproach that assailed her. For now, she would not consider herself guilty of lying by omission. Circumstance required it. "I only ask that you grant me the same privacy," she continued. "I know better than anyone what it feels like to be judged not on merit but on...appearances." At least that was the truth.

He had the grace to redden slightly. "Yes," he said slowly. "That's fair."

"Thank you." Though if the worst happened, if her true identity was discovered, she doubted that he would still agree. She didn't think he would be quite so benevolent should she be revealed as a rich, titled woman.

"You should know that Lady Cecelia was—is—a woman with unlimited wealth and vast connections. She is an enthusiastic patron of the arts," Rutledge said with a twist to his lips. "And as such, there are many who accused me of using her to advance my career. Accused me of sleeping with her to gain entrance to the hallowed halls of society where our sort will never be welcome."

"You don't need to tell me—"

"I want to." He had a strange expression on his face. "You are bound to hear it eventually, and I would prefer you hear it from me. I would prefer that—" He stopped. "I did not use her. She used me. Fancied me as nothing more than a wicked diversion, something more scintillating than the civilized gentlemen who pursued her. And something easily cast aside and replaced when she tired of it."

"I'm sorry." This time Charlotte did say it. Because being cast aside by those who were supposed to love you was something that she understood better than anyone.

His lip curled, and he looked down at his mug. "Just heed my advice, Mr. Beaumont. Do not do what I did. Do not trust your ambitions and your dreams and your secrets to another. If you are to survive in this world, you need to fight all your own battles. Every single one. You need to have your own back."

"I agree," Charlotte said simply.

Rutledge's eyes slowly climbed back to hers, a wary look in his eye like he had been expecting her to argue. "Lady Cecelia was..." He stopped and shook his head.

"A mistake," Charlotte said.

"A mistake," Rutledge repeated as though he thought Charlotte might be mocking him.

"A mistake," she said again, feeling the weight of this exchange. "A mistake to be treated in the exact same manner that you treat a success." She ignored the incredulous look he was giving her. "Mistakes and successes both have the same power—to be destructive or constructive. Dwell on either too long and they will both prevent you from moving forward. Learn from your mistakes and your successes in equal measure, and they will both make you better."

"Grand words for one so young," Rutledge remarked after a long minute.

"I've learned a few things the hard way."

"I see." His skepticism was apparent.

He didn't really see anything, Charlotte thought with a sudden frustration that clawed through her like physical pain. The insane impulse to tell him everything gripped her just as swiftly. What would happen if she were to tell him her name? If she took his hand in hers and told him that she understood more than he could imagine how it felt to struggle and hope, only to be shut out and cast aside?

"Do you see? Really?" She knew she should end this conversation, but she couldn't seem to stop the words that had built up within her, and she was no longer sure if she was speaking about Rutledge or herself. "Lady Cecelia was not your first mistake, I would think, and probably not your last," she said. "But neither she nor anyone else, no matter what they've done, diminishes you. Not your skill, your talent, or your ambition. It's all still there within you."

She knew she'd said too much. Said all the wrong things. Charlie Beaumont from Aysgarth would not have spoken in such a manner. Charlie Beaumont would likely have made a crude joke at Lady Cecelia's expense and then suggested that they both get thoroughly foxed to forget her.

"What do you want, Mr. Beaumont?" His question was sudden.

"I beg your pardon?"

"You speak of ambition, and I'm curious what sort of ambition it is that you harbor." He waved his hand in the direction of the panel. "When you are done with this commission, where will you go? What will you do?"

Charlotte ran a finger around the edge of her mug, trying to decide how to answer that. Amid all this candor, it was reasonable for him to press her for details about her own life. Her own ambitions and failings and struggles and...mistakes. Details she could never share.

This was exhausting, all this lying without lying.

She took a sip of tea and then another. "I don't know," she finally said with utter honesty. She didn't know where she would go, but she could not bring herself to imagine ever returning to the cold loneliness of London or

Aysgarth. Though that was not something she could tell him. "What of you, Mr. Rutledge?" she asked instead, deliberately turning the conversation back in his direction. "Where will your ambitions ultimately take you?"

"Italy," he said quietly and without any hesitation. "After this commission is complete, I will go to Italy."

"Italy?" She wasn't sure what she had expected, but given what little she knew of Rutledge and the astounding aptitude she had already seen in his Madonna and his defiant St. Michael, she wouldn't have been surprised if he had declared his intent to become a portraitist sought by royalty. "To do what?"

"To study. To learn." He paused, his voice hoarse. "To see the Baptistery. The church of St. Augustine. The Uffizi gallery." He met her eyes. "And more than anything, the Sistine Chapel."

Charlotte looked down at the dregs of her tea, recalling their earlier conversation about just that. And remembering how bleak he had looked when she'd admitted she'd been there. She set her empty mug aside.

"What are you doing?"

"I have something that you should see." Before Charlotte could second-guess the wisdom of what she was doing, she ducked into her room and retrieved the long canvas tube she had set in the corner. She passed it to Rutledge.

He took it gingerly. "What is this?"

"A piece of the Sistine Chapel," Charlotte said.

He remained motionless.

"It's only fair that you delve through some of my work," Charlotte said lightly. "Since I've already done the same to you."

He shook his head. "I shouldn't have—"

"Just open it," Charlotte interrupted, not wishing to revisit anything to do with the topic of Flynn Rutledge's mistress. And what they may or may not have done together.

Rutledge set his own mug aside before untying the leather strings and sliding the top off the tube. He set it on the long table and carefully slid the canvases out, letting them unroll flat on the surface. Charlotte could see her copy of the Van Dyck on top and moved to push it away, but Rutledge held out a hand and stopped her.

"Is this yours?" he asked.

"Yes," Charlotte said. "It is but a copy of an original work."

"A copy."

"Yes. Of a Van Dyck. But it is not that that I wish to show you. Look at the small one beneath it."

Rutledge continued to gaze down at the portrait of the young girl, and Charlotte wondered if he'd even heard her. Eventually, with what looked like reluctance, he moved it aside, and she heard him catch his breath as the smaller painting was revealed.

"*The Creation of Adam*," Charlotte said quietly. "My favorite of all the chapel scenes because it is, for all its divinity, inherently human. I made more sketches than I care to admit, and when I returned to England, I painted it. I have a...er, knack for reproductions, but you'll have to forgive my memory for any color inaccuracies you discover when you visit it yourself."

Rutledge was tracing the lines of Adam's arm as he reached up, his fingers hovering just over the canvas, careful not to touch the paint. He was completely silent, his expression giving nothing away. She wasn't sure how long they stood there, Rutledge not speaking and Charlotte wrestling with uncertainty that she had done the right thing by showing him.

"It's incredible," Rutledge said.

Charlotte felt something warm blossom inside of her. She had done the right thing.

"It is," she agreed. "In my opinion, Michelangelo's work is second to none—"

"No, I mean this is incredible. What you've done. This painting."

"It's only a copy," Charlotte said, shaking her head.

Rutledge was scowling fiercely. "It's a glimpse of something most people will never have the chance to see."

"Perhaps," Charlotte allowed.

Rutledge held it up reverently.

"Keep it," Charlotte said on impulse.

His head snapped around. "I can't."

"Of course you can. I'm giving it to you." As much as Charlotte had initially doubted the wisdom of showing it to him, gifting him the painting came with a sense of certainty.

He was shaking his head. "I won't—"

"Keep it to look at whenever you need to remind yourself that your ambitions and dreams are always yours. Return it to me when you return from Italy if you must." Not that that would ever actually happen, because Charlotte couldn't begin to imagine what she might be doing months or years from now that would still involve Flynn Rutledge. That thought was oddly dispiriting.

"Why would you do that for me?" he asked, and he was gazing at her with that familiar intensity that made Charlotte fear he was looking right through her. Butterflies were suddenly beating a frantic tattoo against the inside of her rib cage.

She turned away from him before she blurted something stupid that a boy from Aysgarth would never, ever say. Before she responded the way a besotted woman might.

She shrugged. "Because I can," she said carelessly over her shoulder. "And because I am hopeful that we might complete this commission as friends, Mr. Rutledge."

He didn't answer, but she could feel his eyes following her every move.

Charlotte reached for her previously discarded scarf that still hung on her scaffold, suddenly anxious to escape the undercurrents of emotion that were threatening her composure and put a much-needed distance between them. "Thank you for the tea, Mr. Rutledge. Enjoy the rest of your evening." She cringed at the complete artlessness of that.

"Wait. Where are you going?" The words came out in a rush.

Anywhere that wasn't here. "I don't know. To get something to eat. I'm famished."

"There's a tavern on the south end of Warwick Lane. It serves a decent stew and a passable ale for a reasonable price."

"Thank you. I'll keep that in mind."

"Would you care for company?" He hesitated. "Because I, too, would like to complete this commission as friends."

Charlotte instantly opened her mouth to refuse until she turned and caught a glimpse at what lurked beneath Rutledge's closed, tight expression.

Loneliness.

Something that had been her constant, awful companion since she was a child. Something that superseded all the promises she'd just made to herself to put more distance between them.

"I'd like that," she heard herself say.

He smiled at her then, a genuine one that crinkled the

corners of his silver eyes and exposed a slight dimple along his left cheek. All the air in the room was suddenly sucked out. Her knees actually went a little weak, and the aching want and need deep within her roared back to life. Charlotte put a hand on the edge of the scaffold to steady herself. She could not do this. She could not harbor this sort of desire for a man she was supposed to be working with. She could not allow herself to become infatuated like a pitiful, moon-eyed schoolgirl when everything she had truly wanted and worked so hard for was finally in her grasp.

She needed to be better. At the very least, she needed to be far more careful than she'd been this far. "We should go," she mumbled.

"Of course," Rutledge said, seemingly not noticing her reaction. "I'll fetch my coat."

Chapter 7

Flynn studied Charlie Beaumont out of the corner of his eye.

The boy had been as skittish as a feral cat since they had left the grounds of St. Michael's and wound their way through the darkened streets, eventually slipping into the welcome warmth of the tavern. As they had walked, Beaumont had kept his head down and had kept a physical distance as though Flynn carried the plague.

Though Flynn couldn't say that he'd been overly relaxed either. Everything that had been said in that studio had left him wildly out of sorts. Not to mention Beaumont's casual gifting of a canvas so exquisite that it had stripped Flynn of words. He had known deep down that Beaumont was skilled—Lisbon had told him as much, even if he hadn't wanted to hear it at the time. What Flynn hadn't realized until he'd rolled out those paintings—paintings Beaumont had dismissed as mere copies—was that the boy was breathtakingly gifted.

And not only gifted but humble. And wise and generous. And kind.

Perhaps that kindness was why he had told Beaumont as much as he had about Cecelia. He'd tried to convince himself that it was because he didn't want to have to defend himself when the boy inevitably heard the gossip. It was better to get ahead of such things. Competitive jealousy and ruthless guile were hallmarks of the art world that Flynn had constantly endured, and his naïveté about his affair with Cecelia and how he would be received in a society that was not his was as shameful as it was frustrating. He had learned his lesson about misplaced trust the hard way.

But the more he had confided to Beaumont, the less difficult the words had become to share. There was something about him that made Flynn want to bare everything. Because Beaumont had simply looked at him with those calm, caramel eyes and had…understood. In his soft-spoken manner, he had put into words what Flynn had been unable to. He had unwittingly forgiven Flynn for actions that Flynn hadn't been able to forgive himself for. Laid out a truth and a reality that his own anger had prevented him from seeing. It had been unnerving, that revelation.

I am hopeful that we might complete this commission as friends.

It had been a long time since Flynn had had a friendship that wasn't layered in hidden agendas or deceit. He had thought Cecelia Mountbatten, with all her professions of devotion and admiration, had been a friend. He knew better now. But had she possessed even a portion of Charlie Beaumont's gentle grace and honor, or a fraction of his wisdom and kindness, Flynn would have been lost. He would have fallen in love so hard and so deep that he probably would never have found the surface again.

As it was, however, he realized he had found his way back. Righted his ship and recharted his course with the most unlikely of allies. Beaumont had drawn Flynn out of the cold shadows of bitterness and regret, and tonight, he had found himself unwilling to let the boy step out into the darkness alone, as if by leaving, he would take all of Flynn's newfound peace with him. The young artist made him better in so many ways. Made him want to do better. Be better. And as he watched the boy across the tavern table, he thought to himself that it would be a lucky soul who would one day capture the incredible heart of Charlie Beaumont.

Their meal was eaten mostly in silence, Flynn lost in the turmoil of his thoughts and Beaumont seemingly content to keep to himself. Normally, the silence would have pleased Flynn to no end. Normally, he would have no interest in dissecting anything remotely personal with another individual. But with Beaumont, his normal seemed to have shifted. He just wasn't sure what to do about it. They had finished their meal and were almost back to St. Michael's before Flynn decided that silence was not at all what he wanted.

"Thank you," he said into the darkness of the night, the air crisp with the promise of winter.

"For what?"

"The painting. I'm sorry if I came across as ungrateful." The wind had died, and his breath rose in a foggy cloud.

Beaumont shrugged. "Don't trouble yourself," he mumbled.

"Do you have siblings?" Flynn suddenly needed to know more.

He saw Beaumont duck his head, and for a moment

Flynn wasn't sure if he was going to answer. "Two brothers," he muttered after a pause.

"And are they artists as well?"

"No."

"What do they do?"

There was another long pause. Somewhere in the distance, hooves clattered. "They work for my father," Beaumont finally said.

"In Aysgarth?"

A hesitation and then a nod, followed by an empty silence.

Flynn frowned. "What does your father do?"

"He manages land."

"A steward then?"

Beaumont shrugged. "Something like that."

Flynn scowled at the ambiguity of his answer, and Beaumont caught his expression.

"I've never been close to my family," the boy said, his eyes slipping away again. "They've never seen value in me or...approved of my...ah...ambitions. For as long as I can remember, I have only ever been a disappointment to them." There was an edge of frustration and sadness that Flynn recognized well. Because Flynn had also had to fight legions of people who didn't think that he would ever amount to anything. He still was fighting.

"I'm sorry." Because as much as Flynn had fought, he'd been armed with the knowledge that his mother, the only family he'd ever had, had believed in him completely and passionately. "Was it difficult to leave?"

Beaumont made a small noise that was difficult to interpret. "There was no one and nothing to leave," he mumbled. "My only regret was that I didn't find the courage to leave sooner."

Flynn stopped abruptly in the middle of the deserted lane, the handful of buildings on either side of them silent and dark. A broken fence listed drunkenly, creating strange shadows across the road. "You were meant to do this, you know," he said to Beaumont's back.

The boy stopped, and he slowly turned to face Flynn. In the dark, it was impossible to see his features clearly. "Do what?" he asked in a voice so soft Flynn almost missed the question.

Flynn waved a hand in the direction of the church, its spire just visible above the shadowed roofs in the moonlight. "You were meant to create, Mr. Beaumont. Inspire. You see beyond the surface." He didn't know what was making him say these things. Maybe it was guilt over his initial conduct. Maybe because he saw part of himself in Beaumont. Maybe it was because he understood that Charlie Beaumont was not an adversary but an ally. A true friend who listened without judgment and whose actions were driven only by kindness. He didn't have pieces of the Sistine Chapel to gift this boy with, but perhaps he could offer words. "Regardless of what you might have overheard me say, you have a gift. You should be proud of what you've already accomplished."

Beaumont had gone utterly silent and utterly still. As the seconds ticked by, Flynn shifted uncomfortably in the cold, feeling foolish. This is what he got for letting his guard down and spouting... feelings. No doubt Beaumont was—

"Thank you." It was a strained whisper that hung in icy crystals before dissipating. "No one has ever said anything like that to me before."

Flynn frowned. Beaumont sounded... off. Like he was going to weep. There was something not quite right about—

He froze, his skin prickling with an awareness that hadn't ever failed him. An awareness that had allowed him to survive for those years when so many others hadn't.

"Step towards me, Beaumont," he commanded.

The boy obeyed either his tone or because he had sensed the same.

From out of the shadows, a figure emerged. Then another.

"Look what we have here." The man who spoke first was barrel-chested, the buttons of his coat straining over the front of his torso. He had a hat pulled down over his ears so it was difficult to see his expression, but it was not difficult to interpret his intentions.

The second man stepped into the narrow lane. He wasn't as big, but he had the build of a man who made his living with hard labor. "An aris-to-crat," he mocked, making it clear exactly what he thought of the upper classes.

Beside him, he saw Beaumont open his mouth.

"That's right," Flynn snapped before Beaumont could say anything. "And I'd trouble you to leave myself and my servant alone." If these two blackguards believed the boy was a mere servant, they'd likely leave him be. His rumpled appearance helped, as did the pallor of Beaumont's face above his scarf and the rapid rise and fall of his chest. A surge of protectiveness hit Flynn with the force of a runaway carriage.

"That's a fine coat you're wearing, mate," the smaller of the two men said to Flynn. "And fine boots. Expensive."

Flynn didn't need to glance at the grey coat or the boots he wore to know exactly how expensive they looked or why he might have been mistaken for a rich toff. The coat was made of superfine, lined and tailored, the boots made of polished, supple leather with reinforced soles. He had bought them with the money from his first large commission because, for as long as he could remember, winter had meant bone-chilling misery, ragged garments, and broken shoes stuffed with paper no match for the incapacitating cold. The coat and the boots had cost him dearly, and they had been worth every penny.

"We'll take yer boots and yer coat and whatever is in them pockets." The bigger man lifted his hand, and Flynn could see that he held a knife.

"You don't want to do this," Flynn said.

The men were laughing at Flynn's words. "I can assure ye, we do. Besides, a bloke like you can afford it." They took a few steps closer. "Now give me yer coat. I don't want to make you bleed all over it."

"Get out of here, Beaumont," Flynn ordered under his breath.

Beaumont's head snapped around. "What?"

"Go. Run. They don't want you. They want me. And I can handle myself."

"I'm not running. I'm not leaving you alone."

Flynn fought back a surge of frustration. "It wasn't a request," he snapped. "And you don't want to see this. Go. Get help—"

The man with the knife sprang at him without warning, catching Flynn off guard, but Beaumont drove his shoulder into the man's barrel chest, making the attacker stumble. Flynn thought he saw the knife flash in the dull light but he was already leaping forward, wrenching the man's thick forearm back and to the side in practiced movements he had not had to use in a long time. He felt the man's shoulder joint pop, heard him scream, and the knife dropped to the ground. Flynn delivered a punishing blow to the man's kneecap with the heel of his boot, and he fell heavily, but not before Flynn had snatched up his knife.

The second man was much faster than his cohort. Flynn felt the air hiss as a blade narrowly missed the side of his face, and he danced back, adjusting his grip on his own weapon. It was clumsy, this knife, unbalanced and bulky, but it would do. Flynn had done more with less in the past. The smaller man shuffled around his writhing, groaning partner, looking for an advantage that Flynn wouldn't give him. He couldn't see Beaumont, and he hoped that the boy was long gone.

"You don't want to do this," Flynn said again.

The man only bared his teeth in response and lunged with his knife. Flynn sidestepped easily, his fingers once again flexing around the wooden handle of his own blade.

"Just leave," Flynn tried. "Take your friend. He's got a dislocated shoulder and a shattered kneecap, and both need attention if he's going to be able to use his arm and leg again."

His attacker ignored him and lunged again, and this time, Flynn spun and brought his blade down, leaving a deep gash across the man's chest. "Stop, please," he said, though he was beginning to lose patience, the old battle fever rising and starting to pound through his veins.

The man shouted in fury and rushed forward, swinging wildly. Flynn dodged, and his blade found purchase in his attacker's upper arm. But the man didn't even flinch, nor did he slow his attack. He just kept coming, his knife whistling back and forth.

Flynn crouched, balanced on the balls of his feet, and let him come, using his forearm to block his opponent and at the same time sinking his blade into the hard muscle of the man's thigh, hoping to slow him down. But as Flynn twisted, the heel of his boot caught on an uneven ridge, and Flynn felt himself pitching backward. He hit the ground on his backside, and in an instant, his attacker launched himself on top of him.

He tried to roll away, but the man was like a wildcat, his movements erratic and frenzied as his knife flashed downward. Flynn waited for his opening as he blocked each thrust, knowing that his attacker could not maintain this for long—

A sharp crack resounded, and the man suddenly pitched forward with a stunned expression on his face, landing face-first on the ground. Beaumont stood over him, with what looked like a piece of broken fence board in his hand. Flynn scrambled to his feet.

"What the hell are you doing?" Flynn demanded, breathing hard, the blood still roaring in his ears. "I told you to go and get help."

"I did." Beaumont was blinking rapidly. "That board was very helpful."

Flynn glanced down at the board in Beaumont's hand and realized with horror that the jagged wood was slick with blood. As was the boy's whole left hand and the entire outer edge of the sleeve of his coat, an ominous dark stain in the low light.

"You're bleeding," Flynn said, reaching for him.

Beaumont frowned and swayed slightly. "I do feel a little funny," he said.

"Shit," Flynn swore, catching the boy under his arm and noticing the gaping tear at the shoulder of his baggy coat. The edges had bloomed dark as more blood soaked into the fabric. The heavy man must have gotten him when he had charged at Flynn. When Beaumont had stepped into his path to stop him.

He switched sides, pulling Beaumont's good arm over his shoulder, even as the boy tried to push his hands away. "I don't need your help," he mumbled, but his words were slurred. "I'm fine." And then his eyes rolled up in his head, his lashes fluttered, and he went limp against Flynn.

"Shit," Flynn swore again. "Shit, shit, shit." How badly had Beaumont been cut? He couldn't see how deep it went. Stitches might be enough to fix it. Provided it didn't go putrid. Provided infection didn't spread down his arm. Provided Beaumont didn't subside into a fever and waste away. Flynn had seen that before. More times than he cared to remember and from wounds that had looked completely innocent at first.

Fear—real fear—coursed through him. He bent and scooped the boy up into his arms, thinking that he wasn't as heavy as he expected. Flynn hurried toward the spire of St. Michael's, trying not to jar the boy too much.

He reached the grounds and hesitated briefly, wondering if he should alert Lisbon. No, that could wait. And there was no guarantee that Lisbon wouldn't insist on summoning a doctor. The sort that poked and prodded with their lancets, drained more blood, and generally made a bad situation worse. Flynn might not be a surgeon or a physician, but he had treated knife wounds more times than he cared to remember, and he trusted himself more than the quacks he had seen in action. After all these years, he still kept a kit in his belongings that contained everything he needed to treat such wounds.

That decided, he veered in the direction of their studio. He crashed through the door, kicking it shut against the cold with his foot, and hurried to Beaumont's room, laying the boy on the bed with as much care as he could manage. He left Beaumont just long enough to fetch both the lanterns from the studio floor and set them on the tiny washstand, dragging it closer to the bed.

Beaumont was pale, a scrape on his temple Flynn hadn't noticed before slowly leaking blood. But he wasn't worried about that. He needed to see what sort of real damage had been done to the boy's shoulder. Flynn's fingers fumbled first with his scarf, pulling it away, before attacking the buttons of Beaumont's baggy coat, and he shoved it open. As gently as he could, Flynn eased his good arm out of its sleeve, rolling him over slightly so he could pull the coat out from under him and away from his left.

The boy groaned slightly but didn't open his eyes.

He tossed the coat to the floor, already reaching for the ties of his equally shapeless and bulky shirt. Against the pale linen, the blood looked more sinister, Beaumont's entire left arm soaked and darkening. Flynn cursed and pulled at the stubborn laces of the ruined shirt, needing to see the extent of the injury. Beaumont groaned again, his head twisting to the side, one of his hands coming up to push at Flynn's.

"Stop," the boy whispered faintly before he went limp again.

"Shut up," Flynn snapped, not certain Beaumont could even hear him. "Lie still." The laces gave way, and Flynn grasped the worn linen in his hands and pulled, the fabric tearing easily. "I can't see where the blood is—" He stopped.

Stopped speaking, stopped moving, stopped breathing.

Though he could see Charlie Beaumont's chest moving up and down. No, he thought numbly, not Charlie. Or Charles, for that matter. He didn't know who the hell was on the bed in front of him, but it wasn't a *he*.

It seemed obvious now, in the way that hindsight makes

complete fools out of otherwise intelligent men. But Flynn hadn't seen it because he hadn't been looking. Because he'd never had a reason to look. Because he'd been so inwardly focused and consumed by his own bitter struggles that he hadn't bothered to look at hers.

The initial shock was starting to fade, and Flynn fought to put his thoughts in order and examine what lingered. The anger that had instantly welled with the unwelcome surprise had also diminished, and he recognized that response was more a product of his damaged pride than anything else. Because with it, there was admiration that she had been able to hide in plain sight so deftly. There was wonder at the measures that she had felt she had needed to take so that she could do what she was clearly born to do.

But most prominent was the peculiar protectiveness he had first felt in that narrow lane. A protectiveness that had suddenly taken on a whole different slant. It was probably better that Flynn had believed himself to be defending a boy named Charlie Beaumont because, had he been defending the nameless woman lying so still before him, he wasn't sure he simply wouldn't have slit the throats of both thieves. Which was a ridiculous sentiment, he knew, because in theory, nothing had truly changed.

And yet everything had changed.

Flynn reached out and pushed a piece of heavy brown hair from her face, seeing her for the first time. She would never be considered pretty by the most conventional of standards, and it was why her disguise had been effective. She had a jaw that was too strong, cheeks that were too sharp, and brows that fell short of elegant. She didn't have long sweeping lashes or a pert nose or a Cupid's bow mouth. Perhaps, in the right clothing and the right accessories, she might be considered handsome, but her height and the span of her shoulders had probably intimidated more than one man. A warrior, he thought, his chest tightening in an unfamiliar way. His warrior. One who hadn't run. One who had defended him. One who had defied him and fought.

One who would answer a great many questions for him when she woke up.

But a warrior who was still vulnerable and bleeding.

Flynn forced himself to shove all other thoughts from his mind for the time being. He ignored the wide strip of blood-smeared linen that bound her small but unmistakable breasts and examined the cut on the top of her shoulder. It didn't look as deep as he had feared, the bulky coat taking the worst of the blade, but it was long and would require stitches. He balled up her ruined shirt and pressed the linen against the wound, winding her scarf under her arm and over her shoulder to keep it in place.

And went to fetch his kit.

Chapter 8

Charlotte was on fire.

No, that wasn't entirely true—her shoulder was on fire while the rest of her was strangely chilled. Amid the merciless throbbing, she struggled to open her eyes as her mind fought to make sense of where she was. She was lying flat on her back, staring up at familiar rough-hewn rafters.

She was back in her room in the studio. How did—

It came back to her in a rush that made her flinch and surge upward.

Except she didn't get anywhere because two hands were pushing her back down with an uncompromising strength. "Don't move," a voice growled in her ear. "I'm not quite done."

A wave of realizations rolled over Charlotte, each worse than the last. She had been in a bloody street brawl. At some point in time, she must have fainted, because she didn't remember the journey back here. She was naked from the waist up, save for the bindings around her breasts. Flynn Rutledge was seated beside her, doing something to her shoulder that felt like he was applying a branding iron.

And there was no way in hell that anyone in this room believed that she was a *he* any longer.

"What are you doing?" she mumbled, while shoring up her defenses and her arguments because she was going to need them all.

"Stitching." His voice was grim. "And I'd be obliged if you refrained from moving again. This will sting."

It was all he said in warning before she had the vague impression of something cold hitting her skin, followed by a searing pain that left her gasping. She turned her head away from the overwhelming stench of whiskey, telling herself that was making her eyes water.

"You should have run when you had the chance," Rutledge said impassively from beside her, leaving Charlotte to guess what he was thinking. "When I told you to."

"And I told you I wasn't leaving you," she gritted. Even though it had become abundantly clear that Flynn Rutledge had been telling the truth when he had said that he could handle himself.

"You could have been killed," he said.

"I wasn't." Her teeth clenched. "Though I hate that I fainted."

"Shock," Rutledge said, bending over her shoulder again. "And you bled like a stuck pig."

"If I had to do it again, I still wouldn't run." That was the truth, and for some reason, she needed this man to know it, even though that decision may have cost her everything. But the passive Charlotte who had allowed others to steer the course of her life for far too long had been left behind in London. The Charlotte who had bargained with a terrifying man named King, trusted a baron she didn't know, and struck out on her own would not apologize for her actions now. Whatever happened from here on out, she would, at the very least, have a voice.

She listened to Rutledge's steady breathing as he worked. "Tell me your name," he said finally.

She felt a tug at her shoulder, and fire erupted anew. "Charlotte," she said through clenched teeth. "Beaumont."

"Charlotte," he repeated, and despite the throbbing at her shoulder, a shiver ran through her at the intimacy of her name on his lips.

Rutledge abruptly straightened and drew a sheet over her bound chest. If she thought his use of her name was intimate, this should have been beyond the pale, being exposed as she was. But somehow, this new Charlotte couldn't bring herself to muster the appropriate horror.

This Charlotte had acted on instinct in a deserted lane, even though she had been terrified. This Charlotte hadn't run away. In fact, she'd fought back—had splinters in her fingers and burning, aching stitches to prove it—and that had left her with a rash confidence of the sort she had never before experienced.

"I'm done." She heard Rutledge's boots move across the floor, and she still couldn't tell if he was furious or not that she had deceived him.

Charlotte tucked her chin and craned her head to see a neat row of stitches marching across the top of her shoulder. "Thank you," she said slowly.

"Don't touch it. It will be sore for a while. And then it will itch like hell. The stitches can come out in maybe ten days, so long as it heals properly."

"How do you know how to do this?" she asked.

He had his back to her, and she could hear the sounds of water in the basin as he washed his hands. At her question, his movements ceased before they resumed again, unhurried. He dried his hands on a rag and finally turned, his eyes the color of storm clouds. He bent and plucked a bottle of whiskey from the floor next to her bed and dragged the chair he'd just occupied toward himself. He sat, crossing his booted foot over his knee, and brought the whiskey to his lips.

"I know how to do this because I grew up in a part of London where a soul might slit the throat of another for the chance to survive another day," he said when he lowered the bottle. "A part of London my mother left every evening so that she could sell herself to wealthy men who preferred not to stray so far into the rookeries. Doctors didn't like that part of London either. Necessity is a powerful motivator." He took another swig of whiskey. "Your turn for a truth, *Charlie*."

Charlotte forced her features to remain neutral, unsure if he was testing her or trusting her with that sudden confession. "As a woman and an artist, the opportunities beyond tepid watercolors are somewhat lacking. I did what I had to do to obtain this commission," she said evenly. "Necessity is a powerful motivator."

Rutledge dropped his gaze, studying the bottle in his hands. He tapped his fingers on the glass; his forehead creased. "Does Lisbon know? That you are a woman?"

"Yes." There was no reason to lie. Rutledge could ask Lisbon himself. "I'm not the first he's hired."

Rutledge seemed to absorb that. "And you didn't think you could trust me with the truth?"

"I didn't know you."

"You know me now."

"I do. And I can tell that you're angry." She couldn't say she blamed him.

His answer was slow to come. "I was," he said eventually.

Charlotte frowned. "But you're not anymore?"

"You lied to me." He said it more as a statement than an accusation.

"I never lied to you," she replied haltingly. "Everything I told you was true. Except my name. That wasn't the whole truth." *And it still isn't*, a small voice in the back of her mind accused. *You haven't yet told him that you're a lady.* Though given how he felt about titled women, she was not about to mention it now and make this worse. That truth would keep for a bit longer.

"It's the same thing," he said, and he wasn't wrong.

Charlotte closed her eyes before staring up again at the rafters. "You have my apologies, whatever they might be worth now. But what would you have done? If you were me? When you knew deep down that you possess all the ability and skill required, but your whole life you've been told that it's not enough? Would you have risked the truth?"

He didn't answer that.

"Will you ask Lisbon to replace me now? Make me leave?" Her question fell like a stone into the silence. But she needed to know. Because if she had to, she would fight for this too. She would not fade passively into the background. Not anymore.

His head came up, and he stared at her. "Leave?"

"It's a fair question."

"It's an insulting question. Do you think I am intimidated by you? By your talent and skill?"

"No." Charlotte shook her head wearily. "I don't think you are intimidated by anything, Mr. Rutledge."

"Then you'd be wrong." His silver eyes pinned her to

the pillows with the sharpness of a rapier. He set the bottle of whiskey aside and abruptly stood, snatching one of the lanterns and striding toward the door. Charlotte frowned in confusion as he made his way across the studio floor to the panel that was still shrouded. Through the open door, she could still see him and the lower portion of the panel.

He set the lantern down, turned and met her gaze across the space, and yanked the sheet from the panel.

Charlotte couldn't see the top of his work, but what she could see was stunning. St. Michael, in all his defiant glory, stared out larger than life from the surface. Everything that Rutledge had captured in his sketch was also visible here. A raw emotion of the sort that made his Madonna portrait so breathtaking.

Flynn retraced his steps back to her room, pacing the tiny space near the end of her bed.

"It's magnificent," Charlotte said honestly. "But I've always known it would be."

"How?"

"Because I knew how much of yourself you'd put into it. And because I know that you have the talent and skill to do that justice. I've seen it." She jerked her chin in the direction of the panel. "You're creating something extraordinary."

"It's because of you."

"I beg your pardon?"

Rutledge stopped pacing long enough to run a hand through his hair. "I haven't created anything like that in a long time. I've been...lost. Unable to find joy in something that has been as necessary to me as breathing for as long as I can remember. And that didn't just intimidate me—it terrified me. And then you showed up. And gave me..." He trailed off, visibly struggling for a word.

"Direction. Made me remember what was important. Gave me back my purpose."

Charlotte felt a strange current skitter through her veins that made her shiver. He was making her sound like she had some sort of magical power over him. "I didn't give you direction, Mr. Rutledge. I deceived you. Ignored you." She rolled her shoulder with a wince. "Disobeyed you."

"You tolerated my less than honorable conduct with a grace I didn't deserve." He was looking at her now with an intensity that was making her pulse do strange things. "And then defended me. Like my very own Jeanne d'Arc." There was an odd note of reverence in his statement, and another shiver streaked through her, even as she told herself that it was the historic maiden, not herself, who held his regard. To think otherwise threatened to scatter her wits beyond repair.

"Jeanne d'Arc was burned to death at the stake for her visions of St. Michael," Charlotte tried, aiming for levity and failing miserably. "I have no such aspirations, I can assure you, Mr. Rutledge."

"Flynn," he said, moving closer to the side of the bed again. "Call me Flynn. And I will call you Charlotte. I think it's about time we got that part right, don't you?"

Charlotte hesitated. "From a professional standpoint, I'm not sure that—"

"I ripped your shirt in two. Strict professionalism might be compromised." He gave her a wry smile.

Charlotte felt herself flush to the roots of her hair. If he was trying to make her laugh or put her at ease, he wasn't doing any better at levity than she had. Because all she could think about now was just how much she might want to do just that to him.

And not while either one of them was insensible.

"Very well," she managed. "Flynn."

The smile abruptly disappeared, and his eyes fastened on hers. He reached out, and his finger slowly traced a path down the side of her cheek. It was such a gentle, tender gesture that it made Charlotte want to burst into tears. It was only the fierce burn of her shoulder that kept her from reaching up and catching his fingers with hers as if that could keep him here forever.

"So you won't make me leave?" she whispered raggedly.

His hand suddenly dropped, and he averted his eyes from her face. "Of course not," he said curtly, stepping away from the bed. "You should rest. Probably for a few days. And for pity's sake, stay off the scaffolding. You've lost a fair amount of blood, and I have no desire to scrape you off the floor if you get light-headed at the top." He retrieved the remaining lantern from the washstand and made his way to the door.

"Thank you," Charlotte said quietly.

"It was nothing. I've stitched up more individuals than I care to remember." He paused in the doorway, though he didn't turn to look at her.

"Not for that. Well, yes, for that too, but for understanding. Thank you for understanding." Her throat was still tight. "And for accepting me. And believing in me."

"I'm only returning the favor," he said and closed the door firmly behind him.

Chapter 9

He had wanted to kiss her.

When Charlotte had said his name, her cheeks flushed and eyes fixed on his, he had almost lost his head. He squeezed his eyes shut. For the love of God, two hours prior to that moment he had still believed her to be a boy. As a boy, Charlotte's genuine friendship and beautiful heart had left him humbled. His steady wisdom and gentle acceptance had left him healed.

As a woman, all of that had left him reeling, his sudden desire to kiss her the only thing that had emerged clearly.

He cursed softly to himself. Was there anything in this world that was less romantic than kissing a woman who lay helpless in a bed, pale and bruised, her shoulder a painful mess of stitches? Was there anything less honorable than fantasizing about kissing a woman who was there as his equal—his colleague? Charlotte was not some loose tavern wench hoping to catch his eye for an evening's entertainment. In fact, she had gone to extreme measures to ensure that that sort of idiocy would never happen. The least he could do as a professional, as a man—as a bloody human being—was respect that. He hadn't even sought Lisbon out to tell him what had happened as though, by avoiding the architect, Flynn could pretend that nothing had changed and they could proceed with business as usual.

Flynn leaned forward and banged his forehead against the edge of the scaffold gently, wondering if he was losing his mind. Because, despite the stern logical lecture, he still wanted to kiss her.

"Could you imagine if we had to use ultramarine? How ghastly expensive that would be?"

The comment snapped his head up and he spun, finding Charlotte standing behind him. She was studying the deep blue of the heavens he had added to the background until he had lost his daylight. The same deep blue that she would eventually start adding to hers once she was ready.

"You shouldn't be up," he grumbled.

"And you shouldn't have to wait on me hand and foot any longer while I stare at the rafters. I'm perfectly capable of seeing to myself."

Her color was much better than it had been two days ago, though she was still a little pale. She had dressed herself in her trousers and another one of her oversize shirts, though the laces were loose to allow room for the bulky bandage he had wrapped around her shoulder.

"Sit then," he said, fetching a chair and setting it at her side.

She made a face but obeyed readily enough. "I can't abide not working. It's not as though the stitches impede my painting hand." She held up her right hand and waved it around.

"Tomorrow," he told her. "One more day."

"But—"

"One more day, Charlotte."

She sighed. "If this whole art thing doesn't work out for you, a career as a surgeon might be an excellent option. A tyrannical surgeon, but a surgeon nonetheless."

He smiled despite himself. "I'll take that as a compliment."

"You should."

"Would you prefer that I did not sleep here?" he asked suddenly. It had been weighing on him since that night he carried her back here, bloodied and broken.

"What?"

"Would you prefer that I seek other lodgings? I just thought that perhaps you might wish to be alone—"

"Does my being here make you uncomfortable?" she asked, her brows furrowed.

Yes, he wanted to say. *Because now I lie awake at night imagining what it would be like to have you beneath me. And above me. And that makes me hot and hard and restless and very uncomfortable.*

"Of course not," he said instead. "I just didn't want my presence to make this awkward…"

"Now that I'm Charlotte and not Charlie?"

"Yes."

"I appreciate your honor, Flynn Rutledge," she said, smiling softly at him and making something deep in his chest ache. "Thank you for asking." She dropped her eyes, her cheeks pink. "But I'm glad you're here," she said. "I don't want to be alone. I don't want you to go anywhere."

Warmth flooded through him, and it threatened to ignite into a different sort of heat. "Good," he said. "I don't want to go anywhere either."

She nodded, her eyes still fixed on her hands clutched in her lap, her teeth worrying her lower lip. Wide, impossibly kissable lips. Lips that had featured prominently in his recent fantasies. Flynn had to look away before he did something that was not honorable at all.

"How do the stitches feel?" he blurted.

"Itchy," she said.

"Good. Then it's healing." He took a deep, steadying breath, bringing his gaze back to hers. "Let me take another look."

She opened her mouth as though she might argue.

"You will not win an argument with a tyrannical surgeon."

That was met with an eye roll. "Oh, very well." She loosened the laces at her throat a little more, and Flynn had to look away again, realizing that this was the height of folly. Last time he had examined her shoulder, she'd been half asleep and covered in blankets. She had not been restless and alert, her eyes following his every move.

He stepped around the back of her chair so that she couldn't see his face or anything stamped across it that might betray his thoughts. Carefully, trying not to touch her skin, he lifted her shirt away from the side of her neck, easing the loosened collar over the bandage on her shoulder. She had beautiful skin, he thought, his eyes tracing the graceful curve of her shoulder where it met her neck. Smooth and soft, begging a man to run his fingers over it. Or press his lips to the sensitive spot just below her ear. It was a crime to conceal such beauty under layers of rough homespun. It should be showcased in silk and satin.

Or better yet, nothing at all.

Flynn gritted his teeth against the arousal that surged through him. His job, at the moment, was only to examine her wound to ensure her health. Not to fantasize about what she would look like sprawled in his bed. Not to imagine what it would feel like to curl his fingers through her thick hair and taste all that gorgeous skin.

He went to work on the bandage he'd secured and gently unwound it. He removed the pad of clean linen he'd placed over the stitches and peered at the cut.

"What does it look like?" Charlotte twisted her head, trying to get a glimpse and blocking his view in the process.

"I can't see with you in the way." Flynn slid his hand along the side of her head just above her ear and tilted it back, her hair as soft as he had imagined it would be under his fingers. Unable to help himself, he placed his other palm against the exposed skin at the back of her shoulder blade. It, too, was as soft as he had imagined it would be.

He, on the other hand, was as hard as a rock.

Beneath his touch, he felt her shiver. "Are you cold?"

"No," she whispered.

It would be so easy to bend his head and place a kiss at the side of her neck. It would be so easy to slide his hands beneath the loose fabric of her shirt to explore more of her glorious skin. To pull away the bindings and trace the slight curve of her breasts. To run his palms over the span of her rib cage to the waistband of her trousers. And in doing so, he knew he would not stop there.

But he would stop now.

Because Charlotte Beaumont deserved better than his libido. She deserved his respect. This wasn't a game to either of them.

"It looks good," he said as evenly as he could. He replaced the bandage and rewrapped it to keep the stitches from catching on her shirt, casting about for a topic of conversation that would distract him from the feel of her body beneath his hands. "Why this commission?" he asked as he finished, stepping away from Charlotte and all the temptation that she was.

"I beg your pardon?" She straightened her shirt and began to tug the laces tighter.

"Why did you come here? Why not take something in London? Something that might gain you more recognition?" He had thrown out the original question without much thought, but now he found himself waiting intently for her answer.

She finished with the ties. "Recognition," she repeated with a slight scoff. "Recognition for whom? Charlie Beaumont?"

"There are women who are successful artists, you know," he said with a slight frown. "Clare Wheatley Pope, for one. She's a very accomplished miniaturist. She's even taught members of the aristocracy. And Maria Cosway has painted—"

"And would the clergy and directors of St. Michael's have consented to having either of those two women on this commission?" Charlotte asked.

Flynn's frown deepened. "Probably not," he admitted.

Charlotte turned in her chair to gaze up at him. "I don't want to paint miniatures. I don't want to teach the aristocracy how to execute watercolor renditions of damask roses. I want..." She trailed off.

"What?" he demanded. "What do you want?"

"I want to create something that is greater than myself. Greater than all of us. I want to leave something behind for those to come. Something that has the power to elicit inspiration and contemplation that will endure the test of time." She paused, her eyes sliding to the panels behind him. "I've spent a great deal of time copying the works of others, and it has taught me everything I know. But now, I want to write my own story."

"Which is what?" Flynn's throat had gone dry at the passion and the fire in her eyes.

"Redemption. Reinvention. And this commission is both of those things." Her gaze came back to his. "Tell me what this commission is to you."

"Reinvention. Redemption." He hadn't understood that until this very moment. And without Charlotte Beaumont, he wasn't sure he ever would have.

He saw her raise a brow.

"I've spent too long chasing the wrong things."

"Like what?"

"The chance to exhibit my work on the walls of the Royal Academy."

"Any number of artists have realized substantial success from that sort of exposure. Portraitists in particular." A furrow had appeared in her forehead. "There is nothing wrong with wanting that, especially when your work deserves a place on those walls."

"Not if it requires me to be a version of myself I no longer recognize. Not if it requires me to be something I'm not."

Charlotte abruptly stood from her chair and went to stand in front of his panel. "Sometimes that is necessary," she said quietly. "If you recall, you addressed me as Mr. Beaumont for a good while."

Flynn shook his head. "You misunderstand me. You have only ever been you, even if you've dressed as a boy. You once told me that who we are and the experiences that go with that are what gives our work life. You were right." The words were tumbling out in a rush in his need to make her understand.

Charlotte turned to look at him, a strange expression on her face. "Flynn, there is something that I should—"

"Please, let me finish," he implored, afraid that, if he didn't say this all now, he never would.

Charlotte fell silent.

"When I met Lady Cecelia, I was blinded with her beauty and infatuated with the ease in which she moved through a world that I thought I needed to conquer. She promised me that with her by my side, I would gain both recognition and respect from the members of the Royal Academy and their wealthy, titled patrons. And she made me believe that she loved me, right up until the day that I proposed to her."

"You asked her to marry you?" She sounded stricken.

Flynn flinched. "Very publicly. And just as publicly, she laughed at me, as did every one of her titled friends. The subsequent scandal sheets and gossip rags reminded everyone that the sons of whores do not marry ladies. That any exposure I had gained as Lady Cecelia's lover should simply be considered compensation for services rendered. The son of a whore should know how that worked better than anyone."

He heard her suck in a breath.

"In the blink of an eye, I went from being considered a serious artist to a plaything for the Lady Cecelias of the world. I was forced to seek commissions outside of London where bored, titled ladies did not propose contracts of a more carnal sort."

"Flynn—"

"I should have known better from the very beginning," he said with a sigh. "Because in all the time that I was with Cecelia, she never let me forget where I came from. She maintained that my past was something that I needed to overcome if I ever wanted to be an individual of importance." He took a deep breath. "But growing up, there was goodness beside the awfulness, love beside the hate, and the sum total of all of that is a part of me. I refuse to sacrifice my sense of self on society's altar of smug self-importance. I don't want to forget where I come from."

"Nor should you ever." She pivoted away from him again. "I feel sorry for her."

"For who? Cecelia?"

"Yes. She must have deeply rooted insecurities of her own to be unable to understand that. To be unable to admire you for you. To admire how far you've come."

Flynn blinked at Charlotte's back. He'd never considered it like that. "Well, she has an Italian count who claims to be an aspiring artist in her bed now to distract her," he said, and then winced at his crudeness.

"Her loss," Charlotte said, gazing up at the stars that were still only chalked suggestions amid the blue heavens.

Flynn scoffed. "Did you not hear me? I said she has an Italian count—"

"Who isn't you. She's an idiot."

Flynn froze. She was still facing away from him, and he couldn't see her face. Couldn't tell if she was simply trying to make him feel better or if she meant more. Afraid that he was making a horrible mistake, he closed the distance between them, coming to stand directly behind her, giving her a chance to move away.

She didn't.

Very gently, he put a hand at the small of her back, again giving her a chance to step away from him. Still, she didn't move, but he could see the rapid rise and fall of her shoulders beneath her baggy shirt. "What are you doing?" she asked so quietly he almost didn't hear her.

"I have no idea," he answered. Gently, he tugged her around so that he could see her face. She was staring at the toes of her stockinged feet, the wool bunched around her ankles. "Look at me," he said.

She kept her eyes on her toes for a moment longer before she lifted her gaze to his. In an instant, Flynn saw the want reflected in her eyes. It sizzled through him, leaving him unable to remember why this couldn't happen. His eyes dropped to her lips, tantalizingly close to his. He imagined that they would be just as soft and warm as her skin. If he moved, simply leaned forward, he could find out. He could taste those lips, and when he had his fill of that, he would taste everything else.

It was Charlotte who moved then, her right hand coming up as if to caress his face. Her fingers stopped a breath away from his cheek, and he nearly came out of his skin, so badly did he need her touch. Without considering what he was doing, he turned his head, pressing the side of his jaw into her palm. Her breathing stuttered, and her fingers slid up over his cheek and higher, to smooth the edge of his brow.

"I've wanted to do that since the moment I first saw you," she whispered. "When you were burdened by so much unhappiness."

"You should have," he croaked.

The corner of her mouth curled. "That might have been...presumptuous."

"Perhaps." He caught her hand with his. "What else? What else did you want to do?"

Her eyes widened even as they went hot, the caramel depths now like molten gold. He saw her throat work as she tried to find words.

"Don't tell me," he murmured. "Show me."

Her lips parted, and her eyes dropped to his mouth. Her

hand slid from his, and now she was tracing the edge of his lower lip with the pads of her fingers. He closed his eyes, every muscle in his body fighting the need to simply take her right there.

He felt her shift, felt the butterfly-light pressure of her fingers vanish. In the next instant, her lips brushed his, soft and unhurried, and that simple touch sent a primal desire crashing through him with enough force to leave him shaking.

"When I first saw you," she whispered, "I thought you looked how an angel ought to. Fierce. Strong."

His eyes opened. "I'm not an angel."

"No," she agreed. "You're real. Fierce and strong and real."

"Charlotte..."

"I imagined how it would feel to be kissed by a man like that. Like you." Her color had risen again, though her voice didn't waver.

Flynn didn't remember moving, but in a heartbeat, he had caught her head with his hands and covered her mouth with his. In an instant, all the hunger and want that he'd been trying to keep banked roared to life. He pushed her back a step, until her back was against the wall, and leaned into her, kissing her as though his life depended on it. And maybe it did. Maybe this woman beneath his hands and his lips, who had given him back what he had feared lost, really was his savior.

All he knew was that in this moment she was his. And that he was hers.

And that she was real and beautiful and perfect.

He felt her melt against him, one of her hands sliding around the back of his neck, her fingers threading through his hair. The other, the one hampered by the stitches on her shoulder, was tucked between them, her fingers splayed over his heart. Flynn tried to pace himself, tried to explore sweetly and softly, but she was opening beneath him, demanding more. He followed the outlines of her lips with his, every erotic fantasy he'd had pounding through his veins and making him groan. He slid his hands down the sides of her neck, taking care to avoid her shoulder, instead letting them trail along the sides of her bound breasts, to her waist and then to her hips. Forget silks and satins. These damn clothes that made every part of her body so touchable and yet so inaccessible would kill him.

He dropped his hands to the back of her buttocks, every glorious curve beneath her shapeless trousers fitting perfectly into his palms.

Charlotte shifted, her hand tightening around his neck, her teeth catching at his lower lip, teasing and tasting. He growled, pulling her hard against him, and was rewarded by a breathless gasp. He caught the sound against his lips, and his tongue explored the heat of her mouth, making this kiss a sexually explicit promise.

Flynn squeezed his eyes shut against the waves of desire that were crashing through him. She fit so flawlessly against him, her body strong and hot and pliant against his. But it wasn't enough. His hands moved from her backside to the waistband of her trousers. He yanked her shirt up, sliding his fingers over the smooth, heated skin of her back. She arched against him, another breathless gasp escaping, and Flynn caught that one too.

She kissed the way she painted, he thought through a haze. Passionately, freely, honestly. She would make love the same way, he knew. And he would give her back everything twofold, watching those caramel eyes as she came apart beneath him, his name on those sinful lips.

"Flynn," she whispered against his mouth.

He dipped his head and traced a path along the edge of her jaw to the hollow of her throat.

"Flynn," she said again more urgently, and he raised his head, a sharp rapping on the door finally penetrating his lust-fogged mind.

"Mr. Rutledge?" Accompanying his muffled name was another round of rapping, more impatient this time. "Mr. Beaumont?"

He released Charlotte and staggered back. "Bloody Lisbon," he cursed under his breath. His eyes flew to Charlotte, who looked back at him, flushed and breathing hard. "A moment," Flynn shouted in the general direction of the door. He put a hand against her cheek. "We're not done," he whispered harshly.

Flynn dropped his hand and stalked to the door. He took a second to smooth his hair back, adjust his trousers, and rearrange his features into what he hoped was bland neutrality, and yanked the door open.

Lisbon pushed past him, rubbing his hands against the chill. "About time. It's freezing outside."

"You could have just come in," Flynn muttered even as he recoiled at the potential consequences of that and feeling, for the first time, a stirring of misgiving. What had he just done? What if he had taken advantage of circumstance and her vulnerability? What if she would come to despise him for it, given the time to reconsider?

The architect shook his head. "I try to retain some level of courtesy, Rutledge," he said crisply, "and leave my artists alone to complete their work in peace. Though I do expect, on occasion, an invitation so that I might gauge how far you've—" He stopped abruptly as his eyes fell on Charlotte.

She had reclaimed the chair that Flynn had provided for

her and was sitting back in it, her stocking foot crossed over her knee, her expression admirably vague. What wasn't vague, however, was the large lump at her shoulder where her bandage sat under her now untucked shirt.

Lisbon's eyes slid between them, eventually settling on Charlotte. "What happened to your shoulder, Mr. Beaumont?" he asked.

"You may dispense with calling me Mr. Beaumont," she said, sounding almost resigned, as though this moment had always been inevitable. "I required...medical assistance, and Mr. Rutledge was kind enough to provide it. Subsequently, the truth was difficult to avoid."

"What happened?" The architect's words were like cut glass. "And why wasn't I informed that one of my artists had been injured?"

"We encountered a bit of trouble on the streets two evenings past," Flynn answered before she could. "And it was my decision not to worry you with something that you could do naught about."

"It's but a mere cut, and Mr. Rutledge has been quite thorough in his treatments and precautions," Charlotte added hastily. "I'm very much on the mend, and I can assure you that it will not hinder my work."

"Trouble?" Lisbon's sharp eyes swiveled back to Flynn.

"Two gentlemen who sought to take something that was not theirs."

He could see the architect's features harden. "I see. I must assume that you also chose not to involve a magistrate? Or any other authorities?"

Flynn inclined his head. "The situation was resolved to my satisfaction. Save, of course, for Miss Beaumont's unfortunate injury."

"I see." Lisbon crossed his arms over his chest, his

eyes darting back and forth between them. "Will this be a problem, Mr. Rutledge?" he asked.

"Will what be a problem?"

"My decision to hire her. And my insistence that she will finish this commission."

Lisbon's decision to hire Charlotte Beaumont had already caused him all sorts of problems, the least of which being that he was suffering from an overwhelming desire for the woman who was sitting in that damn chair. He was tormented by a possessiveness that seemed to be getting worse with each passing minute. And he was plagued with the knowledge that he was both unable and unwilling to keep his hands off her.

None of which he would share with Henry Lisbon.

"Of course not," he said, hoping he sounded suitably offended. "She is here on her own merit. Her gender and station in life are inconsequential."

"I see." He turned to Charlotte. "I must ask at this juncture if you would prefer other living arrangements?"

"Mr. Rutledge has already very gallantly offered. And like I told him, no, I do not wish other arrangements." She still hadn't looked at Flynn once. "This...unfortunate event will affect nothing."

"Fine," Lisbon said, glancing in Flynn's direction briefly before returning his attention to Charlotte again. "I will honor your decision. However, I must stress that, as long as you are here, you will continue to be addressed as Charlie Beaumont. No one outside of this room shall be privy to the truth. I, for one, do not have the time to begin a search for a new artist with your skill should our clients object to your presence. I have promised that these paintings will be completed and mounted in time for the Christmastide services. Is that understood?"

"Of course," Charlotte said. "Again, nothing has changed, I assure you. I simply won't allow it. It will be like nothing ever happened."

Flynn looked down at the toes of his boots, a deep disquiet settling into his gut, suddenly unsure if she was speaking of their work or their kiss.

"Excellent." Lisbon moved farther into the room toward the panel, reaching for a lantern. "Now show me what you've done."

Chapter 10

Charlotte stood and stared at the exquisite painting of the Madonna.

She'd slipped silently into the church to look at the painting, and it still sent chills down her spine, much the same way it had the first time she had seen it. It was of a quality that museums across the Continent sought for their walls, the sort of work that art teachers referenced to their young pupils. Here, in the soft light of her candle, Mary's expression took on a haunting, ethereal quality, and Charlotte almost expected her to raise those soulful eyes and gaze at Charlotte.

And what would she see?

A woman balancing on the fine edge of ecstasy and terror.

Which was, of course, the aftermath of discovering exactly what it felt like to be kissed by Flynn Rutledge. Ecstasy because she had never, in all her life, been kissed the way Flynn Rutledge had kissed her. He had kissed her with a need and a passion that made her want to believe in happily ever afters of the heart. He had kissed her with the conviction of a man who had finally found what he'd been searching for.

And that ecstasy was coupled with a dread-filled terror that he would reconsider and declare that kiss a monumental mistake. And then in the next breath, a hope-fueled terror that he wouldn't. Both of which catapulted her into unknown territory where expectations, professional and personal, were murky at best.

This new Charlotte, the one who took what she wanted, hadn't stopped to think things through. Hadn't stopped to think that she would fall as far as she had. Far enough to know that she couldn't lose him, no matter what the cost. There was still a small voice demanding that she tell him who she really was, but everything else in her rebelled at that notion. She didn't ever want to be Lady Charlotte again. That passive, unhappy, lonely creature had vanished forever in a pretty blue Haverhall sitting room, leaving behind only Charlie, a woman who fought for who and what she believed in.

A woman who had fallen in love.

Charlotte closed her eyes. Ecstasy and terror. Terror and ecstasy.

Rutledge had left with Lisbon after he'd viewed the panels, offering no explanation but both men instructing Charlotte to rest on their way out, and Flynn refusing to meet her eye. Charlotte had paced restlessly for a handful of minutes before she found her boots and coat and fled the confines of the studio. She'd wound up here, alone in the front of the empty church, as if she might find answers in the silence of the space. But the cavernous darkness only pressed in on her tiny cocoon of candlelight, leaving her trapped with her thoughts.

"You're supposed to be resting." His voice came out of the shadows and made her jump.

Awareness crackled through her like a tempest.

"Corpses have rested less than I," Charlotte mumbled, trying to conceal the tremble in her voice. "I was cut, not run through and disemboweled." She glanced over at Flynn as he came to stand directly beside her, his shoulder brushing hers. He wasn't wearing a coat, and in the meager candlelight, it was difficult to see his features.

"Mmmm." He didn't argue further.

A silence descended between them, not uncomfortable but heavy with things unsaid.

"Who was the woman in this painting?" Charlotte asked, knowing she was being craven by not addressing what needed to be aired but unable to do it quite yet.

Flynn shifted, and she could feel him looking at her. Eventually he turned, granting her a small reprieve. "My mother," he replied.

Charlotte studied the woman who was gazing down at her son with such adoration. Who had clearly been adored in return. And even though she had started this conversation as a diversion, she needed to know more. "Tell me about her."

"I've already told you enough," he said, his words sharp in the darkness.

"No, you told me what she did," Charlotte said quietly. "You never told me who she was."

She heard Flynn release his breath on a sigh. "She was my most ardent supporter. The one person in the world who believed that I was destined for greatness."

Charlotte remained quiet.

"Her . . . clientele was generally comprised of rich gentlemen. Some more gentle than others who found a penny's worth of amusement in the sketches and drawings of her young son. By the time I was ten, I was selling small pencil-and-chalk pastel portraits on the docks, mostly to seamen anxious for a memento of their wives and lovers. By the time I was fourteen, I had secured a handful of commissions from wealthy industrialists. It was enough to help keep us from starving when my mother fell ill."

"I'm sorry," Charlotte said helplessly.

"I'm not. Necessity is a powerful motivator. I may have mentioned that before."

Without considering what she was doing, she found his hand in the darkness and threaded her fingers through his.

"My mother insisted that one day my paintings would hang in the Royal Academy. That one day, the titled men who had laughed and paid mere pennies for my work out of pity would look up at those walls and know that they could never afford another. That her son would become greater than they because of talent and not an accident of birth. That was her dream for me."

"She was right. Your work belongs there," Charlotte said with utter conviction. "Your paintings—this painting—deserve to be there."

"Perhaps. But I think that, with talent, there is always a component of fortune that is required for true success. An alignment of the stars, if you will—the outcome of which neither you nor I can control."

Charlotte pondered that silently, wondering at the way her own path had altered the moment she had discovered a painting of a young girl hidden in the attics of Jasper House.

He was still staring at the Madonna. "Before she died, I promised her that I would make it happen—an exhibit at the Royal Academy. And in failing to accomplish that, I feel like I've let her down."

"You haven't let her down. She would still be so proud of what you've done. Proud of you and the man you've become."

"That's kind of you to say."

"That's not kind. It's the truth, Flynn."

Flynn let go of her hand, and Charlotte felt the loss of his touch like a blow. "I've come to accept that some things are simply out of reach. No matter how much you want them, you can't wish them into being. Shouldn't, perhaps, wish them into being."

There was something in his tone that suddenly made her doubt that he was speaking of art or family anymore. The razor edge of terror and ecstasy that she still balanced on cut hard toward the former.

"What else do you want, Flynn?" she whispered, asking the question that she should have asked at the very beginning.

He reached for the candle and turned away from the painting. "It's cold. We should get back," was all he said.

* * *

She left the church and made her way silently through the darkness, Flynn at her side, his head down against the chill. He ushered her wordlessly into the studio, setting the candle on the mantel and bending to add more coal to the glowing embers.

He held his hands out to the warmth, and Charlotte found herself riveted by the sight of his long fingers silhouetted against the glow. Beautiful, long capable fingers that had just held hers. Fingers she had already felt on her skin. Fingers that she desperately longed to feel on her body again. Everywhere.

"Flynn." She spoke his name into the silence, and it hovered somewhere on the verge of a question, addressing everything that had not been said since the moment he had kissed her. Addressing everything that still needed to be said.

"It's late. You must be exhausted. Perhaps you should rest," he said stiffly, straightening though he continued to gaze down at the fire.

"Rest," she repeated.

"Yes." He sounded strained and Charlotte recognized the choice he was offering her.

The gallant bastard.

"Is that what you want, Flynn? Me to retreat into my room and close that door on you? On us?"

He put a hand out on the mantel, as if anchoring himself to something. "Charlotte."

"Tell me what you want from me." She would give him no quarter. "Tell me what you wanted when you had your hands on my skin and your mouth on mine."

He looked up at her then, his eyes glittering in the low light. "Too much."

Charlotte fought for a breath. "Then take it. Because you were right. We are not done."

He closed the distance between them, his steps predatory. He caught her chin in his fingers and tipped her head up, his eyes fierce and feverish and wildly possessive. A new wave of arousal ripped through her and settled low and hard in her belly. All of that hunger was for her and only her. It made her feel powerful and reckless all at once.

"I need you to be very sure about this," he rasped. "Because if I start, I don't think I'll be able to stop. I don't think you understand just how badly I want you."

She could feel the anticipation wavering in the space

between them, thick and electric. "Don't tell me," she whispered. "Show me."

"Charlotte." Her name sounded strangled, and it was all he said before his mouth came down on hers. He slid a hand to the back of her head, his fingers tangled in her hair. He didn't touch her anywhere else, just made love to her mouth with his, and it was indecent and incredible and intoxicating.

His tongue delved deep, the velvety richness of it teasing and tasting, desperate at first and then becoming more deliberate. She had her eyes closed, her entire body vibrating with need as his lips moved from her mouth to her neck, sucking and licking his way down the column of her skin. Her head tipped back, and she shivered.

His lips left her then, and she opened her eyes to find him watching her. "Why did you stop?" she whispered.

His fingers slid from her hair. "I haven't stopped," he said roughly. "I'm just getting started."

He began working on the buttons of her coat, his fingers deft and sure. Careful of her shoulder, he peeled the coat from her body, letting it drop to the floor. Gently, he tugged her toward the hearth, stopping her in front of the heat. He went to work on the laces at her throat, pulling the linen over her head. His hands came back to span her ribs, and she leaned into his touch impatiently.

He bent, his lips against her throat again, his hands working on the bindings at her breasts. And then they, too, fell away, and now his palms were cupping their slight curves, his thumbs circling her hard nipples, pleasure streaking through her like lightning. Her hands came up to his shoulders, needing to hold on to something.

She looked down breathlessly as his head dropped lower still and he took the nipples he had just been caressing into his mouth, his tongue swirling around each peak. She didn't recognize the sound that escaped from her, but she recognized the pulsing dampness that instantly throbbed at her core. And perhaps he recognized it too, because his fingers were on the fall of her trousers, and they were sliding down her thighs, Flynn lifting his head just long enough to yank her boots and her trousers from her legs.

He was kneeling before her now, his hands wrapping around the back of her legs and then over her buttocks, and his tongue was tracing a trail of fire over her navel and to the top of her curls. She watched as his hands came around her hips, brushing her mound and sliding along the inside of her thighs, urging her legs farther apart. He slid a finger through her folds, and Charlotte gasped, her own fingers clutching his shoulders as everything clenched deep inside.

"Perfect," she thought she heard him murmur, but the uncontrollable pounding of the blood in her ears was making it difficult to hear.

He was stroking her now, insistent circles over the pulsing spot that was twisting her insides tighter and tighter. The heat at her back from the hearth was nothing compared to the heat that was building inside of her. And then his fingers slipped away, but before she could protest, his mouth was there, right where she needed it, sucking and licking and making her vision dim along the edges.

"What are you doing?" she gasped.

"Tasting you," he growled without stopping. "All of you."

Charlotte hadn't thought herself a virgin, but under Flynn's hands, she was. She had never been seduced like this. Had never known that such excruciating pleasure was even possible. She should be mortified, she knew, at the way her legs shook where they were spread, at the way her hips tilted helplessly with want, and at the way her hands left his shoulders and gripped his hair, holding him exactly where she needed.

"Flynn." It came out somewhere between a plea and a groan.

He sucked hard once and then again, his tongue flicking with unerring precision, and Charlotte felt her world explode in a haze of white light. Pleasure radiated through her in merciless waves, and she whimpered, her entire body shuddering. Flynn didn't relent, his hands unyielding at her back, and still the spasms kept coming, leaving her panting and shaking and sobbing.

It could have been hours or minutes before she managed to come back to herself, and she folded gracelessly to her knees, her legs unable to hold her any longer. She extracted her fingers from his hair, wrapping them around his neck, her forehead resting on his shoulder. Belatedly she realized that he was breathing as hard as she, every muscle in his body rigid beneath the clothes he still wore.

She wondered if she ought to be embarrassed about this as well, the fact that she knelt in front of this man, stark naked and boneless, while he was yet fully dressed. When she could collect her wits, she would give it more thought. But not right now.

"That was perfect," she whispered.

Flynn made a harsh sound and nodded.

She lifted her head and gazed at him. In the light from the hearth, she could see his eyes squeezed shut, a grimace across his face. "Flynn?" she whispered.

"I just need a second," he said hoarsely. "Watching you...that was like nothing...just let me..." He shifted on his knees and groaned softly.

Charlotte glanced down to the fall of his trousers, where she could clearly see the bulge of his straining erection.

She slipped a hand from around his neck and stroked him through the rough fabric. Flynn jerked and hissed.

"Charlotte." She recognized his plea because it was the same as the one that had fallen from her own lips. Exhilaration and hunger flooded through her, knowing that it was she who had brought him to this brink.

Carefully, she took her hand away, her fingers going to the laces of his own shirt. When she took him over that edge, she wanted to see him the way he had seen her. Beneath her touch, she could feel him trembling, his muscles flexing. His eyes were on hers now, darkened silver full of need and want. She slipped his shirt over his head, letting it fall to the rug, sliding her palms over the expanse of his chest. The scattering of hair over the lean ridges of muscle tickled the pads of her fingers, and Charlotte pushed him back gently so that he was sitting before her. She went to work next on his trousers, loosening the fall and sliding them down his legs the way he had done with hers, casting them and his boots aside.

And caught her breath at all the masculine glory that was laid out before her. He was leaning back on his hands, his broad shoulders gilded in the glow, faint ridges of muscle descending from his chest across his abdomen. The hair she had felt across his chest descended too, creating an ever-narrowing trail to where his erection jutted between long, lean thighs. He was watching her. Watching and waiting.

She hesitated, wanting to do this right. Not sure where she should start. Suddenly uncertain that she would be able to give him the kind of pleasure he had wrung from her.

"Come here, Charlotte," he said.

She crept toward him on her hands and knees, and she saw something shift in his expression. He shoved himself off his hands, reaching for her, and hauled her into his lap unceremoniously. She could feel the unyielding muscle of his thighs beneath her where she straddled him and could feel the hard weight of his erection where it lay trapped between them.

"I want to make this perfect for you too," she whispered.

"This is perfect," he said. "You are perfect."

"Tell me what you want."

"I want you to touch me."

Charlotte shifted, sliding back a fraction, and wrapped her hand around his erection. Flynn closed his eyes, and his head fell forward, his hands coming to rest on her thighs. Charlotte slid her fingers up the rigid length, watching his expression, gauging his reaction. Her thumb caressed the head, and she heard him grunt, his hips flexing beneath her, pushing himself harder into her hand. She leaned forward and caught his mouth with hers as she stroked down, catching his moan against her lips.

His eyes opened. "I can't wait," he gasped against her lips. "I thought—"

She kissed him hard, an open-mouthed, hungry kiss that he returned with a fierce desperation. She raised herself on her knees, positioning the head of his cock at her entrance, feeling a new pressure coil through her body as he pressed into her with a muffled moan. His hands moved from her thighs to cage her hips, hard and urgent, guiding her all the way down until he was seated deep within her, filling and stretching her completely. She twined her arms around his neck and rolled her hips slightly, sparks of pleasure instantly igniting.

Flynn made a feral sound and thrust up against her, and the sparks ignited into a wildfire. Charlotte closed her eyes, letting him control the pace, surrendering to the timeless rhythm, feeling her body once again reaching inside itself as Flynn rocked into her. Against her ear, she could hear him breathing, harsh, rapid breaths that spoke only of his need. The tips of her breasts rubbed against his chest as he moved, adding to the maelstrom of arousal that was now burning out of control.

Her orgasm, when it came, was just as devastating as the first. It tore his name from her lips as she ground helplessly against him, the rhythm broken. He thrust up hard once again before his hands tightened like a vise on her hips, and he lifted her forward, slipping from her heat and finding his own release between them with a guttural shout.

Their breathing slowed eventually, the sheen of perspiration Charlotte could feel trapped on their skin cooling them even in front of the hearth. She rested her head in the crook of his neck, her fingers tracing the smooth line of his collarbone. She didn't ever want to move. Didn't ever want to leave this man.

"Come with me." His voice rumbled against her ear.

She lifted her head. "I beg your pardon?"

"Come with me to Italy."

"Just like that?"

"Just like that." His hands slid up her back.

Charlotte shivered. "What are we doing, Flynn?"

"I don't know. All I know is that the stars brought me to you. And the thought of letting you go is unbearable."

"Flynn—"

"Promise me you'll think about it."

Charlotte couldn't imagine a time when she wouldn't be thinking about it. But there was a debt to be paid, the one that had brought her here.

Be careful what you promise, my lady. Circumstances can change and make promises difficult to keep. It was what King had said to her. She hadn't understood then. She understood now.

"I promise," she whispered.

Chapter 11

They had retreated to his bed, and Flynn had fallen asleep at some point, because the suggestion of dawn was starting to creep through the rafters when he woke. He should get up. Add some more coal to the hearth. Boil a kettle of water. But he did none of those things because Charlotte was curled around him, her head nestled against his shoulder, the heat and solidity of her body warming something deep within him as surely as it warmed his own skin.

He turned his head and gazed down at her. Her lashes lay across faintly flushed cheeks, her kiss-swollen lips were parted slightly, and her short hair was sticking up in all directions. He had never experienced a sense of rightness—of perfect peace—as the one that had settled over him at this moment. In this makeshift studio, in a town far away from where he had been born, covered in borrowed blankets on a borrowed bed, he had finally found home.

She was home.

He brushed a kiss across her forehead and she stirred.

"Good morning," he whispered.

"Mmm." Her hand slipped across his chest.

He stroked his own hand down the length of her arm, careful of the stitches at her shoulder. The blanket fell away from her long limbs, leaving glorious expanses of skin glowing like alabaster in the silver light of dawn. Her hand left his chest and tried to pull the covers back up.

"Don't," he said, brushing her fingers away. "I want to look at you." He shifted, propping himself up on an elbow so that he could gaze down at her. He pushed the blanket farther over her hip, his fingers lingering, his body already straining for a woman he was never going to be able to get enough of.

"Flynn—"

"I'm trying to decide how I will paint you," he said, flattening his palm against the tautness of her abdomen. He slid it up unhurriedly, circling one nipple first and then the other. She whimpered and arched into his touch, and he bit back a groan as his cock jerked. He was as hard as marble, and every tiny sound she made tested his restraint.

"I don't want to be painted," she said a little breathlessly.

He lowered his head and pressed a kiss at the hollow of her throat. "I will paint you the way I will always see you. Bold. Beautiful," he mused, ignoring her protestations.

"Don't be absurd," she said. "I'm not beautiful. I'm not even pretty."

Flynn lifted his head and stared down at her, a curl of what felt like anger rising through him like black smoke.

She gazed back at him unapologetically. "It's why Charlie Beaumont was possible," she said. "And I would have it no other way."

"Define pretty," he said.

"I beg your pardon?"

"Tell me what pretty looks like."

Charlotte shrugged. "From your drawings, I'd say Lady Cecelia was very pretty."

"Perhaps," Flynn mused. "Midnight-sky hair, pink-rose lips, chalk-white skin, sea-blue eyes."

"You just made her sound like a travel advert for the shores of Kent County."

Flynn chuckled. "I did, didn't I? And yet not one of those things makes a woman beautiful. Pretty, perhaps, but pretty is a superficial thing. A puddle of piss looks pretty if it is reflecting a sunset."

Charlotte snorted. "My, but you have a way with words," she laughed. "Perhaps if art and medicine fail, you could try poetry."

"Listen to me and listen carefully. You, Charlotte Beaumont, are beautiful."

He felt her go still under his touch.

"Your beauty, the sort that comes from within, has made me a better version of myself," he said, searching her caramel eyes. "Because your beauty defies mere description. It is something far more intangible and something far more precious."

She gazed up at him, her features set into deep shadows, but he didn't miss the way she suddenly blinked at the dampness that had gathered in her eyes. "It's funny, in a way," she said slowly, "because I came here to seek a better version of myself."

"And did you find it?" he asked, catching her hand in his and squeezing.

"Yes," she replied. "In pieces."

"Pieces?"

"I found one part in a church when I refused to listen to a man who had his doubts about me."

His fingers tightened on hers. "Charlotte, I should never have—"

"Shhh," she said, cutting him off.

He fell silent.

"And then I found another part in a studio when that same man took a good look at my work and made me critique it as his equal. Arresting and hopeless in corresponding measure," she said with a small smile.

"I stand by my assessment of your poker-wielding angel," he murmured.

She sniffed, and her smile widened before it faded again. "And then later, I found a little more when he made me believe in myself. When a man who I admired very much told me I was meant to do this." She took an unsteady breath. "And then he compared me to his own Jeanne d'Arc, and I knew I had found the rest."

He brought his hand up and traced the side of her face.

"So thank you," she whispered, "for helping me become that better version of myself."

He leaned forward and caught her lips with his, kissing her tenderly, his heart hammering in his chest, emotion pushing thick and sharp into his throat. She let go of his hand and wrapped her good arm around his neck, pulling him closer, demanding more. He moved over her, his body fitting perfectly against hers.

He deepened his kiss, and she opened beneath him, taking and giving. Her hips tilted against his, and he slid inside, burying himself deep. He heard her moan softly and broke their kiss, lifting his head to watch her face. Her hand slipped from his neck to touch his face the way she had done the very first time.

"Don't stop," she whispered. "Don't ever stop."

"I won't," he promised.

Chapter 12

S oldier and savior.

Both completed and both to be left behind on the morrow. The scaffolds had been taken apart and removed, the tables of paints and brushes and thinners tidied and packed. The clergy and the church directors had been brought through the studio yesterday for a final viewing, and Lisbon had relayed that they had been utterly astounded and captivated by the finished paintings.

As they should, Flynn thought with steady appraisal. This portrayal of an archangel rising up in furious defiance was Flynn's finest work yet. And on the other side, another portrayal of that same archangel reaching out across the heavens, offering a soul a chance at redemption. On their own, each painting was extraordinary. Together, they were breathtaking.

Which described the last two months entirely. Months that had been unlike anything Flynn had ever experienced, and it was because of Charlotte. She had been his friend and his lover. His teacher and his student. The one person who managed to argue and encourage all at the same time. She had never asked him to be anything he wasn't. Never allowed him to doubt himself. Believed in him wholeheartedly.

And though it was a bittersweet moment to leave these paintings behind, he knew that he would never, ever, be able to leave Charlotte Beaumont.

They had not spoken of love, and Flynn had cursed himself for his lack of courage. For all the emotion that he had poured out onto that panel for utter strangers to gaze upon, he had been unable to expose what lay in the very depths of his heart to the single person who mattered most. He would remedy that now, he vowed. She needed to know how he felt about her. How he had fallen completely, helplessly in love with her. Because he was not ready for them to be over. He didn't think he ever would be.

A familiar knock sounded. "Come in, Mr. Lisbon," he said over his shoulder.

Henry Lisbon let himself into the studio, his boots echoing as he hurriedly crossed the floor. "Admiring your work, Mr. Rutledge?"

"Yes," Flynn said simply.

"As you should. I can't wait to see these hung. You and Beaumont have outdone yourselves," Lisbon said with satisfaction as he took his sleet-covered hat from his head.

Flynn only nodded.

"Is Beaumont here?" Lisbon asked, jerking his head toward the room that Charlotte hadn't slept in for a long time.

"She is not. She has gone to post a letter."

Lisbon made a face. "That's too bad. I could have

saved her the trip. I was just there." He reached into his coat pocket and withdrew a missive sealed with a blob of scarlet wax, a small emblem of a crown pressed into its surface. "This was waiting for her." He passed the letter to Flynn. "I trust you can see that she gets this?"

"Of course," Flynn replied. Idly, he turned the letter over in his hands, *L. C. Beaumont* written in neat, precise script across the front. Idly, he wondered what the *L* stood for.

"I wanted to thank you again for your progressive objectivity, Mr. Rutledge," Lisbon said. "There are many men who have and would have refused to work with a woman. Your decency and honor once her identity was revealed are to be commended."

Flynn continued to stare down at the neat lettering, quite sure Lisbon wouldn't think him honorable or decent if he knew just how much of Charlotte Beaumont had been revealed. And how much she had enjoyed every minute of it. Repeatedly. He had made sure of that.

"Given your tribulations with the Lady Cecelia and her ilk, I wasn't sure you would be quite so forgiving," Lisbon said.

Flynn raised his head, frowning. "Charlotte has absolutely nothing in common with Lady Cecelia," Flynn said, a little harsher than he had intended.

"I'm glad you could recognize that," Lisbon said with a brisk nod, "given the trouble she went through to hide both her gender and her title for this opportunity." The architect jammed his hat back on his head. "I must be off again. See that our Charlie gets her letter, aye?"

Flynn might have nodded, but ice had crystallized in his veins and everything seemed to have slowed. Betrayal cut deep, confusion and hurt and anger bleeding from the gaping wound.

Outside, the wind rattled a shutter somewhere, and sleet continued to batter the windows. Minutes passed. Or maybe it was hours.

"Flynn?" The sound of his name brought his head around. Where Lisbon had been, Charlotte now stood, pink faced from the cold, wrapped in a warm coat and looking at him with concern. "Are you all right?"

"You lied."

"I beg your pardon?"

"What is your name?" he hissed.

"Flynn, what—"

"What is your name?"

"Charlotte. Beaumont." Her face had gone pale. "Why are—"

"Your whole name."

Her warm eyes dropped to the paper in his hands. He could see a muscle working along the side of her cheek. "Lady Charlotte Beaumont," she said evenly. "Daughter of the Earl and Countess of Edgerton." Her eyes climbed back to his. "Is that what you wanted to hear?"

It was suddenly hard to breathe. She wasn't at all who she had pretended to be. Every whispered promise, every shared confidence, every piece of what he had believed to be real had been built on a foundation of lies. He had been played the fool.

Again.

He tossed the letter in her direction. "That was what I wanted to hear months ago. Before you lied to me and then kept lying. You're one of them."

"I'm not."

"Was I an adventure for you too? A titillating, erogenous experience on the wrong side of civilized before you wed a man twice your age for his money and his wealth?"

"You think I'm like her? Like Cecelia?" she whispered, her eyes pools of brown against a pale face.

He didn't think that, did he? But fury and shame were making it hard to think. She had lied. Over and over. And he had trusted her. Trusted her with his secrets and bared all the dark parts of his soul where insecurity and fear and vulnerability lay.

And she hadn't even trusted him with the truth. With her bloody *name*.

"You would think I would have learned by now," he said, running a hand through his hair in agitation. "You would think I'd be able to know when I am being used."

"I never used you."

"I don't believe you."

"You want to know why I didn't tell you who I was?" she asked, her voice rising. "Because Lady Charlotte no longer exists. Lady Charlotte was a miserable, isolated woman who was nothing but a disappointment and a duty to her family." Her expression was stark. "It was simply Charlie Beaumont from Aysgarth who came to Coventry. To stand on her own two feet and to be judged by her work and her character, unfettered by bias." She took a shuddering breath. "I am exactly who you know me to be."

"I have no idea who you are."

She looked as though he had struck her. "I am the woman who loves you."

"Loves me?" he sneered, something withering in him. "You don't love me. You never even trusted me."

She looked at him sadly. "And if I had told you my name at the very beginning? Would you have reacted any different than you have now? Would you even have spoken to me? Or would the demons from your past have simply become mine earlier?"

Flynn's fists clenched and unclenched. He spun, heading for the door. He couldn't stand here in the face of her duplicity. Worse, he couldn't stand knowing that he didn't have an answer to her question.

"I regret that I didn't tell you my name. I regret that mistake, and I regret that you've chosen to believe the worst of me," she said to his back.

He paused at the door, pride not allowing him to turn around.

"But I don't regret falling in love with you, Flynn."

He stepped out into the sleet and didn't look back.

Chapter 13

"Lady Charlotte." King glided into the room with sound-less stealth. His eyes slid over her altered appearance, though his expression didn't change. "You look...well."

Charlotte remained mute.

King stopped near his desk and leaned on his walking stick. "I was beginning to think that perhaps you didn't receive my summons. Or perhaps you had had...second thoughts about our agreement. I was becoming concerned that you had chosen to travel elsewhere from Coventry." There was a brittle quality to his words that Charlotte didn't mistake as anything other than a threat.

She lifted her chin, strangely unafraid. Maybe because she had already lost everything that mattered. "My apologies if my temporary absence caused you undue worry. I can assure you I have no intention of reneging on our agreement."

King eyed her coldly and silently.

"But you are partially correct. I did not travel to London directly from Coventry," she continued. "I stopped at Jasper House to collect something that I think will interest you." She gestured to the two covered canvases that were propped up against a massive bookcase behind her.

"I'm not interested in more forgeries." His fingers were drumming on the silver top.

"And I'm not interested in showing you any."

Curiosity flickered. "You have my attention once again, Lady Charlotte," he replied.

"The Royal Academy."

"What of it?"

"If one wished to have a painting exhibited, could you make that happen?"

King gazed at her. "I never took you as vain, my lady."

"Answer the question."

Pale eyes narrowed. "Have a care, Lady Charlotte."

"Please answer the question," she amended tonelessly.

A faint line appeared in his forehead. "Of course I can."

Charlotte closed her eyes briefly before she turned and lifted the smaller of the two canvases. She pulled the wrapping from it and set it against his desk, feeling his eyes following her. She stepped back.

King's eyes lingered on her before he turned his attention to the painting. "Very evocative," he said slowly. "Masterful use of light and color. A contemporary piece, yet I see shadows of Raphael in this."

Charlotte only nodded, her voice suddenly choked by the sadness and regret that rose hard and fast.

"But not your work, I think," King continued, stepping closer to the painting.

She shook her head. "I have merely borrowed it for a time."

"It surpasses everything currently on those pretentious Somerset walls," he murmured.

"I know," Charlotte managed. "That's the idea."

King turned to gaze at her in consideration as the Madonna continued to stare down in adoration at her son. "I can see it done."

"Thank you."

"Tsk, you get ahead of yourself with your gratitude." He smiled an empty smile. "You have not yet provided me with something that makes my service worthwhile."

Wordlessly, Charlotte returned to the bookcase and pulled the cloth from the second painting. She let the fabric fall to the floor, and the silence that followed was absolute. The woman in this painting gazed past her nude reflection in a mirror, as if searching for someone just beyond the frame. Her fingers played wistfully with a single strand of pearls at her throat, each tiny orb as lustrous as her skin. She sat against a background of deep midnight, a robe of rich garnet covering her lap, both the perfect foil for her fairness.

"You know what this is," Charlotte said into the deafening silence.

"Yes," King replied quietly, his eyes not straying from the painting. "I was told that this version was lost. And it was certainly not in the attics of Jasper House. My men would have found it."

"No," she said. "It was hidden in my rooms. My aunt had ordered it destroyed. Nudity of any sort offends her."

King hadn't yet moved. "This isn't a forgery."

"No," Charlotte agreed, unsure if that was a question. "I have not yet attempted a Titian."

The clock in the corner ticked on.

"There are two conditions that go with this painting," Charlotte said into the quiet.

She saw King's hand tighten on the top of his walking stick. "Conditions from a woman who comes begging my favor?"

"I trust a lost Titian should recompense any insult."

His impenetrable gaze slid back to her then.

She didn't wait for him to respond. "One, at no point in time should my name ever come up in conversation outside this room," she said, repeating the words he had said to her what seemed like a lifetime ago. "Invent an acquisition story for this work that does not involve me."

"And the other?" He looked almost amused now.

"When you sell this painting, you will not auction it off like a pretty mare in a Tattersalls ring."

His amusement slipped, and red-gold brows rose. "And just what, Lady Charlotte, do you propose I do with it?"

"Sell it to someone who understands the deeper story that lies within this canvas."

"Which is what?" He was studying her keenly.

"That love cannot be found in a beautiful reflection."

King regarded her, his austere features revealing nothing of his thoughts. "Very well," he said. "I will meet your conditions, and your Madonna will grace the walls of the Royal Academy within a fortnight hence. With all the appropriate fanfare."

"Thank you."

"You've changed, Lady Charlotte," King said abruptly.

"Yes," she replied, because it was the only thing she could say.

She would not discuss how Flynn Rutledge had changed her. She would not examine the love and the joy that had set her heart and her mind soaring. She would not dissect the trust and the faith that had made her believe—truly believe—that she could do more. That she could be more.

She would not dwell on the knowledge that she had been gifted with all those things and had let them all slip away. Because in the end, she hadn't been brave or confident or courageous. In the end, she hadn't reinvented herself at all. In the end, she had been a coward.

She withdrew the original missive that he had sent her and set it on the desk. "May we get on to the business at hand?"

King watched her for a moment more before he moved, settling himself behind his desk. "By all means, Lady Charlotte."

"I prefer Charlie. Charlotte, if you must." She held her head high, as if that gesture could overcome the relentless pain that had lodged deep within her heart and would never leave. "Lady Charlotte posted a letter to London from Coventry informing her family that she was seeking her fortunes abroad. Lady Charlotte, as she once was, no longer exists."

"Very well." His eyes slid from her hair to her baggy coat and trousers once more.

"Good. I understand you have a painting for me to forge."

* * *

Flynn looked around the cramped space of his rented London rooms.

There was nothing that he wished to take with him. Nothing that he regretted leaving behind.

Liar, a little voice in his head whispered. He was leaving love behind.

His eye fell on the small canvas that lay flat on the top of a table, the figure of Adam reaching out to be touched. Unable to help himself, he picked it up. He hadn't known what to do with it. He still didn't know what to do with it. He couldn't bring himself to destroy it, nor could he bring himself to pack it away. Instead, he found himself gazing at it more than was healthy or smart. Because every time he looked at the painting, doubt crowded in, making him question his decisions.

He closed his eyes, unwilling to think on it any longer. No matter her protestations and declarations, love meant trust. Trust meant truth. And in the end, Lady Charlotte Beaumont hadn't been able to give him that. He needed to forget her.

He set the painting inside an open trunk and slammed the lid with too much force. Charlotte Beaumont was nothing but a mistake.

Then why was this so hard? And why did leaving feel like the mistake?

There was a soft knock on his door, and Flynn almost tripped in his haste to answer it. God, he needed a diversion. Any sort of diversion. He yanked open the door.

And recoiled. Any diversion but this.

"Flynn," Lady Cecelia greeted, stepping into the tiny flat. Her pretty mouth made a predictable moue of distaste at the small confines before she smiled at the sight of his trunks. "Thank God. You're finally moving. It's about time. I've always told you that these rooms are beneath you."

Flynn didn't budge from the door, as baffled as he was repelled at her presence. "What do you want?"

Cecelia fluttered her lashes and sauntered back in his direction. "That's not much of a welcome for an old friend, Flynn." She reached out an expensively gloved hand and stroked his forearm.

Flynn stepped back. "We are not friends."

Her eyes narrowed slightly before they widened again.

"Don't be like this, Flynn. We both know that we were quite spectacular together." She advanced another step closer. "We could be again," she breathed.

"I'm sure your Italian count might have an opinion on that," he said coldly. "Good day, my lady." He held the door a little wider.

"That Italian does not possess half the skill you do," she purred, seemingly undaunted by his rudeness. "In the studio or otherwise." Her sooty lashes were fluttering again. "I admit, I should never have let you go."

"You didn't let me go, Cecelia. I left."

She waved her hand as if she hadn't heard him. "I always knew you were destined for great things, Flynn."

"Well, right now, I am destined for Italy. And I need to finish packing. Goodbye."

She blinked, this time in what looked like genuine surprise. "Italy? What are you thinking?"

"That Italy is far away from London." *And you*, he refrained from adding.

"But you can't leave. Not now."

Flynn was hanging on to his patience by a thread. "Watch me."

"But you're famous. Together, we'll be feted like royalty."

"I can assure you, Cecelia, that I am no more famous now than I was a year ago. Just a whole lot smarter."

She was shaking her head. "Now is not the time to be humble, Flynn," she snapped. "Not when you have princes offering patronage. Now is the time for you to embrace your celebrity." She preened slightly. "And I will be there at your side every step of the way."

Flynn was frowning. "I have no idea what you're talking about. And I certainly don't need you anywhere, least of all at my side."

Cecelia laughed, and it wasn't a pretty sound. "Come now, Flynn. Start acting like a gentleman and not an ignorant urchin from the stews. Your exhibit that's opening at the academy this afternoon will only get you so far—"

"I beg your pardon?" Flynn felt himself go hot and cold all at the same time.

Cecelia's lips twisted. "Manners, Flynn. They must be as flawless as your work. I believe I've mentioned this in the past, and it's clear that I need to do so again." She poked a finger at him. "You need me now that you're going places. Though I would suggest that you stay away from exhibiting subjects that have a religious context in the future."

There was a dull roaring in his ears that had almost completely drowned out the sound of her voice. He could feel the edge of the door cutting into the palm of his hand, and he held on, afraid that if he let go, he might simply spin away. The room around him seemed to steady then, and a curious calm descended. He straightened, his limbs oddly numb but obeying the commands of his mind nonetheless. "I have to go," he mumbled, urgency propelling him through the door and down the stairs, heedless of Cecelia's furious shrieks.

He had to go. Before he made another mistake.

Chapter 14

The Royal Academy's exhibition hall, housed in Somerset House, was thronged.

Those of the upper classes who hadn't traveled to a country pile for Christmas were out in droves in the city, seeking their own entertainment. And a new artist, one who was rumored to have garnered the attention of royalty at home and abroad, was always a draw.

Flynn had no idea where those rumors had come from, nor did he care. He skirted the crowd, his hat pulled low over his brow, his eyes fixed on the far wall where a massive knot of people milled, gesturing and chattering. He ignored the noise, slipped through the crush, and came to an abrupt stop, robbed quite suddenly of breath.

His Madonna had been hung in the center of the hall above a raised dais used only for the most illustrious of exhibitors. High above him, winter light streamed in from the windows and fell across the painting, illuminating the

Madonna's gentle expression with an unearthly brilliance. It was dramatic, it was celebrated, and it was everything his mother had always wanted for him. The gift he had always wanted for her to reward her unflagging love and belief, even if she never had the chance to see it.

Charlotte had done this, he knew. He didn't know how or when, though those details could be guessed at. What wasn't fathomable was why. Why had she done this for him after everything? After he had walked away from her?

Because she loved you, the voice in his head hissed. *And you didn't believe her. Didn't believe in her.*

Didn't allow her to make a mistake.

He raised his hands to his face and pressed his fingers into his eyes hard enough that spots danced. He cursed and let his hands fall, spinning quickly enough to startle a flock of well-dressed matrons who were pressing toward the dais. He ignored the infuriated gasps as he shoved his way back through the crowd. He would fix this. He would find her and—

"Mr. Rutledge."

The man was standing just inside the hall, as though he had been waiting for Flynn. He could have been a Tudor prince, given his expensively tailored clothing, his aquiline features, and the confident ease in which he moved, an ebony walking stick held loosely in his hand.

"I'm afraid you have me at a disadvantage," Flynn replied.

"Hmmm." The man made no effort to introduce himself but merely gazed in the direction of the portrait on the far side of the room, impossible to see now behind the crush. "I must say, your work did not disappoint. Haunting. Compelling. You have bent the light to your will with a mastery very few possess."

"Thank you." Flynn frowned. "But if you'll excuse me, I—"

"Leaving in such a hurry?" The man tapped his fingers on the head of his walking stick. "I would have thought you'd wish to linger. Bask in your newfound success, as it were. Even without the rumors of royal patronage, you'll have lords and ladies falling all over themselves for a piece of you. It was, after all, the purpose of this exercise, was it not?"

"No. It wasn't the purpose at all."

"Ah." Pale blue eyes probed his. "I wondered."

Flynn bit back a retort. This man didn't know him, and Flynn certainly wasn't about to explain himself to him, whoever he was. Nor was he going to waste any more time. He needed to find—

"Charlie Beaumont."

For an agonizing moment, Flynn thought his heart might have stopped in his chest. "I beg your pardon?"

"Mr. Charlie Beaumont. I understand that he was your partner for the St. Michael's commission."

Flynn felt a peculiar feeling winding through him. "Yes. How did you know that?"

"You might find it of interest then to know that I have since hired him," he replied, ignoring Flynn's question.

"For what? Where?" Flynn was trying to keep his expression neutral, but even he could hear the rough desperation in his voice. "Where is s—he?"

"Ah. I wondered at that too," the Tudor prince murmured, almost too quietly for Flynn to hear. "He was here, as a matter of fact. You just missed him," he said more clearly. "If you hurry, you might catch—"

Flynn didn't hear the rest. He was already running.

* * *

The carriage was as fine as any Charlotte had ever seen in her life.

But given King's blatant predisposition for fine things, she shouldn't have found this surprising. Sleek and well sprung, and painted a glossy ebony with scarlet trim, it was only missing a coat of arms. Not something that a boy from Aysgarth, dressed in a loose pair of trousers and a baggy coat with a canvas bag slung over his back, should ever have at his disposal.

Charlotte handed her bag to the goliath of a driver, dressed just as sleekly in ebony livery, and tried to offer him a word of thanks. It came out as a strained whisper because the emotion that was threatening to suffocate her was making it equally difficult to speak.

She had stayed in that hall only long enough to see that the Madonna had been hung as she had wished. Long enough to hear the rumors swirling through the expensively dressed crowds speculating about the man behind the painting and arguing over who might have discovered him. Long enough to know that, if nothing else, Flynn would know that she had loved him.

And then she had escaped to the carriage that waited for her, because the tide and the ship that would take her from England waited for no one. She climbed into the plush, darkened interior and reached for the door, only to have it yanked open, away from her grasp. A body hurtled through the opening into the carriage, and the door snapped shut. Charlotte swallowed a shout of startled alarm.

"Don't go." Flynn was crouched in front of her, his hands braced on either side of her legs, breathing hard.

Charlotte closed her eyes, willing her breathing to steady

and wondering if she might be imagining this. She opened her eyes and discovered he was still there, illuminated by the daylight filtering in along the edges of the closed curtains. A familiar brew of terror and ecstasy bubbled up to fill her chest. "What are you doing here?"

"Trying not to make another mistake," he said hoarsely.

"Another mistake?"

"My first mistake was letting you go once. I'm not going to repeat it." His eyes were the color of pewter in the dim light, filled with anguish.

Charlotte looked down at her hands, her heart hammering against her ribs so hard that she feared they would crack. "In all fairness, I made the first mistake."

His fingers caught her chin, forcing her eyes back up to his. "And it was yours to make and mine to forgive. And I didn't. And for that, I ask your forgiveness."

"This is a very circular conversation," she sniffed, a sound that was half laugh, half sob escaping. "All these mistakes and forgiveness."

"Yes. Because we're going to make more mistakes," he said. "And we're going to forgive them. Because that is what people who love each other do."

Charlotte caught her breath, her throat tightening even further.

"I love you. All of you. Charlotte, Charlie, Lady Charlotte. Whatever you wish to call yourself, it matters not to me."

"Yours," she whispered. "I want to call myself yours."

He kissed her then, a hard, possessive kiss that stole whatever was left of her composure. Her hands slipped around his neck, and she held on tightly, not ever wanting to let go.

He pulled her closer against him. "I can't ever repay

what you did for me in that gallery," he said against her neck.

"I didn't just do it for you," Charlotte replied. "I did it for me. I did it for a woman I never got to meet, but who loved unconditionally."

"Charlotte." He pressed his forehead to hers.

"I have a commission waiting," she whispered. "I have to leave England."

"I know. I heard that Charlie Beaumont had been hired."

"Come with me—"

"Yes."

"You don't even know where I'm going," she sniffed with a smile.

He pulled back from her and wiped a tear from her cheek that she hadn't realized had fallen. "It doesn't matter."

Charlotte caught his fingers with her own. "I love you, Flynn."

"And I you. Don't ever forget that." He smiled softly at her. "Tell me where we're going, Lady Charlie."

She kissed him, love for this man suffusing every corner of her being. She raised her head and saw that love reflected in his own eyes with the promise of forever. "How do you feel about Italy?"

About the Author

Kelly Bowen is a three-time RITA Award–winning author who grew up in Manitoba, Canada. She attended the University of Manitoba and earned a master of science degree in veterinary physiology and endocrinology. But it was Kelly's infatuation with history and a weakness for a good love story that led her down the path of historical romance. When she is not writing, she seizes every opportunity to explore ruins and battlefields. Currently, Kelly lives in Winnipeg with her husband and two boys, all of whom are wonderfully patient with the writing process. Except, that is, when they need a goalie for street hockey.

Learn more at:
    www.kellybowen.net
    @kellybowen09
    Facebook.com/pages/Kelly-Bowen/636626389706813

DON'T MISS THESE OTHER GREAT READS BY KELLY BOWEN

The Devils of Dover

A Duke in the Night

Last Night with the Earl

A Rogue by Night

A Season for Scandal

Duke of My Heart

A Duke to Remember

Between the Devil and the Duke

The Lords of Worth

I've Got My Duke to Keep Me Warm

A Good Rogue Is Hard to Find

A Lady's Guide to Skirting Scandal: A Short Story

You're the Earl That I Want

Looking for more historical romance?
Forever brings the heat with these sexy rogues.

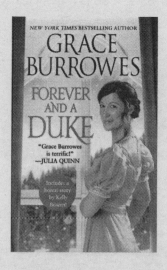

FOREVER AND A DUKE
by Grace Burrowes

Wrexham, Duke of Elsmore, is overrun by family obligations, and when he finally carves out a moment to evaluate his family's finances, he learns that he—and his sisters—are on the verge of social catastrophe. When Rex enlists the help of creative accountant Eleanora Hatfield, what starts out as an unwanted assignment soon leads to forbidden kisses and impossible longings. But as Ellie begins to understand the severity of Rex's money troubles, the less likely it becomes that their passion will add up to anything more than heartbreak. Includes a bonus story by Kelly Bowen!

Discover bonus content and more on read-forever.com.

Find more great reads on Instagram with
@ReadForeverPub.

WHEN A ROGUE MEETS HIS MATCH
by Elizabeth Hoyt

After a decade of doing the Duke of Windemere's dirty work, Gideon Hawthorne is ready to be his own boss. But the duke isn't going to make leaving easy—he wants Gideon to complete one last task. And as payment, he offers the one thing that could seriously tempt Gideon: Windemere's niece, Messalina Greycourt. Includes a bonus story by Kelly Bowen!

Follow @ReadForeverPub on Twitter and join the conversation using #ReadForever.

THE HIGHLAND EARL
by Amy Jarecki

Mr. & Mrs. Smith meets *Outlander* in this action-packed Scottish romance as a marriage of convenience leads to secrets that could be deadly. Lady Evelyn has no desire to wed the rugged Scottish earl her father has chosen, but at least she'll be able to continue her work as a spy—as long as her husband never finds out. Yet the more time Evelyn spends with John and his boys, the fonder she grows of their little family, and the last thing she wants to do is put them in danger.

Connect with us at
Facebook.com/ReadForeverPub

A ROGUE BY NIGHT
by Kelly Bowen

A doctor by day and a smuggler by night, Harland Hayward is determined to rescue his family from financial ruin. But when his next heist brings him side-by-side with Katherine Wright, he must choose between saving his family and being with his perfect match.

HIGHLANDER EVER AFTER
by Paula Quinn

As the clan chief's son, Adam MacGregor is duty-bound to marry a royal heir. Yet when he meets his bride—a beautiful but haughty lass who thinks he's nothing more than a common savage—he realizes she's more than he bargained for.